KU-299-342

Candlenight

PHIL RICKMAN was born in Lancashire and lives on the Welsh border. He is the author of the Merrily Watkins series, and *The Bones of Avalon*. He has won awards for his TV and radio journalism and writes and presents the book programme *Phil the Shelf* for BBC Radio Wales.

ALSO BY
PHIL
RICKMAN

THE MERRILY WATKINS SERIES

The Wine of Angels
Midwinter of the Spirit
A Crown of Lights
The Cure of Souls
The Lamp of the Wicked
The Prayer of the Night Shepherd
The Smile of a Ghost
The Remains of an Altar
The Fabric of Sin
To Dream of the Dead
The Secrets of Pain

THE JOHN DEE PAPERS

The Bones of Avalon
The Heresy of Dr Dee

OTHER TITLES

Candlenight
Curfew
The Man in the Moss
December
The Chalice

PHIL RICKMAN

Candlenight

CORVUS

First published in Great Britain in 1991
by Gerald Duckworth & Co. Ltd.

First published in E-book in Great Britain in 2011
by Corvus, an imprint of Atlantic Books Ltd.
This paperback edition published in Great Britain in 2013 by Corvus,
an imprint ofAtlantic Books Ltd.

1 3 5 7 9 10 8 6 4 2

A CIP catalogue record for this book is available from the British Library.

Paperback ISBN: 978 0 85789 694 0
E-book ISBN: 978 0 85789 688 9
Printed in Italy by Grafica Veneta S.p.A.

Corvus
An imprint of Atlantic Books Ltd
Ormond House
26–27 Boswell Street
London WC1N 3JZ
www.corvus-books.co.uk

Candlenight

PART ONE

PORTENTS

CHAPTER I

Laughter trickled after him out of the inn.

Ingley's mouth tightened and he would have turned back, but this was no time to lose his temper. In a hurry now. Knew what it was he was looking for. Could almost hear it summoning him, as if the bells were clanging in the tower.

Besides, he doubted the laughter was intended to be offensive. They were not hostile in the village – yes, all right, they insisted on speaking Welsh in public all the time, as if none of them understood anything else. But he could handle that. As long as they didn't get in his way.

"Torch," he'd demanded. "Flashlight. Do you have one I could borrow?"

"Well . . ." Aled Gruffydd, the landlord, had pondered the question as he pulled a pint of beer, slow and precise as a doctor drawing a blood sample.

The big man, Morgan somebody, or somebody Morgan, had said, very deadpan, "No flashlights here, Professor. Blindfold we could find our way around this place."

". . . and pissed," a man called out by the dartboard. "Blindfold and pissed."

Aled Gruffydd laid the pint reverently on a slop-mat and then produced from behind the bar a big black flashlight. "But we keep this," he said, "for the tourists. Rubber. Bounces, see."

Morgan laughed into his beer, a hollow sound.

"Thanks," Ingley said, ignoring him. "I . . . my notes. And a couple of books. Left them in the church. Probably there in the

3

morning, but I need to know." He smiled faintly. "If they aren't, I'm in trouble."

The landlord passed the rubber torch across the bar to him. "One thing, Dr. Ingley. Batteries might be running down a bit, so don't go using it until you need to. There's a good bit of moon for you, see."

"Quite. You'll have it back. Half an hour or so, yes?"

"Mind the steps now," Morgan said.

There was a short alleyway formed by the side of the inn where he'd taken a room and the ivy-covered concrete wall of an electricity sub-station. From where it ended at some stone steps Thomas Ingley could hear the river hissing gently, could smell a heady blend of beer and honeysuckle.

This pathway had not been built with Ingley in mind. The alley had been almost too narrow for his portly body, now the steps seemed too steep for his short legs. On all his previous visits to the church he'd gone by car to the main entrance. Hadn't known about the steps until somebody had pointed them out to him that morning. The steps clambered crookedly from the village to the church on its hillock, an ancient man-made mound rising suddenly behind the inn.

As the landlord had said, there was a moon – three parts full, but it was trapped behind the rearing church tower (medieval perpendicular, twice repaired in the nineteenth century) and there were no lights in the back of the inn to guide him up the steps. So he switched on the torch and found the beam quite steady.

Ingley had lied about leaving notes in the church. Kept everything – because you couldn't trust anybody these days – under the loose floorboard beneath his bed. He wondered what the hell he would have done if one of the regulars had offered to help him. Can't go up there on your own in the dark, Professor –

break your neck, isn't it? He'd have been forced to stroll around the place, pretending to search for his documents, the tomb tantalisingly visible all the while, then have to wait for the morning to examine it. Too long to wait.

He never put anything off any more. If one had a line to pursue, strand to unravel, one should go on regardless of ritual mealtimes, social restraints, the clock by which man artificially regulated – and therefore reduced – his life.

And depressingly, with Ingley's condition, one never knew quite how much time one had left anyway.

He set off up the jagged steps.

A bat flittered across the torchbeam like an insect. Bats, like rats, were always so much smaller than one imagined.

Ingley paused halfway up the steps. Had to get his breath. Ought to rest periodically – doctor's warning. He scowled. Stood a moment in the scented silence. Did the sense of smell compensate for restricted vision in the dark? Or were the perfumes themselves simply more potent after sunset?

A sudden burst of clinking and distant clatter, then a strong voice in the night. A voice nurtured, no doubt, by the male choir and the directing of sheepdogs on windy hills.

"Professor! Dr. Ingley! Where are you, man?"

Morgan. Dammit. Dammit. Dammit. Snapping off the torch, he held himself very still on the steps. Or as still as one could manage when one was underexercised, overweight and panting.

"Prof, are you all right?"

Of course I am. Go away. Go away. Go away. Thomas Ingley stayed silent and clenched his little teeth.

Another voice, speaking rapidly in Welsh, and then Morgan said, "*O'r gorau.*" OK, then – must mean that, surely. And the heavy front door of the inn closed with a thunk that sounded final.

Ingley waited a while, just to be sure, and then made his way slowly to the top of the steps. Emerging onto the plateau of the churchyard, he stopped to steady his breathing. The sky was a curious moonwashed indigo behind the rearing black tower and the squat pyramid of its spire. A dramatic and unusual site in this part of Wales, where most people worshipped in plain, stark, Victorian chapels – rigid monuments to nineteenth-century Puritanism. Even the atmosphere here was of an older, less forbidding Wales. All around him was warmth and softness and musty fragrance; wild flowers grew in profusion among the graves, stones leaning this way and that, centuries deep.

Not afraid of graves. Graves he liked.

"*Dyma fedd Ebenezer Watkins,*" the torch lit up, letters etched into eternity. "*1858–1909.*"

Fairly recent interee. Ingley put out the light again, saving it for someone laid to rest here well over four centuries before Ebenezer Watkins. Excited by the thought, he made straight for the door at the base of the tower, straying from the narrow path by mistake and stumbling over a crooked, sunken headstone on the edge of the grass. Could fall here, smash one's skull on the edge of some outlying grave and all for nothing, all one's research. "Don't be stupid," he said aloud, but quietly. He often gave himself instructions. "Put the bloody light back on."

Followed the torchbeam to the door, which he knew would be unlocked. "A hospice, sanctuary I suppose you would say, in medieval times," Elias ap Siencyn had told him. "And today, is there not an even greater need for sanctuary?" Impressive man, ap Siencyn, strong character and strong face, contoured like the bark of an old tree. Too often these days one went to consult a minister about the history of his church to be met by a person in a soft dog collar and jeans who knew nothing of the place, claiming Today's Church was about people, not architecture.

At the merest touch the ancient door swung inwards (arched

moulded doorway, eighteenth century) and the churchy atmosphere came out to him in a great hollow yawn. He was at once in the nave, eight or nine centuries or more enfolding him, cloak of ages, wonderful.

All the same, was it not taking tradition too far to have no electricity in the church, no lights, no heating?

Inside, all he could see were steep Gothic windows, translucent panes, no stained glass, only shades of mauve stained by the night sky. He knew the way now and, putting out the torch, moved briskly down the central aisle, footsteps on stone, *tock, tock, tock.*

Stopped at the altar as if about to offer a prayer or to cross himself.

Hardly. Ingley didn't sneer this time, but it was close.

Table laid for God. A millennium or more of devotion, hopes and dreads heaped up here and left to go cold. Confirmed atheist, Thomas Ingley. Found the altar just about the least interesting part of the church.

He'd stopped because this was where one turned sharply left, three paces, to get to the secret core of the place, the heart of it all. Simply hadn't realised it until tonight. Been up here five times over the weekend. Missing, each time, the obvious.

Decidedly cool in the church, but Ingley was sweating in anticipation and the torch was sticky in his hand. A sweeping sound, a skittering far above him in the rafters: bats again. Then a silence in which even the flashlight switch sounded like the breach of a rifle.

Clack!

And the beam was thrown full in the face of the knight.

Like a gauntlet, Thomas Ingley thought, in challenge. Slap on one cheek, slap on the other. This is it. Lain there for centuries and nobody's given a sod who you were or what you were doing here. But you've slept long enough. Taking you on now, sir, taking you on.

The stone eyelids of the knight stayed shut. His petrified lips wore a furtive smile. His stone hands, three knuckles badly chipped, were on his breast, together in prayer. The beam of light tracked downwards, over the codpiece to the pointed feet.

"All right, friend," Thomas Ingley said, speaking aloud again, laying the torch on the effigy, taking out a notebook, felt-tip pen, his reading glasses. Nuts and bolts time. "Let's get on with it."

He made detailed notes, with small drawings and diagrams, balancing the notebook on the edge of the tomb beneath the light. He drew outlines of the patterns in the stone. He copied the inscriptions in Latin and in Welsh, at least some of which he suspected had been added later, maybe centuries after the installation of the tomb. Tomorrow, perhaps, buy a camera with a flash, do the thing properly. Tonight, just had to know.

Finally he took from his jacket pocket a retractable metal rule and very carefully measured the tomb. It was about two feet longer than the effigy. The inscription in stone identified its occupant as Sir Robert Meredydd. An obscure figure. If indeed, thought Ingley, he had ever existed.

The main inscription, he was now convinced, had been done later, the slab cemented to the side of the tomb; he could see an ancient crack where something had gone amiss, been repaired. He put away rule, notebook, pen, spectacles. Picked up his torch from the knight's armoured belly.

Got you now, friend. Yes.

For a moment, in the heat of certainty, all his principles deserted him and he wanted to tear the tomb open, take up a sledgehammer or something and smash his way in.

Involuntarily, he shouted out, "Got you!" And now he really did slap the effigy, full in its smug, smiling face.

A certain coldness spread up his arm as the slap resounded from the rafters.

Ingley stepped back, panting, shocked at himself. He felt silence swelling in the church.

The knight's cold face flickered. The torch went out.

Batteries.

Couldn't say he hadn't been warned. Too absorbed in his work to notice it growing dim. He shook the torch; a mean amber glimmer, then it died.

Mission accomplished, anyway. Retreating into the aisle, he glanced over his shoulder at the stone husk on the tomb, its dead lips luminously purpled by the colour of the night through the long windows. He would go now. He hurried down the aisle, *tock, tock, tock.*

As if to guide him on his way, five yards distant, at the entrance to the nave, close to the font (heptagonal, nineteenth-century replacement) a meagre flame appeared, like a taper. When he moved forward to try and see it more clearly, the small light moved with him, as if whoever held it was backing away.

"I'm sorry," Ingley said, raising his head and his voice, authoritative, irascible, producing an echo. "Who is there?"

there . . . there . . . ere . . .

He registered, disturbed, that the little flame cast no ambience. It was like the light through a keyhole, something on the other side of the dark.

Then it went out.

Was somebody with him now in the church? Somebody who'd seen him by the tomb, who would tell them what he'd been doing? Who'd now doused his light to. . . .

Blindfold we could find our way around this place . . .

More likely he was simply overexcited and overtired. He

stood very still, disgusted at his heart for suddenly pulsing in his chest like some squirming animal. Pills, where were his pills?

"Finished now. Leaving," he said to nobody.

ving . . . ing . . .

Back in the inn, that was where they were, the pills. On the dresser in his room.

". . . Leaving, all right . . . ?"

. . . ight.

There was nobody. Nobody at all. He walked down the aisle to the great door, which was open a crack – had he left it like that? Thought perhaps he had, certainly didn't remember closing it. He glanced back into the church, towards the altar and the tomb, neither visible now. Saw only the tall Gothic windows tinctured in amethyst. He grasped the iron ring handle and hauled the door closed behind him, hearing the muffled echo of the latch from within.

Out then, gratefully, into the remembered warmth of a summer night, into the churchyard's terraced circle, from where one could look down on the yellow glowing of the village. Relieved, he took a great gulp of the soft night air.

The air was hard and slammed into his throat and locked there.

Ingley spun round, blinking.

No lights.

No village.

No moon.

He clutched at the stone porch and the breath came out of him like razorblades.

The circular cemetery was an island in a dark, polluted sea. The sky was black, and something was swirling about him, plucking playfully at his jacket.

He hauled in another breath; it didn't want to come. He

slapped at his jacket where the dark wind was fingering it like a pickpocket.

The breath came up like an anchor through mud. His chest seemed to creak. Cold too out here now, and damp. No sweet smells any more.

Then the true essence of the place came to him, faint at first, and shocking because . . .

"Oh, Christ!" The little fat man, clamping a cupped hand over his mouth and nose, was thrown back by the stench.

Stench?

Yes, yes, vile, decaying, putrid . . . as if the season had betrayed them and the scented flowers had choked and bloated on their stems. He knew that stink, had always known it. He knew it from hospital wards and his stricken mother's bedroom, from dustbins in summer and the yard behind his father's butcher's shop. And he knew, sad and angry now, that it was not as it seemed. It was within him – had to be – the blackness, the smell, the withering.

His own lights going out.

Poor old Ingley, historian, antiquary, awkward customer, abrupt sometimes, knew it – but so little time to do things, always so little time. Hang on to things. Hang on to reality – single-chamber church with tower to the west, perpendicular, wooden bell-stage, pyramidal two-tiered roof . . .

Then, at first vaporous and indistinct, above a middle-distant grave, possibly the grave of Ebenezer Watkins, rose the little flame. Rose up and hovered, steamy and flickering as if in the hand of a still, dark figure, waiting. And blue this time, a cold and gaseous blue.

Ingley began to sob, and it was bitterly painful in his chest.

CHAPTER II

The corpse wore a shroud and a silly smile, and its hair was sticking out like wires. The five people standing around its coffin were gloomily dressed in black or dark brown – but they too were smiling.

Bethan was not smiling. It ought to have been comical, but it seemed all the more sinister and graphically real without the benefit of perspective. With the figures ludicrously out of proportion, big heads like grinning toffee apples on black sticks, it resembled some crude medieval engraving.

She turned over the exercise book to look at the name on the cover, and she was right. Sali Dafis, it said unevenly in capitals. She turned back to the drawing. Underneath it the childish script said in Welsh,

Old Mrs. Jones, Ty Canol, died on Friday. We all went in to see her. She was in her coffin. It was on the table. Nain said she knew Mrs. Jones would die soon because she saw the cannwyll gorff in the churchyard and it went all the way to Mrs. Jones's door.

On the facing page, another drawing showed a white gravestone against a sky crosshatched with dark-blue crayon. In the sky were a half-moon and several stars and something that looked like a bigger star hanging over the grave. Underneath this one was written,

Here is the cannwyll gorff over the grave of Mr.
Tegwyn Jones. He is sending it to fetch his wife.

"God," Bethan said and slapped the exercise book face-down on the sofa.

She'd told the children to pretend they were working for the *papur bro*, the community newspaper in Pontmeurig, and to write about something that had happened in their own village which they thought people ought to know about. Of the results she'd seen so far, most had been predictably innocuous. Carys Huws had written about the haymaking and how the farmers were hoping to have it finished in time to go to the Royal Welsh agricultural show. Bobi Fon had described the chairman's chair his father, the carpenter, had made for Glanmeurig District Council.

But both Cefyn Lewis and Glyn Jones had described the *Gorsedd Ddu* meeting in the oakwoods at dead of night to judge the traitors and the cowards – writing as if it had really happened, although both were old enough to know the difference between history and legend.

And now Sali had written again of some sinister, imaginary aspect of death.

Slowly, to calm herself, Bethan poured out a mug of tea. Yesterday she'd overheard Glyn and Cefyn telling little Nerys Roberts about the *toili*, as if it were a regular feature of village life. Nerys was big-eyed and pale. Bethan, furious, had sent the two boys out into the yard, from where they'd grinned slyly at her through the window.

Buddug, she thought. Buddug is behind this.

She sipped the tea; it was horribly strong and bitter. Bethan grimaced. Corpse candles, phantom funerals. The knocking, the moaning, the bird of death. It was insidious.

The tea in the pot was as dense as peat. She went into the kitchen to make some more, pulling the rubber band from her black hair, shaking her head and letting the hair fall softly, comfortingly around her shoulders. She felt very alone.

Waiting for the kettle to boil, Bethan stood by the window, wondering whether to take up smoking again, and she thought, I hate weekends.

Outside the window it was Saturday night in Pontmeurig. Only eight miles – and yet a whole world – away from the village of Y Groes. Barely four thousand people lived in this town now, but it still had seventeen pubs. Considering how much of the population was either too young, too sick or too ostensibly clean-living to go out for a drink, that left . . . well, it made Bethan wonder how they'd all survived, the seventeen pubs.

She took off her glasses and rubbed at her eyes, smudging the remains of her make-up and not caring; she would not be going anywhere tonight.

Just before ten o'clock, Guto Evans phoned.

"What are you doing then, Bethan, at this moment?"

"Nothing illegal," Bethan said cautiously.

"That's a shame," Guto said. He paused, hesitated. "Look, the night, as they say, is young. Why don't we go out and paint the town? Any colour you like, except for grey, which nobody would notice."

Bethan pictured him with the phone tucked into his shaggy beard, like a big terrier with a bone, his stocky frame wedged into a corner of his mother's front parlour amid hundreds of plates and china ornaments.

"I don't think so," Bethan said solemnly into the phone. Her glasses slipped and with one finger she pushed them back along her nose. "I have my reputation to protect. You would lead me into bad ways."

"One drink, then? A chat?"

"I'm sorry, Guto, I do appreciate it. It's just . . . well, I've such a lot of work to catch up on."

And she drew him away from the subject by asking if he'd

heard about the unfortunate incident at that afternoon's protest demo by some of their mutual friends in the sometimes militant Welsh Language Society. The society had targeted a particular estate agent in Aberystwyth who specialised in selling country cottages in Welsh-speaking areas to affluent English people looking for holiday homes.

"It got seriously out of hand, of course," Bethan said. "Some of the boys had collected FOR SALE signs out of people's gardens and heaped them up outside Hughes's door. And what should someone do but pour paraffin over the pile and set them alight. If the fire brigade had not arrived in time, who knows, the whole building might have gone up."

"Would have been no great loss. Bloody Emyr Hughes. Him and his new Mercedes. And a helicopter now, did you hear?" Guto snorted. "Traitorous fat bastard. Grown fat on English gold."

Bethan smiled. Guto sharpening up his rhetoric, now, because it was rumoured Burnham-Lloyd was a very sick man and there might soon be a by-election. "So Dewi and Alun Phillips were arrested," she said. "They will probably be charged tomorrow. Wilful damage, I hope. Not arson."

"Of course, I would have been there myself," Guto said. "But I am keeping a low political profile until such time as I am called."

"Well, there's sensible," said Bethan, in mock-surprise. She paused. "Um, it was nice of you to ask me out."

"Yes," said Guto. "I am a nice man, this is true."

"But I must get back to my marking."

"Should I call again some time?"

"Yes. When I'm not so busy."

"And when will that be? No, no, it's all right. I might be nice but I'm not daft. Goodnight, Bethan. *Nos da*."

"Guto, have you ever found . . . ?"

"What?"

She had been going to ask about the *cannwyll gorff*. She stopped herself. What could she say? Guto, I'm scared. There is something badly wrong in the village and I don't think I can handle it.

"Hello . . . Bethan . . . ?"

But if she said any more then Guto would say it was quite clear that in her state of mind Bethan should not be spending the night alone, and so . . .

"Are you still there, Bethan?"

"Yes . . . I . . . It doesn't matter," she said. "*Nos da*, Guto."

"You take care of yourself," he said.

It would have been nice to go out for a drink. And a chat. Just a chat. She wondered: did I say no because it would not be seemly for a widow of less than a year to be seen out with Guto Evans on a Saturday night in Pontmeurig?

No, she decided. If I'd thought that, I would have gone.

Saturday night was probably the reason the seventeen pubs survived.

They had come into Pontmeurig now, from all the outlying villages and the hill farms, sometimes six or seven of them in a single Land-Rover. Farmers, farmers' sons, farmers' grandsons. Even a few women, these days. Some of the men would get quietly and expertly drunk. A handful would make a macho celebration out of it, and there would perhaps be a fight, a smashed window, a beer glass flung into the street, splintering against the kerb or somebody's head.

A yellow haze of smoke and steam, beer fumes and chip fat settled on the street below the lighted window of the apartment over Hampton's Bookshop. In the window, Bethan was a still silhouette.

She drew the thin curtains, turned back to the sadly over-crowded sitting room, drank tea and glared at the dark-green cover of the book lying on the sofa. Sali Dafis. Aged seven.

A bright child. Confident too – winner of the recitation prize for her age-group at this year's Urdd Eisteddfod, where three other children from the school had also won prizes. Which was incredible for a little village school with just twenty-four pupils. One of the judges had commented that this was clearly a school where children were encouraged to be imaginative. He could say that again, Bethan thought. She remembered Buddug, huge and beaming, in the audience. Buddug, quite rightly, taking all the credit because Bethan had been away looking after a sick husband.

Then mourning for a dead husband.

She was back now. She didn't have to return, she'd terminated her lease on the cottage. She could have gone anywhere, stayed in the city, where there was no silence and no sense of a gathering darkness.

Parting the curtains, Bethan looked down into the street, watched four youths standing outside the Drovers' Arms nursing beer glasses, admiring a motor bike. She thought, I should have gone. Maybe it was my last chance. I've been too long with death.

Irritated and restless now, she snatched the green exercise book from the sofa. Sali Dafis was the daughter of the man who ran the garage. Her mother had died when Sali was a baby; the child had been raised by her grandmother, Mrs. Bronwen Dafis, a withered crone who dispensed herbal remedies and told fortunes.

And who, Bethan thought, frowning, was also a friend of Buddug's.

She got out her red pen, intending not to mark Sali's exercise but to write, "See me after school" at the bottom of it, because the child needed help. She had a vague memory of Sali's mother, a little blonde-haired secretary from Essex whom Dilwyn had met on holiday.

As she started to write "*gwel . . .*" at the bottom of the second drawing, Bethan's red ballpoint pen ran out. Without thinking, she bustled into the bedroom to pinch a pen from the inside pocket of Robin's jacket in the wardrobe. Stood there with the wardrobe door half-open, a hand inside feeling from coat to coat. *Her* coats. Realising then that Robin's jacket had never been in this bedroom, had gone long ago to the Oxfam shop, probably with the pens still in the pocket.

I'm not going to cry, she told herself. I'm going to laugh. But she couldn't make her lips go through the motions.

She heard a scornful, trailing cheer from the street outside, as she went back into the living room, edging around cumbersome furniture she didn't need any more. A male voice hooted and a girl screamed in excitement as Bethan sat down at the table to continue her note to Sali in pencil.

"Geraint, don't . . . !" the girl squealed in the street, and Bethan knew that, whatever it was Geraint was doing, the girl really didn't mind. It was about romance.

Bethan looked up from the table. By the wan light of the Victorian brass standard lamp, their first Christmas present from Robin's mother in Durham, she saw a little attic flat over somebody else's failed bookshop in a town which had been falling apart for five centuries.

Single person's accommodation, Bethan thought.

She broke down then, a hot rush of despair, over the horror-comic drawings of Sali Dafis, aged seven.

For three nights before Robin died, the village women said, the *cannwyll gorff* had been seen. First in the churchyard. Then over the river.

Finally, hanging solemnly in the still air outside their cottage.

When Bethan raised her head from the table she saw that the pages of the exercise book were crumpled and tear-stained.

I spilled tea on your book, she would tell Sali on Monday. I shall have to give you a new one. I'm sorry. All your nice drawings.

Feeling suddenly light-headed, she almost rang Guto back to say yes, she would go out with him and they would get very, very drunk.

She didn't, though. It was not the time.

CHAPTER III

Above him the whitewashed ceiling gleamed faintly between beams as thick as railway sleepers. The heavy bed of Victorian mahogany was creaking below like the timbers of a sailing ship.

Sinking.

Head rolling back on the pillow, he closed his eyes.

... And his mind was alive with images, burgling his brain like fragments of a dream getting through from the other side of sleep, as if they couldn't wait. Black tower in a purple sky, perpendicular tower, wooden bell-stage, in tiers ...

Always ends in tiers, he thought ludicrously. Opening his eyes again, he tried to calm his thoughts, remembering pushing at the door of the inn to escape from the cloying dark. Then the yellow light, beer haze, oak beams, the ceaseless banter – the overwhelming relief of it, of being back amongst these tiresome people with their impenetrable language. Still not closing time when he'd returned. How had he made it back so quickly?

Pounding pain in his chest now. He reached to the bedside cabinet for a Trinitrin. Slipped it under his tongue. How had he got back? He remembered the stink of decay all around him in the churchyard. Remembered trying to find the steps in the mist. Then nothing until the door and the yellow light. Inside, they had seemed almost pleased to see him.

"All right then, Professor?"

"Well, hell, man, you look cold . . ."

"Course he's cold, Morgan. Bloody church – sorry Reverend – always cold, that church. No heating, see. Get him a drink, for God's sake, Aled."

"Oh, I'm so sorry, Dr. Ingley. Should have replaced these batteries weeks ago, but you know how it is. Look, my fault, have a drink. What is it to be now, nice drop of brandy? Best Welsh brandy, mind . . ."

"Thank you, no. I think I'll go directly to bed."

"Big mistake, Professor. First time this year Aled's offered anybody a free tot of his precious bloody brandy. Never see it again."

"Leave him be, Morgan. Poor man's knackered."

"Oh aye, leave him be, now, is it, Aled? Any excuse, you bugger."

"I'm sorry, I . . . good night."

"Night, Professor."

"*Nos da i chi!*"

Still the pain.

Another Trinitrin. Worked in seconds, they always worked in seconds. He lay there in the bed, not moving, the pill under his tongue. It was a small room; just beyond the bed was a lumbering Victorian wardrobe, to its right the uncurtained window hanging open for air, bringing in the sounds of glasses jingling as they were collected in the bar below, laughter, oaths, a *nos da* or two.

He was uncomfortable and tried to roll over. But when he moved the pain ripped through his chest like the roots of a tree being torn out of the ground.

Christ.

Breathe. Come on, breathe steadily.

His eyes closed by themselves.

Creaking of the bed. Wooden bed. Wooden bell-stage,

moulded doorway eighteenth century, heptagonal font, perpendicular tower . . . black on purple . . . falling . . . Oh God in heaven, I don't know where I am . . .

Blindfold we could find our way . . .

Calm down. It wasn't a candle.

candle, andle, ndle . . .

Sharp, probing pain now, deep in his chest, like a slender knife going in . . .

. . . and his eyes came open, to show him there *was* a candle. At the bottom of the bed. Just above his feet. The flame did not waver.

He shut out the image in frozen panic. It was only a symbol, a motif summoned by his subconscious, an hallucination, a manifestation of the corruption in his system – a sick body's attempt to bring down the mind to its own level of decay.

Dying people, he thought in silent hysteria, conjured up choirs of angels, all that nonsense. Chemicals. And his own chemicals now, flooding about uncontrollably, mixing their toxic cocktails, how ironic they should throw off such an image. The corpse candle. Harbinger of death. Flickering from the periphery of his scholarly probings into a society still obsessed with its own mythology.

He could make this candle go away. He could send it back to his subconscious. He was furious now. He would not submit to this invasion. And he would not die. Damned if he would.

Damned if he . . .

Ingley squeezed his eyes shut, trying to squeeze rationality into his thoughts . . .

and found himself walking up the aisle of the church, footsteps on stone, *tock, tock, tock* . . .

Turn back, turn back, turn back . . . !

tock, tock, tock . . .

Can't . . . Can't go on . . . Must go back . . .

Drawn steadily down the aisle towards the steep windows leaking livid light into the nave.

He struggled frantically to open his eyes, didn't care now what arcane symbol they would show him, so long as it could pull him out of this place of old, forgotten, stinking evil. He felt himself rolling about in the bed, sweating cold fluid, screaming inside. But his eyelids, fastened down like heavy blinds, would not move. He remembered as a boy being shut by older boys inside a wall cupboard where there was barely room to breathe and heaving at the door in helpless panic, his first experience of claustrophobia, the stifling terror.

tock . . . tock . . .

Please. Let me go. I'm sorry, oh God, I'm sorry.

It was cold in the church. The altar cloth was white, with a mulberry splash, like an old bloodstain, where it caught the light through the long windows. The altar was where you turned left, three paces to . . .

"No . . . !"

Three paces.

tock . . .

The air thickened and vibrated with a frigid energy.

tock . . .

No. Please . . . Can't . . . Jesus Christ, let me out!

tock

A long black shadow arose in his path. He screamed. Screamed to get out of the church. Screamed for his eyes to open. But it was as if, while his mind was elsewhere, both eyelids had been very precisely stitched up.

. . . but the stone eyelids of the knight sprang open, and his eyes were of cold amethyst light. His hands unclasped from prayer, chipped knuckles, white bone beneath the stone, seeking one's throat. His stone mouth splintered into a grin.

Thomas Ingley threw all that remained of his strength into

the fight to re-enter his bedroom at the inn, like pushing and pushing at a seized-up manhole cover to escape from some fetid cellar, the strain tearing at his poor exhausted heart, stretching and popping like rotted rubber.

Don't want to know who you are. Don't care any more who you are! But please . . . don't let it happen here, not here, to be held for ever among the deep shadows and the misty mauveness . . .

The stone hands locked around his windpipe. His eyeballs bulged.

And his eyes opened.

Lids flicking up with a butterfly motion. Effortless.

The room was quiet and the air was still. He could see the wardrobe in the corner by the door. The moon through the uncurtained window. The luminous green hands of the travel alarm clock, although he couldn't make out how they were arranged. Inside his chest he felt nothing at all. The bed was silent now, no creaks. He expected to find the bedclothes in knots, but the sheets were still stiffly tucked in around him. Hospital corners. He lay calmly motionless and listened to his breathing, steady now. Nor could he feel his heart pounding any more.

So peaceful.

The relief was so great that he didn't try to move, just let his head sink into the pillow and his gaze drift up to the ceiling, where the little light hung in a frosty miasma about six inches above his temple. He went on watching the light, fully resigned now, as it turned from blue to pink . . . to blood red.

He tried to scream then, his face twisting, but it came out as a parched rattle.

CHAPTER IV

This was the thing about Wales. Some places seemed cursed – filthy weather, soil you could hardly grow dandelions in – and some places, like this village, had it all. The change, when you came out of the forestry, the other side of the Nearly Mountains, was dramatic and yet subtle too . . . the landscape greener, the weather milder, the whole atmosphere all-round mellower.

It embraced you, he thought, like a good woman.

The better to appreciate it, Dai Death, the undertaker from Pontmeurig, stopped his hearse in the middle of the road, where it left the forestry, and looked down on the village in its little cwm. Sunday afternoon. No hurry. It had looked like rain in Pontmeurig, but the sky over Y Groes was as deep a blue as you could ever expect to see in Wales. The cottages were a clutch of eggs in a nest; the church a benevolent old bird.

A clutch of eggs, yes. Nice metaphor. Dai liked to write a bit of poetry and aspired to the crown of the Glanmeurig Eisteddfod. Sitting at the wheel of his hearse, window wound down and the sunlight warm on his bald head, he lit a cigarette, feeling happy because he liked doing business in Y Groes and it wasn't often he got the chance – not because nobody died here, but because they had little use for undertakers. He wondered, not for the first time, how anyone could look out at such a place from his deathbed and hold on to any hopes of going to a greater paradise.

By all accounts, though, today's customer had been in no position to dwell upon the relative merits of a hypothetical heaven and the village of Y Groes. He'd gone in the night, when, Dai supposed, Y Groes looked much the same as any other village.

An engine grumbled at him from behind. In his wing mirror he saw a tractor that couldn't get past, it being a narrow road and the farmer not wanting to sound his horn because he could see a coffin in the back of Dai's hearse and how was he to know it was empty?

"All right, man, I'm off."

Dai tossed his cigarette out of the window, raised an apologetic hand and put the hearse in gear. Normally he might have let out the clutch sharpish like, and shot off with a spurt – bouncing the pale utility coffin into the air and giving the bugger on the tractor one hell of a shock. But he didn't like to do that now.

Not here.

For Dai's greatest aspiration, even closer to his heart than the thought of wearing the plastic crown at the Glanmeurig Eisteddfod, was to get himself a cottage in this village, to retire one day to paradise.

He was on his own today, his brother Harri still in Bronglais Hospital with his back. So he had to ask the landlord to give him a hand with the customer.

"Police sent you, is it?" said Aled Gruffydd.

Dai nodded. "Said could they have him stored until they find his relatives down in England." He lifted up the tailgate of the hearse and pulled out the lightweight fibre-glass coffin with one hand. "Well, see, I don't mind jobs like this, even on a Sunday. Sooner or later some bugger pays the bill." He smiled slyly. "English prices, isn't it?"

The bedroom was almost directly over the bar. It had a very low ceiling and wasn't really big enough for three men, even if one would be forever still.

"Above and beyond, this is, Dai." Aled grunted as they laid the body on a plastic sheet next to the coffin. It was going to be a tight fit. "Not what I'd call a small man, the Professor. Also, seemed to smell a good deal better, if I remember, when he was alive."

"Obviously went off in a bit of a sweat," Dai observed.

The customer was somewhere between late middle-aged and elderly. There was a touch of froth, which nobody had bothered to wipe away, at the side of his mouth.

"Professor, you say?" Dai said conversationally, trying not to react to the expression on the face of the customer. He was reminded of the time he'd removed a body from a dentist's chair, a man, who – mortally afraid of dentists all his life – had expired at the very moment of extraction.

"Well, of sorts." Aled was small, but wiry and strong enough to take the corpse's weight at the shoulders. "Big Morgan, it was, first started calling him that. Retired teacher, I suppose, or a college lecturer. Some sort of historian. Always walking around making notes, looking at things, never at people, you know the kind. Oh, Christ, I forgot they did that. Pass me that cloth, will you, Dai."

"Sorry, Aled. Should have thought." In this part of the world most people still knew the basics of it. They had not grown up with funeral parlours; laying out their relatives was something most of them had had to learn, like changing a wheel. Not only was it uneconomical to pay somebody like Dai to prepare a corpse, it was also still considered in many homes – and particularly, he'd found, in Y Groes – to be less than polite to the deceased.

"Can you do anything about that?" Aled asked, nodding at the face. "Or does he have to go to his maker looking as though somebody was amputating his leg without the anaesthetic?"

Dai made a professional appraisal of the customer's blue and twisted features, working out how they might be rearranged. "Easy," he said loftily. "Piece of piss. What was it, anyway?"

"Well, heart. Angina, something of that order. Dr. Wyn said he was not surprised at all. Been coming here for months, see. Had his pills through Dr. Wyn regular."

"Why was that?"

"Well, convenient, I suppose."

"No, no, I mean why did he come here? The fishing?"

"No, I was telling you. Historian or something. Into old churches."

"Not old houses?" In Dai's experience, most of the English people who persistently returned to this area were looking to buy a piece of it, some little stone cottage with an inglenook and a view of the mountains. "Buggers go crazy over places like this."

"Do they now?" Aled said. "Well, well."

"Name your price, man, place like this. Name your bloody price."

Aled made no reply. Dai looked for an expression in the landlord's compact face, but none was apparent. All the same, he decided this was as good an opening as any, and so he said carefully, "You know . . . I was only thinking to myself, well, I wouldn't mind retiring to Y Groes, me and the wife. Nowhere quite like it, see, for the peace and quiet." Casual like. In passing. Not sounding as serious as he really was. "But hell, man, I don't suppose I could afford it any more, even with selling the business, the way things are going, the prices."

"Where do you want him?" Aled asked, as if he hadn't heard any of this. "In that thing, is it?"

"In the shell."

"The what?"

"Shell. What we call it. Utility job, see. Just to get him to the warehouse, and then the relatives choose something more tasteful."

Dai tapped the side of the light-coloured coffin to show how cheap and flimsy it was, then returned, hopefully, to his theme. "What's the answer, though? What is the answer? Local boy wants a home of his own, priced out of the market before he starts. Got to go, isn't it? No option. Winds up in bloody Birmingham or somewhere and all the rich buggers who couldn't tell a Welsh mountain ewe from a Beulah speckle-faced if you drew 'em a diagram are moving in and building bloody squash courts. Well, of course, I have nothing against the English, as a race . . . Right, now, you get the other side and we'll . . . Ah, lovely job."

Both men stood back. Dai Death mopped his bald head with a handkerchief. "So, tell me, purely out of interest, like . . . How much are they fetching?"

"Beulah speckle-faced?"

"Houses, man! What would it cost for me to get a place here? How much did the last one go for?"

"I can't remember. It was a long time ago."

"Oh, come on now!" Dai was getting a bit exasperated. What Aled was supposed to say was, well, Dai, funny you should bring that up because there's this very interesting little place I know of, not on the market yet, but if they thought you were keen – you being a local boy, a Welsh-speaker and a respected professional man – I'm sure a nice quick deal could be arranged, no fuss, no estate agents.

"That it?" Aled demanded. "Finished, have we?"

"I can't credit that at all," Dai said. "Bloody hell, in Pont, I'm not kidding, the estate agents' signs have been going up faster than the TV aerials when we got the first transmitter."

"So they tell me," said Aled.

"But not here."

"No." A note of finality. "Not here."

Dai was baffled and felt slighted. What, he wondered, had happened to Tegwyn Jones's place now his wife was also dead?

Every village always had a couple of houses ready for the market, especially now, when the English would pay a small fortune for something you wouldn't keep chickens in. And what about – now here was a point – what about the judge's house?

"Having the lid on, are we, Dai?"

"I'll deal with that. Tricky, this sort. Professional use only." Dai straightened up, gathering what was left of his dignity. They only ever called him out here for the foreigners, like that chap Martin, the curate. And poor Bethan's man.

He sniffed. For Judge Rhys there'd been a coffin custom-made by Dewi Fon, the carpenter, gravestone by Myrddin Jones, the sculptor. He went out to the landing and returned with a rectangular strip of fibreglass, which he slotted into place, concealing the dreadful face of the Professor. Wondering gloomily who would be doing this job in ten years' time when he and Harri had retired, Harri being a bachelor and Dai's son away at university to study engineering. No doubt the business would get taken over by one of these national chains with colour brochures of coffins and off-the-peg shrouds. Well, bollocks to that.

"So what happened," he asked bluntly, "to the judge's house?"

"Well done, Dai," said Aled, ignoring the question. "Look, come and have a drink before we take him down." He towed the coffin away from the bedroom door so they could get out. "There, see . . . getting soft, I am, helping you with your bloody corpse then offering you a drink." He smiled. "Stiff one, is it?"

"Very funny," said Dai Death. "I'll have a pint and I'll pay you for it."

"Good God. Epidemic of something fatal, is there, in Pontmeurig, that you're so wealthy?"

"The judge's house," Dai reminded him, annoyed now and showing it. "Just tell me what happened to the fucking judge's house?"

*

30

Driving away, customer in the back, Dai took careful note. And, yes, it was true enough. Not a FOR SALE sign anywhere in the village. He shook his head in disbelief, afflicted by the usual aching longing as he took in the mellow stone and timber-framed dwellings, the crooked stone steps and walled gardens, the soft fields and the stately oaks, the wooded amphitheatre of hills sloping to the Nearly Mountains. Even the bloody Nearly Mountains, wind-blasted and conifer-choked ... even they looked impressive when viewed from Y Groes.

He looked back towards the lane which led to the judge's house. It would have been perfect. Not too big, not too small, nicely screened. But a lost cause. Christ, he'd never even heard of the old chap having a granddaughter. Recluse who never left the village, never even went into Pontmeurig. Maybe – he brightened momentarily – maybe she'd want to sell. But then – his spirits sagging again – what would she do but advertise it in the London papers?

It was, he thought, only a matter of time. They were bound to discover this place, the English. Some young stockbroker-type would cruise out here in his Porsche and spot a derelict barn, ripe for conversion, and make the farmer an offer he'd be a fool to refuse. And another farmer would hear about it and he'd sell *two* of his buildings. Then some poor widow would be staggered at how much she could get for her cottage. And, in no time at all, there'd be a little colony of English, enough to hold a bridge party with After Eight mints.

Dai gave Y Groes a final rueful glance before turning into the forestry.

And in time, he thought, the little clutch of eggs will turn rotten in the nest.

PART TWO

NOT MEANT TO
BE THERE

CHAPTER V

ENGLAND

Lying back, red hair all over the pillow and the cane headboard too, Miranda applied the Zippo to the end of her cigarette and said, "So, how was it for *you*, Miranda?"

Berry Morelli said, "Huh?" the sweat on his back was merely damp now, and chilly. It was an hour before dawn, the bedroom half-lit from the street.

In a dreamy voice, Miranda replied, "Well, since you ask, Miranda, not too wonderful. I can say, with some degree of confidence, that I have definitely had better. I suppose, as rapes go, it was not *without* consideration . . ."

"Rape?" Berry Morelli sat up. "You said *rape*?"

"Well, if it was meant to be love-making," Miranda said, "it was distressingly short on the customary endearments. In fact, now I think about it, it was entirely silent, bar the odd sharp intake of breath."

"Hey, listen, I . . ." Berry leaned over her and helped himself to one of her cigarettes from the bedside table.

". . . And then I began to detect in this rapist a . . . sort of underlying absence of joy, would that describe it? One's first experience of *pre*-coital tristesse. Or perhaps it was simply lack of interest, which would be *considerably* less tolerable." Miranda turned onto her side to face him, looking pale and fragile – which she wasn't – in the hazy streetlight from the uncurtained window.

"OK," she said. "What's eating you, Morelli?"

Berry hauled black hair out of his eyes. The hair was still wet. From the rain not the sweat. "Listen, I'm sorry."

"Oh, please . . . not the apology. I expect I enjoyed it more than you anyway." She covered up a breast and stared into space, smoking.

This Miranda. You could never figure out if she was deeply wounded or what. Berry rolled out of bed and into his bathrobe. "You want some tea?" He was fully into tea now, no coffee these days. Very British.

"No sugar," Miranda said. "No, wait . . . make that two sugars. I suspect, God help me, that the night is yet young."

"I'll fetch a tray. Black?"

"Morelli, we haven't all got the zeal of the converted."

"OK." While Berry's hands moved things around in the tiny kitchen, his head was still walking the streets. There'd been cabs around the hospital but he'd needed to walk. Death did that to you, he thought. You had to keep moving, proving to yourself you still could.

A bad night, in the end.

And he'd lost a friend.

He couldn't afford to lose a friend in this country. It only left one, if you didn't include Miranda. Which he didn't, yet.

"Biscuits, too, Morelli," she called imperiously from the bedroom. Miranda, whom he'd often find in his bed but whom he hesitated to call his regular girlfriend. Who'd gone home with him the first time because, she explained, she liked the sound of his name, the way you liked the sound of Al Pacino and Robert de Niro. There were dukes in Miranda's family and her aunt had once been a temporary lady-in-waiting to Princess Anne. Berry liked the sound of Miranda's name too, the way you liked the sound of cucumber sandwiches and Glyndebourne.

"Morelli!"

"What?"

"Biscuits."

"Yeah, I heard."

"The chocolate ginger things from Sainsbury's, OK?"

"Right."

Earlier tonight Miranda's good mood had blown like a light bulb after she'd produced tickets for Peter Gabriel and he'd told her he wouldn't be able to make the gig on account of it was old Winstone's farewell binge. Old Winstone, his friend.

She hadn't believed him. "What's he doing having it on a Sunday night?"

"All about Monday morning. If he gets smashed, he doesn't wake up till way past the time he normally goes to work. Thus avoiding the initial trauma of his first day of retirement."

"You think I'm awfully stupid, don't you, Morelli?" Miranda had said.

"Listen, I'm . . ."

"Sorry. Yes."

Berry put on the light as he carried the tea tray into the bedroom. "I didn't figure on you being here when I got in."

"I suppose that explains it," Miranda said. "You thought you were shagging someone else."

"You never came back before. Not the same night. Not after a fight. How'd you get in anyway?"

"I'm frightfully unpredictable," she said, sitting up, breasts wobbling at him and somehow making the trayful of cups jiggle in his hands. "It's part of my appeal." She giggled, a sound like Chinese bells, signifying things were OK again, for the time being. "And I'm not going to tell you how I got in, because I'm also terribly clever and rather mysterious."

Mysterious, she wasn't. In spite of everything, he grinned,

wishing he could say she was his girlfriend. Why was he so goddamn insecure? He set the tea tray down on the bed and Miranda reached across to pour. "Too strong as usual, Morelli. You're an awfully selfish bastard."

He flinched a little. It was what his old man had said, leading to Berry's decision to leave the States. *You're a goddamn selfish bastard. You don't have to agree with a fucking thing I stand for, but when you screw things up for me to further your own pissant career, that's indefensible, boy.*

"Listen, I guess what happened was I used you," he confessed to Miranda, "to reinforce my hold on life. How's that sound?"

"Pretentious."

"It was kind of a heavy night."

"You're not pissed, though, are you?"

"No, I . . . Jesus, this guy – a friend – he just died on me."

"To be quite honest I thought somebody was dying on *me*," Miranda said. "Don't do it again. Wake me up first, I might've missed it."

"Yeah, I'm . . ." Shit, he seemed to spend half his time apologising to people. Maybe he should apologise for apologising too much. He felt he could still hear the ambulance siren, the efficient clunk of the rear doors after they'd loaded the stretcher. The finality of it. He'd known then that it was final.

"Oh, for God's sake, Morelli . . ." Miranda drowned her cigarette end in the dregs of her tea, a small rebellion against her refined upbringing. "Tell mummy all about it. Who died on you? You don't mean really died? As in, you know . . . turning up one's toes?"

Berry drank his tea, not quite knowing where to start. He detected mild amusement in Miranda's green eyes. How could it be really serious if he'd strolled in afterwards and screwed her, however perfunctory that had been?

"I ever tell you about this guy I know, Giles Freeman?"

"The political reporter? I met him, if you remember, that time at Verity's. Very dashing and sporty, but terribly earnest. Quiet little wife, a bit hamsterish."

Berry admired the way Miranda took in the essence of people she'd met only in passing. Ought to have been a much better actress than she was – maybe she just found it hard to let her own outrageous personality be submerged by lesser ones.

"You're saying Giles Freeman is dead?"

"Huh? No, shit, Giles is fine. That is . . ." He put the empty cup on the teatray and set it down on the carpet. And then he asked her, because this really was the bottom line, "You ever get to Wales?"

"Wales?" Miranda patted around the duvet for her cigarettes. "What's Wales got to do with it?"

"You ever go there?"

"Morelli," she said, "do I look like the kind of person who has Welsh connections? Like someone who reads the Bible all the time, plays rugby and eats seaweed?"

Berry thought about this. "Maybe not," he conceded. He found her cigarettes in a fold of the duvet, lit two and passed her one. "Folks do that in Wales? They eat seaweed?"

"So it is said. They make some kind of bread from it. I went there once, but it was depressing. It rained."

Miranda. If she visited the Taj Mahal during a monsoon it would forever be depressing.

"But this is Britain, right?" Berry said. "This is Wales, England? Same island. What I mean . . . Welsh folks live in England, English folks live in Wales."

"If they're desperate enough. Or they've been offered some terribly lucrative job out there, and there can't be many of those. Why do you ask?"

"OK," Berry said. "Hypothetical, right? If you had friends aiming to move to Wales, what would you say to them?"

Miranda's mouth twitched impatiently. "I'd probably say au revoir rather than goodbye because most of my friends wouldn't even survive in Dorking. Morelli, what is all this about?"

Berry sighed. "Listen, forget the hypothetical shit. What it's about is there's this guy moving to Wales and I find myself in the position of having to try and prevent that. I mean, Christ, I never went there, I don't plan to go there, but I got to talk this guy out of it. Guy who wants to make his home there more than anywhere else in the world, however bizarre that sounds to you. That's it. That's the situation."

Under the duvet Miranda ran a hand across his thigh and back again. "Nothing doing, then?" she said, affecting a squeaky East End accent.

"Gimme a break."

"Morelli, I'm sure there's an awfully interesting story behind all this but I don't somehow think I want to go into it after all. It sounds frightfully complicated, and –" she reached over to her teacup on the bedside cabinet and tipped her cigarette into it half-smoked "– quite honestly, I find the whole subject of Wales the most awful turn-off."

Miranda snuggled down, poking her bottom into Berry's right thigh and within a minute was asleep, leaving him to switch off the light and stare uncertainly into the blotchy dark, trying to figure out how this situation came about.

CHAPTER VI

That evening, seeing Winstone Thorpe flick open his ancient hooded eyes, Berry had thought of an old tomcat on a back-porch alerted by the flutter of wings.

"Where's that then?" Winstone had asked in that tired, diffident way he had.

"It's a smallish country sort of welded onto the side of England, Winstone," Giles Freeman explained, and he giggled drunkenly. "It's where the M4 peters out. They've got mountains there. Play rugby. Sing a lot."

"Oh ..." Old Winstone Thorpe chuckled and his chins wobbled. "You mean Wales. Sorry, old boy, must've misheard."

Sure you did, you old bastard, Berry thought affectionately. He looked at Winstone across the pub table. Then he looked at Giles, who was clearly too drunk to realise he was being set up. Several of the other journalists, who knew Winstone of old, glanced up from their drinks and grinned. "Wales, eh?" Winstone said. "Oh dear."

There he goes, Berry thought.

"All right," Giles Freeman said testily. "What's that supposed to mean?" Giles had drunk maybe five pints of beer, and he wasn't used to it. His fair hair was in disarray and his long face was hot and shiny, freckles aglow. He was too drunk to realise how bored they all were with hearing about his incredible piece of luck – well, Claire's actually, her inheritance. But an utterly amazing old place, splendid countryside, absolutely terrific atmosphere. Just being there

41

made you realise how totally cardboard and artificial your urban environment was.

So Giles had fallen heavily for some backwoods shack. And now old Winstone Thorpe, who had retired that day after more than half a lifetime on the *Daily Telegraph*, was blinking lazily beneath eyebrows like thatched eaves and saying, "Oh dear."

"Well, come on, Winstone." Giles was leaning aggressively across the table now. Berry had never seen him like this before; somebody had hit a nerve. "If you've got something to say, just bloody say it."

"But, dear chap . . ." Winstone put down his empty whisky glass and looked around vaguely until Ray Wheeler of the *Mirror* slipped him a replacement. "Ah, a fellow Christian. Thank you. No, you see – am I stating the obvious here? You're an Englishman, old boy."

Somewhere a clock chimed. It was eleven o'clock, and there was a momentary silence in the battered Edwardian bar of what old Winstone Thorpe maintained was the last halfway decent pub in what used to be Fleet Street.

Berry found himself nodding. Aside, perhaps, from old Winstone himself, Giles Freeman was just about the most English guy he'd ever met, even here in England.

"Now look, Winstone." Giles took an angry gulp of his beer. "That is just incredibly simplistic. I mean, have you ever even been to Wales? Come on now, tell the truth?"

Wrong question, Giles, thought Berry. You just walked into it. He leaned back and waited for Winstone Thorpe's story, knowing there had to be one.

"Well, since you ask . . ." The venerable reporter unbuttoned his weighty tweed jacket and lifted his whisky glass onto his knee. "Matter of fact, I *was* in Wales once."

"No kidding," Berry said and then shut up because there were guys here who still had him down as a no-talent asshole on the

42

run. Things had changed since his last time here, as a student in the seventies. People had gotten tighter, more suspicious – even journalists. They were coming across like Americans imagined the English to be – stiff, superior. And they were suspicious of him because he wasn't like Americans were supposed to be – didn't drink a lot, never ate burgers. They weren't programmed for a vegetarian American hack who'd come up from the Underground press and dumped on his distinguished dad. Berry looked around the three tables pushed together and saw complacent smiles on prematurely florid faces. These were mainly Parliamentary reporters like Giles. In this job, after a while, after long hours in the Westminster bars, journalists began to look like MPs.

"Early sixties, must've been," Winstone said. His face had long gone beyond merely florid to the colour and texture of an over-ripe plum. "Sixty-two? Sixty-three? Anyway, we were dragged out to Wales on a Sunday on the sort of story that sounds as if it's going to be better than it actually turns out. Somebody'd shot this old farmer and his son, twelve-bore job, brains all over the wall. Lived miles from anywhere, up this God-forsaken mountain. Turned out the housekeeper did it, sordid domestic stuff, only worth a couple of pars. But that's beside the point."

Berry glanced over at Giles who was trying to look bored. Giles caught the glance and rolled his eyes towards the ceiling. Berry got along OK with Giles, who was less clannish than the others.

"Point is," Winstone said, "locals treated us as if we were lepers. Here we are, sitting in this grim, freezing so-called guest house like the lost bloody patrol – Sunday, so all the pubs are closed, can you imagine that – and all we can hear is the rain and the natives jabbering away at each other in Welsh, which is just about the world's most incomprehensible bloody language. We try to quiz the landlady: 'Are you sure you didn't know them,

Mrs. Davies, they only lived two hundred yards away, surely you heard the shots, didn't you?' Everybody in Wales is called Jones or Davies, terrible interbreeding. 'Will you take your tea now?' she says. 'It's nearly time for the chapel.' Then she waddles out on us. And she'd been to chapel twice that day already!

"And we're there for hours and bloody hours, Freddie Payne of the *Express*, Jack Beddall of the *Sketch*, and me, knocking on the doors of these broken-down farmhouses, trying to drag a statement out of Chief-Inspector-bloody-Davies-no-relation. Trying to cultivate the local reporter who didn't even drink, even when it wasn't Sunday. Getting absolutely nowhere. Dreadful times, old boy."

Giles Freeman sighed. "Look, that's . . ."

A restraining hand went up. Nobody deflected old Winstone Thorpe from his punchline.

"So, what I did in the end, I went over to the local chapel and picked a name off a bloody gravestone. Emrys Lloyd – never forget it. And I wandered back to the pub and button-holed one of these local shepherd-types. 'Look here, I suspect this is a long shot, old boy, but I don't suppose you knew this great-uncle of mine. Emrys Lloyd, his name. Told he used to live in this neck of the woods . . .'"

He paused while everybody laughed, except Giles.

"Told 'em my name was Ivor Lloyd and I'd been born in Wales but moved out at an early age, always regretted I'd never learned the good old language, all this bullshit . . . Well, dammit, you couldn't stop the sods talking after that. Gave me everything I wanted. No longer one of the enemy, you see. I could be trusted. They even felt sorry for me because I was a bloody exile in England, can you believe that?"

"No," said Giles Freeman loudly, something catching fire behind his freckles. "It's utter bollocks. You made it up. You've always made things up, you old bastard."

Winstone Thorpe looked hurt. "Not a bit of it, old boy, that was precisely what happened. And the thing is –"

"Utter balls," Giles said contemptuously. He glared across the table at Winstone. "You're just a boring old con-man."

And that, Berry perceived, was the point at which the other guys decided that Giles, irrespective of the amount of booze he'd put away, had overstepped the mark and should be dealt with for pissing on a national monument.

Giles didn't notice the guys exchanging glances. "You know why the Welsh are suspicious of the English?" he demanded, slapping the table, making waves in all the glasses.

"Actually," said Shirley Gillies, one of the BBC's political reporters, "I once –"

"Just hang on a minute, Shirley. Listen, I'll tell you why. Because we're so . . . bloody . . . smug. We think we're the greatest bloody race on earth. We think we're great by tradition. And the idea of people here in Britain, in our island, who don't want to speak English . . . we think that's a joke. Because ours is the language of Shakespeare and Keats and Barbara bloody Cartland . . ."

"Actually," Shirley Gillies repeated, as if Giles was some stray drunk who didn't really belong in their corner, "I had rather a similar experience of being frozen out in Wales. Only I wasn't as clever as you, Winstone. I rather left with egg on my face."

And this mention of egg reminded Charlie Firth, of the *Mail*, of the time he and his wife had gone into this Welsh snack bar for a meal just as it was about to close. The waitresses had muttered to each other – in Welsh, of course – and eventually served Charlie and Mrs. Firth a couple of scrambled eggs which had left them both with seriously upset stomachs. "Had to stop off at about seven public lavs on the way back," Charlie said. "Like, you expect it in Spain, but . . ."

"Poisoned," said Max Canavan, of the *Sun*. "They poisoned you on account of you was English, yeh?"

Voices had risen, everybody grinning, suddenly having fun thinking up horror stories about Wales. Or more likely, Berry figured, *making them up* as a communal putdown for Giles. Other hacks in the bar, not part of Winstone's farewell pissup, were gathering around, sensing that electric change in the atmosphere, noses almost visibly twitching. The pack instinct was always strong among British national journalists. Guys from papers which were bitter rivals hung out together like a street gang.

"Oh dear me, look," old Winstone said. "I didn't want to start –"

"Always been like that," said Brian McAllister of the Press Association. "I remember once I was in Colwyn flamin' Bay . . . Anybody ever been to Colwyn Bay?"

"Called in once, but it was closed," Charlie Firth said.

"Bloody Welsh," one of the newcomers said. "Frogs, Krauts, Eyeties – I can get along with all of 'em, but the bloody Welsh . . ."

"Right." Giles was on his feet, swaying, freckles ablaze. "I've fucking had enough of this." He was very angry and began to extricate himself from the table. "Bigoted, racist bastards . . ."

"No, mate, they're the racists," Ray Wheeler of the *Mirror* said gleefully. "The Welsh. Ever since we beat the brown stuff out of 'em back in, when was it, I dunno, Edward the First and all that."

"Piss off," Giles snarled, and slammed his glass down so hard that it cracked in two places. Giles being Giles, he paid for it on his way out.

Berry hesitated a moment, then followed him.

CHAPTER VII

Giles had been pacing the pavement under a mild summer drizzle. As Berry came up behind him he swung round murderously. Berry swiftly put a lamp-post between them.

"Who the hell's that?" Giles said.

Berry stepped out from behind the post.

"Oh," Giles said. "You."

"Yeah."

"If it was that fucking Firth I was going to –"

"Sure."

Giles grinned, white teeth flashing in the headlights of a Bentley whispering somebody home. "Bit pissed. Sorry. Those bastards." He pushed fingers through his heavy fair hair. "Feel a bit of a prat now, actually. Shouldn't have let them wind me up. Shouldn't have gone for old Winstone like that. Not like me. Am I very pissed?"

Berry looked him up and down. "Smashed outa your skull," he said.

Giles laughed. "You're probably quite a decent guy, Berry, for an American. You didn't say anything bad about Wales."

"That's because I never went there, Giles. It most likely is the armpit of Britain."

"Bastard."

"Sure."

The pub door opened and Giles swung round again in case it was somebody he felt he ought to hit. Ted Wareham, of the

47

Independent, came out grasping a bottle of Scotch. He didn't notice them.

"So you're leaving us, Giles," Berry said.

Giles said rather wearily, "I don't know. Don't know what to do. For a while I've been looking around and thinking it's time I moved on. Where do you go? It's a trap."

"Trap?"

"The money for one thing," Giles said. "We moan sometimes, but, bloody hell, where else can you collect on this scale in our job? Plus, it's an addictive sort of life. Policing the Great and Good, or whatever it is we do. But the thought of spending another thirty years around this bit of London, drinking with the same blokes, getting older and shabbier and ending up, at best, as some lovable father figure with a face full of broken veins and a knackered liver . . ."

"That wouldn't happen to you, Giles," Berry said, meaning it. "You're not in that mould."

"What's that mean?"

Berry shrugged.

"Anyway I reckon we've been thrown a lifeline, Claire and me. To pull us out of our complacency. Just came out of the blue. Something we'd just never thought of. We drove out there – couple of weeks ago – first thing in the morning. Quite a grey morning, everything really drab. But by the time we got there it was a gorgeous day, and it got better and better. And we found the cottage almost straight away, just as if we were being guided. Up the street, over the bridge, past the church, along this shady country lane and there it was. I felt –"

Giles hugged the lamp-post in a burst of passion, then pulled away. "Bloody beer. This is not like me, not like me at all. You'll go back in there and tell them what I said and all have a fucking good laugh."

"Aw, Giles, come on . . ."

"Sorry, sorry . . . an injustice."

"Those guys didn't even notice me leave, 'cept for Winstone. So what did you feel?"

"What?"

"When you saw the place. What did you feel?"

"Look, here's a cab. I'll have to grab it, OK? Excitement, Berry. Only more than that, much more. I didn't want to come back. Course it was all locked up, we couldn't get in that day, just peering through the windows like Hansel and bloody Gretel. It was enchanting. I'd have stayed there all day and slept on the grass when it got dark." Giles got into the taxi. "Tell the buggers that, why don't you. I don't care."

Berry watched the cab's tail-lights vanish into the traffic along what used to be Fleet Street.

Then he went back into the bar.

"Those stories," Berry said. "All shit, right? Kind of, let's put the frighteners on ole Giles."

"Yes and no, old boy." Winstone Thorpe said. "Yes and no."

"Meaning?"

"Meaning, probably, that nobody poisoned Charlie Firth. Can you really see that man dining on unlicensed premises?"

At close to midnight, old Winstone and Berry Morelli were the only two left, Berry because he thought he had nobody to go home to tonight and Winstone because – as he'd told them all earlier – he suspected that when he walked out of the bar this time he'd never come back. People had been shaking his hand and promising to look in on him sometime. Berry didn't think any of them ever would.

"And no?"

"No what?"

"You said 'yes and no'."

"Ah." Winstone finished off his last Glenfiddich. At this hour even he wouldn't get served again. "I suppose . . . Well, I was drinking with our property chap the other day. Do you know how many English people have bought homes in Wales over the past few years? Tens of thousands, apparently. Mind boggles. Got them cheap, you see – well, cheap compared with the south-east. Plenty of spare cash about down here these days. So it's holiday homes, retirement homes, views of the mountains, views of the sea."

Winstone put his glass down, sat back. "Backs to the wall, now, the Joneses and the Davieses. Getting driven out, along with what's left of their language, by all these foreigners searching for the old rural-idyll bit."

Like Giles.

"Very pretty and all that, apparently, this cottage of Claire's. They're so enchanted with the place, they're talking about leaving London altogether and trying to make a living out there . . . or even commute, for God's sake."

Winstone shook his head sadly. "Pretended I was asleep, but really I was the only one listening to him. Oh dear . . . Bad news, old boy. Going to get ugly. Seen it before. Nothing drives people to loony extremes more than religion and national pride."

"We never learned much about Wales at school, back home."

"A hard and bitter land, old boy. Don't have our sensibilities, never been able to afford them. We go there in our innocence, the English, and we're degraded and often destroyed. I'm talking about North Wales and the West, where they've always danced on the edge of the abyss. Look, this is most unlike me, but is there some club we could go on to?"

Berry smiled. "It isn't the end, Winstone. They said you could freelance for them, right?"

"Not the same, old boy. Wife gone, kids abroad. Paper's been my family." Winstone put a hand on Berry's arm and the ancient eyes flickered. "Look, you put the arm on young Giles. Persuade

50

PHIL RICKMAN

him to get the bloody place sold. Soon as he can. We're really not meant to be there, you know, the English. Stop him. I mean it. You have to do this for the boy. He won't survive. *Listen* to me, this is not the drink."

Berry met Winstone's urgent, bloodshot gaze and saw some long-buried sorrow there. "C'mon," he said. "I know somewhere." He thought Winstone was suddenly looking too old and too sober. "Anyway, you try and talk Giles out of something, he just gets more determined."

"He's a decent chap, compared to most of us," Winstone said. "But naïve. Innocent. Throw everything away if somebody doesn't stop him. You see – as an American you may not understand this, but the thing is, Giles made the big time too soon. What's he now, thirty-three, thirty-four? My day, you were lucky if you'd made it to the nationals at all by that age. So now Giles is looking around and he's thinking, where on earth do I go from here? What's there left to do? Sort of premature mid-life crisis, everything comes younger these days. And of course he can see all the editors getting alarmingly younger too. One day his copy's being handled by some chap who only shaves twice a week. Or worse still –" Winstone got unsteadily to his feet and reached for his raincoat "– not shaving at all, if you see what I mean."

"Women," Berry said.

Winstone scowled. "So he's looking for a new adventure. But he thinks – fatal this – he *thinks* he's looking for his soul."

"In Wales?"

"Insanity." Winstone paused in the doorway, took a last look around the almost deserted bar. His face was pale, his jowls like tallow dripping down a candle. "The boy was right. I talk too much nonsense. So now nobody believes my stories any more."

"Winstone, Giles was smashed."

51

The old journalist smiled wistfully and walked out into the street, where the night was warm but rain was falling.

"You know, old boy," he said after a moment, turning and looking around him in apparent confusion, "I must say I feel rather odd."

"It's gonna pass, Winstone, believe me, it's gonna pass. You just got to find a new . . . Hey –"

Winstone gripped the lamp-post which Giles had hugged in his drunken excitement. "Do you know what, old boy?" he said conversationally. "I think I'm having another stroke."

"Huh . . . ?"

Winstone Thorpe quietly slid down to his knees on the wet pavement, as if offering a final prayer to the old gods of what used to be Fleet Street.

"Shit," Berry breathed. He stared down at Winstone in horror. The old man smiled.

Berry dashed back and stuck his head round the pub door. "Somebody call an ambulance! Listen, I'm not kidding. It's ole Winstone!"

He rushed back to the old man. "Hey, come on, let's get you back inside, OK?"

But, as he bent down, Winstone toppled – almost nonchalantly, it seemed – on to his face. As if his prayer had been answered.

CHAPTER VIII

"Dead?" Giles said. "But that's wonderful."

Claire passed him his coffee. "Oh, Giles, let's not get –"

"I know, I know, I'm sorry, it's the beer. Bit pissed. But it is rather wonderful, isn't it? Not for the old boy, of course, but we've all got to go sometime and, bloody hell, he couldn't have chosen a better time for us, could he?"

"You can't say that yet," Claire said. "They might not even let you do it."

She'd been waiting up for him with the news, that mischievous little tilt to her small mouth; she knew something he didn't. It was as near as Claire ever came to expressing excitement.

Giles had both hands around his coffee cup, squeezing it. "Let them try and stop me," he said. "Just let the bastards try. Did it say on the news what his majority was?"

"I don't think so. They may have. It was still dawning on me, the significance of it, you know."

"Right then." Giles sprang to his feet. "Let's find out."

"Will you get anybody? It's nearly one o'clock."

"No problem." He was already stabbing out the night-desk number on the cordless phone. Standing, for luck, under the framed blow-up of Claire's first photograph of the cottage, the one taken from between the two sycamores at the entrance to the lane. They'd taken down a Michael Renwick screenprint to make space for it on the crowded buttermilk wall above the rebuilt fireplace.

"Peter, that you? Oh, sorry, look, is Peter there? It's Giles Freeman. Yes, I'll wait."

There were blow-ups of five of Claire's photographs on the walls. None of the award-winning Belfast stuff, nothing heavy. Just the atmosphere pics: the old woman collecting driftwood on the shore, the shadowed stillness of a cathedral close at dusk, that kind of thing. The picture of the cottage was the only one that hadn't appeared in a paper or a magazine. Giles loved it. He was still amazed by Claire's ability to move at once to the right angle, to link into a scene.

"Peter. Listen, sorry to bother you, but I've just heard about Burnham-Lloyd, the MP for Glanmeurig. Was there time for you to run it in the final?" Giles sniffed. "Well, I think you should have, Peter, I really do, even if it *is* only Wales." He and Claire exchanged meaningful glances. "Anyway, listen, Peter, what was his majority?"

Giles waited. Claire perched on the edge of the sofa and cupped her small face in her slender hands, short, fair hair tufting through the fingers. She wore a cream silk dressing gown and wooden sandals. Giles, re-energised by the news, eyed her lustfully.

"Bloody hell," he said. "That's not bad. That's not at all bad. Thank you, Peter, thank you very much indeed."

He cleared the line and made a whooshing sound.

"Narrow?" Claire asked.

Giles said, very slowly and precisely, "Eight hundred and seventy-one." His freckles were aglow again. He tossed the phone almost to the ceiling and caught it. "Eight hundred and seventy fucking one! It's marginal, Claire! Plaid's been slowly gaining on him for years! Oh, God, I really do feel something's working for us."

"I suppose," Claire said thoughtfully. "I feel a bit scared now. It's all coming at once. Propelling us into something. Out of our control." She was still feeling upset, actually, by her mother's reaction. She'd phoned her while Giles was out, to explain about the inheritance, tonight being the first opportunity since her parents had returned from their cruise.

Giles was hungrily pacing the carpet. "What I'll suggest is a bit of a recce. Zoom up there this weekend. Take the air. Talk to people."

"I can't. I've got that thing for the *Observer* in Norwich." Claire was glad to put it off. She'd been frightened by her own emotional response when they'd first gone to look at the cottage. The feeling that somehow she was *meant* to live there. Now she wanted to slow things down, give them time to think. Giles, however, had to be firing on all cylinders or none at all.

"Well, all right, *next* weekend," he said impatiently. "You see, what we have to do is build this up as a really significant midterm by-election, knock off a couple of prelim pieces, hype it up a bit. We can have the cottage as our base, save them hotel bills and stuff. And while we're there . . . I mean, with the run-up and everything, we're talking well over three weeks for a by-election campaign. So we can do all the groundwork, either for persuading them they really need a full-time staffer in Wales or setting up some decent freelance outlets. I would have sounded people out tonight, but they were all being so bloody snide and superior."

Slow down, slow down, Claire yelled inside her head. But Giles in overdrive was not open to reasonable argument. She wanted to tell him about her mother, but in his present state of drink-enhanced euphoria he wouldn't take it in. And even when stone cold sober, hearing what she'd had to say – the bitch – would only harden his determination.

As expected, her mother had been stiff and resentful, so Claire herself had gone on the attack.

"Mother, why didn't you tell me he was dead? Why did I have to find out from the solicitor?"

Elinor made an impatient noise. "Because . . . Oh, look, we only found out the day we left. I mean, really, what was I supposed to do, put it in a postcard from Greece? Weather fine, old Rhys dead?"

Old Rhys. Claire's grandfather.

"But – I can't believe this – he was your *father*."

A distant snort.

"I know, I know," Claire snapped. "But that doesn't alter anything, does it?"

"It clearly altered things for him, if he's left his awful hovel to *you*. He only ever saw you once. I wonder what he did with his money."

"It seems," Claire said icily, "that he left most of it to the Church."

There'd been a silence, then Elinor gave her a short, false cackle. "Oh dear, do excuse me. It's simply that the idea of God and my father discovering each other in that ghastly Welsh backwater is rather too much to take at this hour of the night."

Claire had expected bitterness, had been ready for *some* of this. But nothing as unpleasant as . . .

"What happened to his whores, I wonder. Perhaps he was predeceased. Do you think he died alone and unloved? I do hope so."

This is awful, Claire thought. She knew her mother did not need the money. But she must, all the same, have hoped for some token in the will, a sign that Thomas Rhys even remembered once having a wife and a daughter . . . as well as a grandchild.

"Did you – tell me the truth now, Claire – did you ever go to visit him, you and Giles?"

56

"Of course not! I mean . . ." There had, it was true, often been times when Claire had felt powerfully drawn to seek out the mysterious Judge Rhys. That tug of curiosity edged with an undefined sense of guilt and longing, whenever she'd come across a picture of Welsh mountains on some holiday brochure. And then there'd been that electric moment when she'd first seen the village – a mere three months ago, but it felt to Claire as if she'd known it all her life in some unexplored part of her soul.

"Then why?" Elinor's voice was flat and hard. "Apart from a desire to spit on your grandmother and me. Why? Can you explain it?"

"No," Claire said in a small voice. "Mother, look, I – I know you must be terribly hurt –"

"Don't patronise me, Claire. I'm extremely glad the old swine's gone, I didn't want a penny of his money and I shall be thankful when you've sold that damned house for as much as you can get."

"Sell it?"

"Well, you're hardly going to live in it, are you?" her mother had said.

"I've been thinking," Giles was saying. "Perhaps we should make contact with a few of the local tradesmen – plumbers, carpenters. Book them in advance. Sometimes guys like that can be jolly hard to find in rural areas, and they need lots of notice. Then we're going to need an automatic washing machine and all that. We shall have to work pretty fast."

"Yes, but, Giles . . . what if the by-election goes ahead before probate's complete. There's no way round that, you know. We can't let workmen into a house that isn't ours yet."

Claire somehow felt she had to create as many obstacles as she could to counteract the awesome pull of the village. To make sure that it was the right thing to do, that it really was *meant*.

"Won't happen," Giles said confidently. "No way there'll be a by-election until all the party conferences are safely over. We're talking November at least."

Claire realised then that this by-election could be quite a good thing after all. It would give them a trial period to see if life in Wales really suited them. Trying to get the cottage into some kind of shape and cover an election campaign at the same time would be quite a testing experience. And if they realised they were making a big mistake they could always come back here and either sell the place or keep it as a holiday home – and feel grateful they hadn't burned their boats.

"I'll tell you one thing, though," Giles said, leaning against the remoulded plaster of the fireplace. "Those bastards tonight, my so-called colleagues. It's made me realise how badly I want to get out of all this. It's a phoney life, a façade, just a garish back-cloth we think we can perform against. Not real at all. I mean, I can't get on with those guys any more. Even Winstone – Christ, I thought he was a friend." He shook his head, mouth tight.

Then he loosened up and flashed Claire a grin. "What have you got on under there?" He tossed the phone into an armchair, threw off his jacket and plunged at the sofa.

Claire let him pull the dressing gown off her shoulders and suddenly quivered.

Nothing to do with Giles. Something her mother had said was replaying itself. She hadn't realised at the time, hadn't seen the significance.

. . . *left his awful hovel to you. He only ever saw you once . . .*

When? Claire didn't remember ever seeing her grandfather. She'd always understood there'd been no contact whatsoever since the day, two years before she was born, when Judge Thomas Rhys had gravely announced that he would be returning to the place of his birth, but his family would not be accompanying him.

So when?

Excitement and dread combined to make Claire shiver.

Giles moaned, lips tracking down her bare shoulder. "Darling . . ." he breathed.

CHAPTER IX

"Look," Miranda said. "I just don't see it. Why don't you come back to bed?"

The sun had emerged, and Miranda looked rosy and warm and inviting.

"I didn't expect you would," Berry said, standing by the window, turning to look into the street three storeys down. "What counts is how I see it." He gazed out towards the Thames. This building did not itself overlook the Thames but you could see some other buildings which did.

"Well, it certainly isn't *my* idea of a dying wish or a last request or whatever," Miranda said. "To make a last request you have to know you're dying. And from what you say, he didn't."

At the hospital, the tired-eyed young doctor on night-duty, jeans under the white coat, had said it looked like a small stroke followed by a second, massive stroke. Happened like an earthquake, or maybe an earthquake in reverse, a mild foreshock and then the big one. Bip, bam! Good a way to go as any, better than most. And he'd had a minor one before, had he? Say no more. Later, the cops had gone through the motions, because of the way it happened.

"I'm gonna call Giles," Berry said. "Maybe we can organise lunch."

. . . *Look, you put the arm on young Giles. Persuade him to get the bloody place sold. Soon as he can.*

"You were going to have lunch with *me*, remember, if you

were in town." Miranda pulled the duvet over her breasts and went into a pout.

Shit, how was he supposed to get this across?

"See, it's just . . . when I first came over here I didn't know England from a hole in the ocean and ole Winstone, he kind of initiated me."

"Is England so complicated?"

"Minefield," Berry said. He'd taken the job with the agency, American Newsnet, without thinking, in his haste to get out. Mario Morelli's son guilty of unAmerican behaviour.

"The English National Press, they were a club I didn't know how to join," he said. "I walked in this bar one night and sat down and all these guys stared at me like I'd thrown up on the table. After a while one leaned over and said out of the corner of his mouth, 'You do know you're sitting in Winstone's chair.'"

"I think I've seen that film," Miranda said.

"So I apologised to Winstone."

"As you would."

"And he became the first one of them I really talked to, you know? I asked him a whole bunch of those questions I didn't dare ask anyone else. By closing time he'd explained how Parliament worked and all those British niceties. Why it isn't done to talk to the Queen without she talks to you first, or label a guy a killer after he's charged and like that. No big deal, but he saved my ass a few times, while certain people stood around waiting for me to fall on it. He was always there, anything I needed to know. He drank like prohibition was starting tomorrow, but it didn't matter to him that I didn't join him."

"So long as you paid for his I shouldn't imagine it would bother him in the slightest," said Miranda. "You're endearingly naïve sometimes, Morelli."

"The only other guy ever spared the time to help me along was Giles," said Berry.

61

Stop him. I mean it.

"Morelli," Miranda said. "You're overreacting. If Freeman is loopy enough to want to throw up his career to go and live in wildest Wales it's his decision. None of your business. And if you think old-what's-his-name is going to come back and haunt you, you must be even simpler than most of your race. Now come back to bed. I warn you – last chance."

We're really not meant to be there, you know, the English.

"How much of a generalisation is it, that stuff about rugby and the Bible?"

"Wales? Who cares? It's still an awfully long way from Harrods."

"You're a big help, Miranda."

"Oh, you are a pain, Morelli. Look, I haven't been very often. It's got lovely mountains and nice beaches here and there. And in the south there used to be a lot of coal mines, and Cardiff's fairly civilised these days but terribly bland . . . But, from what you say, your friend is off to one of the primitive bits, about which I'm really not qualified to comment. You know me and the primitive. Admittedly, there are *times* for being primitive . . ."

Miranda put on her most lascivious smile which, Berry had to admit, was pretty damn lascivious.

"Yeah, OK," he said. "Maybe I'll call Giles later."

CHAPTER X

WALES

It was the third headline on the BBC Radio Wales news at 8 a.m.

". . . and Sir Maurice Burnham-Lloyd, Conservative MP for Glanmeurig for more than thirty years, is dead."

Guto Evans felt unexpectedly nervous. He lay in bed and waited for the full report. By the time it came on, he'd convinced himself that he definitely wasn't going to get the Plaid nomination. Dai Death had been right: no chance.

The whole report lasted just over one minute. After a summary of the high points of Burnham-Lloyd's career (Guto wondered how they'd managed to pad it out to twenty seconds) there was a short clip of the Secretary of State for Wales speaking over the telephone to the studio.

". . . but most of all," crackled the Secretary of State, "Maurice was a constituency man, a farmer among farmers. He was always *deeply* concerned that people in London and in Brussels should be *aware* of exactly how their policies would affect a sheep farmer in the heart of Glanmeurig."

Guto groaned, snapped off the radio and pushed back the covers. "Mam!" he shouted, hearing the clatter of a pan from downstairs. "Mam, no breakfast for me, I've got to go out right away, OK?"

Bethan. He had to see her before she left for school or he'd spend the day in a state of advanced paranoia. Being a widow seemed to have endowed Bethan with a certain aura of wisdom.

63

He found her making her way across the car park below the castle ruins. She was carrying her briefcase and a pile of exercise books to the little green Peugeot.

"What should I do then, Bethan?" Guto demanded without preamble.

"Now," said Bethan thoughtfully, leaning into the car. "Do you think I should put all these books into the boot or will they stay on the back seat without falling over?"

"Do I phone anybody or do I wait for them to contact me?" said Guto in agony. "Don't want them to think I'm pushing, see."

"I think what I shall do," said Bethan, "is put them on the back seat and prop them up behind the briefcase."

"I've got to be well placed for it. I mean, I'm pretty well known locally."

Bethan straightened up. She was wearing a black cardigan over a white cotton dress, and big gold earrings. Guto felt a pang of something not connected with politics.

"Well, Guto," she said. "There you have identified the problem. You are *exceedingly* well known locally."

They stared at each other across the roof of the little car.

"What are you getting at?"

"Well, who in this town has not heard you ranting on at length about the English and what we should do to keep them out? Ah, they say to strangers, you know who that is, don't you? That is Guto Evans, the famous extremist."

"Well, good God, woman, they all *agree* with me."

"Of course they don't, and neither does the party. Guto, the one thing you must never suggest these days is that Welsh nationalist means anti-English."

"I know that, but . . ."

"And a by-election! In-depth scrutiny by the media of all the candidates, especially ours. Muck-raking. Well, think about it

64

– can Plaid credibly be represented by a man who once had a homing device attached to the underside of his van so the police could keep track of his movements?"

"Oh, now, that was a mistake. They thought I was –"

"But it will come out. So will the pub brawl –"

"I was never charged, for God's sake –"

"Only because all your friends lied through their teeth. Now, Guto, I'm not saying that, in one respect, a man of your talents would not be the best hope in a by-election. But you have a lot of work to do. Have to change your image, Guto. People must get used to seeing you around in a smart suit and a tie. And er –" Bethan smothered a giggle "– kissing babies."

"Aaaargh," growled Guto in disgust.

"English babies too." Bethan slid into her car.

Guto watched her drive away, dragging a cloud of early-morning exhaust across the Pontmeurig bypass and on to the mountain road to Y Groes. Though still warm, it was the first grey morning in three weeks. There was rain in the air and mist on the hills.

"Damn it, Bethan," Guto mumbled wistfully, shambling back into the town, past the castle destroyed by his hero, Owain Glyndwr. "If I could have you, they could stuff the bloody nomination."

Impossibly, as Bethan drove out of the forestry, the mist appeared to evaporate and the church tower of Y Groes shimmered in a shaft of gold.

It's a blue hole, this place, Bethan thought, but she took no great pleasure in the thought these days.

The school was on the other side of the river in a little lane of its own, screened from the village by a row of elms which had somehow survived successive epidemics of Dutch Elm Disease when nearly all the others for miles around had succumbed.

Bethan liked to get to school at least ten minutes before the first of the children, but Guto had delayed her and there was a small group of them around the wooden gate, chattering in Welsh. They stopped when they saw Bethan and chorused dutifully, "*Bore da*, Mrs. McQueen."

"*Bore da, blant*," said Bethan, shouldering the gate open, arms full of briefcase and books. The children followed her in, all good Welsh-speaking children from Welsh-speaking families, not a single English cuckoo. Which disappointed Bethan in a way, because she used to enjoy the challenge of taking a handful of children from London or Birmingham at the age of five and then sending them on to the secondary school completely fluent in Welsh, even starting to think in Welsh.

The school had been lucky to survive so long with only twenty-four pupils. Twice the education authority had attempted to close it down and transfer the children to Pontmeurig. But that would have meant an eight-mile journey for them along a mountain road that was often impassable in winter, and the local councillors had won the day.

Bethan waded into the school through a puddle of children, the smallest ones pulling at her skirt to attract her attention. She never discouraged them. The school had a warm family atmosphere.

"*Bore da*, Mrs. Morgan," the children sang, as Buddug entered, the deputy head teacher or Bethan's entire staff, depending on how you saw it. Buddug, a big woman in her middle fifties, a farmer's wife with red cheeks full of broken veins, like a map of the London Underground, had taught at Y Groes for over thirty years and was regarded as the head of the school by everyone except the county education officials who'd appointed Bethan.

"*Eisteddwch!*" Buddug commanded, and the children squeezed into their seats and snatched a final few seconds of chatter as Buddug strode across to the piano for the morning hymn which was only changed once a week and was limited to the three tunes Buddug could play, except at Christmas when carols were sung unaccompanied.

"Buddug," said Bethan in her ear, "can you spare me a couple of minutes during playtime? Something is bothering me."

Buddug beamed and nodded and crashed her stiffened fingers down on the keyboard like a butcher cleaving a side of beef.

"It's this," said Bethan determinedly, and opened the child's exercise book to reveal the drawing of the corpse and the corpse candle over the grave.

"Yes, isn't it good?" said Buddug. She turned over the exercise book to read the name on the front. "Sali Dafis. Her writing has improved enormously over the past few weeks, and look at the detail in those drawings!"

"I'm not objecting to the quality of it," said Bethan. "It's more the content. I asked them to pretend they were working for the *papur bro* and to write about something which had happened in the village."

"Excellent," said Buddug. "And were any of the others as good as this one?" She stared insolently at Bethan out of dark-brown eyes.

"Oh, Buddug, what are you trying to do to me?"

"I don't understand. What are you objecting to? What sort of ideas have you brought back from the city? Would you rather the children wrote about one-parent families and lesbians?" Buddug laughed shrilly.

Bethan snatched back the book and turned away, blinking back angry tears. Seeing, out of the window, the children in the playground, seeing a certain corruption in their eyes and their milk-teeth smiles.

"I accept," she said carefully, still looking out of the window, her back to Buddug, "that a child has to learn about death. I don't believe that being taken to view a neighbour in her coffin and being informed that her dying was foretold by the corpse candle is a particularly healthy way of going about it."

She gathered her resolve and whirled back at Buddug, who was wearing an expression of mild incomprehension now, like a cow over a gate.

"I don't believe," Bethan said furiously, "that little children should see the woods not as the home of squirrels and somewhere to collect acorns but as the place where the *Gorsedd Ddu* hold their rituals. I don't believe that when they hear the thunder they should think it's the sound of Owain Glyndwr rolling about in his grave. I don't want them looking at storm clouds and not seeing formations of cumulonimbus but the Hounds of Annwn gathering for the hunt. I just don't believe –"

"You don't believe in anything!" Buddug said, smiling, eyes suddenly alight. "And this is not a place for people who do not believe in anything. Playtime is over. Time to bring them in."

She rang the brass handbell with powerful twists of an old milkmaid's wrist.

CHAPTER XI

ENGLAND

The rolling countryside of the Cotswolds was turning out to be good therapy for Berry's car, which had been a mite bronchitic of late.

He drove an old Austin Healey Sprite of a colour which, when the Sprite was born, was known as British Racing Green. He loved this car. It coughed and rattled sometimes and was as uncomfortable as hell, but it was the fulfilment of a dream he'd had since seeing an old detective show back in the States called *Harry O*, whose hero drove a British MG sports car and was, even by Californian standards, very laid back.

The Cotswolds, also, were laid back, often in a surprisingly Californian way: rich homes sprawled languidly behind lush foliage which was not so lush that you couldn't admire the beautiful bodies of the houses and their gorgeous Cotswold tans. Was this what remained of olde England: a burglar alarm and a Volvo estate car outside some cottage originally built for farmworkers who couldn't afford their own cart?

Touch of therapy for Berry too, to be out here. Distances were negligible in Britain. Couple of hours ago he'd been in the office, the combination of events and Miranda ensuring that by the time he arrived at work he was already feeling overtired. This had cut no ice at all with American Newsnet's London bureau chief, Addison Walls, who'd ordered him to go at once to Gloucestershire, where the Government's Energy Secretary had his country home. The Minister was to give an unofficial Press conference explaining why he'd chosen to resign over the Oil Crisis.

"Anybody in the States give a shit about this?" Berry had asked, and Addison Walls looked at him like he was crazy.

"Morelli, watch my lips. The Oil Crisis. O–I–L."

"Yeah, yeah, OK. Just tired is all."

"Get outa here," muttered Addison Walls. "Fuckin' radical."

When he finally arrived at what turned out to be quite a modest Cotswold farmhouse – barely an acre of land around it – Berry learned he'd missed the Press conference by a good twenty minutes. He found two reporters chatting by their cars in the lane. One was Shirley Gillies of the BBC with a black Uher tape-recorder over her shoulder. The other was Giles Freeman, his wheat-coloured hair uncombed and grey circles under his eyes.

"Don't worry about it, mate," he told Berry, waving a weary, dismissive hand. "Wasn't worth coming. Terse statement, nothing new in it. Wouldn't answer questions. Posed for a few simpering pictures with his wife. Didn't offer us coffee."

"Giles rebuked him for wasting our time," Shirley Gillies said. "I'm afraid if I spoke like that to a Government Minister, the next farewell piss-up would be mine, but he as good as apologised to Giles. Who can be quite impressive when he's sober."

Giles, who was wearing a crumpled cream suit, shrugged in a what-the-hell kind of way. The attitude of a guy who wasn't planning to be around much longer, Berry thought. He hesitated then said, "Ah, talking of farewell piss-ups. I suppose you . . ."

Giles sighed. "It was all round the office. What can I say? I feel awful. Easy to say, 'If only I'd known.' I mean, God –"

Berry wondered if this might be the time to fulfil his obligation to put the arm on Giles. He couldn't, however, say anything with Shirley around. Couldn't think, anyway, how to start. Suppose old Winstone was simply paranoid?

"Still, I suppose if he'd had a choice of where to snuff it," Giles said, "he'd probably have opted for the pub."

"I gather you were still there, Berry," Shirley Gillies said brightly, "when it happened."

"Yeah," Berry said. "Tell you about it sometime."

"Yes," Shirley said, clearly meaning no. "Look, I must go. See you around, Giles."

Giles and Berry stood in silence in the Cotswold lane as Shirley loaded her gear into her car. It was a soft, dull summer morning, still moist from last night's rain.

"Bloody awful smug place, this," Giles said. "Not exactly nature in the raw, is it? Not like –" He broke off.

"You gonna give me the Minister's statement?"

"Sure. Let's find a pub. You don't have to rush back?"

Berry shook his head. Giles said abruptly, "We're nowhere near bloody Painswick, are we?"

"Now how would I know that?"

"Claire's mother lives near Painswick. Wouldn't like to run into the old bat. Not just now. I wouldn't be responsible."

Berry followed Giles's silver BMW in his beat-up Sprite. They motored through shimmering ochre villages before pulling up at Hollywood's idea of an olde English pub, outside which Giles had detected an obscure Real Ale sign. They sat on upholstered wooden stools at the bar, the first customers of the day. On Giles's recommendation, Berry ordered two halves of something even thicker and murkier than Hollywood's idea of English beer.

"Hair of the dog," Giles said. "Bloody animal."

"He'd hate you to feel bad about this, Giles. He was very fond of you and Claire. Winstone, I mean."

Giles found a lop-sided smile. He told Berry a couple of funny old Winstone anecdotes from way back. Berry had heard both before, but he chuckled over them anyway, for Giles's sake, assuring him again that Winstone had in no way been offended by the way he'd stormed out of the bar and no, there was no way it had caused any stress which might have hastened the stroke.

"That story he told," Berry said, fishing for a reaction, "about the domestic murder and the Welsh landlady and all. I guess it was kind of a Winstone parable. He'd been hearing about how bad things were over in Wales. Folks feeling their heritage was being ripped off. Dumb foreigners on a back-to-nature trip stampeding the sacred cows."

"Yes," Giles said. "But don't you go thinking we're going to be like that, Claire and me. We aren't going to march in like bloody yuppies on the make. We'll learn the language, the whole bit. Go, er, go native. Well . . . I . . . You're not really interested in hearing this, are you, Berry?"

"I am, Giles."

"You sure? I think people were bored last night."

"No way, Giles. Jealous is all."

"You think that?"

"Sure. Tell me about Wales, Giles."

Giles shrugged and had a slurp of Real Ale.

"Well, for a start, even though she'd never even been there before this, Claire has very strong family links with this village, Y Groes. So we feel we're . . . reviving something. And reviving ourselves in the process. Do you know what I mean?"

"When I was a kid," Berry said, "they used to tell me my great-grandpa made the best pasta in Venice. That doesn't mean that to find eternal fulfilment I have to be a fucking gondolier."

Giles gave him a warning look and started rocking on his bar stool. "Look, poor old Winstone struck a nerve when I was pissed. I'm sorry about that, but it doesn't change anything. You hear about Burnham-Lloyd?"

"Who?"

72

Giles told Berry about the impending by-election. It seemed to restore his mood. "Brilliant timing, don't you think? Not just another mid-term by-election, old son." He was holding his beer to the light and nodding appreciatively at tiny specks in the umber fluid. Berry pushed his own glass away in disgust.

"Burnham-Lloyd," Giles said. "Tory, OK? Held that seat for over thirty years on the strength of being a local chap, well in with the farmers, all that. But Plaid Cymru – that's the Welsh nationalist party – have been slowly gaining on him for years. The other parties haven't much support, so it's a two-horse race. Going to be a cracker. Gives me a chance to go in there as a reporter, meet the local people, discover all the key local issues. So when we move we won't be going in cold."

Berry nodded. Maybe Giles wouldn't get along with the local people, would discover he was out of sympathy with the local issues. Well, maybe . . .

"What about you, Berry? Has it got Newsnet potential? I'll tell you – mass-immigration by English people is sure to be a major issue. And the one that could give the seat to Plaid. Absolutely fascinating."

"What are we looking at here, Giles? Beginnings of an Ulster situation?"

"Oh, good God no. They're just after devolution to begin with, power to run their own affairs. Then to become a free state within Europe. Not a huge step for Wales – or Scotland, for that matter. And, in spite of the odd bits of terrorism, it's not a nation inflamed by anti-English passions, whatever old – whatever people say."

"Yeah," Berry said non-commitally. Most Americans didn't even realise Wales was a separate country. If they mentioned it at all they talked about "Wales, England", like it was some district.

"We were going to drive out there this weekend," Giles was

saying. "Make a few political contacts and have a little drool over our cottage at the same time. Won't be ours for a couple of months yet – legal red-tape – but it's a wonderful feeling, just standing in the lane gazing at it through the trees, making plans."

Berry noticed the grey circles under Giles's eyes had shrunk and his freckles were aglow.

Look, you put the arm on young Giles.

"Only we can't go because Claire's saddled with this job for the *Observer* in East Anglia –"

"Too bad," Berry said.

"Unless … Hey, look, Berry, what are you doing next weekend?"

Playing with Miranda. "Nothing fixed," Berry said.

"Feel like taking a drive out there?"

"To Wales?" She'll kill me, he thought.

"You could get it on exes, surely? Bit of research?"

"Well, I –"

"And you could come and see our cottage, see Y Groes – and then you'd realise why we're so excited about it."

Persuade him to get the bloody place sold.

"Come on, Berry, it'll be fun."

Not meant to be there, the English.

"What do you say?"

Stop him. I mean it.

"Yeah, OK," Berry said. "Why not?"

CHAPTER XII

WALES

"Miss Sion!"

Bethan turned at the school door, the key in her hand. "You decided you'd better come back then, did you, Sali?"

She was small for her age, Sali Dafis, and looked more fragile than other members of her family. Her father, Dilwyn, and her *nain* had coal-black hair, but Sali's was wispy brown. A legacy from her mother, the secretary from Essex whom Dilwyn had met on holiday at Butlins, Pwllheli.

"It's a bit late now, though, isn't it?" Bethan said. "And I'm not Miss Sion any more, remember?"

They were alone in the yard. It was a gloomy afternoon now. Overcast. A reminder of how rapidly the days were shortening. Locking the school door, Bethan had heard a child's shoes tripping across the yard towards her and wondered if it would be Sali.

"See me after school, please," she'd finally written in the exercise book, but Sali had gone off with the others half an hour ago. Now she was back, alone. An indication that she didn't want her friends to know she was seeing the teacher.

"But, Miss Sion, your husband is dead."

Bethan breathed in sharply, as if stabbed. Children could be vicious.

"Mrs. McQueen, if you don't mind. I won't tell you again. We don't go back to our old names just because –" Bethan

75

had a thought. "Who told you to start calling me Miss Sion again?"

Sali Dafis looked at her feet and said nothing.

"Never mind," Bethan said. "I think I can guess. Look, why don't we talk to each other tomorrow. We don't want your *nain* wondering where you are." Or the old hag will put a curse on me, she thought, then decided that wasn't funny.

Sali looked up at Bethan very solemnly and seemed about to say something.

"Well?"

"Mrs. McQueen," said Sali innocently, "would you like to see a dead body?"

Bethan put the key in her bag and snapped it shut. "All right, we'd better have our talk right now. You wait there while I put my things in the car, then we'll go for a walk."

She was definitely not in the mood for this.

They followed the river from the rear of the school towards the oak woods, most of which were coppiced by Meirion, the forester whose father had done it before him. It was like entering a huge, entimbered medieval cathedral. Awesome in the right light, but dim and heavy now, the trees immense and gnarled, prickly bushes in the shade of some of them. The river entered the woods and then went off on its own, away from the path.

"So whose was the dead body – the one you thought I might like to see?"

Bethan knew very well that nobody had died in the village recently, except for the antiquarian at the *Tafarn* and Mrs. Tegwyn Jones, Ty Canol, over a week before that.

"Don't know," Sali said.

"Why would you think I might even want to see this . . . this dead body?"

"Don't know," Sali said.

76

They were approaching the thick wooden gate draped with creepers that said on it one word.

Rheithordy.

The rectory. It was the only house in the wood. Well, not quite in the wood: the house itself was in a green clearing, but the encroaching oaks had claimed most of its garden, heavyweight sentinels around it. The rectory was itself hugely timber-framed, and Bethan found it all a bit ominous, as if the beams in the house's skeleton had only been borrowed from the wood.

Hurrying the child past the gate, because the rector also tended to give her the creeps, Bethan said, "You know what a dead body is, don't you, Sali?"

She saw the child nod without looking up. This was not going to be easy. Why did she feel, uncomfortably, that the big trees were listening to her with more attention than Sali?

"Do you really know what a dead body is? It's nothing to do with the person who used to be in the body. That is why we bury them – because they are no use to anyone any more. What people are is nothing to do with their bodies. The really important part is something that just uses the body to get around in. And when it's too old or badly damaged, we discard it, throw it away."

Bethan felt inadequate to the task of explaining to a seven-year-old the things that few adults claimed to understand. This was no time to be trite or patronising.

"When someone brings an old car or a Land-Rover into your dad's garage, he . . . he mends it. If he can. And if it's just too old and tired out, then he has to send the car to the scrapyard. And the driver gets a new one. That's what happens to our bodies when we've used them up – we get rid of them and then we get a new body – a heavenly body." This is pathetic, Bethan thought.

"I know *that*," Sali said scornfully, kicking at the dirt. "My *nain* can see people in their heavenly bodies."

Bethan stopped walking.

"Sometimes," Sali said, walking on then turning round on the path, "she asks me if I can see people in their heavenly bodies."

Dear God.

"But I can't," Sali said. "Well, I don't think I can. *Nain* says that is because my mam was English. She says the English haven't got the gift."

Lucky them, thought Bethan. They were following the path deep into the wood. It would soon be strewn with acorns. Season of mists and mellow fruitfulness and nature rambles and autumn leaves to press. Once, autumn had excited Bethan – the scent of burning leaves, logs gathered for the fire, newly made toast. Someone to eat it with. She thought, that's right, burst into tears in front of the child.

Instead, she sat down on a big tree stump and pulled Sali towards her, gripping the girl's arms. "Sali, look at me."

Sali gazed into Bethan's face. Disturbingly, she was reminded of the way Buddug had looked at her that morning. Condescending.

"Sali, some . . . some people don't want to let the dead go. Do you remember last year . . . my husband died."

The child stood stiffly between Bethan's hands. She did not seem interested.

"I was very sad," Bethan said. "I didn't want him to be dead. I used to think about him all the time. I still –"

"He was only English," Sali said.

"I – what did you say?"

Sali pulled quickly away and ran off.

"Sali! Come here!"

The child had vanished, as if the woods had absorbed her. Alone now in this sombre place Bethan thought, I've blown it. We're on different sides of some invisible barrier. She's gone to Buddug and Mrs. Bronwen Dafis.

"Sali, come back now, we have to go home."

The child had disappeared.

"Sali, where are you?"

The wood was heavy with age and stillness. No birds fluttered in the undergrowth. Overhead the branches formed a great canopy of darkest green, no breath of autumn yet among the foliage.

"Sali! This instant!"

Bethan had risen to her feet, feeling cold now in her white cotton dress. She stepped off the path and a bramble ensnared her shoe, pulling it off.

"Damn you, Sali –"

She tore her shoe away from the spiny tendril, scratching her hand, drawing blood. What was she bothering about? The kid probably knew every inch of these woods, and there were no marauding paedophiles in Y Groes.

"I'm going home now, Sali. If you want to stay here all night, that's up to you."

What if she'd fallen somewhere? Pushing on through the bushes, Bethan suddenly became aware of the sound of rushing water.

What if she'd fallen in the river?

"Sali! Shout if you can hear me!"

She saw where some of the undergrowth had recently been flattened, and she moved towards it. Overhead, the sky had darkened and mingled with the interwoven leaves. There was a harsh spattering of rain. She could hear it but couldn't feel it yet.

"Shout, Sali!"

She prised her way through the bushes towards the sound of water and felt her dress tear at the hem.

"Damn you, Sali, if you're –"

A blackberry had been squashed against her hip and she

looked down and saw bubbles of juice like dark blood. Then she slipped and fell down the river bank, rolling over and over.

The crows had taken his eyes.

That was the first thing she saw.

She was winded by the fall and lay on her back, a few yards from the water. Pain rippled up her left leg: ankle twisted.

A muddy boot swung gently about a yard above her head. She must have caught it as she rolled past. The boot made a sort of click as it swung against the other boot.

Bethan retched.

"I said, didn't I, Miss Sion?"

Sali Dafis was standing at the edge of the river looking proudly up at where he hung, nylon climber's rope under his chin, knotted around the branch, his tongue out, black now, and a dried-out pulp where the crows had taken his eyes.

CHAPTER XIII

Pontmeurig was eight miles from Y Groes, on the other side of the Nearly Mountains. A slow, messy drive, especially for a hearse.

It was an untidy town, mottled grey and brown, something that had rolled down from the hills in the Middle Ages and was still rolling, new housing estates and factories spilling over the old boundaries on either side of the river.

Still puzzled by the attitude of Aled Gruffydd, Dai Death drove the corpse into town past the cattle mart and the new car park and past what was left of the medieval castle, looming grey in the dusk. Sometime in the early fifteenth century the castle had been burned down by Owain Glyndwr, it was said, in retribution for something, and had never been rebuilt because nobody could remember why the hell they'd ever needed a castle in Pontmeurig anyway.

In a street squashed behind the ruins, almost opposite one of the town's three chapels, was an offensive new fast-food take-away, The Welsh Pizza House, owned, of course, by English people. Next to it was a small yard with a sign that said: V. W. Williams and Sons, Funeral Directors. Dai was parking the hearse under the sign when the police car drew up alongside and a constable wound down his window.

"You've done it again, Dai. He's not yours yet, he's ours."

"Oh, bloody hell," said Dai. "I'm sorry, Paul. Automatic pilot I'm on today. You back into the entry and I'll turn around."

"Daft bugger, Williams," he told himself, switching his lights on, then putting the hearse into reverse. Understandable, though; it had been a year since the Dyfed-Powys police had last used him as a meat wagon.

He pulled out into the main street and drove past the police station to the cottage hospital at the bottom of the town. The forecourt wasn't very big and was packed with cars, because it was visiting time, so he had to park on the pavement outside. He got out, hoping the police would find him a space. He didn't like having a fibre-glass shell seen in public; people would think he specialised in cheap coffins.

A thirtyish couple walked past in identical outsize lumber-jack shirts and baggy corduroy trousers with turn-ups. The man had a baby strapped into a sort of sling around his chest. "Pity, really," he was saying. "Super view, I thought." The voice carried across the quiet street.

"Look at that," Guto Evans said, walking up behind them on his way to the Drovers. "The Ethnic Look. Designer working clothes. And of course they have to pretend they can't afford a bloody pram. Evening, Dai."

"What do they call those things?" Dai asked him. "Something Red Indian."

"Papoose," said Guto in disgust. "The day you show me a Welshman with a papoose around his neck is the day I emigrate to Patagonia." He peered into the back of the hearse. "Who have you got in there?" His black beard split into a wide, carnivorous grin. "Burnham-Lloyd himself, is it?"

Dai did not find this funny. He'd had a vague hope that he, the local man, would have been chosen to handle the Burnham-Lloyd funeral, but the more he thought about it the less likely it seemed.

"Let me tell you something, Guto," he said. "Even if, through some insane aberration, they were to make you the candidate, I don't even think your mother would vote for you. It's a hiker."

"What is?"

"Him. In the back. They found him in the woods by Y Groes."

"English?"

"Probably."

"Second one in just a few days. Bloody hell, Dai, might as well be working for the council, the times they send for you to cart away the rubbish."

"Anybody can tell, Guto, that you are a natural politician. That sense of fair play, of diplomacy, the way you choose your words so as not to cause offence." Dai opened up the tailgate of the hearse so fast that Guto jumped back. "How would you like to help me carry him in?"

"Me? Carry a coffin? An Englishman's coffin?"

"Don't like the thought of death, do you, Guto?"

"Get lost," said Guto.

Dai nodded knowingly. Most people were made instantly uncomfortable by the arrival of himself and his hearse. Except for those in professions touching on the death business – doctors, nurses, solicitors, monumental masons. And the police.

By the time Dai had arrived the body had been cut down and lay on the river bank in the manner of a determined sunbather, vainly stretching out his head to catch what remained of the light.

Then Dai saw the rope still dangling from the branch and realised what this was all about.

"Oh dear," he had said to Chief Inspector Gwyn Arthur Jones, and the policeman nodded.

"I've never understood why they come out here to do it," Gwyn Arthur said, taking out his pipe. "Three or four a year, I reckon. If it's not here it's the Elan Valley. If it's not a rope over a tree it's a rubber pipe from the exhaust."

Dai did not mention that it was his personal ambition to die here too in case the Chief Inspector got the wrong idea. "Well, they come here for holidays. Happy memories, isn't it. Want to go out where they were happiest."

"Bottle of pills and a photo album would save us all a lot of mess," said Gwyn Arthur.

The corpse looked to be in his mid-forties and quite a seasoned hiker, judging by his clothing and well-worn boots.

"Who found him?"

"What's her name – the teacher. Pretty girl."

"Bethan? Oh God."

"Well, one of the kids it was originally. Anyway, Dai, we want to have a little poke around the woods, just to make sure he was alone. Then you can cart him up to the hospital mortuary. Why don't you go and bang on the *Tafarn* door and get Aled to give you a pint. If you leave your casket on the bank, by there, my boys will have filled it up for you by the time you get back."

Dai made his way back to the hearse. He'd managed to squeeze it into a bit of a clearing by the roadside so it wasn't very far to carry the coffin down to the river – not as far, anyway, as it would seem to the coppers carrying it back.

It was less than a quarter of a mile to the village, so he walked, feeling the air – so much lighter, somehow, than the air in Pontmeurig.

He strolled across the bridge to *Tafarn Y Groesfan*. It was just gone six. Aled rarely opened before seven-fifteen. Dai rapped briskly on the pub door. Forgetting, until the pain stung his knuckles, what a solid oak door this was.

For a long time there was no response.

Dai was about to knock again when the door opened slowly and unwillingly, and in the gap he saw Aled's worried face. His white hair was uncombed; he had a hunted look about him.

"Coffee, Aled?"

"What?"

"Coffee. I won't ask you for a pint, but I wouldn't mind a coffee."

"What are you doing here?"

Dai was thrown by this. All right, he was early and some landlords could be expected to be inhospitable. But not Aled. Aled was flexible.

"Something wrong, is there?"

"No . . . Well, Gwenllian's not so good. Bad throat. Awake half last night. Got a bit behind, we have."

"Oh, I'm sorry. In that case I won't bother you."

"No, no," Aled said, opening the door wider. "Come in. I want to talk to you."

Aled made him coffee in the bar. There was no sign of Gwenllian. But then, in Dai's experience, there rarely was; she kept herself to the kitchen and served infrequently in the bar.

"Another body then," Dai said.

"What?" Aled dropped a saucer.

"A body. Up by the woods. Hiker. Strung himself up, poor bugger."

"Oh." Aled was staring at the broken saucer as if someone else had dropped it. He began to pick up the pieces.

Dai drank his coffee in silence, burning his mouth in his haste to be away. There was clearly something wrong here, more than a bad throat.

Aled said, a bit hoarsely, "How did you get on with Dr. Ingley?"

"The Prof? Shipped back to – where was it now? Basingstoke."

"Gone?"

"Gone," said Dai.

"Where did you keep him?"

There was an odd question.

"How do you mean?"

"Where did you put the body?"

"Well, chapel of rest."

"No . . . no problems?"

What the hell did that mean?

"I was asked to embalm him. Usual thing. Why do you ask?"

"No reason," Aled said. Though it was not quite dark yet, he moved to the switches on the wall and put all the lights on.

Blinking in the sudden glare, Dai thought at first he must be seeing things when he noticed how badly the landlord's hand was shaking.

PART THREE

SICE

CHAPTER XIV

"I know what you're thinking," Giles said.

They were driving inland on roads that became narrower, through countryside that got bleaker. Camouflage country, Berry thought. Weathered farmhouses were hunched into the hillsides; tough, cynical-looking sheep grazed mean fields the colour of worn khaki. And then the forestry began, rank upon regimented rank of uniform conifers, a drab army of occupation.

"But you're wrong." Giles was trying vainly to stretch his legs. Claire had taken the BMW to Norwich while her own car was being serviced, so they'd come in Berry's little old Sprite, lanky Giles wedged awkwardly with his knees around his chin because of the bags and stuff behind his seat.

They were passing a derelict lead mine in a valley, broken grey walls and tin-roofed shacks. A thin river seeped along the valley bottom, tired as a drain.

"Just you wait," Giles promised.

Berry's first time in Wales. They'd driven in from the south-east, which he found pretty much like England, except more of it was rural. Wherever they stopped for a meal or cigarettes everybody seemed to speak English too, in quite intelligible accents.

Then they'd hit the west coast, checking into a hotel in Aberystwyth where quite a lot of the people around them were speaking a language Berry didn't understand. It sounded European, but it had a lilting quality, and the speech of people in the street was flecked with English phrases. They were only a couple hundred miles from London. Weird.

"So this cottage," Berry said. "All comes down to Claire, right?" He was quite enjoying himself. A whole new scene.

They came to a T-junction. A sign pointing right said Pontmeurig 5 miles.

"Go left," said Giles. "Yes. What basically happened is that sometime back in the fifties Claire's grandparents split up, and the old man – well, he couldn't have been that old then – he came back to his native Wales. Back to the actual village where he'd been born."

"How Welsh does that make Claire?"

"Not very. Second generation, or is it third generation? Point is, Claire's mother was furious at Granddad, just buggering off like that, so they never had anything to do with him again. But then he dies – and he leaves his house to the granddaughter he never knew. Rather romantic, isn't it?"

"How far now?"

"No more than four. Of course, Claire's kicking herself now that she never came to see the old chap while he was alive."

"He, ah, had a lot of dough?"

"He was a judge," said Giles. "Qualified as a barrister in England, worked in London and the South East for years, then became a circuit judge or a recorder or something – one of those chaps who used to take the old Quarter Sessions in provincial towns, it's all changed now. But yes, he did all right. She's English, of course, his wife, Claire's granny. She did all right, too, out of the settlement. Nobody in the family talks much about why they split up. He'd just retired. Maybe he wanted to come back to Wales and she didn't."

"Kind of a drastic solution."

"Ha. When you see the village, you can imagine people doing pretty drastic things to get back."

"Not if it's like this," said Berry.

There was forestry now on both sides of the road. Berry liked country roads, as did the Sprite. But this route was no less claustrophobic than some concrete canyon in Brooklyn.

"Here?"

The sign said Y Groes 2. Giles gave a confirmatory grunt.

They turned left. At the entrance to the road another sign had a broad red line across it: dead end. After Y Groes – nothing. For over a mile the forestry stayed close to the road on both sides.

"What's it mean, this place? The name."

"Y Groes?"

"Yeah."

"It means The Cross," said Giles.

"Like in religion?"

"Must be. It has a very impressive church. Look, there it is – see?"

"Oh, yeah. Hey –" Berry's head swivelled. "Where'd the forest go?"

Something lit up underneath Giles's freckles.

"Great, isn't it, the way you come out of the forestry so fast and everything changes. Notice how the trees are all broadleaf now? Look at the variety of wild flowers on the verges, don't see that in many places nowadays. And, look – what about the *sun*, for Christ's sake!"

"What *about* the sun?"

"It's come out!"

"Big deal," said Berry.

All the same, he was getting an idea why Giles was so excited. Something in the light, was that it? Maybe it was because the journey across the hills had been through such harsh and hostile country that Y Groes seemed subtly translucent and shimmering like a mirage. Maybe the sun looked suddenly brighter and warmer here because, along the road, its rays had been absorbed by the close-packed conifers. Something like that.

They drove on down, and it got better.

Most of the other villages Berry had seen on the way from Aberystwyth had consisted of a single street, with cold-looking houses, a shop and a big grey chapel all strung out like damp clothing on a frayed washing line. Here, chunky, timber-framed cottages were clustered below the old church in a way that seemed somehow organic, like wild mushrooms in a circle. An image came to Berry of the cottages pushing themselves up out of the ground, chimneys first, each one in its naturally ordained space.

Weird thought, but kind of charming. And natural – none of that manicured Cotswold gloss. You went behind that ochre Cotswold stone and you were in Hampstead. Here . . . he didn't know.

For the first time this weekend, he wished Miranda were here. She'd approve, although she hadn't approved when he'd said he would not be seeing her that weekend and explained why. "Morelli," she'd snarled, "as far as I'm concerned you don't ever need to come back. You can bloody well stay out there with the leeks and the seaweed bread and the Bibles." Then things had gotten heavy.

"Looks like a nice old pub too," Berry said, slowing down, wondering where they'd got the stone from because it seemed to have a more softly luminous quality than the rocks they'd passed. Although the soil here seemed lighter too, so maybe . . .

"I've never been in the pub," said Giles. "I was sort of saving it." Giles was hunched forward in his bucket seat, excited in a proprietorial kind of way, pointing out this feature and that, the natural amphitheatre of hills, the steps leading up behind the inn to the churchyard, the path to the river.

Berry eased the Sprite over the narrow river bridge, the inn directly ahead. Its sign, swinging from a wooden bracket – or it would have been swinging if there'd been a wind – had a fading picture of the same church tower they could see jutting out of the hilltop behind. The inn sign said *Tafarn Y Groesfan*.

"Just carry straight on up the hill, as if you're heading for the church."

Two old men with flat caps and sticks leaned against the side of the bridge. Berry gave them a wave and, to his vague surprise, one returned a cheery, gap-toothed smile and the other raised his stick in greeting.

Giles raised a friendly hand to the two old men and grinned delightedly. "You see . . . absolutely nothing like old Winstone's picture of Wales, God rest his soul. Super people here; everybody you meet has a smile."

Backs to the wall now, the Joneses and the Daviesses . . .

Yesterday Berry had been to Winstone's funeral. The old reporter had gone down into the flames just like he always said he would and all the hacks had gone back to the last halfway decent pub in what used to be Fleet Street and drunk, between them, what Berry figured must have been several gallons of Glenfiddich in memory of one of the Scottish distillery's most faithful supporters. Giles had been unable to attend, having been sent to cover a much-heralded speech by Labour's shadow chancellor at some local government conference in Scarborough. Berry suspected he was glad to have avoided the occasion. Somebody – Firth or Canavan – would have been sure to make some discreet reference to Giles's behaviour on the night of Winstone's death.

Berry could still feel Winstone's hand on his arm. *Stop him.*

But this village wasn't helping.

He'd been hoping for somewhere grey and grim. Instead, he was charmed. There was a surprising air of contentment about the place.

The Thorpe funeral had been conducted by a retired Fleet

Street chaplain, the Revd Peters who'd known Winstone from way back. In the bar afterwards Berry had bought the old guy a drink, and it had emerged he was Welsh, from the industrial south-east of the country. This had been a surprise because the Revd Peters had seemed seriously English to Berry, hearty and genial and built like Santa Claus with a matching white beard. He'd laughed when Berry had told him of Winstone's gloomy warnings. His part of Wales, he'd said, had the warmest, friendliest folk you could wish to meet.

Up the short street Berry could see just two shops. Three women stood chatting outside one, shopping baskets on their arms. One woman had a cloud of fluffy white hair and wore a white summer dress with big red spots. Berry just knew they were speaking in Welsh. Something about the way they used their hands.

"Hey, Giles –" He'd been trying to work out what it was made Y Groes different from anywhere else, even allowing for the absence of tacky modern storefronts among the old buildings.

He realised. "Giles, we're the only car here!"

"That's right. What do the villagers need cars for? Going to drive fifty yards to pick up the groceries?"

"What I'm saying is, village this attractive – how come there're no tourists, 'cept us?"

"Well, it's not on a tourist *route*," said Giles. "Lots of attractive villages don't get hordes of visitors simply for that reason. I mean, we're in the middle of some pretty rough countryside, the sort that tourists just want to get through quick to get to somewhere else. I suppose they get a few walking enthusiasts and people of that sort, but obviously not enough to be worth catering for – as you can see, no souvenir shops, no cafés, no snack bars. Don't even think the pub does overnight accommodation."

"Shame."

"Not for me," said Giles. "I hate bloody tourists. Pull in here. We'll walk the rest of the way."

A track led between two outsize sycamore trees. It was blocked after about twenty yards by a rusted metal farm gate.

"OK to park here?"

"Private road," said Giles. "*Our* private road. Or it will be."

They got out and stood looking down on the village in the vivid light of early evening. To the left of them stood the church tower, like a monolith. The church was built on a big hump, around which cottages fitted – or grew, as Berry liked to fantasise – in a semi-circle. The church tower had a short pyramid for a spire with timbers around the belfry. It seemed very old, older than the village. Older than the goddamn sky, Berry thought, for some reason.

"This is not typical, in Wales, right? Like, big churches, stained glass and all?"

"Chapels," Giles said. "That's what you have mainly in Wales. Ugly Victorian chapels, presided over by hellfire preachers rather than Anglican vicars. Non-conformism – Baptists and Methodists, Puritanism, Fundamentalism – all that just stormed through Wales around the turn of the century. Trampling on history. And it didn't go away. Bit like your Bible Belt, I suppose."

"How come this place escaped?"

"I don't know," Giles said. "But I'm bloody glad it did. There's supposed to have *been* a Victorian chapel here, but it's obviously gone. One of those little mysteries. Y Groes is full of them."

A palpable silence lay over the scene, like a spell. No dogs barked, no radios played. It was calm and mature and the air was scented. The sycamores framed the view as if they'd been arranged by some eighteenth-century landscape painter.

"Nice," said Berry. "Hey, pal, I apologise, OK? You were right."

"Yes," said Giles.

"This is some place."

"Isn't it."

They stood in silence for almost two whole minutes.

Birds sang. Butterflies danced up and down invisible staircases of warm air.

"You really gonna commute?" Berry asked. "Can you *do* that?"

"The way I see it," said Giles, "I'm working this four-day week, OK? So, let's say I'm working Monday to Thursday. I get up really early and drive down Monday morning. On Thursday night I drive back. That means I only have to spend three nights in London."

"Lot of travelling, ole buddy."

"I don't care. I just want to spend as much time in this bloody glorious place as I can wangle."

"Sounds good to me," said Berry, wondering if it really did.

He thought, could I go for this, all this rural-idyll stuff, four nights out of the rat race? Well, maybe. Maybe, with the right lady. Maybe for a few months. Maybe in the summer.

You put the arm on young Giles. Persuade him to sell the bloody place, soon as he can . . .

But what would Winstone Thorpe have said if he'd seen this place?

"Tell you what," Giles was saying. "Why don't you come down for a weekend, or even a holiday, when we're settled in? Bring whoever it is you're with these days."

"Miranda," said Berry doubtfully.

"Oh yes, the one who –"

"Thinks I look like Al Pacino. When he was younger, of course."

Giles, face bright with pride, opened the iron gate and carefully closed it when Berry was through. Then he led the way along a track no more than eight feet wide, lined with hawthorn and holly.

They came at last to the house. And that was where, for Berry Morelli, the idyll died.

CHAPTER XV

The dead lower branches of the close-packed conifers, pale brown by day, were whitened by the headlights – the only kind of direct light they'd ever known, Berry thought. He was aware of just how narrow a channel the road made between the bristly ranks. Like driving down the middle of a toothbrush. He wondered what it would be like in the frozen days of January.

Berry shivered.

"You thought of that?" he asked, needing to talk.

"Thought of what?" said Giles.

"How it'd be in winter. Like when you have to get up at 5:30 on some freezing dark morning and drive to London on ice-bound roads and wonder how you're ever gonna make it back if there's snow. You ever think about that?"

"Nothing's without its problems," Giles said. "If you start to dwell on things like that, you never try anything new."

The forestry was thinning out now. Berry braked as a rabbit scooted across the road. How about that, something alive in this place. He shivered again.

Pull yourself together, asshole.

It wasn't so dark yet, not when you got through the forestry. When they cleared the next ridge they'd get the benefit of the light coming off the sea. A sign said Pontmeurig 5, Aberystwyth 16. One-horse resort or not, he'd be glad to see Aberystwyth again. Least it had a few bars and a pier with coloured lights and gaming machines. Familiar, tacky things.

"Berry?" Giles said.

"Uh huh?" He turned briefly to look at Giles, saw only a hunched-up shape in a space too small for it and the glow at the end of a cigarette.

Giles said, "Are you trying to put me off?"

"Put you off?"

They came into the valley of the disused lead mine, stone towers black against the western sky. It looked powerfully stark, quite impressive now it was too dark to see all the drab detail. Wales's answer to Monument Valley.

Yeah, he thought, damn right I'm trying to put you off.

Berry snapped the headlights on again. This was going to need careful handling.

It had seemed, in all the obvious ways, a good house. Barely fifty yards off the road, but nicely private, screened by laurels and holly and hawthorn, hunched into the hillside, protected from the wind. It had a view of the church hill some 250 yards away. Below that was the village; on winter evenings they'd be able to see the smoke spiralling from the village chimneys, warming the grey sky.

Nice. Cosy.

So the cottage looked, too, from the outside. Its walls were that warm, rusty grey that softened the outlines of the whole village. Its windows, six of them on the front, were small and quartered like in the picture books.

And clean. Somebody had been and cleaned the goddamn windows.

Not only that, they'd taken care of the garden too. It should have been overgrown, yet the small front lawn had been mown, the flowerbeds tended, even the roses dead-headed.

This did not look like the empty house of a man deceased.

Berry had said, "You're sure we got the right place here?"

"No, I just thought we'd poke around somebody else's garden first, to pass the time. Of course it's the right bloody place!"

"Only somebody's taking good care of it for you. Why would they do that?"

"It was the judge's house, Berry. People respected the man." As if to make his own mark on the garden, Giles bent down to a clump of pansies, and pinched off a couple of dead flowers. "Perhaps the gardener and the cleaner wanted to maintain the place as he'd have wanted. Maybe they got a little something in the will."

"I get it," said Berry. "So the lawyer wouldn't give you a key but he gave one to the cleaner so he or she could keep the place like the judge was still around."

Giles clearly hadn't thought of this. Visibly miffed, he turned and walked off round the side of the cottage.

Berry caught him up.

"Hey, don't worry about it, fella. What d'you expect? You're English."

"Now look!" Giles snarled. He spun round and shoved under Berry's nose an elegant English finger. "Just stop trying to wind me up, all right? Me being English doesn't come into it." And then he strode off across the back lawn that would be *his* lawn, olive-green waxed jacket swinging open to reveal his olive-green army-officer's pullover. An urban man who thought his life would be made suddenly healthier by driving an extra five hundred miles a week.

Berry looked at the cottage, soft-focus through the bushes. It was like most of the others in Y Groes, seemed as if it had grown out of the soil, its timbers forming together, like a developing bone structure.

Inevitably, the thought came to him: Giles might need this house, but the house doesn't need him.

Giles strode back across the lawn. He wore a wry half-smile. "Sorry, mate. I'm touchy, OK? It means a lot to me. To be accepted. To be, you know, part of all this."

"I can buy that," said Berry. "It's a good place to have."

Maybe good wasn't quite the word. It was its own place.

They peered through a few windows, but even though the glass was clean and sparkling it was too dark inside to see much. One downstairs room they couldn't see into at all.

"That's the study," Giles said. "Somebody must have drawn the curtains to protect the books from too much light."

"Thoughtful of them," said Berry.

And that should have been it. He should have told Giles how nice the cottage looked and what a lucky man he was and they'd have walked around a while then maybe gone down to the pub, had one drink, then off back to the coast. They would have done just that if, while strolling by the rear of the cottage, he, Berry dumb-ass Morelli, had not spotted a dark line along the edge of a window. Now the late Winstone Thorpe had himself a firm ally.

"Hey, Giles – you want to get in here?"

"What d'you mean?"

"See, if I go fetch a screwdriver from the car, I can slide it into this crack, push up the lever and maybe – well, just a thought, ole buddy . . ."

"Ha," said Giles. "One in the eye for Mr. Goronwy Davies, I think. Well spotted, Berry."

"Who's Mr. Goronwy Davies?"

"The lawyer in Pontmeurig. The chap who won't give us a key until probate's complete."

"Ah, right."

And from then on they'd been like two schoolkids on an adventure. The goddamn Hardy Boys strike again.

*

"You did like it, though?"

"Oh, yeah. Sure. It looked in pretty good condition. All things considered."

"That's not what I meant."

"We still on the right road, Giles? It looks different."

"Just getting dark. Bound to look different. You seem a bit nervy tonight, Berry."

"Me? Naw, tired is all. Been a long day."

"I'm not tired. I'm exhilarated. It always seems to renew me, going back there. I feel it's my place. Becoming more like my place all the time. And Claire's of course, I mean –"

"Sure," Berry said.

No, he thought. It's not your place at all. It's somebody else's place. Always be somebody else's place.

CHAPTER XVI

He'd dropped to the floor and found himself standing next to a sink. An old-fashioned sink of white porcelain sticking out of the wall. No cupboards underneath, just a metal bucket. It was gloomy in here, but there was no smell of damp. Two spiders raced each other along the rim of the sink. Spiders didn't like damp either – where had he read that?

It had been quite a squeeze getting through the window, which was only a quarter pane. It seemed unlikely that Giles would be able to manage it.

"Listen," he'd shouted through the open window, "why don't I come round, open the back door?"

"Good thinking," said Giles. "Only, don't shout, all right? We don't want to advertise ourselves."

Berry threw the screwdriver out to Giles and carefully closed the window.

"Always knew I could've made it in the CIA," he said aloud, and was surprised at how firm his voice sounded in here. You expected an echo in an empty house, but this was acoustically very tight, like a recording studio. He looked up, saw heavy oak beams and more beams sunk into the walls. That was it: timber-framing, low ceilings. A vacuum for sound.

Also, it wasn't an empty house. Much of the furniture, it appeared, was still here.

He looked around. The kitchen, right? It was quite small. Probably all cottage kitchens were small when this place was built back in the – when, 1800s, 1700s . . . earlier? Whenever,

102

no dinner parties in those days. Was there going to be room here for the dishwasher, the freezer, the microwave oven and all the other sophisticated stuff he was pretty sure Giles and Claire must possess?

Berry chuckled, which was a very intimate sound in here. He stifled it.

In one corner he could see a big Aga-type stove, the only substantial piece of the twentieth century, if you didn't count the faucets and the electric light, which was just a bulb with a white porcelain shade shaped like a plant pot.

There were two doors. He opened one and found some kind of storeroom or scullery. He hit his knee against a stack of shelves, still loaded with provisions. A packet fell off and he caught it. Paxo sage and onion stuffing. Judge Rhys's concession to haute cuisine?

The other door led him into a dim hallway, low ceiling, beams black and sagging. He could have used some light in here, but the power wouldn't be connected. The passage led straight through to the front of the house and ended at the front door and some narrow stairs. So which way was the back entrance? There were more doors on either side of him, so he tried one and found himself in a room where the light was rationed by drawn curtains. The judge's study.

"Christ," Berry said.

It could have been a homely room: fireplace, book-lined walls, low ceiling with beams. Place where you could come and put your feet up, have a TV dinner, glass or two of beer. Warm your ass by the fire.

Except the fireplace was Victorian, an ugly iron thing, cold and dead, and the black beams seemed to press down like the fingers of a gloved hand.

And the books. Well, as Berry saw it, there were basically two kinds of books. There were warm, friendly books with bright dustjackets that gave you the come-on, brought a room alive.

And there were books like these.

Thousands of them. The shelves ran floor-to-ceiling, taking up most of two walls, dark oak shelves of dark old books, heavy, black-spined books. The kind of books you felt it would be a breach of protocol to take down without you were wearing a tie.

It was a coldly austere room, this study, like . . . what? Some old-fashioned classroom? Air of discipline. Severity.

The window, quite small, was set uncommonly high in the wall, faded grey curtains pulled across as if for a passing funeral. Opposite the window was a huge old desk, like a monument; behind it a chair, thronelike, with a tall back and carved spindles. Heavy, dour, forbidding.

No, not a classroom, Berry thought suddenly. A courtroom. It's like a very small courtroom. Is this what happens when old judges retire and have no lowlife scum to send to jail any more? They have to bring with them that ambience of old-fashioned judicial disdain?

Above the fireplace was a single picture, a framed photograph of what he took, at first, to be a gathering of the Ku Klux Klan, everybody in long white robes. Then underneath he saw the words *Eisteddfod Genedlaethol 1963*. Ah, the annual Welsh festival of poetry and song and stuff where all the head guys dressed up like Druids. Was Judge Rhys one of the men in white?

Berry stood in the middle of the floor, which was stone-flagged, a single rug beneath his feet, on it a threadbare red dragon spitting faded fire.

He hesitated, then crossed to the shelves and pulled down one obese volume, expecting a small dust storm. It didn't happen. Even the damn books were still being cared for. In case the judge came back from the grave and had nothing to read?

When that thought – a typically trivial, facetious thought –

occurred to Berry Morelli, he felt a chill that came and went, like the door of a freezer opening and closing with a hiss. A cold hiss, like the hiss in ice . . . *iiiiice*. Did he hear that, or did he imagine it?

He opened the book, and that hissed too, tissue-thin pages whispering secrets denied to him . . . because every word was Welsh. He quickly pulled down three more fat, black books at random – and they were all in Welsh too. Hard to imagine so many books being published in a language spoken by so few. But then it *was*, according to Giles, supposed to be the oldest language in Europe. And these were real old books.

As he returned the book to the shelf, he felt suddenly guilty. And furtive, like a kid who'd left sticky fingermarks on the school Bible. He thought, somebody's watching, and he spun around and there was nobody. But in his mind the freezer door opened and closed again. With a hiss . . . *iiiiice* . . .

It was darker, too, he was sure the air itself had got darker. And yet there was a sunset out there (so why are the damn curtains washed with grey?).

Berry's gaze travelled across the patchy gloom, from the ranked books, to the drab lumps of furniture, to the picture of the procession of men in white. He felt the weight of something old and hallowed.

He didn't care for it.

In the room, and yet beyond the room, he felt kind of a coiled malice. And the air was too thick. How could the air be thick in a room with no dust?

The air came in shifting shades of black and grey and a poisonous off-white, like dirty milk. And it hissed, short gasps, like bellows. He felt, with an astonishing wrench of panic, that, if he stayed in here much longer, Judge Thomas Rhys would materialise, fully robed, in the tall gothic chair, his eyes giving off dull heat, a bony finger pointing, trembling with a focused fury.

"*Sice!*" he'd breathe, the word coming out in a short, hideous rasp, like a cobra rearing to strike.

And the air hissed, the bellows, the freezer door opening and closing. The air said, "*SICE!*"

"Fuck this," Berry said, suddenly very scared. He stepped back into the hallway and closed the door of the study firmly behind him, then backed off, afraid to look away in case it should open by itself, releasing the air, the wafting hate.

CHAPTER XVII

The door hung ajar.

Aled Gruffydd stepped back quickly, as if afraid something would reach out and snatch him inside.

"I will not go in there with you," he said. "You do understand?"

The tall man with white hair only smiled.

"Did not happen immediately, see," Aled said. "Quiet it was, for more than three days after Dai took the Englishman's body away."

It was gloomy on the landing, the day closing down.

"We cleaned out the room and stripped the bed," Aled said. "Gwenllian said to burn the sheets, but I said no, isn't as if he had anything contagious."

The tall man looked at the opening and did not move. He was very thin and his greasy suit hung like leaves blackened by a sudden overnight frost.

"So she took off the sheets for washing and brought clean ones and put them on the bed. And as she is tucking in the sheets, it flew off the bedside table. The vase. She had sweet peas in it, to sweeten the air, see."

The white-haired man silently put out a forefinger to the door but did not quite touch it.

"Flew off the table, flew within an inch of Gwenllian's head. Smashed into the wall. Gwen came tearing down the stairs, almost falling over herself."

Aled looked over his shoulder, down the stairs. His companion said, "And then?"

"I came back with her and we picked up the pieces of the vase and the flowers. All quiet. No disturbance. I would not doubt her, though. I shut the door and locked it, and we came downstairs and did not go in again until this morning."

With a small coughing sound, the bedroom door moved inwards, revealing a slice of white wall. Aled recoiled. "There – can you smell it?"

The Reverend Elias ap Siencyn remained motionless. His pale eyes did not blink. His long nose did not twitch at the stench, which included, among other odours, the smell of hot decay.

"We have not been in since," Aled said. "We've left it the way we found it this morning."

"Only this room? He has not come to you in the night? Or to Gwenllian?"

Aled gripped the banister. "Oh, good God." He was shaking at the thought. "No. Nothing like that."

"I doubt if he knows, you see," the rector said. He had a sur-prisingly high voice, though with a penetrating pitch, like organ pipes. "Sometimes it takes quite some while before they can fully accept their condition."

"I don't want him, Reverend. I don't want him here." Aled tried to make a joke of it. "Not as if he's paying me now, is it?"

The rector had not taken his eyes from the door. "Tell me again. What you found."

"Oh Christ – sorry, Reverend. But can't you smell it?"

"Bodily fluids?"

"Shit, Reverend. And the other stuff. Slime. Mucus. All over the sheets. Soaked in, dried stiff. And splattered on the walls. Like those prisoners in Ireland did to their cells."

"All right, Aled. It's clear this spirit is disturbed and angry and frustrated. The English think they have a right to know everything; Ingley is dead and still knows *nothing*. His spirit is unsatisfied and so it wants, pathetically, to register a protest. But it's frightened, too – more frightened, perhaps, than when it died. It's a week, you say, since he left us?"

"A week ago tonight. Exactly."

"Very well. I may need assistance. Perhaps you could fetch Mrs. Dafis. Or Buddug Morgan from the farm."

"Yes indeed," Aled said, clearly glad to have an excuse to go outside. He went downstairs very rapidly, but at the bottom he turned and shouted back, "I swear to God, I locked the door! I put the key in the glass with the others. In the bar, see. I swear to God, nobody could get in."

"Aled, I *believe* you."

"So how can it be? He's *dead*, Rector. Dead and gone. I know there are things the dead can do, but this . . . How can it be?"

"Because," said the Reverend Elias ap Siencyn, "he cannot adjust. And he cannot contain his fear and his – I don't know, there is something else."

With a single finger he pushed open the door.

"Also," he said quietly, when Aled had gone, "like others of his race, he is vermin. Vermin make a mess."

The rector walked into the bedroom and looked around.

The sheets and the walls were spotless. Whatever Aled had seen was gone. But the stink remained. The stink was obnoxious, and carried a sense of fear and pain and suffering. As well as deep frustration, a helpless rage and a terrible confusion.

"Alien contaminant," he muttered to himself, a fragment of an old verse, "a foul disease now chokes the oakwood."

He stood at the foot of the bed and spoke, with the clarity and resonance of the first words in a sermon.

"You expect my pity?"

He smiled coldly, putting down a scuffed attaché case. Then

he straightened up and looked at the bed, at a spot just above the pillow.

"You can't stay here," he said. "You are over. The air's too strong for you, the light's too bright."

CHAPTER XVIII

When they drove at last into Aberystwyth, the coloured lights were on at the entrance to the pier. Green and yellow lights, rippling up and down in a sequence. It wasn't Coney Island, but it made Berry feel a little happier.

"Giles, I – You ever talk to anybody about the house? Anybody local?"

"How d'you mean?"

"– 'bout its history. Anything."

"No, not really. We didn't like to go round asking questions. Nosey newcomers. Why?"

Berry took the first left after the pier and found a parking space in a sidestreet, a block or two away from the hotel. He could see its sign and an illuminated advert for Welsh Bitter. He switched off the engine and lay back in his seat and let out a sharp breath.

"Look, what's up, Berry? You're behaving pretty bloody strangely tonight."

"Giles, you're gonna think I'm crazy –"

"I always have."

"Listen," Berry said. "You remember old Winstone Thorpe –"

"Oh no!" Giles snapped. "We're not going into that again."

Berry had come out the way he'd got in, landing this time less easily, on a gravel path, ripping a hole in his jeans and grazing a knee.

Giles had found him on the lawn. He must have looked like hell, but Giles didn't seem to notice.

"Berry, you cretin," he'd said when Berry told him he hadn't been able to open either the front door or the back door. "Why didn't you shout? There's a back-door key in the bottom of an old vase in the scullery. I remember seeing the solicitor put it there when he was showing us round. You'll just have to get back in through the window."

Berry was already shaking his head. Uh huh. No way. No time now. Gonna be dark soon. Anyway, had plenty time to look around. Let's go, OK . . . ?

"Well, go on," Giles snapped. "Say it. Say what you've got to say."

His lean, freckled face, lit up by the headlights of a passing car, looked aggressive, affronted and defiant, all at once.

A girl with luminous green hair and a man in a tight silver jacket, as worn on the Starship Enterprise, walked past the car, laughing at each other, but probably not because of the jacket and the hair. They went into the hotel.

"C'mon, let's go in," said Berry. "Get a drink."

The hotel bar was quite crowded, but they managed to find a table, one people had avoided because it was next to the men's room. Giles went to get the drinks and Berry leaned back in his chair and closed his eyes, letting the voices wash over him, soporific, like surf. He could hear people speaking in English and in Welsh and even, he was sure, in Japanese. University town. Kind of a cosmopolitan town. He liked that. Made him feel secure. Like New York, except if you closed your eyes in a New York bar you'd open them half a minute later to find you'd lost your wallet or your watch or, where applicable, your virginity.

There was a crush of people around the bar; it took Giles a while to get served. Berry sat quietly, half-listening to the multi-lingual voices and half-hearing his own voice talking to him, saying all the real obvious things.

112

. . . you dreamt it, it was your imagination, you're making it up . . .

No way.

Something had been in there, something heavier than the desk, harder than the oak beams, blacker than the books.

"Here we are," said Giles. He put down two beers. "I know how you like to try local brews, so this is . . . dammit, I've forgotten the name, but it was in a bottle with a yellow label with a red dragon on it."

"Thanks, pal." He hated local brews. "I was just thinking, I could quite get to like this town. Good mix of people here, you know?"

"Yes," said Giles. "But what about Y Groes? What about my cottage?"

"Hell of a place," said Berry. "*Hell* of a place."

So, OK, he thought, let's work this out rationally, bearing in mind that, at the end of the day, this is not your problem. Tomorrow you drive out of here and you don't come back. Let Giles find out for himself. It is *his* problem.

So you didn't like the cottage. No, get it right, there was nothing so wrong with the cottage, it was the room you didn't like. You didn't like the furniture. You couldn't understand the books. You were inexplicably disturbed by a photograph which, in other circumstances, might have seemed faintly comic, bunch of old men in christening robes.

So how come you were squeezing out that window like some guy breaking jail. Grown man, smooth-talking wise-ass reporter, scampering away like a puppy, oh, Jesus, this can't be happening, too bewildered to crank up the mental machinery to attempt to analyse it.

"Berry, are you going to come on like the rest of them. Like Winstone Thorpe – 'But you're an Englishman, old boy, you don't belong there.'"

"No," Berry said uncertainly. "That's not how I –"

"Fuck 'em all, that's what I say." Giles stared into his beer. "I've had it with all these smug London bastards. They're the ones who're out of touch, you know. Had it with Westminster too. And newspapers that try to tell the public what's important in life, what they should be concerned about. This is a place where you can't bargain on London terms. Listen to this – I wasn't going to say anything about this, I thought you'd snigger –"

Giles leaned back, drew in a breath and said, *"R'wyn dysgu Cymraeg."*

Berry stared at him, expressionless.

"Means 'I am learning Welsh.' Been working at it for several weeks now with cassette tapes. When we move in here I'm going to take proper lessons. What d'you think about that?"

"Let me get you another drink," said Berry.

He pushed his way through to the bar and said to the barman, "Gimme a couple of those beers with the dragon on the label."

It was worse than he'd thought.

So Berry said casually, "Listen, Giles, that . . . study. You didn't feel it was a mite depressing in there, all that heavy furniture, those old books?"

Giles put down his glass and laughed in amazement. "Depressing? That study has to be absolutely the best part of the house. Super atmosphere. Real old Welsh. Stark, strong –"

"Yeah but, Giles, what if . . . what if it was, you know . . . ?"

He couldn't say it. He just couldn't bring himself to say it. "So you're learning Welsh, huh?" he finished lamely.

"We have these cassettes," Giles said. "We play them in the car, Claire and I. Try and talk to each other in Welsh, over breakfast. *R'wyf i eisiau un siwgwr.* I should like one sugar."

"Could be real useful that, Giles, you have to use a teashop making so much money they can refuse to serve people who don't place their order in Welsh. What else can you say? How about, 'Don't spit in my beer, I can't help being English.'"

"You're not into this at all, are you, Berry?"

Berry smiled sadly.

"*Cwrw*, that's beer. *Peint o gwrw*. Pint of beer. The C in *cwrw* mutates to G after a vowel. More or less everything mutates in Welsh; once you grasp that you can start making progress."

Berry lost patience with him.

"OK, then, Giles, ole buddy. You go over to the bar and order us up a couple half pints of whatever it was, guru, right?"

"I *could* do it, I expect," Giles said. "If I really had something to prove."

"Ten pounds says you won't go through with it."

Giles, eyes flashing, pushed back his chair and rose decisively to his feet.

"Right," he said. "Put your money on the table."

Berry pulled his wallet out of the hip pocket of his newly torn jeans and placed a ten-pound note under the ashtray.

Giles put on his stiff-upper-lip expression. "Right, you listen carefully."

Aw, hell, Berry thought. Can't you ever keep a hold on your mouth, Morelli?

Through his fingers, he watched Giles march to the bar. Two men in front of Giles who'd been conversing in Welsh ordered a pint of lager and a whisky and soda in English. Berry saw Giles stare down his nose at them. When it was his turn he said loudly, *"Hanner peint o gwrw, os gwelwch yn dda."*

Lowering his voice and pointing at the bottle with the dragon on it, he added, "Er, make that two."

Berry thought he'd never seen so many wry smiles turned on at once. It was like a *chorus* of wry smiles. You had to feel sorry for Giles; he was a brave man and a born fall-guy.

He was still cringing on Giles's behalf, when, at the adjacent

CANDLENIGHT

table, the young man in the Starship Enterprise jacket nodded towards Giles and said laconically to the girl with the luminous green hair, "*Sice.*"

Berry spilled a lot of beer. He felt himself go pale.

Within a minute Giles was back, red-faced, slamming two glasses on the table and snatching the tenner from beneath the ashtray.

"Bastard," he said.

"I'm sorry, ole buddy. I didn't plan to set you up."

"You're a bastard," said Giles. "I think I'll go to bed."

"What about your beer?"

"You drink it," said Giles. "I'll see you at breakfast."

"Giles, what's '*sice*' mean?"

"Piss off," said Giles.

"Come on, Giles, I'm serious, what's it mean?"

"Piss off, you know what it means."

"Aw, for Chrissakes, Giles, if I knew what it meant would I be asking you?"

"*Sais,*" Giles hissed. "*Sais.*"

"Yeah, right, *sice.*"

"English," said Giles. "It means English. Often used in a derogatory way, like the Scots say Sassenach. Satisfied now?"

"I don't know," said Berry. "Maybe, I . . . I don't know."

"I'm going to bed," said Giles. "OK?"

PART FOUR

CROESO

CHAPTER XIX

ENGLAND

Four or five times Berry had picked up the phone, intending to call Giles, each time pulling back. In his head, he'd almost had it figured out. "See, Giles, I've always been sensitive to atmospheres and I just had the feeling there was something badly wrong in there. Humour me, OK? Have a priest take a look." Every time he heard himself saying that, he chickened out. A priest! Had he really been about to say that?

From the Newsnet office, the day after they'd got back from Wales, Berry had called Giles's paper and asked if he was around. "It's Gary Willis here," a guy said. "Giles has taken some leave. Gone to move some of his stuff out to this place he's got in Wales."

"When's he gonna be back?"

"I don't know, mate, and Roger's not here at the moment. But it can't be more than a week or two."

Berry stood at his apartment window, looking out at the block from which you could see the Thames. He clenched his fists.

All the way home from Aberystwyth, he and Giles had discussed their respective careers in journalism, the differences between the British and American media and even the rift between Berry and his dad and what had caused it, the ethics of the job, all this stuff.

Everything, it seemed, except the cottage in Y Groes, Giles's future there, Berry's feelings about the place. It was clear that

Giles, having brought Berry to see the house without getting the expected result – "Gee, Giles, this is just amazing, you're a lucky guy, I can't tell you how jealous I am" – had been studiously avoiding the issue.

While Berry . . . Well, what was *his* excuse?

You asshole, Morelli, he told himself. You blew it again. All ways, you blew it.

This was three days ago. It was now Wednesday night. It was well into October. It was dark. He had nobody to talk to.

Miranda had landed a part in a TV commercial for perfume. Although the perfume was made in Wolverhampton, they were making the commercial in Paris. She'd left a message on his answering machine to say she might be back by the end of the week if she didn't run into any vaguely interesting Frenchmen looking for a little fun.

Berry sat down and tried to watch a re-run of an episode of *Cheers*. Even that didn't lift him out of his private gloom. When it was over, he switched off and lay down on his bed, missing Miranda, haunted by the same crazy question.

Am I psychic or just neurotic?

"*The kid's neurotic*," Mario Morelli had said. It was the first time he was conscious of hearing the word. He'd been – what? Nine, ten? The year he went to summer camp and was so unhappy they sent him home, scared – he heard his dad telling his mom – that he was going to walk off on his own and drown himself. After that, Mario took no chances; he wasn't having a son of his bringing down scandal on the family.

His career. Really, he was afraid of what it would do to his career.

In subsequent years they reluctantly took him with them on vacation, which was how he first saw London. He'd been happy then, although he knew things between his parents were not good. He'd pretended he was there alone, pretended it was his town. Felt the history of the place; imagined he was part of it, not part of his dad's vacation, which seemed to be full of inefficient service and lousy Limey food.

How long after that was The Gypsy?

Whenever, that was the year the vacation coincided with his mom being in hospital having this Ladies' Surgery – he never did find out whether it was a hysterectomy or new tits – and his dad had to take custody of the kid. Berry had spent this dismal fortnight down in Florida, where Mario – already a high-profile newsman with NBC – had borrowed a beach house from a friend. Come to think of it, this friend had been a senator, the bastard already getting too close to politicians for a guy who was supposed to be ruthlessly impartial.

Anyhow, that had been the summer of The Gypsy. He didn't know if she *was* a gypsy, but that was how he always thought of her. He didn't know, either, if she was a phoney. Just always hoped she was. Better to be a basic neurotic than what she said.

He remembered the nights spent holding the pillow around his head to muffle the sound of Mario humping Carmine, his mistress, in the next room. One night he didn't go back to the beach house, just walked until dawn, a night of spinning pin-balls and hard coloured lights and cheap music. And The Gypsy.

She was this mid-European lady, with a sign over her door covered with coloured moons and stars. He couldn't imagine now how the hell he'd found the courage to walk in there with his five dollars. She'd said, "You not a happy boy, you mixed up." He thought she was about to use the word neurotic, like his old man. But she went on, "It affect you more on account of you sensitive, right? Have eyes inside, yes?" Berry staring at her blankly. "One day something happen to you. Wow! Crash! Boom! And then you know what you got."

Crazy. The lights, the hot music and The Gypsy. Sometimes – occasionally in the years before The Gypsy and increasingly afterwards – he'd gotten feelings about things or places. Small things, stupid things. Feelings that said: don't get closer to this, back off. And The Gypsy's words would come back to him, and he'd laugh. Try to laugh, anyhow. She'd been called Rose-something, weren't they all? She'd taken his money, but afterwards given it back to him. "You and me, we in same shit. You find out. Good luck, huh."

Most likely, she was neurotic too.

The thing that really got to him was old Winstone. Put the arm on young Giles, stop him, not meant to be there, all that crap. The sequence of events leading up to him standing in a dark, cold room permeated by hatred.

Or maybe simply a perfectly ordinary room with a certifiable neurotic standing in it.

On Friday night Miranda called Berry from her mother's house in Chelsea to say she was home.

"Did you get my message?" she asked him.

"Did you get a Frenchman?"

"They all tried too hard," Miranda said. "I wanted one who really didn't want to know, but they all tried too hard. I'm afraid Paris has become rather tedious."

"As tedious as Wales?"

"Do me a favour. How did you get on, anyway?"

She seemed to have forgotten about telling him not to bother coming back.

"Oh, you know, OK," Berry said. "Interesting place, good scenery. Crazy language."

"And you spelled it out for him? As stipulated in the dying wish of old what's-his-name?"

"It was complicated."

"Complicated. I see. What you're saying is you didn't sort it out. You didn't, did you? You really didn't tell him. You spent the whole weekend poncing around with a lot of Celtic sheep-shaggers and you didn't say a word."

"That isn't quite fair, Miranda. What happened . . . Listen, can I see you?"

She hung up on him.

Angrily, Berry broke the line and tried to call her back. Then he changed his mind and called Giles at home. This was it. The end. He'd lay the whole thing on him, the whole Winstone bit, the bad vibes in the judge's study, everything.

Giles's phone rang five times and then there was a beep.

"This is the London home of Claire and Giles Freeman. We're not here, so you can either leave a message after the tone or ring us on Y Groes 239."

Beep.

Berry put the phone down.

Y Groes 239.

"Shit," he said, dismayed.

Giles had complained it would be months before all the legal stuff was complete – what did they call it, probate.

"They're living in that goddamn house," Berry said aloud. "They moved in."

He'd blown it. He'd let everybody down again. Giles, Winstone. Even Miranda.

You're a waste of time, boy. You know that?

Mario Morelli's words, of course.

You got no guts is the problem.

CHAPTER XX

WALES

One of the first things they did was to go into Pontmeurig and choose a bed.

Nothing else. Not yet, anyway. Any changes, they had agreed, should be dictated by the cottage itself. They felt that after they'd spent a few weeks there they would know instinctively which items of new furniture the judge's house might consider permissible.

But a new bed was essential. There was only one in the place, an obvious antique with an impressive headboard of dark oak which was possibly Claire's grandfather's death-bed. Hardly be seemly for the pair of them to spend their first night in Y Groes squashed into that.

So they ordered the new bed from Garfield and Pugh's furniture store in Stryd y Castell, Pontmeurig. It wasn't the kind of bed they would have bought under normal circumstances – it had a headboard of shiny pink vinyl – but there were only three to choose from and Giles was adamant that they should support local traders.

"We can soon pick up a new headboard somewhere," he whispered to Claire. "I mean, it'd look pretty bad if we walked out now without buying one."

Young Mr. Pugh, son of one of the partners, was standing no more than four feet away with a contemptuous smile on his pale, plump face. He had obviously heard every word and was not bothering to conceal the fact.

"I cannot see us having anything that would suit *you*," Mr. Pugh had told them bluntly. "No brass bedsteads here. No pine. Nothing – how can I put it – nothing *cottagey*. Have you tried Aberystwyth or Lampeter?"

"We'd rather shop locally," Giles had replied stiffly. "Now we're living here." He was furious. This youth was treating him like one of the mindless incomers who wanted to turn Wales into an English colony. He imagined a headline in the local paper.

SNOOTY LONDONERS SNUB LOCAL BEDS

"We'll have this one," Giles said. "Nice cheerful head-board."

Mr. Pugh shrugged. "We can't deliver until Monday."

"That'll be fine," Giles said, wondering where the hell they were going to sleep over the weekend.

"*Blaen-y-cwm*, is it?" Mr. Pugh asked.

"What?"

"Mrs. Harris's old place. Where you're living?"

"No," Giles said. "We've taken over my wife's grandfather's house at Y Groes. Judge Rhys."

"Oh, I see," said Mr. Pugh, with a little more interest. "*Siarad Cymraeg*?"

"I'm afraid not," Giles said. "But we hope to learn."

"They don't speak much English in Y Groes," Mr. Pugh said with a smirk.

"Good," said Giles.

When they left the shop, Claire said, "Not very friendly, are they? He didn't particularly want to sell us that bed."

"He's probably sick to death of posh English people buying things and then seeing something better and cancelling their order."

"They weren't very friendly in the Drovers' Arms either."

"They were OK. They didn't all start speaking Welsh or anything when we walked in."

"Oh yes, most of them were speaking English," said Claire. "But not to us."

"For God's sake –" Giles snapped. "Give them a chance, can't you?"

Claire's small face was solemn, and Giles's mood softened. He knew she was looking for reasons not to stay here. Not because she didn't want to, but because she did want to, very badly.

"Look," Giles said. "We can't expect them to rush out and welcome us with open arms. We're just another English couple in love with a dream. They've seen us before. That's what they think."

Claire smiled. "I doubt if anyone has seen you before, Giles," she said.

Giles ignored this. "We've got to persuade them we're not the usual kind of pompous self-satisfied shits who come in and throw money about until they get bored and move to Provence or somewhere the weather's better." He put an arm around Claire. "Come on, let's go home."

He loved the sound of that. Home.

Y Groes was home now.

Giles had taken a fortnight's leave to coincide with the move, which had become possible far sooner than they'd imagined. It turned out that the usual six months' probate period did not apply in the case of property bequeathed to a close relative.

Suddenly the judge's house was theirs. The weather was still warm, the travelling was easy. There'd never be a better time, Giles had maintained, freckles aglow, hustling Claire.

So they'd done it.

As they were retaining their London flat – for the time being, at least – and the cottage was already furnished, there wasn't a great deal to bring, and the removal firm had used its smallest van.

Now, as they drove back from Pontmeurig with groceries and things in the boot of the BMW, Giles was once again aware of the difference in atmosphere as they came out of the Nearly Mountains.

It wasn't simply the transition from the bleak forestry to the broadleaved haven of the village. It was the striking difference between Y Groes and Pontmeurig – a town Giles had never actually visited before today.

He tried to explain it to Claire. "A definite air of depression. I don't mean the people. The shops weren't exactly overstocked. And there was quite a lot of, you know, not exactly dereliction, but peeling paintwork, that sort of thing."

"Not a prosperous town," Claire conceded.

"Dying on its feet, if you ask me. All right, there were a couple of shiny new shopfronts – the bookshop and that awful pizza joint. But you get the feeling they won't be there this time next year – or they'll be replaced by other experiments in the art of retailing."

"Not enough money," Claire said. "Because there aren't enough people. I bet . . . I bet all the incomers get their provisions from the supermarkets in Aberystwyth. They're used to travelling a fair distance on shopping trips back in England – big discount furniture places and hypermarkets."

"Well, *we* won't be doing that," Giles said firmly, turning into the track between the two sycamores. "I don't care what it costs or how many different shops we have to go to. These people deserve our trade."

They found the gate already open and two women by the front step. Oh God, Giles thought. What have we done wrong?

If there were neighbours outside the flat in Islington, they'd usually come to complain.

He remembered what young Mr. Pugh had said about Y Groes. "*Bore da*," he said uncertainly, then realised it was no use wishing them good morning at three-thirty in the afternoon. He tried again.

"Er . . . *Prynhawn da.*"

The first of the ladies came forward, smiling, hand outstretched. "Oh, Mr. Freeman, good afternoon," she said. "We are terribly sorry to trouble you, but the telephone people arrived to reconnect your line and could not get in. I am Mrs. Huws, from the post office, this is Mrs. Hywels."

Mrs. Huws and Mrs. Hywels both shook hands with Giles and with Claire. "Pleased to meet you, Miss Rhys."

"Oh gosh," Giles said. "I mean, there was no need for you to come all the way up here just to –"

"Well, they could hardly ring to tell you they had been to connect your telephone," said Mrs. Hywels.

"We are delighted to help in any way we can," said Mrs. Huws. "Moving house is such a trial. You must be exhausted."

"What you must do," said Mrs. Hywels, "is to tell Mair when it is convenient for the telephone people to come to you, and she will ring them."

"Good God, no." Giles was glowing with pleasure at their kindness. "There's a phone box in the village. I'll ring them. We can't put you to that kind of trouble."

"Now, Mr. Freeman," said Mrs. Huws severely. "We are a very close village. When you come to live amongst us, you are part of our community whether you like it or not, isn't it. Now is there anything you need for tonight. Tea? Sugar? Bread?"

"Thank you," Giles said. "But we're fine. We've got everything. Everything we could wish for."

The small dark eyes of the women were darting about like

bluebottles, over Giles and Claire and the BMW beyond the gate.

"Would you like a cup of tea?" Claire asked. "Before you go?"

The ladies said they would not put her to such trouble but when Mr. and Mrs. Freeman had settled in they would be pleased to accept their hospitality.

"Super," said Claire.

Walking the ladies to the gate, then holding it open for them, Giles asked how well they'd known Claire's grandfather. They told him the judge was a very quiet and dignified man, who never came out, even in the height of summer, without a jacket and a tie and a watch and chain. Claire, they said, would have been proud to know him. And he, they were sure, would have been very proud of his granddaughter.

"Er, we . . . we don't know an awful lot about the judge," Giles admitted. "That is, his death . . . The solicitor, Mr. Davies, implied it had been fairly sudden. Quick, I mean."

"And without pain, wasn't it, Eirlys," Mrs. Huws said. "Very weak, he was though, at the end. Weak in body, mind, not in spirit. And he was over ninety. Dr. Wyn wanted to send him to the hospital in Pont, but he refused. He knew he was going, see, and would not leave Y Groesfan."

"In case his spirit could not find its way back," Mrs. Hywels said.

Giles smiled, acknowledging that no spirit in its right mind would want to leave Y Groes.

"Don't forget now," Mair Huws said. "If you find you have run out of anything, come to the shop and knock on the door if we are closed."

"Great," said Giles. "Er, *diolch yn fawr*."

"Goodbye then, Mr. Freeman. "And welcome to Y Groesfan."

Giles went back to the house, his gratitude brimming over.

Life in Y Groes was already turning out exactly as he'd hoped it would.

That night they built a big log fire in the inglenook (Giles, with a howl of delight, had uncovered what looked like a year's supply of cut, dry logs in a shed) and spread two sleeping bags on the living-room floor. Claire, ever efficient, had brought them just in case. The house really was remarkably clean, and Giles was surprised how generally trauma-free the move had been. They hadn't had a single row – although Claire was the sort of quietly efficient professional person it was hard to pick fights with anyway.

Giles did get rather angry with himself as he discovered he had no natural ability when it came to making log fires and had to keep getting up in the night to feed the thing. At this rate what looked like a year's supply of logs would probably last about six weeks. Altogether Giles reckoned he got about three hours' sleep, and he awoke next morning with a slight headache.

Of course, the ache began to fade as soon as he looked out of the window and saw the hills freshly speckled with early sun. He pulled on his trousers and went barefoot through the primitive kitchen to fill the kettle with spring water which came, apparently, from their own private supply and in as much quantity as if it were from the mains. He cupped his hands under the tap and tasted it – probably better than the stuff they bought in bottles from Sainsbury's – and rubbed the rest into his eyes, rinsing away the remains of his headache.

He went back into the living room and stared down at Claire, still sleeping, curled foetally in her yellow sleeping bag. He didn't think he'd ever seen her looking so relaxed, so untroubled. Even her hair – short, blonde, business-like – mustn't have it flying over the lens, ruining a shot – seemed to have loosened up and was fanned out over the edge of the sleeping bag and onto the hearthrug below. She really did, he thought, look reborn.

Giles felt his lungs expand with something he identified as joy. It felt quite strange and moving.

"This, my darling," he said softly, a little chokily, "is where it really begins."

Claire slept on.

CHAPTER XXI

On Sunday evening, Giles decided to make his first visit to his new local, *Tafarn Y Groesfan*. Claire watched him walk out of sight down the hill before setting off alone to chase the spirit of the place in the only way she knew how: by taking pictures of things.

She walked out of the front garden gate and did not look back. She wanted to photograph the cottage last of all. That was the natural sequence. She didn't want to take its picture until she'd made other connections . . . out there.

Feeling as if she were descending into a dream, Claire walked into the last burst of brilliance from the setting sun. It forced her to look downwards, denying her a view of the church, denying her a picture too, because from this side the tower would be hard against the light and it was too bright yet to make any dramatic use of that.

There was nobody on the main street. Dark blinds were down in the windows of the post office – *Swyddfa'r Post*, it said above the door, without a translation. Claire took a picture of the post office, with herself reflected in the dark window, a slender, crop-haired woman, face semi-concealed behind the battered Nikon. This was a picture to prove that she really was here, an image in the window along with two terraced cottages and a black cat. Part of the scene.

She photographed interlocking beams in the end wall of the general store, pushing out like bones under a taut white skin.

Then she became aware of a very distinguished old oak tree,

standing at the bottom of the street, above the river bridge. She filled the frame with the stern expressions on its trunk, and then took another shot on wide angle, to get in a heavy tractor looking flimsy and transient in its shade. Claire could almost feel the ancient male arrogance of the tree, its roots flexing in the earth.

That made her wonder about her own roots, how deep *they* were here.

She'd phoned her mother to explain that they would be spending a few days at the cottage. Not yet telling her, however, that they actually intended to make it their permanent home – although Giles had thought they should. Indeed, he seemed to be looking forward to it. "Christ, I'd love to see the old bag's face when she finds out," he kept saying. Giles, who had never got on with his mother-in-law, was taking full advantage of her being out of favour with Claire as well.

"You're doing what?" Elinor had said.

"It seems only right, Mother. He *did* leave it to me. Do you really think I could sell it without a second thought?"

"You can't sleep there. It'll be damp."

"Why should it be? It hasn't been empty long. I gather he hadn't been in hospital for more than a few days when he died."

"And dirty."

"We'll clean it."

Elinor was breathing very hard.

"Mother . . ."

"What?" Elinor snapped.

"You said my grandfather had only seen me once."

"When did I say that?"

"When I rang you two weeks ago."

"Well, I – I've told you about that, surely."

"No."

"I must have."

"You haven't."

"Well, I don't want to talk about it now."

"Oh, Mother, please – this is ridiculous."

"You don't know what that man was like, Claire."

"I expect I'll find out this weekend then. I shall ask people in the village about him. I'll find out from them when I saw him. Somebody must know –"

"No!"

"What?"

"Listen . . . We went to see him just once, your father and I," her mother said, "when you were a very small child, three or four. I've told you before, I'm sure, but I don't suppose you were very interested at the time. Anyway, we thought he ought to see his granddaughter. Just once, for the sake of –"

Appearances, Claire thought.

"– the family. Old times. I don't know why we went really."

Because you wanted a good snoop, Claire thought.

"But – my God, we soon wished we hadn't. It was *the* most embarrassing day I can ever remember. He seemed to have nothing to say to us. A *stranger*, a strange man to me – my own father. Just some old, some old . . . Welshman. Who didn't even look the same, somehow. His . . . housekeeper prepared this very basic lunch of ham salad, I remember. She also did most of the talking. And then after lunch he said, let's go for a walk, something like that. And your father got to his feet and the old devil waved at him to sit down. Not you, he said. The child and I will go. I was speechless."

"And what happened?" asked Claire.

A silence.

"You went," her mother said coldly.

"Really?" Claire had been expecting to hear how she'd burst into tears and clung to her mother's skirt, demanding to go home. She was thrilled. "I really went with him?"

Elinor didn't reply this time. She obviously regarded it as an act of almost unbelievable treachery.

Claire said, "You never told me that before. I know you never told me."

"Why should I? It's hardly been a fond memory."

"Mother –" Claire thought, *that feeling . . . the feeling that it was meant . . .* I was simply *remembering . . .* "What happened," she said, "when I went for this walk with my grandfather? I mean, where did we go?"

"Claire, it's thirty years ago, and it's not something –"

"Oh, come on, Mother, you must remember. You remember everything else that happened."

She heard Elinor drawing in a long, thin breath. "All I remember is that you were both gone for what seemed an awfully long time and I ran out of things to say to this frightful woman, the so-called housekeeper, and your father got increasingly embarrassed, so we went outside to look for you. George was getting rather worried because it was hardly a big place and yet we couldn't see you anywhere. And then the old swine came up the lane from the church. He was holding your hand and we could hear him – well, I was disgusted. I snatched you away at once."

"Good God, Mother, what on earth –?"

"I put you in the car and I made your father drive us away from there. We didn't bother to say goodbye. We'd been insulted enough."

"But what was he doing? Did he say something to you? To me?"

"And we swore never to go back there again, ever. And we never did."

"But what –?"

"I don't *know*!" her mother had almost screamed. "He was talking to you in *Welsh*, for God's sake!"

*

135

The old oak tree stood there, as if it were absorbing her thoughts and her emotions and considering what to do about her.

Claire looked up the lane towards the church and pictured a distinguished gentleman in a black suit walking slowly down it, a little girl clinging to his hand.

But, of course, this was all imagination because Claire had no idea what her grandfather had looked like. She'd never seen a single photograph of him. Her mother wouldn't have one in the house.

CHAPTER XXII

Walking towards *Tafarn Y Groesfan*, Giles felt undeniably nervous. For some reason, he started to think about Charlie Firth, of the *Mail*, and the allegedly poisoned eggs. All that absolute nonsense.

But, bloody hell – if, in parts of Wales, there *was* a lingering suspicion of the English, was it not amply justified by people like Charlie Firth and the others? If the locals were suspicious of *him*, better to find out now. Show his face, let them get used to it.

It was the last week of British Summertime. The evening sun was losing strength, although it was still remarkably warm, as Giles approached the huge oaken door which hung ajar, giving direct access to the bar. As it swung open, the heads of three men inside slowly pivoted, as if they were part of the same mechanism, and three gazes came to rest on Giles.

He blinked timidly.

The bar was so small and – well, *woody*, that it was almost like being inside an ancient, hollow tree. Beams everywhere, far thicker than the ones in the cottage. It was lit only by the dying sun, so it was dark. But dark in a rich and burnished way, rather than dim like, say, the judge's study.

It was palpably old. The phrase "as old as the hills" – a cliché too hackneyed for Giles ever to use in an article – suddenly resounded in his head, making dramatic sense.

All the richness came from the age of the building, for it was very plain inside. No brasswork, no awful reproduction warming pans.

In a most un-publike silence Giles approached the bar. From

beneath a beam the shape and colour of a giant Mars bar, a face peered out.

The landlord, if indeed it was he, was a small man with white hair and a Lloyd George moustache. Aled Gruffydd, it had said over the door. What Giles had presumed was the familiar line about Aled Gruffydd being allowed to sell liquor pursuant to sub-section whatever of the Licensing Act had been given only in Welsh.

Either side of the bar a man stood sentinel-like. Giles tentatively flashed each of them a smile and recognised one immediately, having almost run out of petrol on the way here in his determination to fill up locally, at this wonderfully old-fashioned grey stone garage. It had tall, thin pumps, no self-service and a small, rickety sign outside which said Dilwyn Dafis and something in Welsh involving the word *modur*, which he'd taken to mean motor.

This was Dilwyn Dafis. He was in his thirties, wore an oily cap and had a spectacular beer belly. The second customer was a contrastingly cadaverous chap with large, white protruding teeth and thick glasses which were trained now on Giles, like powerful binoculars.

Giles had to bend his head because the great beam over the bar was bowed so low. Too low for an Englishman's comfort. All three of them stared at him.

Should he try greeting them in Welsh? *Nos da*? No, that was good night, said when you were leaving. *Nos . . . nos . . . noswaith da*? Was that it? Was that good evening? Bloody hell, he ought to know something as simple as that, he'd learned a whole collection of greetings weeks ago. *Noswaith da*. It was close but it wasn't quite there.

The three men went on staring at him in silence.

Giles began to sweat. Come on, come on, say *something*, for God's sake.

"Er . . . evening," he said lamely. "Pint of bitter, please."

The landlord nodded and reached for a pint glass.

"And please," Giles added earnestly, flattening his hair as if trying to make himself shorter and thus less English, "absolutely no need to speak English just because I'm here."

Christ! What a bloody stupid, patronising thing to say. Especially as nobody, as yet, had spoken at all. He wanted to go out and never, ever come in again.

Still nobody spoke, but the white-haired barman gave him an amused and quizzical look, into which Giles read withering contempt.

"I mean –" he floundered, feeling his face reddening. All those years a journalist and he was going red! But this wasn't an assignment, this was the first faltering step into his future. "If I want to know what's going on around here, I'll just, er, just have to learn *your* language, won't I?" Christ, worse and worse . . .

Dilwyn Dafis, the garage man, chuckled quietly.

Aled the landlord stepped back to pull the pint. The pump gurgled and spat.

It was the thin man with the sticking-out teeth who finally spoke. He said, "Well . . . *there's* a thing."

What the hell did that mean? For the first time, Giles came close to wishing he were back in London.

Aled Gruffydd topped up Giles's pint, leaned across the bar with it. "Nobody expects that, man."

"I'm sorry . . .?"

"I said nobody expects you to learn Welsh. Right, Glyn?"

"Good God, no," said the thin man.

"No indeed," said Dilwyn Dafis, shaking his head and his oily cap.

Giles inspected the three faces, found no hint of sarcasm in any of them and was nonplussed. "That's very generous of you," he said. "But I *want* to learn Welsh. I believe it's the least one can do when one comes to live in a Welsh-speaking community." How pompous it sounded, how horribly, unforgivably, tight-arsed *English*.

Aled Gruffydd said, "Why? What is it you think is going to happen if you don't?"

"Waste of time for you, man," Dilwyn Dafis said. "We speak it because we grew up speaking it, the Welsh. No great thing, here. Just the way it is, see."

"Have a seat," said Glyn. A faded tweed suit hung limply from his angular frame. "Tell us about yourself. We won't bite you."

Giles sat down rather shakily on a wooden bar stool. The whole atmosphere had changed. He'd walked into silence and stares, and now they were making him welcome and telling him there was absolutely no need to learn Welsh – in a village where little else ever seemed to be spoken. He was confused.

"Where is your wife?" Aled Gruffydd said.

"Oh, she's . . . out. Taking a few pictures."

"Photos, is it?"

"That's what she does. She's a photographer."

"Well, well," said Aled.

Giles had the feeling Gruffydd knew this already. A feeling there was very little he could tell them about himself that they didn't already know. But he explained about his wife's inheritance and they nodded and said "well, well" and "good God" a few times as if it was the first they'd heard about it. They were unbelievably affable. And this made it more important for them to know he and Claire were not just going to be holiday-home-owners, that this was now their principal residence and they were going to preserve its character; there'd be no phoney suburban bits and pieces, no patio doors, no plastic-framed double-glazing, no carriage lamps . . .

"Good house, that is, mind," thin Glyn said. "Been in that family for . . . what is the word in English? Generations."

"You mean the Rhys family?"

"Generations," said Glyn. "Many generations, the Rhyses."

Bloody hell, he'd never thought of that – that he and Claire were actually maintaining a family chain of ownership going back possibly centuries. They really didn't know anything, did they?

"Gosh," Giles said. "I suppose – I mean, is that why Judge Rhys came back? Because somebody left *him* the house?"

"Well," said Glyn. "I suppose that was one of the reasons. From England, he came, as you know, having spent most of his life there."

This was actually marvellous. This gave them a solid, copper-bottomed basis for residency. This gave them a right to be here.

"What is that other word?" said Glyn. "Continuity. We believe in that, see, in Y Groesfan. Continuity."

Giles understood now. When he first came in they weren't quite sure who he was. Now they knew he was the husband of a Rhys. Knew he belonged. He settled back on his wooden stool and began to look around. What a superb old place it was. He remembered Berry Morelli telling him on their way back to London how the buildings in Y Groes had struck him as having grown out of the landscape as part of some natural process. This pub was like that, its oaken interior so crude and yet so perfect. He felt privileged to be here. And proud too, now.

He bought them all drinks.

They told him about the village.

They told him it had about two hundred and fifty people, if you included the outlying farms.

It had two shops, the general store and the post office. One garage, one school, one church.

They told him the original name of the village was Y Groesfan

– the crossing. But when non-conformism had taken Wales in the nineteenth century a chapel had been built and the name shortened to Y Groes – the cross – because it seemed more holy. When Giles said he hadn't noticed a chapel, Dilwyn Dafis smiled. Glyn, who apparently was something of an historian, said non-conformism had been a passing phase here, although nobody had bothered to change the name back.

Giles wondered briefly why the old name should have referred to a "crossing place" when the village was in fact a dead-end and apparently always had been. And would, he hoped, be the end of his own search for a spiritual home. He also wondered – very nervously – how these chaps would react to *that*. He realised there was only one way to find out.

"I suppose," he said, as steadily as he could manage, "that you must be pretty sick about all these English people moving in."

"What English is that?" Aled said. He took a cloth from a shelf below the bar and began to polish glasses.

"Well, you know ... I mean, we were in Pontmeurig this morning and at least half the people we met, half the shopkeepers for instance, were incomers. I just hadn't realised it was that bad. I mean, it must irritate you, surely."

"Ah, well, see, that is Pontmeurig," said Dilwyn Dafis.

"Pont is different," said Glyn. "They are always moaning about the English in Pont. But we don't moan about them here, do we, boys? No cause to."

Aled Gruffydd shook his head. Glyn drained his beer glass and Giles seized the opportunity to buy everyone another drink. He was dying to ask all kinds of questions but settled on just one more as the glasses were passed over and the three Welshmen said "Cheers" rather than *Iechyd Da!* out of deference to their English companion. They really were remarkably accommodating. Indeed, if everyone was as gently hospitable as these chaps and Mrs. Huws and Mrs. Hywels it was really no wonder the country was being overrun by the English.

But they hadn't been like this in Pontmeurig. Only in Y Groes. A special place.

"So, what," Giles asked, "is the actual percentage of incomers in Y Groes? I mean, you know, roughly."

Dilwyn Dafis looked puzzled. "How's that, like?"

"What he means," Aled said, "is how many English compared to Welsh."

"In this village?"

"Right," said Giles.

"What English?" said Dilwyn.

"You mean –?" The truth hit Giles like a brick. "You mean that the entire immigrant population of Y Groes is –"

Glyn smiled, his large front teeth standing out like a marble cemetery in the moonlight.

"– *us*?" said Giles.

"Well, there we are," said Dilwyn Dafis, raising his glass to Giles and smiling slowly. "Makes you a bit of a novelty, like, isn't it?"

CHAPTER XXIII

Claire climbed into the riverside field by a convenient stile to photograph a lone sheep, somebody's initials SE scrawled across its back in lurid crimson, like a splash of fresh blood. The sheep was lying apart from the rest of the flock, benign head lifted, gazing beyond the field to the village street. Through the lens, Claire followed the sheep's gaze but saw only a litter bin attached to a low wall with grass growing out of the top. She took a picture, the sheep dark in the foreground.

The river was beautiful. It splashed and fizzed amiably over the rocks, calling out so strongly to Claire that she just had to scramble down the bank, camera bouncing around on its leather strap, until her feet slipped into the soft, cool water. One shoe floated off and she had to rescue it. Then, on impulse, she put the blue shoe back in the river and took a photograph of the clear water swirling gently around it, in the background the river-washed stonework of a bridge support.

The river, the bridge, her shoe – part of the scene.

She should have come to see him. If she'd known about him wanting to take her, just her, for that walk, down the lane to the village, past the church; if she'd known that, she would have come. She imagined him talking to her softly, musically, in Welsh – how beautiful. If she'd been told about that, she would have come. No doubt her mother had thought of that. Bitch. Until that phone call Claire had assumed she'd never met her grandfather, never been to Y Groes in her life. No wonder the village called out to her to come back.

Bitch.

Y Groes – always "some ghastly God-forsaken place in the middle of nowhere" or "some damp, dreary hellhole". If only she'd known . . .

It was her own fault. Such a placid child, people always said. Incurious about everything until her teens, when she began to take photographs and the world opened out like a huge flower. And then always too busy: leaving home, catching up on everything she'd missed, carving out a career in what then was still seen as a man's world. And forgetting for years at a time that she had a grandfather on her mother's side, an estranged counterpart to good old Reg with his garden and his golf.

And here, unknown to her – all this.

Bitch.

Sitting on the river bank, in the lengthening shadow of the bridge, strange, conflicting emotions crowded in on Claire and she wept silently. Not soul-wrenching, God-cursing tears, as often wept by Bethan, whom she did not as yet know, but quiet tears of regret.

Another shadow fell across her and she looked up, a tall figure blocking the dying sun.

It's *him*.

Claire's heart leapt in fear. Fear and –

– and longing.

The voice was soft and high and sibilant, like the wind in a cornfield.

"I'm afraid I don't know your name. So I shall just call you Miss Rhys. How are you, Miss Rhys?"

CHAPTER XXIV

Three-fifteen. Home time.

Bethan was bustling about the school hall attending to children's major crises: the four-year-old boy whose shoe-lace had come undone, the girl of six with a broken nail.

"Try not to get it wet or it will come off," she said, adjusting the Band-Aid round the child's finger then turning to help a small boy who'd buttoned his coat all wrong.

A handful of mothers were waiting for the smallest children. They watched her with indulgent smiles, none of them rushing to help her. Perhaps they thought this was the kind of therapy she needed to cure her of widowhood.

The mothers took their kids and left, leaving Bethan with just three small pupils waiting to be collected and a strange woman standing hesitantly in the doorway, clutching one of those slim, garish packages in which prints and negatives are returned from processing.

"Mrs. Freeman," Bethan remembered. "You rang this morning. You wanted to see me."

"Hello," the woman said. She looked down at the photo envelope. "I usually do my own or take them to someone I know in London," she said half-apologetically. "I've been to one of those fast-print places in Aberystwyth. Just, you know, wanted . . . to see how they'd turned out."

She seemed embarrassed. Bethan couldn't think why. She smiled at the woman. "Come in," she said. "Try not to fall over Angharad, she thinks she's a sheepdog."

Buddug had left early, to Bethan's relief. In the emptying school hall, where an electric kettle was coming gently to the boil on the teacher's table, Bethan looked at the woman and the woman looked at Bethan. They were around the same age, one dark, one blonde, one Welsh, the other . . . well, very English, Bethan thought, but who could really say?

"I'm still rather feeling my way in the village," the blonde one said. She was dressed like a very urban explorer, in fashionably baggy green trousers and red hiking boots. "I don't know quite how I should behave."

Good heavens, Bethan thought, they aren't usually like that, the English, when they move into Pontmeurig, joining this and organising that and introducing themselves everywhere and even buying people drinks, sometimes.

"Don't be silly," she said, pouring boiling water into a chunky earthenware pot. "Sit down. Have a cup of tea."

"Thank you," the judge's granddaughter said, lowering herself, quite gracefully under the circumstances into a tiny chair designed for a seven-year-old. "That's kind of you, Miss Sion."

"Mrs. McQueen."

"Oh, I'm terribly sorry, I was told –"

"Bethan. Call me, Bethan."

"Oh. Yes. Thank you. I'm Claire Freeman, but everyone seems to know that." She laughed. "Although they all seem to call me Miss Rhys – the women in the post office and Mr. ap Siencyn, the rector. My grandfather, you see, he was –"

"I know," Bethan said. "I'm afraid I never really met him. A bit before my time. He was staying in his house most of the time, when I was here. He used to study a lot, people said. In the village, I believe, he was very much . . . well, revered."

This had the desired effect of pleasing Claire Freeman, who told Bethan how wonderful it had been to discover in the cottage and in the village this whole new aspect of her ancestry, long hidden, like the family treasure.

"But you said you didn't really know him," Claire said. "So you can't have been here all that long yourself."

Pouring tea into a yellow mug, Bethan told her she'd been here nearly a year, then left, then come back. No she hadn't been here all that long, when you added it up.

"But it's different for you," Claire said, "and that's what I've come about, I suppose." She'd opened the envelope and was flicking through the photographs without looking at them, still rather ill at ease, the child, Angharad, scampering around her feet.

"Milk?" said Bethan.

"Just a little."

"Sugar?"

Claire passed. "*Dim siwgwr*. Is that right?"

"Yes," said Bethan, smiling a little, passing her the mug of tea. "But only if you're trying to lose weight. Can I see?"

"I haven't really looked at them yet. They won't be very good. They're just snaps."

Bethan pushed back her hair and adjusted her glasses. She opened the envelope and saw clear water swirling around a bright-blue shoe. It was a startling picture. She drew it out and below it saw the judge's cottage, twilit. Then she saw the village street looking very still, with deep shadows; various close-ups of the timber-framed houses – including the tiny terraced cottage where she and Robin had lived, with the setting sun floating in its upstairs front window. Then a solitary sheep, a view of the darkening hills, of the rigidly upright figure of the rector standing in the grass above the river, of Mair Huws outside her shop, of the church tower braced against the dying light and photographed from a steep angle that made it look as if it was falling towards you.

She felt something at once in the photograph. This woman had plucked ripened images of Y Groes out of the air like apples from a tree, and caught the glow.

"They're wonderful," Bethan said. "They're like something out of a magazine. No, that's inadequate, that cheapens them."

"Oh dear," said Claire, "I was hoping they'd be like holiday snaps. I can't seem to take snaps any more."

She looked so seriously disappointed that Bethan had to laugh, quite liking her now. Out of the window she saw two mothers appear at the gate, and excused herself and rounded up the remaining three children – "*Dewch yma, Angharad*, wuff wuff" – gently pushing them out of the door into the playground, waving to the mothers.

When she returned, Claire was thumbing rapidly through the photographs, looking puzzled.

"Anything wrong?"

"No, I – a couple seem to be missing, that's all. My own fault, I should have waited to have them done in London. That is –"

She looked embarrassed again, as if expecting Bethan to say, Oh, so our Welsh film processing isn't good enough for you, is it, Mrs. Posh Londoner?

"Well," said Bethan, "they *are* a bit slapdash, some of these quick-processing outfits."

Claire looked grateful. "What I've come about – I – somebody in the pub told Giles, my husband, that you were rather brilliant at teaching English children to speak Welsh, and so we wondered –"

Bethan explained that it wasn't a question of being brilliant; English children, the younger the better, picked up Welsh surprisingly quickly. By the age of seven or eight, if they attended a Welsh-medium school, they were often quite fluent. Claire said they had no children yet, but when they did have a baby she would like it to be raised in a bilingual home, and so – "It's

149

funny really, some people in the pub told Giles there was no need to learn Welsh in Y Groes."

Bethan raised an eyebrow. "They told him that?"

"I think it was because we seem to be the only English people in the village. I think they were just being kind, probably."

"Probably," said Bethan, thinking how odd this was.

"We'd fit in, of course, with your arrangements," Claire said.

Bethan thought about it. "I've never done it before, taught adults."

"Is it so different?"

"I don't know," Bethan said.

"They say the brain starts to atrophy or something, when you pass thirty. Isn't that what they say?"

"Well," said Bethan, pouring herself a mug of strong, black tea, coming to a decision, "let's prove them wrong. I could come to your house after school for a short time, how would that be?"

"That would be super. I mean, Giles will have to go back to London during the week, but I'll be staying here, and I could bring him up to date at weekends on everything I've learned."

Bethan said slowly, "I'm . . . often free at the weekend too." All too free, she thought. "The thing to do is to work on it every day if you can, even if it's only for twenty minutes. I'm sure we could do that most days. And perhaps at weekends we could have a revision session, with your husband."

Claire flung out a big smile, and Bethan thought she was going to hug her. "That's absolutely marvellous, Bethan. I mean, we'll pay whatever you think is –"

"Don't worry about that. I'll enjoy it, I think."

Bethan had caught a breath of something from this woman, something she realised she missed, a sense of the cosmopolitan, a sense of *away*.

*

150

Bethan closed the school door behind her and looked around her nervously, half expecting to find another child inviting her to inspect a dead body. She shivered, although it was a pleasant evening, still warmish, still no sign of the leaves fraying on the trees. In Pontmeurig many already were brown and shrivelled.

The arrival of Claire Freeman and her husband had, she thought, opened up the place, making a small but meaningful crack in its archaic structure. All villages needed new life, even one as self-contained as Y Groes. *Especially* one like Y Groes.

Learning the language was good – and something that few of the incomers to Pontmeurig bothered to attempt. But she found herself hoping (Guto would be horrified) that the Freemans wouldn't try *too* hard to fit in.

As she drove the Peugeot out of the school lane towards the bridge, she saw Claire Freeman standing in the middle of the village street gazing out at the river. Nobody else was on the street. Claire looked abstracted, a wisp of blonde hair fallen forward between her eyes.

Bethan paused for a second before turning the wheel towards the Pontmeurig road, and Claire saw her and began to run towards the car, waving urgently.

She wound down her window.

Claire, flushed and panting, leaning against the car, said, "Bethan, I think I must be going mad. I can't seem to find my tree."

"Your tree?"

"It's a huge oak tree. Very old. It's . . . I'm sure it was in that field. You see, I took some pictures of it, but they weren't there, with the others."

"Perhaps they didn't come out."

"My pictures," said Claire, "*never* don't come out – I'm sorry, I didn't mean – but they don't. I've been through the negatives and the tree pictures aren't there either. And now the tree's gone too. I'm sorry, this must sound ever so stupid."

"Well, perhaps –" Bethan was going to say perhaps somebody chopped it down, but that made no sense either and she wasn't aware of there ever having been a tree down there anyway.

"The tractor!" Claire exclaimed. "Look, see that yellow tractor . . . *that* was there when I took the picture, standing next to the tree. The tree was *there*!"

"Well, that explains it," said Bethan. "Somebody has moved the tractor and confused you. Your tree is probably further up the bank."

"No –" Claire's brow was creased and her mouth tight. "No, I don't think so."

There is more to this than photos, Bethan thought.

"I'm sorry," Claire said, pulling herself away from the car. "It's professional pride, I suppose. You always know exactly what you've shot, and there are a few things on that film I don't – Look, I'm delaying you again, you're probably right, the tree's somewhere upstream and it doesn't matter anyway, does it?"

Claire tried a weak smile. "Perhaps my brain really is starting to atrophy," she said.

Bethan didn't think so.

CHAPTER XXV

Giles was setting up his word processor in his new office, plugging the printer into the monitor and standing back to admire.

It was all just too bloody perfect.

Well, all right, *almost* too perfect. His one disappointment had been not being able to organise his office in the old man's study. He'd pictured himself in the Gothic chair behind that monster of an oak desk, surrounded by all those heavy books in a language which he couldn't as yet understand – although that was only a matter of time.

Last night, after returning from the pub, Giles had unpacked his word processor and was struggling into the judge's study with the monitor in his arms, fumbling for the light switch, when he found there wasn't one.

There was no electric light in there!

Not only that, there were no bloody power points either.

"Bit of a primitive, your granddad, was he?" he'd said in some irritation.

Claire's reply had been, "Oh, didn't you know about that?" Which could have meant anything. Giles had resolved to contact an electrician. He really wanted that room.

Meanwhile, he'd decided to adopt the smallest of the three bedrooms for his office, and he had to admit there were compensations.

Not least the view, through a gap in the trees (an intentional gap, surely) and down over the rooftops of the village towards the Pontmeurig road. The church was just out of sight, seemingly behind the cottage at this point, but he could sense its presence, somehow.

There was another window to the side and it was against this one that Giles had pushed his desk, which was actually their old stripped-pine dining table from the flat in Islington, one of the comparatively few items of furniture they'd brought with them. Claire had insisted they should eat at her grandfather's dining table, which was a terrible fifties-style thing with fat legs. Giles himself would have chopped it up for kindling; he hated its lugubrious lack of style.

Through the side window he could look out from his desk on to an acre of their own land sloping down towards the river. The neighbouring farmer apparently had some sort of grazing right, and the field was full of fat sheep. Giles was thrilled. He could gaze on all this and the enclosing hills with one eye while keeping the other, so to speak, on the VDU. He was, he felt, in the vanguard of journalism: living in this superb rural location, yet in full and immediate contact with London. Or he would be once he'd installed a fax machine.

He didn't think he'd ever felt so happy or so secure. For the first time in years the job was not the most compelling thing in his life. And he knew that if he did have to quit the paper and go freelance like Claire – a freelance specialising, of course, in honest features about the *real* Wales – they'd be cushioned for the foreseeable future by the no doubt astonishing amount of money they'd get for the flat in Islington.

Giles was feeling so buoyant he told the computer how happy he was, typing it out on the keyboard in Welsh: *R'wyn hapus.*

He examined the sentence on the screen. It wasn't right, was it? It didn't look right at all. He hadn't had much chance to work on his Welsh since moving to Y Groes. Awkward bastard of a language; back in London he'd been sure he was going to have it cracked in no time at all.

Still, no doubt it would start to improve again now Claire was arranging a teacher for them. "Well, all right then, why don't you have a word with Bethan at the school," Aled in the pub had said finally, when he'd emphasised how determined they were to learn the language. "She used to teach a lot of English kids in Pont. Must be good at it."

"Right," Giles had said. "Tremendous. Thanks." Getting somewhere now.

"I'll go and see her," Claire had said that morning, when Giles got up with another headache. "Then I'll drive over to Aberystwyth and get my film processed and get some food and things. You take an aspirin and sort out your office."

The headache had completely vanished now, the office was in order, everything was fine. He rather wished he'd gone with Claire. He'd been wondering which of the teachers this Bethan was, what she looked like – just hoping she didn't turn out to be that female-wrestler type he'd seen stumping down the lane to the school. He understood she was called Mrs. Morgan and was in fact their neighbour, wife of the farmer who raised sheep in their field. Mrs. B. Morgan. Bethan Morgan? He did hope not.

Giles leapt up in alarm when, down in the living room, the phone rang for the first time since the Telecom blokes had reconnected it. He charged downstairs, thinking he'd get them back to scatter a few extensions around when he and Claire had worked out which rooms they were using. At present the only phone was on a deep window ledge in the living room.

"Hullo, yes. This is, er, hang on – Y Groes two three nine."

"Giles? Is that you, Giles?"

"Certainly is."

"Giles, this is Elinor. Could I speak to Claire?"

Oh hell. He should have known it was all too good to last.

"Sorry, Elinor, Claire's out with her camera. I'm not sure when she'll be back. Might be staying out late to photograph badgers or something."

"Don't be ridiculous, Giles. Now tell me what on earth you're doing *there*. Why is there a message on your answering machine referring people to *this* number? What's going on?"

Giles smiled indulgently into the phone. "Going on? Nothing's going on. That's the whole beauty of this place, nothing *ever* goes on."

"Giles –" the voice of his mother-in-law had acquired a warning weight "– am I to expect any sense at all out of you? Or should I call back when my daughter's in? Look –" Being reasonable again, the old Mrs. Nice and Mrs. Nasty routine, Giles thought. "I'm aware that hovel may not be in a fit condition to sell, but surely you could afford to pay someone to *do* something with it. You didn't have to go there yourselves."

"It's already in good enough condition for us, old darling," said Giles. "Well, virtually. I mean, it needs a few minor alterations, mainly of a cosmetic nature. Anyway, look, I may as well tell you. Expect Claire's been too busy to fill you in about our plans, but the current situation is that we're actually living here now."

The silence lasted nearly half a minute, it seemed to Giles. Why did she always have to phone when Claire was out? He'd have to suffer it all twice now – the heavy threats over the phone from Elinor and then, when he'd told her about the conversation, half an hour or so of Claire pacing around saying what an old cow her mother was.

"Elinor, you still there?"

"In . . . in that house?" She was sounding very far away. "*His* house?"

"No, Elinor. *Our* house."

"Oh, Giles." Unexpectedly her voice had turned itself down

low, with apparent anxiety rather than anger. "What about your work, both of you?"

"No problem," said Giles, enjoying talking about this bit, as he always did. He explained how fate had intervened in the form of the Glanmeurig by-election, how he was taking a fortnight's holiday by the end of which, with any luck, they'd be into the campaign. Could be weeks before he'd have to return to London, give or take the odd day, and then, afterwards –

"And *then* you'll sell it, that's what you're saying, when this election is over. Because –"

Giles mentally battered his forehead with an exasperated hand. "Good God, no, you're not getting this at all, are you? We'll still have our base here. I'll travel to London during the week, Claire will work directly from here – good as anywhere – and then we've got a few long-term plans to make sure that Wales remains our home. I mean for good. For ever. Got it now?"

There came a stage with Elinor when only brutality would work. He heard her breathe in sharply and then force herself to calm down and reason with him.

"Giles, listen – before this nonsense goes any further –"

"Oh, bloody hell, it isn't . . ."

"– I – I *can* talk to you, can't I? I've always thought I could – most of the time." She drew a long breath. Christ, Giles thought, get me out of this. "Now, I assume this is some insane idea of Claire's . . . You have to talk her out of it, do you understand? I can't do it, never could once she'd made up her mind about something – now that's an admission, isn't it, from a mother? Giles, please, I'm relying on you, and one day you'll thank me for this –"

"I'll do it now, in case we don't see you for a while. Thanks, Elinor. Now if you don't mind –"

"Giles, don't you dare hang up on me! Listen –" The old girl was racing along breathlessly now. "You could probably get rid of it – the house – quite quickly, if you put your mind to it. I'm sure, if you really want to live in the country, you could get quite a nice property in . . . in Berkshire or somewhere, for the money. Isn't there some land to sell?"

"Strewth," Giles said. "We don't want to live in bloody Berkshire. I mean, don't worry, we'll still come to see you at Christmas, it's not exactly the other side of the world."

Christ, how could somebody as balanced as Claire have a mother like this? She reflected all the worst aspects of Home Counties womanhood – smugness, snobbery, inability to conceive of civilised society anywhere north of –

"Giles, this is not funny. You must fetch Claire home at once."

He felt a warning ripple behind his forehead.

"Home? Home? Listen, Elinor, if you want the truth –" the headache was coming back, bloody woman "– if you really want the truth, I've never felt more at home in my entire bloody life. OK, sure, we all know you and the old man were not exactly close but – well, it's not as if he's still here, is it?"

"Isn't it?" his mother-in-law said, sounding suddenly strained and old and tired.

Then she hung up on him.

"All fixed," Claire said. "Starting tomorrow evening."

"What's she like?"

"Very pleasant."

"I mean, is she young or . . . not so young?"

"I suppose," said Claire, "that depends on what you mean by young."

Getting a bit cryptic these days, Claire. Must be exposure to the Welsh.

"What's she called? I mean, what's her last name?"

"Something English. McQueen – or is that Scottish? Although, obviously, she isn't. Anyway, she's going to pop round after school as many nights as she can manage. We didn't get round to agreeing a fee, but I'm sure it'll be reasonable."

"Doesn't matter," Giles said. "Where else would you get Welsh lessons in your own home? But, look, we've got lots to talk about, so why don't I light a fire? Brought some more logs in. Marvellous logs, you know, these, dry as bone."

Going dark earlier these nights. Colder too, Giles thought, glad Claire was back; it was good to stride around the place during the day but he could never go too long without a spot of company. He was dismayed when Claire said, "I have to go out again."

"Go out? Where?"

"I've got some more pictures to take." A wry little twitch of the mouth. "I'm photographing my way into the community, aren't I?"

"Christ, haven't you got enough pictures yet?"

Claire didn't reply. She began to load a film into her newest Nikon as if leaving for a major assignment in the jungles of Nicaragua. It had been like this all day, as though he didn't really exist. She'd just announced what she was going to do and then done it.

Giles said plaintively, "I was waiting to light the fire, have a discussion about, you know, the future. I mean we've hardly had much chance to talk, the past few days. Also, your m–" No, he wasn't going to go into all that Elinor business. Not now.

"We can talk later," Claire said. "I have to catch what's left of the light, OK?"

"Bugger all left, if you ask me. Why not leave it till tomorrow?"

"Also," Claire mumbled, snapping the camera shut, "I have to find my tree."

"I see. And which tree is that?"

"Just a tree I shot last night, and then it went missing."

"I see," said Giles, gritting his teeth. "Now look, Claire, I really do think –"

But Claire had shouldered her camera and was off before he could even tell her about the call from her mother.

Fuck her, thought Giles, and then realised he hadn't done that for quite a while either.

CHAPTER XXVI

Through the living-room window, Giles watched Claire approach the iron gate. The trees seemed to close around her, and it was as though she were passing quietly into some other dimension. Claire opened the gate without effort and went through, and the landscape appeared to absorb her on the other side. She fitted. She blended with the scene. It welcomed her.

Croeso.

As if she's lived here all her life, Giles thought.

The illusion frightened him. He thought, has she ever really blended with me like that? For the first time since they'd come to live in Y Groes he felt heartsick and alone. And vaguely jealous of the village, which was ridiculous.

He was becoming aware of how differently they regarded this move, this new life. It had been, for him, the big adventure, the great expedition into the unknown, a terrific challenge. It had filled him with energy just thinking about the future. Now he felt his wife was not tuned to quite the same wavelength.

With her it was not elation. It was less of a fun thing. Here they were, just the two of them in a totally strange place and, far from getting closer, confiding more in each other, there was a hazy space between them. Well, not so much between them as around Claire, who had always been so practical and clear-sighted. Now she was altering in unpredictable ways. Like tonight, doing what she'd never done, in his experience, before: going out to take pictures, not in a professional way, but just snapping things, looking for some special sodding tree, for

161

God's sake! This, especially, had got to Giles because only rarely could Claire be persuaded to get out her camera for holiday photos and family occasions. He remembered once suggesting she might knock off a few pics at the christening of his cousin's new baby and she'd gone very huffy indeed, asking him how he'd feel about being asked to write features for the local parish magazine.

Giles sat down at the bloody awful fat-legged dining table and looked into the fireplace which he'd laid with paper and kindling and three small logs and didn't feel like lighting any more.

He ought to try to understand her instead of feeling sorry for himself. She was obviously preoccupied, something here she was struggling to come to terms with. A responsibility to her surroundings that she'd never felt before? Because of her grandfather, yes? Filling in for a missing generation, her mother, who had spurned everything the old man wanted out of life? And what *had* he wanted out of life except for a bit of peace and quiet, back among his compatriots?

For the old man perhaps, this had represented peace and quiet, but for English people it was a lot more demanding, Giles thought, only now realising how clean-cut their life in London had been. *That* was the simple life, when you thought about it, for people with their background. He was a hack. Claire took pictures for money. Professionals. The flat in Islington had been like a station waiting room where they'd passed the time until trains took them in different directions. Maybe he only knew Claire as a kind of intimate colleague.

Stuff this! Giles stood up angrily and reached on the deepset window sill for a box of kitchen matches. He struck two at once and flung them at the fireplace, watched the paper flare, listened to the kindling crackle. Life. Energy.

Early days. Give it time. Be positive. Be practical.

In the diminishing light, he moved purposefully around the

house, thinking about the improvements they could make without spoiling its character. He took with him the slimline pocket cassette-recorder he used sometimes for interviews.

The living room – well, that was more or less OK. Beams, inglenook fireplace – great. A wood-burning stove might be useful in the inglenook, more energy-efficient. It would save a lot of work too; amazing how many logs you got through on an open fire, and most of the heat went up the chimney anyway.

Giles went out into the hall, trying to remember where he'd seen a shop specialising in woodstoves.

"Was it Aberystwyth?" he said into the slim, leather-covered cassette machine. "Check in Yellow Pages."

The hall, too, was basically all right. Bit dark, and you had to walk permanently stooped or risk collecting a pair of black eyes from the low-slung beams.

"Hall," he said. "Perhaps some diffused lighting under the beams."

He came back through the living room to the kitchen. This, of course, would need the most attention. In Giles's view only the solid-fuel Aga-type stove was worth keeping. It hummed and belched a bit, but he liked that. Also, it took both coal and wood.

"OK," Giles said into the recorder. "New sink, for starters. Fitted units, maybe the wall between the kitchen and the pantry knocked out. Discuss with Claire . . . *if* she can spare the time."

Right, OK . . .

The study.

"Now, we shall have to be a bit careful here," Giles told the machine.

After all, one wrong decision and they could easily ruin what was undoubtedly the most interesting room in the house. Again, he found himself groping for the light switch before remembering.

"Unbelievable," he said. "How the hell did the old boy manage without any power in here?"

Wrong there, Giles, he thought. There's certainly power in here. Shelves full of it. But how did he read without a light?

He almost bumped his head on the answer, a big oil-lamp of tarnished brass Claire had found in the pantry. It was now hanging from the central beam – she must have done that this morning. He tapped the lamp and gave it a swing, trying to find out if there was oil in it. It didn't sound as if there was. The lamp just rattled. It needed polishing up, too.

"OK, memo: buy paraffin. Also chase up that electrician."

It was darker in here than anywhere else in the house, and yet the room was facing west. Must be all the books, no light reflected from the walls. He wondered if the books were valuable. He wondered how he was going to make space in here for his own books when he brought them up from London. OK, they'd look a bit odd, glossy paperbacks among the stark black spines of Judge Rhys's library. But if it eventually was going to be his office, the judge would just have to move over a bit.

It was chilly in here too. Giles wondered if they could run a radiator from the kitchen stove; it wouldn't be far to bring a pipe. First things first though: let there be some bloody light.

"Suggestion," he said to the tape. "What about removing some of the shelving in the middle of the two side walls and installing some wall-lights? Have to be tasteful ones of course. Convert a couple of antique oil-lamps or something."

He glanced up at the framed eisteddfod photograph, full of dignified, white-clad bards and shivered pleasurably, remembering how this room seemed to have spooked Berry Morelli. Great. That picture was definitely going to stay. He wondered which of the bards, if any, was his grandfather-in-law.

The picture seemed dusty and unclear in the dim light and he took a tissue from a hip pocket of his jeans and rubbed at the pale faces of the bards, thinking perhaps he might catch an image of Claire in one of them. Peering at the picture, he felt a dull throb behind his eyes. Bloody headache again. The strain of trying to make out details in semi-darkness.

He backed off, rubbing at his eyes. The room was all shadows now and the only light seemed to be coming out of the picture, out of the white robes of the bards, who appeared to be walking slowly towards him in solemn procession, as if they were about to drift out of the picture and into the room to stand around Giles like a chalk circle and then to melt into the blotchy air.

Back in the picture, meanwhile, the bards had turned black.

"Aspirin," Giles mumbled. He left the study and closed the door behind him and gave it a push to make sure it really was shut.

Where was she?

Giles looked out of the window and it was utterly black, he couldn't even see the lights of the village. How could she take pictures in this? He was pretty sure she hadn't taken a flash unit with her. He looked at his watch and saw it was nearly eight o'clock – she'd been back by seven last night.

He felt a pang of anxiety, unable to shake the ludicrous image of Claire being absorbed by the trees or the village or the night or some numinous combination of all three. And then thought: of course, somebody must have asked her in for a cup of tea, that's what's happened. A bit bloody silly worrying about her being out after dark in Y Groes when she'd survived the streets of Belfast and photographed call-girls on the corners and junkies in the darkened doorways of the nastier crevices of London.

All the same he went out to the porch to wait for her and found the night wasn't as dark as it had seemed from inside. There was a moon, three parts full, and the tallest village roofs were silvered between the two big sycamores. Giles moved out onto the dampening lawn and the church tower slid into view, the tip of its spire appearing to spear the moon, so that it looked like a big black candle with a small white flame.

Giles's heart thumped as a shadow detached itself from the base of the tower and came towards him, as if a piece of the stonework had come alive. But it turned out to be Claire herself, camera hanging limply from the strap curled around a wrist.

"Bloody hell," Giles said. "I didn't know you were going to be so long. I mean, all right, muggings are decidedly uncommon in this area, but all the same –"

"Darling," Claire said briskly. "Go back inside, will you, and put all the lights on for me. *All* the lights."

"People will think we're extravagant," Giles protested – half-heartedly, though, because he was so pleased to have her back. "I mean, not a good image to have around here."

"Oh, Giles –"

"All right, all right –"

Giles switched on everything, even the light on the little landing upstairs, thinking, we'll change some of these old parchment shades when we get time, they're more than a touch dreary. All the upstairs windows were open and he could hear Claire darting about, aperture wide open, shutter speed down. Thock . . . thock . . . thock. A great tenderness overcame him, and when she came in he kissed her under the oak beams of the living room, next to the inglenook where they'd have log fires all through the winter. His headache had receded and with his arms around Claire's slim functional body he felt much better.

"Sweetheart, where precisely have you been? Your hair feels all tangled."

Claire laughed and Giles heard a new boldness in that laugh, all the London tightness gone. Earthy too.

He joined in the laughter.

"You're really happy, aren't you?" he said.

Claire pulled away from him and went to stand by the window.

"Yes," she said. "I'm very happy."

Giles said, "Did you find your tree?"

"Yes," said Claire. "I found my tree."

And then, without a word, switching lights off on the way, she led him up to bed . . .

. . . where they made love for the first time since their arrival, the first time in the new bed. And it was really not how Giles had imagined it would be in this pastoral setting. Nothing languid and dreamy about it at all; it was really pretty ferocious stuff, the old fingernails-down-the-back routine, quiet Claire on the initiative, hungry. Nothing distant now.

Giles told himself it had been very exciting.

CHAPTER XXVII

He was exhausted and slept like the dead and woke late next morning. Woke with another headache and this one was a bastard. Eyes tightly shut, he ground his head into the pillow. It was as if somebody were slicing his skull down the middle with a chainsaw.

"Change of air," Claire diagnosed. "You're just not used to it yet."

She swung both legs simultaneously out of bed and walked naked to the door.

"Yeah, sure, air like bloody wine," Giles groaned into the pillow. "Air that gives you a bastard hangover."

A few minutes later, he was slowly pulling his trousers on, the sight of the pink vinyl headboard making him feel queasy, when Claire returned from her bath, still naked, tiny drops of water falling from her hair onto her narrow shoulders. She seemed oblivious of her nakedness which, for Claire, was unusual: to be nude, in daylight, when Giles was obviously feeling too lousy to be turned on.

"I may stop rinsing my hair," said Claire, looking out of the window. "What do you think?"

"I think I need a cup of strong tea," Giles said.

"There's no point in being artificially anything around here," Claire said.

Giles looked up, a pinball of agony whizzing from ear to ear with the movement.

"I like you blonde," he said. "I always have."

Claire just went on gazing out of the window, across the village to the Nearly Mountains and the neutral sky.

In a bid to lose his headache, Giles took a couple of paracetamol tablets and went for a walk down to the village, where autumn, it seemed, had yet to begin – even though tonight would see the end of British Summertime.

"*Bore da*," he said, as cheerily as he could manage, to Glyn, the angular historian chap, doing his Saturday shopping with a basket over his arm.

"Good morning, Mr. Freeman," said Glyn with a flash of his tombstone teeth.

"Wonderful weather," Giles said, not failing to notice that Glyn, like everyone else he spoke to in the village, had addressed him in English. He'd never learn Welsh if people kept doing that.

"Well, yes," said Glyn, as if warm weather in October was taken for granted here.

Perhaps it was, thought Giles. He walked across the river bridge, past the entrance to the school lane and on towards a place he'd never been before: the great wood which began on the edge of the village.

Sooner than he expected he found himself in what seemed like an enormous wooden nave. He was reminded of the ruins of some old abbey. It was almost all oak trees, freely spaced as if in parkland. Oak trees bulging with health, with the space to spread out their muscular limbs, no decaying branches, no weaklings. Some of the oaks were clearly of immense age and had a massive, magisterial presence.

Giles wondered if this was what Claire had meant when she talked of "my tree". Had she come up here alone at dusk?

It occurred to him that he was standing inside a huge ancient monument. Most of these trees were centuries old, some perhaps

169

older than the castles the English had built to subdue the people of Wales.

And this was what most of the Welsh forests used to be like, from pre-medieval days to the early part of the twentieth century, until the now-ubiquitous conifers had been introduced – quick to grow, quick to harvest, uniform sizes. Drab and characterless, but easy money for comparatively little work.

This wood was awesomely beautiful. This was how it should be. Giles felt a sense of sublime discovery and an aching pride. He felt he'd penetrated at last to the ancient heart of Y Groes. Surely this was where it had all begun – the source of the timber-framing of the cottages, all those gigantic beams, the woody spirit of the place.

Giles felt, obscurely, that this place could take away his headache.

He wandered deeper among the trees, which were still carrying the weighty riches of late summer. The wood seemed to go on and on, and he realised it must form a great semi-circle around the village.

He came upon two great stumps, where trees had been felled. Between them, a young tree surged out of the black soil. The wood, obviously, was still being managed, still being worked as woodland had been in the old days. Whereas, else-where in Wales, it sometimes seemed as if all that remained of the great oak woods were knotted arthritic copses used by farmers merely as shelter for their sheep, devoid of new growth because the sheep ate the tiny saplings as soon as they showed.

No sheep in here. No people either, except for Giles.

He'd heard talk of foresters in Y Groes and assumed they were blokes who worked for the Forestry Commission in the giant conifer plantation along the Aberystwyth road. Obviously they were in charge of maintaining this huge oak wood, selecting trees for unobtrusive felling, planting new ones so the appearance of the place would never change from century to century. He also knew there was a carpenter, a Mr. Vaughan – or Fon, as it was spelled in Welsh – who made traditional oak furniture. And Aled in the *Tafarn* had mentioned that a new house was to be built near the river for Morgan's eldest son and had laughed when Giles expressed the hope that it would not look out of place. "When it is built," Glyn had said, "you will think it has always been there."

God, Giles thought, the village is still growing out of this woodland just as it always has. An organic process. Morelli had been right when he said it was like the place had just grown up out of the ground.

Giles raised up his arms as if to absorb the soaring energy of the wood but felt only insignificant among the arboreal giants and decided to turn back. It was too much to take in all at once. Especially when he wasn't feeling awfully well, nerves in his head still jerking, like wires pulled this way and that by a powerful magnet.

He almost got lost on the way back, taking a path he was convinced was the right one until it led him to a pair of blackened gateposts where the oaks formed a sort of tunnel. At the end was something big, like a huge crouching animal.

A house. Somebody lived in the middle of the wood.

Well, what was so odd about that? Lots of people lived in woods.

Yes, but this wood was special. The village was down below; this was where the *trees* lived.

There was no gate but on the left-hand post it said, carved out of the wood, *Rheithordy*.

Above the word, which Giles had never seen before, a rough cross had been hewn.

"*Helo.*"

Giles stopped, startled, as a small dark figure darted out from behind the gatepost.

"Hello," Giles said. "Who's that?"

It was a little girl – maybe eight or nine – and she was dressed mainly in black – black skirt, black jumper, black shoes. Even so, she seemed to fit into the backcloth, like some woodland sprite. "*Pwy y chi*?" she demanded.

"Sorry," said Giles. "'Fraid I don't speak Welsh. Yet."

The child had mousy hair and a pale, solemn face. "Are you English?"

Giles nodded, smiling ruefully. "'Fraid so."

The child looked up at Giles out of large brown eyes. She said seriously, "Have you come to hang yourself?"

"What?" Giles's eyes widened in amusement. "Have I come to –?"

But she only turned away and ran back behind the gatepost.

Giles shook his head – which hurt – and strolled on. Soon the path widened and sloped down to the village. It was easy when you knew your way.

There was only one paracetamol left in the packet, but he took it anyway and sat down at the fat-legged dining table. They were going this morning to Pontmeurig, where Giles was to meet the chairman of the local Conservative Party to get a bit of background for a feature he was planning in the run-up to the Glanmeurig by-election. It wouldn't be long now before a date was set.

"And while we're in Pont," he shouted to Claire, who was in the bedroom, changing out of her old, stained jeans into some-thing more respectable, "there're a few things we could be on the lookout for, if you're agreeable. I had a walk around the place last night, making a few notes on tape."

"Super," Claire said, appearing at the living-room door,

still wriggling into clean white denims. "*Da iawn*. How's your head?"

"Could be worse. Don't you want to hear the list?"

"Oh, I hate it when you put ideas on tape and we have to unscramble all this distorted cackle. Why can't you write it out?"

"All right. I mean o'r . . . o'r . . ."

"*O'r gorau*," Claire said, zipping up her trousers as she went through to the kitchen.

While still in London they'd taken to peppering their conversations with a few Welsh phrases. Giles now tried to think of a suitable comment to make in *Cymraeg* but nothing came to him and his head still hurt. How long had they had these bloody paracetamol? Maybe they were losing their potency.

He found his pocket cassette-recorder and ran the tape back to transcribe the aural memoranda into a notebook. Concealed lighting for the hall, electrician, plumber . . .

". . . and the pantry knocked out," his voice crackled back at him from the tiny speaker. "Discuss with Claire . . . *if* she can spare the time . . ."

Giles hurriedly lowered the volume, hoping she hadn't heard the last bit from the kitchen. He put his ear to the speaker in case he'd said anything else vaguely inflammatory, but there was nothing.

Nothing at all.

Hang on, where was the stuff he'd recorded in the study, something about wall-lights, right?

It had gone.

He must have wiped it by mistake.

Bugger.

And yet – turning up the volume as high as it would go – he could still hear the ambient sounds of the room, the hollow gasp of empty space, as if it was only his own voice which had been wiped off. Which was stupid; he must simply have left the thing running.

"Recorder batteries," he wrote in his notebook, at the head of the list. Better make sure of that before he started doing any actual interviews. Over the past few years Giles had relied increasingly on pocket tape-recorders; his shorthand was all to cock these days.

Not that the batteries seemed low, but there was an awful lot of tape hiss.

sssssssss, it went. *sssssssssssssssssssss*

CHAPTER XXVIII

Bethan had never been to Judge Rhys's house before.

She'd been past it enough times – shepherding the children on nature rambles up in the hills, trying to spot the Red Kite, Britain's rarest bird of prey, which nested there.

Occasionally, over the hedge, she'd seen the judge in his garden. Not actually gardening, of course. Other people did his gardening. Simply standing there, not moving but not really looking as if he was admiring the scenery either.

He used to be like that in church too, always in the same pew, two rows from the front, very still in the black suit, not visibly singing and not visibly praying.

Strange man.

Now there was only the house to stand there gazing towards the hills, its windows darkened. As she lifted up the metal gate and pushed it open, Bethan was trying to imagine what it would look like here when Claire had her children and there were toys all over the lawn and perhaps a swing.

She really could not see it.

A fine dusk was purpling into night as Bethan walked up the path. A light came on in a front window, and by the time she reached the front door, arms full of books and things as usual, it was open. A tall, fair-haired man was there in a sleeveless V-necked pullover over a checked shirt, looking, she thought, distinctly relieved when he saw her.

"Great. Hi. Giles Freeman. Bethan, right?" Standing back to usher her into the warm living room with the Welsh dresser and the inglenook and a muted glow from a reading lamp with a brown ceramic base. "Super of you to do this for us, it really is."

"Super of you to *want* to do it," Bethan said. "Not many of you – your – people who move in from England –"

"Bastards," Giles said vehemently, closing doors. "No sense of where they are. We – Ah, here's Claire."

She wore a grey skirt and a white blouse, looking like a schoolgirl, no make-up. She did not smile. "Bethan, hello. Coffee now? Or later?"

"Whichever suits you." Had there been a row? she wondered.

"How about during?" Giles said. "I'll make it."

"I'd like to start, I think," Claire said. "We don't want to delay you. You'll want to get home to your husband."

"My husband is dead," Bethan said casually, standing in the middle of the floor looking for somewhere to put down the pile of books, pretending not to notice the familiar silence which always followed this disclosure.

"Oh," said Claire mildly, as Giles was saying, "I'm awfully sorry. We didn't know." The unspoken question was hanging around, so Bethan answered it.

"He died about a year ago. Leukaemia."

"That's really terrible," said Giles. "That really is a bastard of a thing."

"It was very quick. By the time it was diagnosed he was dying. Three weeks later, he –" Bethan made a mouthsmile. "Right. That is over with. I am at the stage where sympathy only depresses me. Look, I've brought you these little books. They're grown-up cartoons with all the bubbles in Welsh and a lot of the everyday kind of words you don't find in the more formal textbooks."

Giles moved to take the other stuff from her (why did people always rush to help as soon as they learned she was a widow?) so she could open a little paperback called *Welsh Is Fun*. She showed him a drawing of a woman in her underwear. Little arrows pointed to things, giving the Welsh, with the English in brackets. Like *bronglwm* (bra) and *bol* (belly).

"I've also brought you some leaflets for *Pont* – have you heard of that?"

Giles shook his head.

"It's an organisation set up to form links between native Welsh people and the, um, incomers. *Pont* means –"

"Bridge, right?" said Giles. "As in Pontmeurig. Rehabilitation, eh?"

"There we are," said Bethan, glancing towards the fat-legged dining table at which only two chairs were set. "That's a start. Now, where shall we sit?"

"Not in here," Claire said quickly.

Giles looked at her. She said, 'I've set up a table in the study."

"What's the use of going in there? There's no bloody electricity!"

"I filled the oil-lamp. And lit the fire. Will you light the lamp, Giles? Please?"

It was a command, Bethan thought.

"Oh, for Christ's sake . . . What's wrong with staying here?"

"It's more fitting," Claire said quietly.

"Goodness," Bethan said, looking at the rows of black books.

"Can you tell us what they are?" Giles was turning up the wick on the big oil-lamp dangling from the middle beam. "Claire, is this really going to be bright enough?"

"If we put the table not quite underneath, it'll be fine."

She'd erected a green-topped card table and placed three stiff-backed chairs around it. A small coal fire burned rather meanly in the Victorian grate. Bethan also would rather have stayed in the living room. She would never have tolerated a classroom as stiff and cold as this. She crossed to the shelves.

"I don't recognise most of these." Taking books down at

random. "They're obviously very old and must be very valuable indeed. See . . ." She held out a page of text. "This is in medieval Welsh. These must be some of the oldest books ever printed in Welsh – although copies, I expect, in most cases. There seems to be a lot of old poetry – Taliesyn, is this? And these three are quite early versions of The Mabinogion. I've never seen them before, although I'm no expert. Oh –"

"What've you found?" Giles wandered over, craning his neck.

"Nothing really, just a modern one amongst all the old stuff. It hasn't got its dustjacket so it looked like all the rest. It's ap Siencyn, one of his early books of poetry."

"What, you mean ap Siencyn, the vicar here?"

"The rector, yes. He used to be a poet." Bethan smiled. "What I mean is, he used to publish his poetry. Many years ago."

"That's amazing," Giles said.

"Not really, there are poets everywhere in Wales and quite a few are ministers."

Giles nodded solemnly. "Exactly. That's the whole point." He folded his arms, rocking back on his heels in the middle of the room on the dragon rug. "What I mean is – We've become so smug and cynical in England because our cultural heritage is so *safe*. We've got the world's number-one language, we've got Shakespeare and Jane Austen and all these literary giants planted in state in Westminster Abbey. But Welsh culture's about ordinary people. I mean, your writers and poets don't spend all their time poncing about at fancy publishers' parties and doing lecture tours of the States. They're working farmers and school-teachers and – clergymen. And they'll never be remotely famous outside Wales because virtually nobody out there can under-stand a word they write. It takes real commitment to carry on in a situation like that, wouldn't you say?"

Bethan watched Giles's lean English face shining with an honest fervour in the unsteady lamplight. How could the issue of Wales be seized on with such vigour by people like Giles and Claire, who had not been brought up in the warmth of a Welsh community, not had bedtime stories read to them in Welsh, sung Welsh nursery rhymes or made their first terrifying public appearance performing a little recitation before a critical audience of neighbours at the local eisteddfod? Did they equate Wales with whales? Were the Welsh suddenly interesting because they looked like a threatened species?

Then Bethan glanced at Claire and drew in a sharp breath. Claire, small face not mellow but stark in the lamplight, was looking up at Giles. And wearing a rigid expression of explicit contempt.

"You know," Giles was telling Bethan enthusiastically, "I wouldn't mind doing a feature sometime on old ap Siencyn. What's he like?"

"He's – *You've* met him, Claire, what did you think of him?"

Giles looked hurt. "Claire, you never mentioned meeting the rector."

"I –" Claire didn't look at him. "Our paths crossed while I was out taking pictures."

"She took *his* picture," Bethan said.

"I didn't see that," Giles said.

"It didn't come out," Claire snapped. "Can we make a start?"

Bethan thought, her pictures *never* don't come out. Besides, I saw it.

"Well, I think I've seen his house," Giles said. "Up on the edge of the woods. Very impressive."

Bethan said, "Sometimes I take the kids up to the woods, but we go the other way. I don't like that part somehow." Especially now, she thought, shuddering at the image, which came to her unbidden, of two leather hiking boots slowly swinging overhead.

"I thought it was magnificent," Giles said, freckles aglow in the lamplight. "You get the feeling that's where the whole village was born – you know, the timber for the cottages. I think it's fantastic the way they're managing it, renewing the trees and everything. I mean, who actually does that? Who are the foresters?"

Claire, face taut, severe in the oil-light, said, with quiet menace, "*Ydy chi'n barod*, Bethan?"

Giles fell silent, looked embarrassed.

"Yes," Bethan said, feeling sorry for him. Why did his innocent ardour seem to irritate his wife so? "Yes, I'm ready." When she'd agreed to teach them Welsh, she'd been looking forward to a chat over coffee with people who weren't a part of this stifling community. Not this formal, frigid atmosphere, this sense of . . . ritual, almost.

It's the house, she thought. It's the damned house.

She opened one of her books on the card table. Aware, on the periphery of her vision, of the old, heavy desk and the Victorian Gothic chair across the room, beyond the dome of the lamplight. As if they were awaiting the arrival of the real teacher.

It was nearly eight o'clock when Bethan left.

There was no moon. It was very dark.

"Where's your car?" Giles asked.

"I left it at the school, it's only three minutes' walk."

"It's pitch black. I'll come with you, bring a torch."

"Thank you, but I used to live in this village, there's no –"

"There is," Giles said firmly, grabbing his green waxed jacket from behind the door, switching his heavyweight policeman's torch on and off to make sure it was working.

"Well, thank you," Bethan said. Oh God, she thought. I don't really want to be alone with Giles now. I don't need this.

Following the torchbeam, they walked down the hill and over the bridge, the river hissing below them. There was an anguished silence between them until they reached the entrance to the school lane.

"Christ," Giles said.

"Look –" Bethan put a reassuring hand on his arm. "Don't worry, all right?"

"Huh –" Giles twisted away like a petulant schoolboy then immediately turned back, apologetic. He expelled a sigh, full of hopelessness, and rubbed his eyes.

"You will soon get the hang of it."

It was too dark to see his face.

"But you don't understand," Giles said desperately, "I thought I *was* getting the hang of it. I've been working at it for weeks. Before we even came, I used to spend all my lunch hours swotting. I mean, you know – I really thought I was getting pretty good. It's just so bloody embarrassing."

"Don't worry," Bethan said. "Everybody has days like that. When they're beginning. A few weeks really isn't very long, you know."

"All right then, what about Claire? I mean, she hasn't spent anywhere near as much time on it as me."

"Look," Bethan said, as they reached the Peugeot. "The very worst thing you can do is worry."

"But I couldn't put together even the simplest sentences! I mean things I know!" Bethan heard Giles punching the palm of his hand in bitter frustration. The violent movement seemed to hurt him more than he'd intended because he gave a small moan of pain.

"Mr. Freeman, are you sure you're all right?"

"Giles. Please. I hate being Freeman, so bloody English. Yes I'm fine. Well, I've got a headache, but that's nothing unusual. I'm sorry, I'm being ridiculous."

"I know it means a lot to you," Bethan said gently. She felt terribly sorry for him. He wanted so badly to be a part of this culture. It had been awful watching him agonisingly entangled in the alien grammar, tongue frozen around words he just could not say, getting stuck on the same ones again and again, stammering in his confusion. Sometimes – his hands gripping the edge of the table until the knuckles were white as bone – it seemed almost as if his facial muscles had been driven into paralysis by the complexity of the language.

"Look," Bethan said. "Get a good night's sleep. Don't think about it. Don't look at any books. I'll see you again tomorrow. Maybe . . . Look, maybe it's something I am doing wrong. I'm so used to teaching children."

"But what about *Claire*?" he cried. "I mean, for God's sake, how do you explain that?"

CHAPTER XXIX

ENGLAND

Berry Morelli had not long been in the office when his boss threw a newspaper at him.

"For your private information," Addison Walls said.

Newsnet's London bureau chief was a small, neat, precise man with steel-rimmed glasses, a thin bow tie that was always straight and an unassuming brown toupée. It was Berry's unvoiced theory that Addison possessed a normal head of hair but shaved it off periodically on account of a toupée was tidier.

"Your buddy, I think," Addison said and went back to his examination of the *Yorkshire Post*. He was a very thorough man, arriving at work each day somewhere between 8:00 and 8:03 a.m. and completing a shrewd perusal of every British national newspaper and five major provincial morning papers by 9:15 when his staff got in.

The staff consisted of a secretary, a research assistant and three reporters including Berry Morelli. Although there would usually be orders for the major stories of the day, Newsnet specialised in features dealing with peripheral issues of American interest which the big agencies had no time to mess with. Occasionally, compiling his morning inventory of the British Press, Addison Walls would suddenly zap an item with his thick black marker pen and announce, "This is a Newsnet story."

Berry noticed the item flung at him had not been zapped,

although the paper had been neatly folded around an inside-page feature starkly headlined,

THE ANGRY HILLS

Above the text was a photograph of a ruined castle which resembled the lower plate of a set of dentures, two walls standing up like teeth. The view was framed by the walls of more recent buildings; a FOR SALE sign hung crookedly from one.

Underneath the picture, it said,

Giles Freeman, of our political staff, reports on what's shaping up to be a dramatic by-election battle in wildest Wales.

Berry smiled and sat down and lit a cigarette. So Giles had pulled it off. They'd let him cover the Pontmeurig by-election. Filing his stuff, no doubt, from his own cottage, probably over the phone from the judge's study. Two weeks had passed since Berry had fled that place. Two weeks in which to consider the possibility that he'd been overreacting. Him and old Winstone both.

He started to read the feature, thinking Giles would be sure to hype up the issue to persuade his editor that this election was worthy of intensive on-the-spot coverage.

It was not the usual political backgrounder. Giles had gone folksy.

Idwal Roberts smiled knowingly as he laid out his leather tobacco pouch on the bar of the Drovers' Arms.

"This," he said, "is going to be a bit of an eye-opener for a London boy. I imagine you've reported a fair few by-elections, but I can tell you – you won't have seen one like this.

"Oh, I know they've had them in South Wales and the Borders

in recent years. But this time you're in the *real* Wales. A foreign country, see."

Idwal Roberts, a retired headmaster, is the Mayor of Pontmeurig, a little market town at the southern end of the range of rugged hills called in Welsh something long and complicated which translates roughly as "the Nearly Mountains".

This is the principal town in the constituency of Glanmeurig, which recently lost its long-serving Conservative MP, Sir Maurice Burnham-Lloyd, and is now preparing for its first ever by-election. Local people will tell you that the last time any-thing really exciting happened in Pontmeurig was in the fifteenth century when the Welsh nationalist leader Owain Glyndwr (or Owen Glendower, as they call him east of Offa's Dyke) set fire to the castle.

The gaunt remains of this castle still frown over the cattle market and the new car park. The fortress was actually built by the Welsh but subsequently commandeered by the English king Edward I. One story tells how the wealthy baron in charge of the castle offered to support Glyndwr's rebellion, but Owain set light to the place anyway on the grounds that you could never trust the word of an Englishman.

The Mayor of Pontmeurig (an "independent" like most council-lors hereabouts) reckons opinions have not changed a great deal in the intervening years.

Giles went on to outline the problem of comparatively wealthy English people moving into the area, pricing many houses beyond the range of locals, often buying shops and pubs and post offices and conducting their business in English where once Welsh had been the language of the streets.

"What say we take a look at this?" Berry said casually, and Addison Walls gave him a wry smile that said no way.

"They may be a big deal over here, but you think back, son,

and tell me how many British by-elections you saw reported in the *New York Times*."

"It's been known," said Berry.

"It's been known if the Government's on the brink."

"I just thought, maybe this language angle."

"Forget it. You compare this situation with Ulster, it's chickenshit."

"Yeah," Berry said.

"Housing and immigration are going to be key issues in this election," Roberts says. "People are getting very angry, seeing their sons and daughters having to leave the area because they can't afford a house any more."

One local estate agent admits that more than sixty per cent of the houses he's sold this year have gone to English people moving to rural Wales in search of what they see as a "healthier" lifestyle.

"There is going to be acrimony," says Idwal Roberts. "Sparks will fly. You can count on that, my friend."

"You can sure count on it with Giles around," Berry muttered. The article went on to discuss the two leading contenders – the Conservative Party and the Welsh nationalist party, Plaid Cymru. The Conservatives had chosen their man, a local auctioneer called Simon Gallier. But Plaid, as Giles explained, had a crucial decision to make.

If Plaid want to play safe, they'll go for Wil James, a mild-mannered Baptist minister from Cardigan. He's well liked, but party strategists are wondering if he really has what it takes to slug it out with a man used to the cut-and-thrust of the livestock sales.

If Plaid want to live dangerously, however, they'll take a chance on Guto Evans, a 44-year-old part-time college lecturer, author

186

and one-time bass-guitarist in a Welsh-language rock and roll band.

Evans is a man not known for keeping his opinions to himself – especially on the subject of mass-immigration by well-off English people.

"Ah, yes," says the Mayor of Pontmeurig, relighting his pipe. "Guto Evans. Now that really *would* be interesting."

And he gives what could only be described as a sinister chuckle.

It's now felt the election is unlikely to take place before December because of . . .

"Addison, I can't help wondering if this isn't gonna get heavy," Berry said.

"Anybody dies," said Addison, "you can go out there."

"Thanks."

"Meantime, listen up, I got something here the West Coast papers could be clamouring for by tonight so I figure we got no time to waste."

"Right, I . . ." Something had caught Berry's eye. It was the picture byline.

It was placed unobtrusively in the top right-hand corner of the photo of the castle and the FOR SALE sign. Tiny lettering, as was normal in Giles's paper, especially when they used a freelance photographer.

It said,

Picture by Claire Rhys.

"Now that's weird," Berry said. "That is real weird."

"What?" said Addison Walls.

"Sorry," Berry said. "You go ahead, I'm listening."

Maybe it wasn't that weird. People often changed their names for professional purposes. Women reverted to their premarital names. Claire, of course, had never been called Rhys, but maybe she thought a Welsh name like that would attract more work within Wales. Also, when people moved to a different country they altered their names so as not to sound unpronounceably foreign. A lot of Poles did that.

But English people called Freeman?

No, he was right first time.

It was weird.

PART FIVE

TOILI

CHAPTER XXX

By mid-November the weather had turned nasty.

There had been much heavy rain, with three Red Two flood alerts for the River Meurig in as many weeks. And it was suddenly much colder. On the tops of the Nearly Mountains the rain fell as wintry showers, leaving premature patches of stiff snow behind the crags.

In its bowl of snow-encrusted hills, the village of Y Groes was, as usual, preserved from the worst of it. A blue hole, they called it. Bethan thought scientists might explain this in terms of changes in atmospheric pressure brought about by the geophysical features of the surrounding landscape. But the truth was she didn't know, so there was little she could say when Buddug told the children that Y Groes was especially favoured by the heavens because it had preserved the old traditions more faithfully than anywhere else in Wales.

"If you pay attention," Buddug said, wagging a fat forefinger, "you will see how clouds shrink away from the tower of our church. As if they are afraid."

Crazy old bat, Bethan thought, leaning moodily on the piano, as Buddug lectured the assembly, two dozen scrubbed, rapt faces.

Later, as she drove home in the sepia dusk, she glanced towards the church tower and noted with some annoyance that the timbered belfry was hard against an almost perfect cloudless circle.

*

191

That day the Conservative Party had moved the writ for the Glanmeurig by-election, naming the day as December 15th – unusually late in the year. A week ago, the prospective Conservative candidate, Simon Gallier, a local auctioneer and valuer, protege of Burnham-Lloyd and well in with the farmers, had officially been adopted by his constituency party in the suitably dignified setting of the Plas Meurig Hotel. The other parties were not far behind – except for Plaid Cymru which, as usual, took its time selecting a candidate, with predictable implications for Guto Evans's nervous system.

"Quite honestly," he lied that night, "I don't bloody care any more. If they go for the soft option and choose Wil James, they won't be the party I joined all those years ago, so it won't matter anyway."

Guto was slumped in the shabby lounge of the Drovers' Arms with Bethan and two other friends, Dai Death, the funeral director, and Idwal Roberts – the "independent" Mayor of Pontmeurig.

In Pont it was raining hard again.

Although the public bar was half full, the less dedicated drinkers had been deterred by the weather and Guto's table was the only one occupied in the lounge. Because of the shortage of custom the lounge bar itself remained closed, its shutters down. This meant they had to fetch their own drinks from the public bar, but it also meant nobody could eavesdrop on what they were saying. Which was fortunate because the little gathering had turned into an impromptu training session for Guto's final interview by the party's selection panel.

It was not going well.

Bethan thought this was not altogether surprising in view of the publication that morning in Wales's daily newspaper, the *Western Mail*, of the story Guto had been dreading.

It was brief but slotted significantly into the front page. It said police had confirmed having interviewed Guto Evans, a short-listed contender for the Plaid Cymru candidacy in the forthcoming Glanmeurig by-election, following an incident in a public bar a few weeks ago, during which a 26-year-old merchant banker had been slightly hurt. The injured man, who came from Surrey, had just bought a farmhouse on the outskirts of Pontmeurig at auction when the incident occurred at the Drovers' Arms in the town centre. He had been treated at Pontmeurig Cottage Hospital for minor facial injuries. However, police said they had no evidence of an offence being committed and charges were unlikely. Mr. Evans had been unavailable for comment last night.

"It could have been worse," Bethan said.

Her companions clearly disagreed. Plaid's riskier option for the Glanmeurig candidacy was miserably mopping beer froth from his beard with a frayed tartan handkerchief. The Mayor, a solid man with crinkly grey hair, sucked morosely on an empty pipe. Dai Death just stared sorrowfully into space in his best graveside manner.

They looked as dismal as the lounge, which was lit by naked bulbs in tarnished brass wall-brackets and smelled of beer and mothballs.

Bethan said, "I accept that over-confidence is not to be recommended, but I can't help feeling . . ."

She sighed and gave up.

"Warning him weeks ago, I was," said Dai Death. "The day of the activist is over, see. Public displays of anger, all this oratory and rhetoric – forget it, man. Plausible on the telly is what it takes now."

"Oratory and rhetoric have rather more to commend them," Idwal Roberts said heavily, "than physical violence. But I follow your reasoning. Give him another question, Bethan."

Bethan looked at Guto, who shrugged and nodded gloomily.

"All right," Bethan said, straightening her skirt and adjusting her glasses to consult the clipboard on her knee. "So, Mr. Evans, there's been a lot of debate about the upsurge of terrorism in Wales, with the burning of English-owned property and a wave of anti-English feeling. Where do *you* stand on this controversial issue?"

Guto cleared his throat. "Well, er . . . I, of course, abhor all terrorism, while recognising that the present economic situation, the price of housing, the shortage of low-cost homes for local people, the mass-immigration – all this, sadly, is an invitation to those for whom democracy seems such a painfully *slow* way of bringing about change. But nonetheless, we – Ah, I am tying myself up in knots trying to avoid saying that while I might deplore their methods I applaud their aims – ask me an easier one, I'll be all right on the night."

"Hmmm." Bethan looked doubtful. "All right, then. So why, if you abhor all terrorism, did you –?"

She stopped when she saw Idwal Roberts pursing his lips and shaking his head.

"That reporter fellow," Idwal whispered, "has just walked past the door."

Giles Freeman had only really called in at the Drovers' to use the lavatory. He'd spent four days at the paper and was on his way home, still wearing his dark suit, still looking and feeling very London. Far too London for the Drovers' Arms, but he really did need a slash.

Feeling better though, the nearer he got to Y Groes – in spite of the weather, the rain coming at the windscreen so hard it was like being permanently stuck in a high-powered car wash.

Feeling better the further he got from London. Feeling especially good because he would not now have to return until after the by-election. When his fortnight's holiday had ended and still no date had been fixed, he'd had no alternative but to spend four days a week in London. And, in these conditions, the journey had been more gruelling than he could have imagined.

On each of the three weekends, he'd started out happily for home. But each time the drive seemed to get longer – perhaps because he was getting used to the scenery, an element of the routine setting in. And when he arrived back in Y Groes the effects of the journey would hit him like an avalanche and he'd feel utterly exhausted, waking up the following morning with a ghastly headache. A couple of days at the cottage – most of them spent recovering in bed – and he'd had to make his way back to the Islington flat and another week on the paper.

"Giles, you look bloody awful," his boss, the political editor, had told him bluntly last week. "Commuting's one thing – I mean we all commute, up to a point – but commuting a couple of hundred miles each way is bloody lunacy, if you ask me."

"Don't worry about me," Giles had said. "It's just there's a lot of extra pressure, what with moving stuff out there and everything."

"You're nuts," said the political editor.

"It'll be OK," Giles insisted. "Soon get used to it."

But he knew he wouldn't. He knew he was trying to marry two totally incompatible lifestyles.

The headaches, he realised now, had been the result of years of grinding tension: smoking, drinking, late nights, junk food, driving like a bat out of hell – his system had adjusted itself over the years to that kind of lifestyle. And now it had reacted perversely to intensive bursts of fresh air, relaxation and healthy eating.

Withdrawal symptoms. A sort of Cold Turkey.

This had become clear over the past few days, after Giles had been ordered to return to London and plunge back into the urban cesspit. His system had reverted to the old routine, the familiar self-destruct mechanism clicking back into place, the body throwing up the usual smokescreen telling him it didn't mind being abused, quite liked it really and, look, here's the proof: no headaches while you're down in the Smoke, drinking, slugging it out with the traffic, pressurising politicians who've been barely on nodding terms with the truth for years.

One good thing, though – the Welsh. Every night in the Islington flat, with no distractions – for the first time he was glad to have the kind of London neighbours who wouldn't notice if you were dead until the smell began to offend them – Giles would sit down and spend at least ninety minutes with his Welsh textbook and his cassette tapes.

And, though he said it himself, it was coming on a treat.

"*Noswaith dda*," he said affably to the young man next to him at the urinal in the Drovers' gents.

Feeling friendly, feeling good about the language again. Glad to be using it.

He'd been left badly shaken by several nights of humiliation in the judge's study, the last one ending with an almost unbearable headache. But now the grammar was making sense again. Bethan was a great girl, but perhaps he was more suited to working on his own than having lessons.

"*Mae hi'n bwrw glaw*," he observed to the youth in the adjacent stall, nodding at the rain dripping down the crevices of the bubbled window above their heads.

"Yeah," said the youth. He smirked, zipped up his fly and turned away.

Incomer, Giles thought disparagingly.

The youth went out, glancing over his shoulder at Giles.

Giles washed his hands and stared at his face in the mirror above the basin. He looked pale but determined.

Already his new life in Y Groes had shown him the things which were really important. Shown him, above all, that London and the paper were no longer for him – unless he could convince them that they needed a full-time staff reporter in Wales. After all, the *Telegraph* had one now. Failing that, he and Claire would flog the Islington flat for serious money and then set up some sort of news and features agency in Wales, supplying national papers, radio, television, the international media. He had the contacts. All he had to do now was make sure this election generated enough excitement to convince enough editors that Wales was a country they needed to keep a much closer eye on in the future.

Giles and Claire would be that eye. Claire Rhys. He liked the way she'd changed her name for professional purposes. Added a certain credibility. One in the eye for Elinor too. He only wished he could call himself Giles Rhys.

He decided to go into the public bar for one drink before tackling the Nearly Mountains. Unfair to use the place merely as a urinal.

Guto said sharply, "Is it that bastard from Cardiff?" He was halfway out of his chair, face darkening.

"That's right," said Dai Death sarcastically. "That's just the way to handle it. You get up and clobber him in public. He's probably got a photographer with him, you could hit him too. Would you like me to hold your jacket?"

Idwal Roberts said, "Sit down, you silly bugger. It's not him, anyway, it's the other fellow, the English one."

Bethan said, "Giles Freeman?"

She hadn't seen Giles for nearly a week. If he was back from London, she wanted to talk to him.

About Claire, of course.

Claire was still wandering around with her camera as the days shortened and the hills grew misty. Bethan thought she must have photographed everything worth photographing at least five times. Before she realised that Claire was just drifting about with the camera around her neck – but *not* taking pictures at all any more.

Then there was no camera, but Claire was still to be seen roaming the village, wandering in the fields, by the river, among the graves in the churchyard.

As if searching for something.

"Is there something you've lost?" Bethan had asked the other day, taking some of the children into the woods to gather autumn leaves for pressing, and finding Claire moving silently among the trees.

"Only my heritage." Claire had just smiled, wryly but distantly, and moved on. Bethan noticed she wore no make-up; her hair was in disarray and its colour was streaked, dark roots showing. She seemed careless of her clothes too, wearing Giles's waxed jacket, conspicuously too big and gone brittle through need of rewaxing.

"Did you ever find that oak tree?" Bethan had asked her on another occasion.

"Oh that," said Claire. "I made a mistake. You were quite right."

And explained no further.

Bethan asked her, "Does Giles never go with you on your walks?"

"Giles?" As if she had to think for a moment who Giles was. "Giles is in London." Her eyes were somewhere else. "He's having great fun," she said vaguely.

"She is a very nice girl," Buddug said surprisingly as they saw Claire one afternoon, flitting like a pale moth past the school gate.

"You've had much to do with her?"

"Oh, yes indeed. She's our nearest neighbour."

"I suppose she must be." Bethan had forgotten the judge's cottage was on the edge of the seventy-or-so acres owned by Buddug and her husband, Morgan.

"She's had her eggs from us. And sometimes a chicken."

Buddug killed her own chickens and occasionally pigs.

"I can't say much about *him*," Buddug said.

"Giles? I like him."

"Well, you would. Wouldn't you?" Buddug had turned away and scrubbed at the blackboard, smiling to herself.

Something had happened, Bethan thought. In a few short weeks Claire had changed from a smart, attractive, professional person to someone who was either moody or dreamy or preoccupied with things that made no sense. There was no longer that aura of "away" about her, that breath of urban sophistication which Bethan had so welcomed.

Bethan stared hard at Buddug's back, a great wedge between the desk and the blackboard. Buddug. Mrs. Bronwen Dafis. The Revd Elias ap Siencyn.

And now Claire.

A chasm was opening between Claire and Giles, with his boyish enthusiasm for all things Welsh and his determination to be a part of The Culture. Bethan wondered if he could see it.

CHAPTER XXXI

"*Hanner peint o gwrw,*" Giles told the barman, pointing at the appropriate beer-pump and climbing on to a bar stool. "*Os gwelwch yn dda.*"

He was pleased with his accent, the casual way he'd ordered the drink. Grammar was all well and good but if you wanted to make yourself understood you had to get into the local idiom, had to sound relaxed.

The barman set down the glass of beer and Giles handed over a five-pound note. "*Diolch yn fawr.*" Running the words together, as you would say thanks-very-much.

Convincing stuff.

The public bar was less than half full. Giles thought of another bar, in Aberystwyth, where everybody had stared at him, amused by his stumbling debut in the Welsh language. Nobody smiled this time. With those few slick phrases nobody, he felt, could be quite sure he wasn't a native.

The barman gave him his change.

"*Diolch yn fawr iawn,*" Giles said in a louder voice, more confident now.

To his right, there was a sharp silence, somebody putting the brakes on a conversation. "What was that?" a man's voice said in the centre of the hush.

"Beg your pardon –?" Giles turned, thinking, damn, should have said that in Welsh, blown my cover now.

On the next stool sat the youth he'd spoken to in the gents. Not looking quite as youthful now. Around twenty-three, twenty-four, thick-set, face pitted, lower lip sticking out like a shelf, eyes deep-sunk under short sandy hair. He nodded towards the bar. "What you ordered."

"Well," Giles replied, holding up his glass to the light. "It should be a half of bitter."

The young man was not looking at Giles's glass, he was looking hard at Giles. He said, "Oh, that's what it was." Behind him was another young man on another bar stool. This one had prematurely thinning black hair and a slit of a mouth, like a shaving cut.

"What I actually said to the barman here was *hanner peint o gwrw*," Giles explained. "I'm learning Welsh." He smiled sheepishly. "Got to practise."

Two mouths went into simultaneous sneers. The eyes were still fixed on Giles, who realised he'd got it wrong; this chap wasn't an incomer at all.

The man turned to his companion. "Learning Welsh, he is, this . . . *gentleman*." Turned back to Giles, unsmiling. "Go on then, say it again?"

"What d'you mean?"

"Go on – *hanner* . . ."

Giles said quickly, "*Hanner peint o gwrw*." Not liking the way these two were looking at him, almost smelling the sour hostility.

A blast of rain splattered a window behind his head.

"Didn't catch that." Slit-mouth. "Say it again."

"*Hanner* . . . oh, come on!"

"No, we want to learn, isn't it?" the other one said. He had a face like the cratered moon. "We want to speak our own language as good as you, see."

"I reckon that's all he can talk about, the beer."

"Oh no, talking to me in the lav, he was. He's an expert. He can do the weather too."

"Maybe he was takin' the piss, Gary."

"Fuck, I never thought of that." Heavily feigned surprise. Still staring at Giles. "Takin' the piss, is it?"

Giles said evenly, "I can assure you I was not taking the piss. If I'm trying to learn the language, I've got to use it, haven't I? Is there any other way? I mean, what am I supposed to do?"

Definitely uncomfortable now – bloody yobs – he glanced around to see if there was anybody he knew even slightly, some group he could join. Didn't recognise a soul. Apart from a handful of men around the dartboard the customers were all sitting at tables. There were no more than fifteen people in the room. The barman was at the other end of the bar, watching the darts.

The silence set around Giles like cement. Clearly, Pontmeurig was just like any other town these days, full of nighttime aggro. All very sad. Disappointing.

"Well now, there's an answer to that," Crater-face said, all casual, elbow on the bar, hand propping his chin. "I can tell you what you ought to do, English. Ought to fuck off back where you came from, isn't it."

"Yes, all right, I will." Giles made himself take a longish drink. He'd finish his beer and get out. This was not convivial. What a country – layer upon layer of resentment.

"We'll come with you," Slit-mouth said.

"That won't be necessary," Giles muttered.

"Least we can do." Crater-face smiled with lurid menace. "Show you the right road, see."

"Hate you to get lost," Slit-mouth said.

"Finish your drink, English," Crater-face said.

He had lowered his voice so as to not be overheard by a stooping man with a bald head who was paying for a tray of drinks: three pints of bitter and a glass of dry white wine.

*

". . . Ah, no, well, that Freeman does not seem a bad chap," Idwal was saying as Dai laid the tray on the table. "Compared with some of them."

The training session had been abandoned.

"That's because he turned you into an overnight superstar," said Guto. "Idwal Roberts, political pundit, social commentator, media personality . . ."

"He *is* actually OK," Bethan said, lifting her wine glass from the tray. "Quite fair minded. Thank you, Dai."

She was sure Giles had learned about Guto and the pub incident. But he hadn't used it in his article – even though it would have underlined the point he was trying to make about Guto being the party hard-man.

"What I mean is," she said, "Giles is sympathetic. He can see what the incomers are doing to Wales and he doesn't want to be that kind of incomer. That is why he's so concerned about learning Welsh."

Dai Death said, "You're acquainted with this reporter from London then, Bethan?"

"Who do you think is *teaching* the bugger Welsh?" said Guto.

"He wants to learn Welsh for the election? There's enthusiasm."

"No, Dai," said Bethan. "He is thinking longer term. He has acquired a house in Y Groes."

A short but volcanic silence followed this disclosure.

"Y Groes!" Dai's voice rose to a squeak. He lurched in his seat, his bald head shining with hot indignation. "How the hell did he find a house there?"

Of course, Bethan realised. A sore point.

Amid muted rumblings from Guto about wealthy bloody incomers being able to find anything they wanted anywhere at a price, she briefly explained how Claire and Giles Freeman had gained admittance to Paradise.

Dai scowled.

"I've never been one to attack the incomers," he said. "Nothing personal, like. But the first house since I don't know when to come available in Y Groes . . . and it goes, without a word, to a bloody Englishman. There is no justice."

"English*woman*," Bethan said.

Idwal Roberts sniffed. "I will tell you one thing," he said, tamping down the tobacco in his pipe. "You would not catch me living there. Godless place, that village, always has been."

Bethan, who had begun her teaching career as a member of Idwal's staff at Pontmeurig's Nantglas Primary School, had heard that since his retirement he had somewhat deepened his commitment to non-conformist religion.

"Godless," he said.

"Only on your terms, man," said Dai, still annoyed. "Just because there is no chapel any more."

"No." Idwal waved his pipe in the air. "That's not –"

"Still a *church* there," Dai said. "Bloody good church."

Guto looked up innocently from his beer. "Still a chapel, too. Had my car repaired there once."

"What?" Dai looked blank for a moment. "Oh, you mean Dilwyn Dafis's garage. I forgot that used to be a chapel. Aye, well, still a public service, isn't it? And plenty of room for the ramp, see, with that high ceiling."

"What I was meaning –" Idwal said.

"What is more," said Guto, deadpan, "give Dilwyn Dafis a couple of quid on top, and you can have your bloody brakelinings blessed."

"This is getting stupid," Giles said.

Light conversation, in both English and Welsh, went on around them, the thump of darts on the board, nobody appearing to notice anything amiss or picking up on the tension. Giles knew how it must look – as if the three of them were having a nice quiet chat about beer-prices or the prospects of the Meurig bursting its banks.

Slit-mouth made a narrow smile. "He thinks you're stupid, Gary."

Getting into the comedy routine. But Giles had had enough. You really did find them everywhere, didn't you, always looking for somebody whose night they could spoil. A few casual remarks in the toilet and he'd set himself up as tonight's target. Well that was it, he wasn't taking any more.

"Look," he said firmly. "I just came in here for a drink. I've moved into the area, I'm trying to fit in. I didn't mean to cause any offence, all right? What else can I say?"

He felt his voice quiver. Bastards.

They were both studying him now with their stone-hard, hostile eyes.

"Got a house, have you? How much you pay for that?"

"Oh, for Christ's sake, this is getting awfully tedious."

"Oh dear," Slit-mouth said, mimicking Giles's accent. "*Awfully tedious*. Oh, my –"

Crater-face said to Giles, "See, I've got this mate lookin' for a house. Gettin' married, he is. And you know what . . . you won't believe this, but this boy, my mate, he's been lookin' all over town for fuckin' weeks and he can't find one anywhere. Not as he can afford. You know why . . . ?"

Leaning forward now, beer-breath sour in Giles's face. "*Know why, English?*"

Oh yes, Giles knew why all right. "Now look, if you really want to talk about this –"

"'Cause they've all been bought by your kind, is why, you bastard."

Giles got an explicit close-up of the angry, pitted skin and the eyes, wells of malice.

"Kid on the way, see."

Giles felt bits of beery spit spatter his face.

"Goin' to be really in the shit, he is, can't get a fuckin' house for his woman."

Edging his stool closer to Giles, he whispered, "I hate cunts like you, think you can buy in wherever you like. Come on, English, finish your drink."

Giles put one foot on the floor. Get out. Get out fast.

"But you think you're all right, isn't it?" Lower lip out and curling. "You think you're laughing, 'cause –" Eyes glittered and the hand shot forward as if reaching for cigarettes or something.

"– 'cause you're learnin' –"

Then pulled casually back, toppling Giles's beer glass, still half full, off the bar and into his lap.

"– *Welsh.*"

"You bast–!"

Leaping up in outrage, beer soaking invisibly into his dark suit, Giles was drowned out by Crater-face crying, "Aaaaw!"

And leaping from his stool too, knocking it over. Crash of the stool, splintering of glass on the linoleum.

"Aaaaaw, I'm sorry! My fault entirely, clumsy bugger I am. See, go in the lav, quick, sponge it off before it stains, I'll get you another – I'm sorry, pal, I really am!"

Everybody in the bar looking up now, vacant grins from around the dartboard. Obvious to Giles that nobody realised they were setting him up.

"Excuse me," he said stiffly and made for the door that said bilingually TOILETS/TOILED.

"– accident," he heard behind him. "No sense of humour, the English . . ."

Stumbled into the passage, but instead of going to the gents he dashed in the opposite direction. A door before him, ajar, LOUNGE on frosted glass, group of people huddled over a table. Giles saw them look up as if disturbed in some conspiracy –

more hostility, Christ. Turned quickly away and saw, to his overwhelming relief, that the passage was empty all the way to the front door. Going to have to get out of here quick before those two went into the gents and found he wasn't there. Giles glanced apprehensively behind, but they hadn't emerged.

Years since he'd been in such a panic. Memory-flash: hiding from older kids in a cloakroom at school. The famous wheedling lie: *Come out, Freeman, we're not going to hurt you . . .*

Giles charged along the corridor, not caring how much noise he made, knocking over an umbrella stand. He looked behind him one more time – thought he saw a pitted face – and then, with his right arm outstretched like a lance, he sent the swing door flying open and lurched into the street, into the hard, stinging rain, slanting golden needles in the streetlights.

He stood in the cold rain, cold beer in his crotch, telling himself, you're never – breathing hard – *never* going to get in that kind of situation again.

And thinking of the ancient wooden warmth of *Tafarn Y Groesfan*, where he was known and welcomed, he turned and ran through the rain to his car, his shiny new Subaru four-wheel-drive, the thinking driver's answer to the Nearly Mountains on a cold, wet night.

They were waiting for him in the shiny wet car park, rainwater streaming down their ghastly, grinning faces.

"What I like . . . out this pub . . ." – words fractured by the wind – ". . . two doors."

Lower lip jutting like a waterspout.

Gargoyle.

Giles mentally measured the distance to the car. Fifteen yards. Might as well have been a mile. Not a hope of making it.

Through the blinding downpour, he sized up the opposition. They were both shorter than he was, but the crater-faced one had a rugby player's physique, wide chest, arms like double-barrelled sawn-off shotguns.

"Look, lads . . ." he said weakly, accepting beyond doubt that he was in deep trouble here. What could one say to people like this?

Rain coming down like nails. Giles was suddenly terribly frightened. And heartsick to think this should happen to him in the land he'd chosen for his own, for his unborn children. He wanted to weep.

The dark one, Slit-mouth, hard water plastering down his sparse black hair, pouring like furious tears down his concrete face, said, "You're dead, you are, fuckin' Saxon git."

Giles folded in two as a big shoe went into his stomach and his hair was torn back and something that could only have been a fist but felt like a steel spike was driven into his left eye.

CHAPTER XXXII

In Y Groes, around midnight, the air was still.

All that night there would be violent rain in Pontmeurig. Over the Nearly Mountains there was sleet. The River Meurig was savagely swollen.

Y Groes, around midnight, was another world.

True, it *had* been stormy and the barometers still registered minimal pressure. But now the rain had stopped and the wind had died. The clouds slid back theatrically and there was a full moon over the church. Wherever you stood in Y Groes, the moon always seemed to be over the church, like a white candle flame.

Just before midnight, Claire came down the ribbon of lane from the church among a group of people. They included the rector, the Revd Elias ap Siencyn, Glyn Harri, the amateur historian, Mrs. Bronwen Dafis, mother of Dilwyn and grandmother of Sali. And the Morgans – Buddug Morgan and big Morgan Morgan.

They walked down towards the river and Claire, seeing the moon on the thrashing water, became excited.

The river had been rising all day and something in Claire had been rising with it. She felt drawn to the water, but a gentle hand held her back.

"*Dim nawr.*"

Not now.

Mrs. Bronwen Dafis explained that if she went down now she might not get back. It was too dangerous. Too dark.

But the moon . . .

Indeed, Mrs. Dafis said cryptically. The moon.

"*Wel, pryd*?" Claire said. When?

"*Bore fori*," the rector said quietly. Tomorrow morning.

He turned and walked away up the hill.

Tacitly dismissed, the group split up in silence. Glyn Harri followed a respectful distance behind the spindly figure of the rector. Then went Buddug and Morgan. Mrs. Bronwen Dafis was the last, a tiny, upright figure, alone. None of them looked back at Claire, who stood staring into the dark water.

The river was still gathering rage, although there was no wind or rain here. As if driven by the moon, it hurled itself at the stone buttresses of the bridge.

No lights now in the village, except for a lone streetlamp with a small yellow bulb under a pan-lid shade. The rector's long shape vanished beyond the light.

She was alone on the bridge, but unafraid. Inside her dwelt a great calm which stilled her thoughts and her emotions. She was content. She was *here*. Home.

At last.

Time passed. True darkness came, as a dense cloud formed around the moon and then a final fold of cloud came down over it like an eyelid. The air was still, but the water rushed and roared, filling the atmosphere with rhythmic sounds. Claire could hear the night now and feel its essence inside her.

Eventually, she began to walk away from the bridge and up the hill towards the church.

Although she was moving further from the bridge, further from the water, the sounds were going with her, swirling around her and then separating, dying off then wafting in. And mingled with the water noise was the sound of singing, uneven and hesitant. A frail organ wail, like cat-cries, and the sonorous rhythm of measured footsteps.

An arm brushed against Claire and a hand touched her shoulder.

Misty people were drifting around her. She was carried among them up the hill.

And they sang. With uncertainty in their fractured, mournful voices, they sang, in Welsh and then in English,

Love is kind and suffers long
Love is meek and thinks no wrong

The amorphous crowd split in two and something long and narrow slid between the two lines and a darker mist closed around it.

As the singing fell away and the people dissolved into vapour, Claire felt a momentary heart-stab of pain. But a cushion of warm air settled around her and the pain became a soft and bearable memory. With no light to guide her, she turned into the track leading to her cottage.

Soon after, the rain returned. But there was no wind until daylight came.

CHAPTER XXXIII

It was probably the cold water that deadened the pain. He was lying in a puddle. Or perhaps it had been raining so hard that the entire car park was a great lake.

A blow. He heard rather than felt it.

Bastards. He cringed. How long would they go on hitting him and kicking him before he lost consciousness? He lay very still; perhaps he should pretend he was already unconscious. Perhaps that would stop them.

no need for you to speak Welsh, man . . .

How friendly they were in Y Groes. How hospitable.

makes you a novelty, like, isn't it . . .

A Rhys. He was a Rhys. Sort of. In spirit.

He was *with* them.

His head imploding as they kicked it. Far away though, now. He closed his eyes, wished he could keep them closed for ever, feeling nothing but the icy balm.

But they wrenched him to his feet again, flung him back against the wall. His stomach clenched, waiting for the pain. He felt the vomit rising again.

White figure swimming towards him.

From the picture. Pale figure from the photograph in its frame in the judge's study. *Eisteddfod Genedlaethol*. White-robed, bardic, druidic.

It shimmered.

"No," he said weakly. "No . . ."

"Giles."

"No."

Bethan pushed back the hood of her white raincoat. "Giles, can you *see* me?"

"No," he said. "No. Get away from me."

"Got him, have you? Where's the other?"

"Don't . . . know. Keep still, you bugger. You bite me again, I'm going to break your nose. What should I do with this one?"

"What you should do is to get rid of him very discreetly before he sees your face. You have enough problems as it is."

"Big bloody help that is. Where am I going to put him?"

"Well, hell, I don't know – drag him over to the castle and throw him in the moat. Take him a good while to extricate himself, by which time we'll all be away."

Guto looked puzzled. "There is no moat any more."

Dai Death looked up into the plummeting night sky.

"There will be by now," he said.

Giles stared at Bethan as if he didn't know whether to push her away or to hit her. As if he couldn't decide if it was really her. Or, if it *was* her, whose side she was on.

In the shelter of the eaves, he was propped into a corner like a broken scarecrow, fair hair spiked and bloody, his suit vomit-soaked, beer-soaked, puddle-soaked and torn in several places. But it was his eye Bethan was most worried about.

"Giles, can you see me now?"

"Yes. Yes, of course I can."

"Can you see me through *both* eyes?"

"I think so. I don't know. Christ, what happened to me?"

"You – you were mugged," Bethan said.

213

"Mugged?" Giles started to laugh and went into a coughing fit, vomit around his mouth, blood in his left eye. "Is *that* what you call it?"

"We knew something must be wrong when we saw you racing past the door, knocking everything over."

"Where are the bastards now?"

"One got away. Guto has the other."

"Who?"

"A friend. Giles, you're going to get pneumonia. We have to get you to hospital."

Giles said, "Am I hurt?"

Bethan said, "Your eye. How does it feel?"

"Cold. A bit cold. My whole head, really. Cold, you know –"

"Idwal, stay with him. My car's over there. We'll get him to the hospital."

"No!" Giles straightened up and stumbled. "I've got to get back to Y Groes. My car –"

"Oh, Giles, how could you drive? Where is Claire?"

"At home. I suppose. I mean, she's not expecting me tonight. It was . . . When we heard the weather was going to be bad we decided I'd travel back on Friday – tomorrow. I – I couldn't wait. Left early. Thing is – I always phone her, you know, every night."

Bethan thought Giles looked as pathetic as seven-year-old Huw Morus had looked that morning after wetting himself in class.

"I'll ring her for you later," Bethan said. "We've got to get you to the hospital."

"Bethan, I'm OK. Really, I am."

"I'll bring the car. Idwal will stay with you. You remember Idwal Roberts whom you interviewed?"

"Hullo again, boy," said Idwal. "Talk about politics, is it?"

*

Pontmeurig Cottage Hospital accepted patients from within a fifteen-mile radius. As with most local hospitals in Wales it did not have a permanent medical staff of its own but was run by the local family doctors. Anybody in need of complicated treatment or surgery was referred at once to the general hospitals in Aberystwyth or Carmarthen.

They took Giles into a small treatment room with white-washed walls. A local doctor was summoned to look into his left eye, which was cleaned up by a nurse and then re-examined. Serious bruising. Permanent damage unlikely.

The doctor, a youngish man of perhaps Middle-Eastern origins, said to Bethan, "How did this happen?"

"Slipped in the car park," Giles replied quickly. "Running to the car through the rain. Fell into a puddle and hit my head on somebody's bumper."

"What about the vomit?"

"Turned me sick," Giles said. "Hell of a blow."

"I see. Were *you* there, Mrs. McQueen?"

"I came along afterwards."

"Did you? Look, Mr. Freeman, I think I'd like to keep you in overnight, OK?"

"Oh, come on – is that really necessary?"

"I don't know," said the doctor, who had an educated English accent. "But let's not take any chances."

"Well, can I get cleaned up?"

"I sincerely hope so. We're not going to admit you in that state, we have our standards, you know. Excuse me a minute."

"Just look at my clothes," Giles said in disgust when the doctor had gone out. "What am I going to do? I can't put these back on."

Bethan thought about this. "What we'll do, Giles – how does this sound? I'll ring Claire and tell her what happened. She can get a change of clothes ready for you and I'll drive over early tomorrow and bring them back."

Giles shook his head. "I can't ask you to do that. You'd have to leave at the crack of dawn to go over there and bring the stuff back and then get back in time for school. You can't go to that trouble. No way."

"How else are you going to get anything. Claire hasn't a car there yet, has she?"

"She hires one from Dilwyn when she needs to go somewhere."

"And I doubt if anything of Guto's would fit you."

"This Guto," Giles said slowly. "Guto Evans by any chance?"

"Shhhhh," said Bethan. "He was not involved, all right? You did not see him."

Giles tried to smile. "Thank him for me anyway. I'd have been half dead if he hadn't – hadn't been involved. Who were those guys, anyway, d'you know?"

Bethan said, "Dai – that's Dai Williams who was with us – he thinks they work in the kitchens at the Plas Meurig. They are not local boys, I am thankful to say."

Sitting on the edge of the treatment table, looking down at his stockinged feet, Giles told Bethan how it had come about, how the whole thing had developed from one swift *hanner peint o gwrw*.

"I'm confused," he said. "I thought if one was making the effort to learn Welsh . . . That's what you want, isn't it?"

Bethan gave a frustrated half-laugh. "Most likely those boys are not Welsh-speakers anyway. Some Welsh people are very aggressively opposed to the language. It's not black and white, you must realise that by now."

"I'm getting better again, Bethan. With the language. I've done a lot of studying."

"Good. Listen, Giles –"

216

"I don't know what came over me before. Tired, I think. Headaches. But I'm much better now."

"Giles, can I ask you a question?"

"Ask away. What have I got to lose?"

"Everything," said Bethan. "That is just it. You have everything to lose. You are a successful journalist with a –" she hesitated "– a good marriage. A good career, plenty of money, I suppose."

"Well, you know, enough to be going on with."

"So why do you want to be part of this mess?" she asked bluntly.

"Mess?" Giles moved along the plastic sheet to detach his sodden trousers which were sticking to it. "I don't think it's a mess. Politically, it's very stimulating. I mean, in England most people just vote for whichever party they think is going to benefit them financially. To be in a place where the main issues are cultural and linguistic – national identity at stake . . . Hey, listen, I'll tell you one thing –" Giles grinned like an idiot, through his pain "– I bet I'm the first ever English guy to get his head kicked in for speaking Welsh in public."

"Oh, Giles," Bethan said. "It isn't fair, is it?"

How could she tell him that tonight's fracas was probably the least of his problems?

Her face must have become overcast, because he said, "Look, Bethan – we should have a proper talk sometime, you know."

The doctor came back before she could fashion a reply.

"Mr. Freeman, we've prepared a bathroom for you. The nurse will help you. How does your head feel?"

"OK. Just cold. Quite cold."

Giles dropped to the floor and winced.

"Do you have pain anywhere else?"

"Nothing much."

"I think," the doctor said, "that you should go to Bronglais tomorrow –"

"No! No bloody way!"

"– if not tonight. We should have X-rays."

"For Christ's sake," Giles snapped. "It was only a fall. It doubtless looks much worse than it actually is."

"All right," the doctor said. "We'll talk about it tomorrow. Now come and get cleaned up. Would you excuse us, Mrs. McQueen?"

"Of course." Bethan went to the door and looked back at Giles. "I'll be back early in the morning."

"You've been wonderful," Giles said. "I think I'm in love with you, Bethan."

"Join the queue," the doctor said.

When Bethan got back to her flat over the bookshop, the phone was ringing. Guto.

She told him how it had come about that Giles Freeman had been assaulted in the car park.

"Bastards," Guto said. "Ought to have handed that bugger over to the cops, but Dai said I could wave goodbye to the candidacy if I was linked to another assault, even as a witness. A minefield, it is, politics."

"You didn't harm that one, did you?"

"Well, the odd tweak, kind of thing. Nothing that will show. I quite enjoyed it, to be honest. Tell your English friend that when I am MP for Glanmeurig I shall recommend we erect a monument on the Drovers' car park to commemorate his historic stand on behalf of the language."

It was an ill wind, Bethan thought. Guto seemed to have cheered up considerably.

She switched on lights, plugged in the kettle and sat down to telephone Claire, wondering what the reaction would be.

Perhaps this would bring Claire down to earth again. Giles would need some looking after.

In Y Groes the phone rang five times. Then there was a bleep, a pause and Claire's recorded voice said, "*Y Groes dau, tri, naw. Dyma Claire Rhys . . .*"

The message, in near-perfect Welsh, said Claire Rhys was not available to come to the telephone but the caller could leave a message after the tone.

Bethan's own answering machine had a message in Welsh, followed by a translation. Thousands of answering machines in Welsh-speaking areas of Wales now carried messages in Welsh, almost invariably with a translation; nobody wanted to lose an important caller because he or she, like the majority of Welsh people, spoke only English.

Claire's message was given only in Welsh. Bethan hung up, troubled.

Three times a week now, she went to the judge's house for the Welsh lesson – with Claire alone, of late, because Giles had been in London. One to one. The oil-lamp hanging from the beam in the judge's study surrounded by the judge's black books. Sombre yellow light. Deep, deep shadows.

And Claire, face gaunt in the oil-light, hair drawn tightly back, showing the dark roots.

A student so brilliant it was unnerving.

She dialled the number one last time.

"*Y Groes dau, tri, naw. Dyma Claire Rhys. . . .*"

Not the kind of problem you could explain to an answering machine. She would get up very early and go to the judge's house.

Bethan put the phone down.

The rain and wind attacked her window.

CHAPTER XXXIV

Like some spurned, embittered lover, the wind-driven rain beat on Bethan's bedroom window all night. She got little sleep; every half-dream seemed to feature Giles's wet and bloodied image. Its screams were frenzied but inaudible, as if it were separated from her by thick glass – a windscreen or a television screen.

Before six o'clock, Bethan was up, making strong, black tea, peering out of the window and half expecting to find Pontmeurig's main street under two feet of water. Ironically the rain, having deprived her of sleep, had now stopped. There were no signs of flooding in the street, although the river must surely be dangerously high.

It looked cold too. Bethan put on her white raincoat, with a long red scarf and a pink woolly hat which she pulled down over her ears as she stepped out into the street.

By six-thirty she was collecting the Peugeot from the car park under the castle's broken tower. She looked down, with some trepidation, into the ditch below the outer ramparts, as if she might see a rigid, clawing hand emerging from the watery mud in which its owner had drowned. On the eve of the selection meeting, it would be just Guto's luck.

Before leaving she had telephoned the hospital, where the sister in charge reported that Giles had had quite a painful and restless night.

But yet, she thought, unlocking the car door, if Giles were writing a report of last night's incident he would deal seriously and sympathetically with the dilemma of the non-Welsh-speaking Welshman.

That English sense of fair play.

The town was quiet, cowed – as though people were deliberately lying low, apprehensive about getting up to find their gardens underwater or their chimney pots in pieces on the lawn. Driving over the Meurig bridge in the steely-grey dawn, Bethan saw that it had indeed been a close thing. Trees sprouted from the water, where the river had claimed its first meadow.

Allowing for weather problems, storm debris on the road, it would take about twenty minutes to get to Y Groes. Bethan knew Claire rose early and guessed she might be waiting for the light to see what pictures she could obtain of storm damage. If she was still actually taking pictures. She'll probably want to come back with me to the hospital, Bethan thought. Another lost opportunity to talk to Giles.

Part of Bethan said it was not her problem, she should keep out. Another part said Giles was a decent man who needed saving from himself. Too many English people had given up their jobs and come to Wales with new-life dreams, many of them to start smallholdings on poor-quality land from which they imagined they could be self-sufficient. She saw a parallel here with Giles, who seemed about to abandon a highly paid post to spend his life ploughing this infertile place for news, in the naïve belief that the public over the border cared as much about Wales as he did.

In Bethan's experience, the only immigrants who really could be said to have fitted in were those who came to take up existing, steady jobs. Like Robin, her husband, who had worked with the British Geological Survey team near Aberystwyth.

Bethan's eyes filled up.

Stop it! Her hands tightened on the wheel. The Nearly Mountains rose up before her, tented by cloud.

*

Bethan had experimented with a number of different methods of tackling these sudden rushes of grief. Anger, the least satisfactory, had usually proved, all the same, to be the most effective.

So she thought about Buddug.

Yesterday Huw Morus, aged seven, had wet himself in class. Bethan had led him into the teachers' toilet and washroom to get cleaned up.

Huw had been very distressed. Bethan had taken him back into her office, sat him on a chair by the electric fire and asked him if he was feeling unwell. Huw had started crying and said he wanted to go. Again.

Bethan had sent him back to the teachers' toilet and then said, "OK, we'll take you home."

"I am sure he'll be happy now," Buddug commented. "Now he's got what he wanted."

"It seems likely to me that he has some kind of bladder infection," Bethan said.

Buddug had sniffed dismissively. "Lazy. He is lazy."

Huw lived in the village where his father was a mechanic, the sole employee at Dilwyn Dafis's garage.

"Did you ask Mrs. Morgan if you could go to the toilet?" Bethan asked, as the boy trotted beside her past the *Tafarn* and the post office to a timber-framed terrace of cottages at the end of the street.

It emerged that Huw had asked Mrs. Morgan at about half past nine by the classroom clock and she had allowed him to go. Then he'd asked her again at about a quarter past ten and she'd told him he could wait until break. He'd barely made it in time.

At about twenty minutes past eleven Huw had again raised his hand and sought permission to go to the lavatory and Mrs. Morgan had shaken her head and told him he must not try it on with her again.

Ten minutes later Huw, by now frozen to the chair with his legs tightly crossed, had appealed again to the teacher. This time Mrs. Morgan had walked over and bent down and whispered in his ear.

Bethan questioned the seven-year-old boy in some detail, because she wanted to be sure about this.

It seemed Buddug had reminded Huw that the end of the yard, where the children's toilets were, was very close to the woods.

Which, as everyone knew, were guarded by the *Gorsedd Ddu*. The dark bards.

And the *Gorsedd Ddu* would view Huw's repeated appearances as a mockery.

If they found him there again they might catch him and take him with them into the woods, and there would be no relief to be found there. Not for a stupid little boy who tried to deceive his teacher.

Bethan, coming down now out of the Nearly Mountains, swung the wheel of the Peugeot to avoid a grey squirrel in the road. The squirrel shot into the forestry.

In Bethan's experience, small children were often terrified by their first sight of a *gorsedd* of bards, those poets and writers who had been honoured at *eisteddfodau* and walked in solemn procession wearing their long ceremonial robes and druidic head-dresses. These archetypal figures, in the garb of ancient pagan priests, could seem quite awesomely sinister to little kids until they found out that under those white robes you would usually find genial grandfatherly figures who would occasionally dispense sweets like Sion Corn, the Welsh Father Christmas.

The *Gorsedd Ddu*, the black bards – there was a difference here. They were *meant* to be terrifying.

The lower slopes of the Nearly Mountains were sparsely wooded and Bethan had to slow down to find a path between branches torn off the trees in the night. She would not have been surprised to find the road blocked by an entire Sitka spruce, its roots ripped out of the shallow soil.

This never happened to the oak trees in the old woods. The reason, Buddug would probably say, was not only that the soil was thick and deep and the area so sheltered. But that the oak woods were protected by the *Gorsedd Ddu*.

Most parents and infant-teachers, in fanciful mood, might tell children the woods were the home of, say, the *Tylwyth Teg*, the Welsh fairy folk. But that would not satisfy the streak of cruelty in Buddug. First she had refused to consider that the child, Huw Morus, might be ill, and then she had made wetting himself seem the safer option by invoking the insidiously horrifying image of the mythical assembly of black-robed bards who were said to convene to judge the traitors and the cowards.

Bethan decided there were certain aspects of the Welsh national heritage which she disliked intensely – and most of them were represented by Buddug, who would not be happy until children were sitting at their desks dressed stiffly in Welsh national costume, drawing pictures of corpse candles and sin-eaters consuming their lunches from the shrouded chests of dead people.

There was still a strong wind, but no trees had been blown down on the lower slopes of the Nearly Mountains, and Bethan arrived in Y Groes well before seven to find the last few lights glimmering in the cottages, the village enfolded in the dark hills like antique jewellery in velvet, under a delicate oyster sky.

But the wind was high, the sky unbalanced, a sense of something wild beyond the horizon.

Bethan parked in the entrance to the school lane and set off across the bridge. Below it the swollen Meurig frothed and spat. "Big, tough river now, is it?" Bethan said. "You never had much to say for yourself in the summer."

She walked past the *Tafarn* and up the lane towards the church and then between the two sycamores to the judge's house.

The iron gate was open, but nobody was in sight. The wind perhaps? Bethan closed the gate behind her, walked up the path, knocked on the door.

She would tell Claire everything, including the probable reasons for the attack on Giles. Everything except the involvement of Guto who must, for the sake of his image, remain an anonymous hero.

Claire could pack a change of clothes and Bethan would take them – and Claire, if she wanted – to the hospital. There should be plenty of time to get back to school before the first children arrived.

The door opened.

"Oh, Claire, I tried to ring you –" Bethan said, then stopped and drew back.

It was Buddug.

CHAPTER XXXV

Buddug did not seem surprised to see her. But then Buddug never seemed surprised.

She wore a high-necked, starched white blouse and – Bethan would swear – a smudge of make-up. As if she had arrived for an Occasion. She filled the doorway. Bethan could not see if Claire was in the room behind her.

"Where is *Claire*?" she said flatly.

Buddug stared impassively at her.

"Where is Claire?"

"Not here," Buddug said calmly.

"Out? So early?"

She'd been out last night too. The answering machine.

"And what are *you* doing here?" Bethan demanded. Her mind could not grasp this situation. Buddug in Claire's house. At little after seven in the morning.

And formally attired. Looking quite grotesque – there was no other word for it.

"Are you alone here?"

Buddug did not reply. There was a silence in the room behind her but it was the kind of silence which implied *presence*, as if a still company was sitting there. Bethan found herself thinking of the drawing in Sali Dafis's exercise book, dark-brown stick-people around a coffin on a table.

"Are you not going to answer me?" Her voice shook. "Where is Claire?"

Buddug did not move. The thought came to Bethan that this

woman was big enough and strong enough to kill her, as simply as she killed chickens and turkeys, huge hands around her throat. A swift, dismissive jerk of the wrists.

"Look, I want to know. Where is Claire? *What have you done with her?*"

Buddug came alive then, bulging out of the doorway, the veins in her face suddenly lighting up like an electric circuit.

"What is it to you?" she shrieked. "Who said you could come here? Get out! Get back to your school, you stupid, meddling little bitch!"

Bethan went pale. "How d–!"

The front door leapt on its hinges, as if hit by a gale, and Bethan lurched back, clutching at the air, as the door crashed into its frame and shuddered there.

A sudden stiff breeze disturbed the giant sycamores and prodded her down the lane. There was a ball of cold in the pit of her stomach as she walked back towards the river.

What she felt for Buddug had gone beyond hatred to the place where nightmares are born.

"You are early, Bethan."

He was sitting on a wooden bench under the *Tafarn* sign, which was beginning to swing now in the gathering wind.

"You are also early, Aled," Bethan said, groping for composure. "For a landlord."

"Could not sleep, girl. The wind rising."

"The wind's nothing here, compared with Pontmeurig. Well, last night . . ."

"Ah, well, see, so little of the wind we get here that the merest flurry we notice. I do, anyway. Because the river is so close, see. The river goes mad."

Aled's hair was as white and stiff as the icy snow on the tops of the Nearly Mountains. Bethan had always found him a droll and placid man, easy to talk to, in Welsh or English. She wondered if she could trust him.

"Do you . . . ?" She hesitated.

He looked quizzically at her.

"Do you find things are changing, Aled?"

"Changing?"

"Here. In the village."

Aled looked away from Bethan, over the oak woods and back again. "Things changing? In Y Groes?" He smiled.

"Perhaps it's me. Perhaps I should not have come back."

"Why do you say that?"

"I don't know. Too many memories, perhaps." Although, of course, that was not it really.

"He was a nice boy, your man. A terrible shame, it was, that he . . . well."

Bethan asked him, "What do you think of Giles Freeman?"

"Nice fellow," Aled said. "Well meaning, you know."

"He was –" No, she could not tell him what had happened. Not even that Giles had fallen in the car park. Not until she'd told Claire.

"I think, Bethan," Aled said. "I think you have a decision to make."

"What kind of decision?"

"Well, as you said . . . about your future. Whether you stay here, perhaps move into one of the cottages."

"There are no cottages for sale."

"No, but . . . well, Tegwyn Jones's old place. It might be available. If you –"

"If I wanted to settle down here?"

"– to settle down, as you say. To become part of our community. It is . . . well, as you know, it is a rare and beautiful place."

"Yes."

"But it makes . . . demands, see."

"Does it make demands on you, Aled?"

There was rarely much colour in his face. He was not an out-door man, like Morgan, or even Dilwyn Dafis. All the same, he did not look well. Bethan had not seen him face to face for several weeks, and she felt a tiredness coming from him.

"Oh yes," he said. "It has made demands on me. Bethan, would you excuse me. I have the bar to clean." He stood up. "Nice to see you, as always."

Face it, Bethan told herself. No one here is going to help you.

Suddenly she wanted to dash back to the Peugeot, shut her-self in, wind up all the windows, lock the door, put the radio on – loud, loud rock music – and race back over the Nearly Mountains to sanctuary and sanity.

I could do that, she thought hysterically. I could have a nerv-ous breakdown. God knows, I'm halfway there. I could go to the doctor, get signed off. Nobody would be surprised. The Widow McQueen. Came back too soon.

Too soon.

Obviously she had come back too soon this morning. What was going on? What had she disturbed?

Did she really want to know?

Had to pull herself together. Her main task was to get clean clothing for Giles. If she couldn't get into the house, it would have to be Guto – he must have *something* that would not look entirely ludicrous on a man six inches taller and at least two stones lighter. Or she could even go to Probert's and buy some things.

She set off purposefully across the bridge to her car.

But made the mistake of looking over the stone parapet.

To where, fifty yards downstream, a woman had her head in the water.

*

Bethan looked around for help but there was nobody on the main street at this hour. She ran across the bridge, crying out, "Aled! Aled!" at the closed door of the *Tafarn*, but the wind ripped the words away and there was no response as she scrambled down the bank to where the woman's head was being tossed this way and that by the thrashing river.

Halfway down, Bethan lost her footing. Her left shoe skated on a grass-slick, the wind seemed to flick her into the air and she was thrown, screaming, full length down the slimy, freezing river bank.

For a moment Bethan just lay there and sobbed with anguish and incomprehension. And that amply justified sense of *déjà vu* which told her she would look up to find two large, muddy hiking boots swinging one against the other.

But the only thing in focus was the hard grey stone of the bridge support. All around her was just a wash of glacial green and white, the abstract colours spinning past her eyes, because this time her glasses had gone.

"Oh no. Oh no, please, God . . ."

Trembling with cold and shock, Bethan put both hands in the sodden, slippery grass and pushed herself to her knees. Then she began to crawl awkwardly up the bank, groping at the grass on either side.

Stricken with the fear that if she slipped again her hands would find somebody's dead skin, the scaly contours of a drowned face. Or chewed-out eye sockets where the crows had . . .

Her hand touched something smooth and wet and she snatched it back in dread, before realising she'd found the glasses. Half retching with relief, she fumbled them on, rubbing the grass and mud from the lenses which were still, oh thank God, apparently intact.

On her knees now, pink woolly hat missing, hair ravaged by the wind, skirt torn almost up to the waist, Bethan looked around her and then down to the river no more than four feet below her.

The woman was naked from the waist up, bent into the river. Either her body was being thrown about by the wind or . . . Bethan, crouching, half sliding, edged her way to the water.

She reached the spitting river just as the woman's head came up, black and dripping, and her eyes were like chips of ice and she was Claire, and Bethan arched back in horror and bewilderment.

Above the frenzy of wind and water, Claire was making a noise as harsh and chill as the river itself. It seemed at first as if she was crying, with great jagged wails. Then Bethan realised, with shock, that Claire was laughing, which somehow was far, far worse.

"Claire . . . ?"

Bethan felt a piercing of fear. Claire just went on laughing, rising up on the bank, breasts ice-blue, marbled with the cold.

"What's wrong? What's happening? What are you doing? For God's sake! Claire!"

Bethan pulled off her raincoat and went to wrap it around Claire, although she was really afraid to go near her. But Claire stood up and backed off. She was wearing only jeans and her red hiking boots.

"You are crazy," Bethan breathed.

Claire's small mouth was stretched wide with grotesque mirth. She ran her hands through her hair, wet and dark as a seal.

Bethan saw that almost all the blonde had gone, just a few jaundiced patches.

"*Dychi ddim yn gweld?*" Claire hissed. "*Dychi ddim yn gweld?*"
Can't you see?

The river writhed among the rocks.

Bethan, face damp with cold sweat and spray, didn't move. She was very scared now, wanting to clamber up the bank and get away, but afraid of somebody or the crazy wind pushing her back to the river, and the river was slurping at the rocks and the bridge support as if licking its lips for her.

She thought of Giles lying restlessly in his unwanted hospital bed, while his wife cavorted like some insane water-nymph.

Claire started to move back along the bank towards the stile that led into one of Morgan's fields. Black cloth, a shawl, hung from one of the posts of the stile and she pulled it off and wrapped it around her. A sheep track curved up through the field and ended near the judge's cottage.

When she reached the stile, Claire turned one last time towards Bethan, tearing at her once-blonde hair, screaming gleefully through the wind. *"Dydwy ddim yn Sais!"* I am not English!

And burst out laughing again, in raucous peels like church bells rung by madmen.

CHAPTER XXXVI

"Forget it," Giles said. "Just forget it, OK?"

"You're being very foolish, Mr. Freeman."

"Look, mate," Giles said, "it's my bloody head and if I don't want it bloody scanned, or whatever they do these days, I don't have to comply. So bring me the sodding papers or whatever I'm supposed to sign."

"All right, just supposing you have a brain haemorrhage."

Giles shrugged.

"I can't stop you," the doctor said. "I can only warn you. And all I can say is, if somebody had given *me* a kicking . . ."

"I *fell.*"

". . . If somebody had given me that kind of kicking, I'd want all the medical evidence I could get." Dr. Tahan, unshaven, was clearly suppressing rage. He'd been awoken by a nurse on the phone telling him Mr. Freeman was threatening to walk out in his underpants if they didn't bring his clothes immediately.

"Look . . ." Giles passed a hand over his eyes. "I'm very grateful for all you've done, but there's nothing wrong with me that sleep won't cure, and I'm not going to get any here. Bring me whatever I have to sign and my clothes. I want to go home."

"Come and see me tomorrow," the doctor said curtly. "If you want to." And walked out of the room.

Not you, Giles said to himself. I'll go and see Dr. Wyn in the village, if I have to. *If* I have to.

A nurse brought his clothes, put them down on the bed, did not speak to him. If you didn't want to play by their rules, Giles

233

thought, they didn't want to know you. The clothes had been dried and straightened out, as far as was possible with all the torn bits, and the lining hanging out of his jacket. Giles held up the jacket and grinned savagely. He felt removed from all this. He felt he was standing a foot or so behind the action, watching himself hold up the jacket, controlling his own responses at arm's length, pulling strings to bring on the savage grin.

In truth he felt awful – physically and emotionally in a similar condition to his clothes.

But he was going home.

Guto was wearing a tie.

An unheard-of phenomenon.

"I borrowed it," he said. "From Dai."

"But it's one of his *working* ties," Bethan said.

"Looks all right though, doesn't it?"

"It's black."

"Reflects my new image. Sober. Caring."

"Take it off, Guto. I shall go and buy you another. Meanwhile, there is something you could do for me."

"No time – to get a new tie, I mean. I'm meeting Dafydd and Gwynfor in Lampeter at ten. Then we are all going over to Rhayader for the selection meeting."

"It's not until tonight, is it?"

"A lot to discuss before then. Hell of a lot."

They were alone in the house, Guto's mam having gone for the early bus to Aber, as she did every Friday. Bethan had driven over from Y Groes in a kind of trance, going deliberately far too fast so that she would have to concentrate hard on her driving to avoid disaster and would not be able to think about anything else.

"There are big green stains on your mac," Guto observed.

"So there are," said Bethan.

It was not yet eight o'clock. No more than half an hour since she'd scrambled up the river bank away from the madwoman who had almost been her friend.

"Guto, Giles might be coming out of hospital this morning. You know the state of his clothes. I was wondering if you had anything that might fit him."

"What about his own clothes? He's got more than that suit at home, hasn't he?"

"Yes, but . . . there are problems in bringing them across."

The central problem, she now realised, was that Giles would actually be going home – she had no illusions that the doctor might persuade him to be examined at Bronglais – and walking into a situation which he might have difficulty coping with even if he were fully fit.

She simply did not know what to do for the best.

"I'll make some tea," Guto said. "You look as if you need it."

"No, you go," Bethan said. "You get off to Lampeter. It's your big day."

"Are you all right, Bethan?"

"Of course I am."

"Listen, go upstairs now. Second door on the left. Just inside the door there's a wardrobe. Some of my dad's old clothes you'll find in there. A big, tall man, he was, my dad. Well, compared with me he was. Take what you like. Bit old-fashioned, mind, but if it's only to get him home . . ."

Guto straightened his undertaker's tie in the gilt-framed mirror over a mantelpiece heavy with cumbersome Victorian pottery. From a chair he took his briefcase.

His *briefcase*! A tie *and* a briefcase. On any other day but this Bethan would have found the spectacle richly amusing.

"I'm off," said Guto. "Just slam the door behind you when you've finished."

"Thank you. Guto . . ."

He looked back, mute appeal in his doggy eyes.

What the hell, Bethan thought, and went over and kissed him. On the cheek, of course.

"Good luck, Guto."

Guto snatched her by the arm and kissed her on the lips. He'd trimmed his beard too.

"There," he said. "*Now* I feel lucky."

When he'd gone, Bethan went upstairs and found his late father's wardrobe. Guto's dad had been a miner in the Rhondda who had suffered badly with his chest. When Guto was twelve or thirteen the family had moved west for his father's health, taking over a small tobacconist's shop in Pontmeurig. Bethan remembered Bryn Evans as a man who coughed a lot and laughed a lot, spent each night in the Drovers' Arms until closing time but was never conspicuously drunk.

Inevitably, as she pulled open the mahogany doors, Bethan remembered going through Robin's wardrobe, packing up all his clothes, taking them to the Oxfam shop in Stryd-y-Castell. Easily the most heartbreaking task she'd ever performed. She remembered folding his beloved sheepskin-lined flying jacket, then changing her mind and taking it out of the cardboard box and stowing it in the bottom of her own wardrobe, where it still lay, and she –

Stop it, stop it, stop it!

On a shelf above the stiff, dark suits, she found a pair of light slacks and a thick, grey rollneck pullover. Could be worse.

With the clothes under her arm, she ran down the stairs and out the front door, shutting it firmly behind her. Five minutes past eight. Not much time. She wondered how Buddug would react if she didn't turn up for school by nine o'clock. And would Buddug herself be on time, or would she be otherwise engaged?

Bethan shuddered at the memory of Buddug, enormous in the doorway, made up like a fat corpse.

She put the clothes on the back seat of the Peugeot and drove to the cottage hospital. On impulse she went into the phone box in the hospital foyer and dialled Y Groes 239.

Last chance to speak sensibly to Claire, otherwise she would have to tell Giles everything.

Tell him everything?

But what was she doing in the river, Bethan?

She was washing her hair, Giles.

I see.

In Y Groes the telephone rang out. Six times, seven times, eight.

Bethan hung up and left the box and walked across to the reception desk.

"Giles Freeman," she said to a woman who had been a couple of years ahead of her at secondary school in Aber.

"You'll be lucky," the receptionist said. "Do you want to speak to Dr. Tahan?"

"What do you mean?"

"I'll bleep him," said the receptionist. "He'll want to talk to *you*, I imagine."

Bethan went cold. "Is Giles all right?"

"No, he's not all right," the woman said smugly. Bethan could tell that, as she spoke, she was busy fabricating an interesting relationship between the schoolteacher and the Englishman. "Not for me to say, though, is it?"

The doctor was more forthcoming. He led Bethan to his office in the new wing and closed the door.

"Delayed concussion, fractured skull, brain haemorrhage, you name it," he said. "It could be any, it could be none. But how are we to know? I don't particularly want to know precisely how he came by his injuries, but I do want him to be fully examined. Call it selfishness. Call it protecting my own back, I don't care."

"Hold on," Bethan said. "You are saying he's gone?"

237

"Your friend discharged himself half an hour ago. There was nothing I could say to stop him. We don't, unfortunately, have powers of arrest."

"Oh God," Bethan said.

"I don't know how much you are in a position to influence him, but if he blacks out and runs his car off the road . . ."

"All right," Bethan said, looking at her watch. Twenty past eight.

She ran down the hospital corridor and did not look at the receptionist on her way to the door.

CHAPTER XXXVII

Tired. Desperately, desperately tired.

He had thought the fresh air would revive him, but walking to the car park was like he imagined it would be for a deep-sea diver staggering across the ocean bed, the air heavy on his shoulders, powerful currents pulling him this way and that. In reality the wind was not so strong any more and the sky all rained out.

Stepping from the kerb, Giles lost his balance and fell sideways across the bonnet of a parked car. People stared at him, as though he were some rare species of breakfast-time drunk.

When he got into his own car, the new Subaru, it felt strange, as if he hadn't driven it in years. When he pulled out of the car park below the ruined castle, his hands on the wheel seemed a long way away, as if he were driving from the back seat.

He steered stiffly across the Meurig bridge and on to the bypass. The Nearly Mountains were above him now, wispy grey clouds around the tops like smoke-rings.

Just hadn't realised what complete fatigue could be like. Except this was more than fatigue: his whole body aching, bloated, lumbering. His head feeling as though it were encased in some huge metal helmet, like the Man in the Iron Mask.

A truck blasted its horn behind him as he swung the car off the bypass and on to the mountain road, and he realised he'd forgotten to signal.

After three miles, Giles began to see double. Twin roads snaked into the hills, two wooden fences sealed off the forestry.

He pulled into a lay-by. Switched off the engine, sat back, and the seat pulled him in and his eyelids crashed down.

He remembered Bethan then. How she was going to fetch him some clothes. He'd forgotten all about that. He must stop her, tell her he was going home. He sat up, hands scrabbling at the carphone. He would call home, tell Claire, get her to ring Bethan or something. Or something.

His fingers kept pushing all the wrong numbers. The carphone squeaked impatiently. He saw the message NO SERVICE printed out across the illuminated panel on the receiver. Giles groaned. He must have passed the point at which the Vodaphone signal faded out. Perhaps it would return. He must remember to try again. Must remember . . .

Really he felt like stumbling off into the forestry and curling up on the brown carpet of dead needles, knowing he would fall asleep there instantly. But he heaved his body into position on the seat, switched on the engine again and drove very, very slowly over the crest of the Nearly Mountains, where the snow snuggled into the crags and hollows. He could have stopped and walked out and gone to sleep in the snow, like Captain Oates. Just going out. May be some time.

He didn't have to analyse why it was so vital for him to get away from Pontmeurig and back to Y Groes. Couldn't have managed any heavy thinking in his state anyway. But he knew why it was. It came down to this: the first seriously unpleasant thing had happened to him in Pont, the thing that backed up everything they'd said, the hacks, at Winstone Thorpe's farewell session. While in Y Groes, everything disproved it. The warmth, the open friendliness, the generosity, the feeling that here were people who were confident enough of their heritage, their place in the world, not to suspect everyone with an English accent of trying to rip them off.

Something like that.

He glanced back at the phone. NO SERVICE it said still, NO SERVICE. Why should it just say NO SERVICE in English? Why not in Welsh, too? DIM ... DIM whatever the hell service was in Welsh.

Down now, into the forestry's gloom. Sitka spruce stamping in dispiriting symmetry down the hillside, stealing the land and the light. Giles clung to the wheel of the Subaru, wipers scraping at the spray thrown up as the car slogged through a roadside river left by the storm. The rhythm of the wipers wafted waves of sleep into his head.

soon-be-home, soon-be-home, soon-be-home.

Only when his chin hit his chest did Giles awake to his peril, violently jerking himself upright, a bumper scraping the forestry fence as he swerved back into the middle of the road.

Breathing hard, he wiped the palm of his hand across the windscreen and smeared cool condensation into his hot, hurting eyes.

Presently, the sky brightened. He pulled down the sunvisor then flung it up again, tears in his eyes, realising this was the brightness heralding home. He saw the church's two-tiered belfry, and he stopped the car, his heart tugging weakly but triumphantly.

The church was a symbol for Giles of what this village was about. Not some grey chapel behind back-street railings, but a great, soaring tower stabbing the sky, announcing Y GROES. The cross. Y GROESFAN. The crossing place.

He had never been to a service at this church, never been to any kind of service since his wedding, but he told himself he must go this Sunday. Renew his faith, give thanks to the village and to its people and to the Almighty for bringing him here.

Battered, beaten up, bedraggled, Giles wrapped both arms around the steering wheel and wept. And looked up and saw, through his tears, two towers, two bridges, two roads. But he would make it now. Back home to sleep. Sleep until church on Sunday. Sunday. When was that? What day was it? Was it Sunday tomorrow?

The car rolled out of the forestry as if someone else were driving it, Giles's senses somewhere around the rear parcel shelf.

Across the bridge, up the hill, past the lych gate of the church, a couple of hundred yards then right, between the two great sycamores in full autumnal glory.

Oh God, thank you, thank you.

Giles almost fell out of the car, heedless of the pain, and breathed deeply of the soft air. The metal gate was open for him. They must have told Claire he was on his way. What he wanted most in the world was to fall into bed, holding her to him, and sleep. Sleep for ever.

"Claire . . . darling Claire . . ."

He realised he'd said that aloud as he staggered up the path. The judge's house – no, *his* house surely, his house now – sat before him, grey stone under a milky sky.

The front door also was open for him. He stumbled gratefully over the step. "Hello, darling, I tried to phone . . ."

There was no Claire waiting for him in the little stone-walled hallway.

Giles went into the living room. It was silent. No fire in the hearth, no cups on the table.

"Claire?"

He shouted out, "Claire!" His voice almost breaking into a wail of disappointment. She wasn't here.

But the gate open, the front door. Couldn't have gone far, surely.

Giles went back outside, looked around the garden, called out, "Claire!"

The wind brought only a sheep's bleat back to him from Morgan's field.

He returned to the house, upset and angry now, feeling deserted. And terribly, terribly tired. Too tired to think sensibly.

"I'm going to bed," Giles said thickly. "Sod you, Claire, I'm going to bed."

He staggered through the passage to the bottom of the stairs, still clinging to the hope that he would meet Claire coming down, smiling with welcome and sympathy and a hot cup of coffee.

Three doors in the passage, the one to the judge's study hanging open. But no light leaked out of the gap into the already dim passage. Irritably he pulled the door closed, but it swung open again as he turned away.

Angrily he spun round and snapped it shut.

In the passage he stumbled over something that should not be there, could not take in at first that this was the pink vinyl headboard, cheap and brash, from Garfield and Pugh in hostile Pontmeurig. What was the bloody headboard doing at the foot of the stairs?

"Claire? Claire!!" He began to climb the stairs. It was too bad. Just too bloody bad of her. Not even a fire lit.

Halfway up the stairs he looked back and saw that the door of the judge's study was hanging open again. He turned away from it and carried on to the upstairs landing.

He went into his office and looked around. Aghast.

His office had gone.

It was a bedroom.

His office was a bloody bedroom again!

Giles squeezed his aching eyes with trembling fingers. Illusion, fatigue, hallucination?

Let it be that. Please let it be that, God.

But when he opened his eyes. It was still a bedroom, and now he recognised the bed. Two green mattresses and a frame of light pine. It was the bed which had come into the house with the ghastly pink vinyl headboard.

"Claire!!" he screamed, his throat choking on the word. He began to cough.

He backed out of the room and threw open the door of their own bedroom, his and Claire's, knowing in an icy part of his stomach what he would find there. Whose bed, with its frowning headboard of carved oak.

"Thank God," Bethan said, seeing Giles's car parked in the track between the two sycamores.

She'd driven straight out of the forestry and into the village at close to sixty miles per hour, knowing that at this time there'd be no children in the road – they'd all be in school by now, wondering where their head teacher was.

At seven minutes to nine, the head teacher had been shattering a wing mirror on the parapet of the bridge as the little Peugeot whizzed across like a frightened squirrel.

All the way across the hills she'd been peering nervously over walls and hedges and fences, expecting to see a car on its side somewhere, or bits of wreckage.

Well, thank God he'd made it. Thank God for that, at least.

For what it was worth.

Bethan thought, on reflection, that perhaps the best thing that could have happened would have been a minor crash, something to get Giles towed back to Pont, deposited safely in the hospital with a broken leg, something minor but incapacitating.

For a few seconds she debated going up to the house to ask if Giles was OK. But really it was none of her business. All right, a bruised and beaten man and an increasingly loopy woman. What could she do about that? She was a primary school teacher, not a psychotherapist or a marriage-guidance counsellor.

Besides it was almost nine o'clock.

Christ. She felt as if she'd put in two full days' work, and it was not yet nine o'clock.

Five minutes or so later, Buddug's hands froze above the piano keyboard as Bethan slid into the school hall.

She stood in the doorway in her white mac with the streaks of mud and the huge grass stains. The children, sitting in five short rows, all turned towards her, and Buddug's head swivelled round slowly, her lips drawn back into a smile of incandescent malevolence.

"*Bore da*," the children chorused. "*Bore da*, Miss Sion."

She sat down at her desk in the hall, still wearing her mac, too weary to say anything as Buddug's hands smashed into the opening chords of the hymn.

Buddug sang with shrill, ferocious zest, hammering the keys like a pub pianist. Energy rippled through the room as the children yelled out the words, gleefully discordant.

Bethan sat in her soiled raincoat and stared at the wall, utterly defeated.

Giles came out of the bedroom and stood at the top of the stairs, swaying.

He could not believe the agony.

Like a flower it had opened out. Bursting free inside his skull like some huge multi-petalled chrysanthemum. And at the end of every petal, a poisoned barb prodding into each tiny fold of his brain, awakening every nerve to the dazzling white light of purest pain.

He could not even bear to scream.

Mercifully, perhaps, the pain had deadened his emotions. Except for one. Which was rage.

Rage gathered in his throat, choking him. Rage against *her*.

And against him.

Her dead grandfather.

He began to walk down the stairs, each soft step detonating a new explosion in his brain.

He walked across the hall, past the pink vinyl headboard, to where the door of the judge's study still hung ajar.

Giles went in.

PART SIX

BLACK TEA

CHAPTER XXXVIII

WALES

NO RACISM HERE – WE'RE BRITISH
by Gary Willis, political staff

Candidates in the Glanmeurig by-election have denied it's going to turn into a bitter Welsh-versus-English clash.

Launching his campaign yesterday, Conservative Simon Gallier said, "I might have been born in England, but I've spent all my working life in Wales. I believe I stand for the quality of independence which has won worldwide respect for the Welsh nation."

And his Labour opponent, Wayne Davies, said, "The main issue here is the threat to the rural economy and the urgent need for new jobs."

It was a quiet start to a campaign expected to produce electoral fireworks. Everyone here is now waiting for the Welsh nationalist candidate to show his hand . . .

"You really write that, Gary?" asked Ray Wheeler, of the *Mirror*, grinning through Guinness froth.

"Do me a favour," Gary Willis said. Twenty-six years old, the only reporter in the pack with a degree in economics and political science. "Do I strike you as being that inane?"

"You'll get used to it, son," Charlie Firth said, lighting a thin cigar.

"But what's the point in sending us out here if they've made up their minds what the issues are? Or, in this case, what the issues are not."

"Don't be so naïve, mate," Ray Wheeler said. "You really think your rag's going to give any credence to people who figure Great Britain needs fragmenting? Take my advice, send 'em the stuff and try to avoid reading what the buggers do with it."

"And console yourself with one thought." Charlie Firth produced an acrid cough. "However hard it is for you to take, it would have been a bloody sight harder for poor old Giles."

"That," said Ray, "is very true. Does this dump do sandwiches?"

"If it's *egg* sandwiches," Charlie said, "count me out. The Welsh aren't poisoning me a second time."

English was the dominant language tonight in the public bar of the Drovers' Arms, where all five rooms had been taken by representatives of the British national Press. Accommodation, reporters were learning, was not plentiful in this area. Max Canavan, of the *Sun*, had been left with an attic, while Peter Warren, of the *Independent*, couldn't find anywhere in town and would be forced to commute each day from a hotel on the seafront at Aberystwyth.

"Bloody BBC," said Ray Wheeler.

"What have we done now?" Shirley Gillies demanded.

"Only block-booked the best hotel in town."

"Advance-planning." Shirley smiled sweetly. "I shall think of you guys when I'm sitting down to dinner at the Plas Meurig in approximately an hour's time. Still, it's awfully, you know, *homey* here, isn't it."

"Piss off, Shirley," said Charlie Firth.

"The Plas Meurig," Gary Willis said, "is where the Tories'll be having their daily Press conferences, yeh?"

"And the Liberals," Shirley said. "It's a big place. They're at opposite ends. I'm not sure where Labour are, but at least you won't have to get up too early to cover the Plaid pressers, will you?"

"They've got bloody great green signs all over the door of the other bar," Ray Wheeler said. "Listen, are we going to tackle the bugger about this assault stuff tomorrow?"

"Assault stuff." Shirley leaned forward. "Do tell."

"Come on, Shirley," Ray said. "Everybody knows about that."

"The merchant banker he filled in." Charlie bunched a fist. "Think you can buy up all our farms and get away with it, do you, you English swine? Take that."

Charlie pretended to hit Gary Willis.

"Oh, that," Shirley said. "Is it actually true?"

"What's that matter to these buggers?" Gary said.

"Watch it, Willis." Ray held Charlie's beer glass over Gary's head and tilted it threateningly.

Just then a customer put down his glass of lager, detached himself from a small group of companions and leaned across the reporters' table in a conspiratorial fashion, like a trader in dirty postcards.

"Not met him yet then, this nationalist maniac?"

Charlie and Ray favoured this native with their open, friendly, reporters' smiles. They couldn't see him very well because the public bar had bad lighting, as distinct from soft lighting.

"Do you know him, then?" Shirley Gillies asked.

"Surprisingly distinguished-looking, he is. Not, you know, tremendously *tall*. But powerfully built. What the Welsh consider a fine figure of a man."

"Like, short and fat?" said Charlie.

"Stocky," corrected the customer. "A good beard on him, too, but tidy. Dresses casual, like, but not . . . not a *slovenly* man."

"Looks a bit like you, then?" Ray Wheeler said.

"Indeed." The man put out a hand. "Guto Evans, my name."

He took a deep breath and, with visible effort, added, "At your service."

A dark-haired man came in through the bottom door and quietly took a seat at the adjacent table, behind Shirley Gillies.

"Hullo, Berry," Shirley said.

"Hi," he said quietly.

"Where are you staying?"

"Dunno yet. I just got here. Where are *you* staying?"

"Plas Meurig," Shirley said smugly. "Beeb's taken about ten rooms, what with all the telly boys and the technicians. Charlie and Ray are awfully miffed." She lowered her voice. "That's Guto Evans, by the way, the Plaid Cymru candidate. Isn't he perfect?"

"You here on your own, then?" Ray Wheeler said to Guto. "No aides, agent, entourage?"

"My local, this is," Guto told him. "I tend not to require any political advice on which brand of lager to select. Can I get you boys a drink, or is the English Press immune to bribery?"

"Son," said Ray Wheeler, "you've obviously got a big future in politics. Mine's a brandy."

"Come and talk to us," Charlie said. "Tell us what this election is *really* about."

"Off the record, is it?" Guto said dubiously. "I've been warned about you boys."

"Oh, sure," Charlie said. "Don't you worry about a thing, Guto. We're all old hands at this game, except for Gary, and his paper ignores everything he writes anyway." Gary Willis looked very annoyed, and Charlie chuckled and offered Guto a cigar.

"Look, I have to walk back to the Plas Meurig," said Shirley Gillies, "or I won't get my dinner. I'll talk to you again, Guto, OK?"

"I'll walk with you," Berry Morelli said. "Dark out there."

*

"Amazing, isn't it," Shirley said, plump body even plumper in an enormous pink padded ski-jacket. "I mean, it's just a village, really. A big, untidy village."

Seven p.m. The lights of Pontmeurig seemed vague and sparse, suffocating in a cold night mist. There was no moon, no stars.

"You were expecting neon?" said Berry.

Shirley shivered and wobbled. "I suppose not. Still . . ."

"Yeah, I know what you mean. That frontier-town feel."

They walked across the Meurig bridge. No lights were reflected in the river heaving sluggishly below.

"Berry, look, I was awfully sorry about Giles," Shirley mumbled. "We weren't very kind to him, were we?"

"Kind?"

"It's horribly ironic, though, isn't it, that we're all out here and he's . . . I mean, I was picturing him in that pub. He'd have been centre stage, holding forth, correcting our pronunciation of Welsh names. Absolutely in his element."

"Yeah."

"I mean, isn't it just so *cruel*?"

They walked down from the bridge and after a few yards there was a right turning, a sweeping drive and pillars supporting illuminated AA and RAC signs. In the middle distance, a flood-lit façade, a colonial-style verandah. The Plas Meurig Hotel. Two-star.

"Thanks, Berry. I don't think I would've enjoyed walking down here alone. Are you here for the duration?"

He shook his head. "Two days."

"So where are you going to sleep tonight?"

"This an invitation, Shirley?" He was being polite.

"Gosh . . ." Shirley simpered. "I suppose it is rather a cold night to spend in one's car. But I think not, really. Not at the *start* of a campaign. I generally prefer to let the excitement build a little before I start to let myself go."

Shit, Berry thought sourly, heading back over the bridge. This was what they meant by election fever?

The thought of even attempting to spend a night in an Austin Healy Sprite made Berry quicken his pace. It hadn't occurred to him that accommodation might turn out a problem.

What he didn't want was to stay in the same establishment as Firth and Wheeler and those guys. He was here on a mission, and it didn't have anything to do with politics.

He speeded up, seeking to stride through his own sadness and guilt, but they were frozen around him in the mist. It had made big, deep razor-slits in his life, this thing. Might have cost him the only person who could still make him laugh.

"Well, really, it's no good, is it?" Miranda had said as he brought down the lid of his suitcase. For once, being low-voiced, low-key, absolutely and uncharacteristically serious. Sitting on a hard wooden chair well away from the bed.

"Honestly," she'd said. "I'm terribly, terribly sorry about your friend."

"But?"

"But I'm not sure I want to be associated with a really crazy person any more."

So, there it was. The bottom line. The boy's neurotic.

"Listen, maybe you're right." Spreading his hands, appealing for some understanding. "Like, I can't say if I'm crazy. How can I know that? I just have to go find out. I got no choice. Not now."

Miranda had looked about as sad as she was capable of looking. Berry had made her take his key in case she needed a nice central place to sleep, throw wild parties.

"Oh God," Maybe a spark of her old self. "I've got the awful feeling I once played this scene in a World War One spoof at the Edinburgh fringe. Go away. Go and play with your ghosts, Morelli. Your *Welsh* ghosts."

Walking back now into this one-horse town in search of some place to sleep. Solitary like Clint Eastwood in a spaghetti Western. Except Clint was tough, needed no friends and no reassurance. Also Clint knew he was not neurotic.

Berry Morelli stared savagely down the underlit street. It was just about the last place anybody could imagine being part of Britain. Sunk so far into its own private gloom that, when people moaned about the place, they moaned in a language nobody outside even wanted to understand. Some deep irony there. He wondered what it would be like for whoever won this election, sitting up there in the Mother of Parliaments, representing *this*. Honourable Member for Shitheap, Wales.

Berry chuckled cynically to himself. As the evening advanced, the town could almost be said to be filling up with people. A Land-Rover disgorged four men and a woman into the main street. Two kids on motor bikes cruised down the street, circled the castle car park and then cruised back. Night life in Pontmeurig. A black-haired woman in a white mac glanced at Berry as she walked past. She had an oval face and heavy eyelids and she looked no more happy than he might have expected, given the surroundings. He wondered if she was a hooker, but decided not.

CHAPTER XXXIX

She poured another cup of tea, having a sour, perverse kind of competition with herself to see how strong she could make it, and how strong she could drink it.

Outside the window it was not Saturday night in Pontmeurig, but it *looked* like Saturday night. That is, there were more than half a dozen people on the streets, the town having come alive in the hour after nine o'clock.

They weren't all here for the by-election. The sudden excitement had brought out local people, hoping perhaps to catch sight of some half-famous politician, here to campaign for Simon Gallier or Wayne Davies. Tomorrow night, two of Plaid Cymru's MPs would be here to support Guto. Big deal, she thought.

Knowing that really she ought to be throwing herself into this campaign, knocking on doors, scattering leaflets. Support your local boy and your local party, you know it makes sense.

Her hands tightened on the window ledge. Streetlight was washing in the pits and craters of a face beneath the lamp.

Bethan drank some dark tea, which was horrible and burned her mouth. It seemed as if every time she looked out of her window she saw one or both of the boys who'd attacked Giles. Shambling out of the Drovers' or into the tobacconist's that Guto's parents used to own. Grinning at each other. Arrogant, like crows.

Or perhaps it wasn't them at all. She didn't trust her own perceptions any more.

*

This morning she had been to County Hall in Carmarthen to see an assistant in the office of the Director of Education. She had asked for Roy Phillips, who was nice and had helped her in the past and who could be relied upon at least to give her a sympathetic hearing. But Roy had taken early retirement, she'd been told. They'd sent her a chisel-faced young man with rimless glasses, like a junior officer in the Gestapo, and she hadn't known where to begin.

Eventually, Bethan had made herself say it, and the junior officer had leaned back in his leather swivel chair and blinked.

"Mrs. McQueen . . . I hardly know how to react. Have you discussed this with the parents?"

"No. They would, naturally, object strongly. Parents always do."

He was looking urbane and half-amused. They were speaking Welsh.

"I confess, this is the first time such a proposition has ever been put to me by a head teacher. I find it rather extraordinary."

"The circumstances are fairly unique. The village is very enclosed. Too self . . . self-absorbed. I've been convinced for some time that the children need exposure to a wider culture. All I am asking is that it should go on the next list. That the possibility should be debated at county level."

"You are aware that this was mooted some years ago, when we were particularly short of money." He had probably still been at university at the time, Bethan thought. "And there was an enormous row. If you remember, the committee decided that this was a good school with a terrific record . . . And, of course, there was the question of transportation in winter."

"I remember, but . . ."

"And now, with the roll approaching a reasonably healthy level for a rural area, the prospect of fifty pupils in a year or two, you come here – one of our, ah, brightest head teachers – to say you think your school should be closed down."

"Yes." Bethan had stuck out her jaw, determined. "I don't think it's educationally viable. I used to believe in small schools. I no longer consider them valid. Not this one anyway."

"Extraordinary," he said. "You would be putting yourself out of a job."

"Yes."

"I think you should put all this in writing, Mrs. McQueen."

Oh God, Bethan thought. What am I doing here? He thinks I'm off my head.

The education official was peering at her over his glasses in the manner of a far older and more experienced man. Bethan hated him already.

"I'm wondering," he said, "if there isn't something more to all this. How do you get on with the other teacher? Mrs. Morgan, isn't it?"

"I am sorry to have troubled you," Bethan said tightly, in English. "You are right. Perhaps I'll put this in writing to the Director."

"It would be best."

She'd left then, her dignity in shreds. She hadn't gone back to the school. Could not face Buddug – who, she felt, would know exactly where she had been and why.

Bethan had gone straight home – just over an hour's drive – where she'd thrown her coat on the settee, put the kettle on and was plugging in the electric fire when the phone rang. It was a welfare adviser in the education department, a woman she knew slightly. They had wasted no time.

"We think you should take two or three weeks off."

"Oh?"

"You've obviously had a very stressful time lately. Finding that body. And the man who . . . Why don't you go and see your

258

doctor? Get him to give you something to help you relax. Some of us thought you went back to work rather too soon after your husband died."

"What about the school?"

"Don't worry about that. We've spoken to Mrs. Morgan, and offered her a relief teacher. But she says she can manage very well on her own."

The phone shook in Bethan's hand.

They had rung Buddug. Well, of course they had. They must have rung her within minutes of Bethan leaving Carmarthen. She could almost hear the shrill babble over the phone . . . "Oh, the poor girl . . . yes, very, very sad, I have tried to help her, but it has all been getting on top of her . . . No, indeed, I don't think she is good for the children in this state, not at all . . . Perhaps a different post somewhere would be the answer . . ."

Bethan had flung her coat back on and walked around and around the town in the dark, feeling like a ghost condemned to an endless circuit. Well, she had to do it. She had to try.

Now there was nothing left to try. She'd returned to the flat over the bookshop and made strong tea, her final bitter refuge.

Standing in the window now, watching the town filling up with strangers. New life out there.

Finding that body. And the man who . . .

. . . had been lying face-down among a scattering of books. Black books. Hands frozen like claws. Hands which had torn the books from the shelves in a frenzy, nail marks scored down black spines.

Morgan had turned him over with one hand, effortless. His bloodless lips pulled back in a snarl. Eyes glazed over but still screaming. How could eyes scream? Bethan had turned her head away and run from the house. Run down the path, between the sycamores, leaving the iron gate swinging behind her.

Oh, Giles.

Oh God.

"Where'd the guys go?"

He was addressing the nationalist candidate, Evans. Nobody else in the bar he recognised, apart from a couple of MPs drinking Scotch and examining a map. "Buggered if I know, Keith," one of the MPs was saying. "By tomorrow night, I'll have done my stint, so I couldn't care less."

"Charlie and Ray," said Guto, "and young Gary . . . have gone for a meal. I recommended the Welsh Pizza House." He grinned malevolently. "Serve them right."

Berry Morelli noticed how Guto's beard split in half when he grinned. The guy looked like some kind of caveman.

"American, eh?" Guto said.

"Sure am," Berry said, like an American. "Just great to be in your wunnerful country," he added wearily.

"Yes, I bet," said Guto. "You want to ask me any questions before I get too pissed?"

"No," said Berry, who wasn't expected to file a story the following day, unless something happened – and Addison Walls's definition of "something" usually meant several people dead.

"Good," said Guto. "Bloody shattered, I am. I think I shot my mouth off again."

"I thought that was what politics was about."

Clearly less inhibited in the presence of someone who was neither English nor Welsh, Guto affected a drawling English accent. "'Seeaw! Tell us about yourself, Guto! Why does it say in your Press handout that you're only a part-time lecturer?'" His voice sank bitterly. "Because this is Wales, pal. I could only get a *full*-time lecturer's job in England."

"You wanna drink?" said Berry.

"Aye, why the devil not. Pint of Carlsberg? What can you say, eh? One day in politics and I've had it up to the bloody eyeballs."

"One day in politics is a long time, buddy."

"You know what else they asked me? What was the name of the rock and roll band I played bass guitar with? *What was the name of the flaming band?* Why the hell would they want to know that?"

"You really are new to this game, aren't you?" said Berry.

"Is it that bloody obvious?"

"They had to know the name of the band so they could have it checked out in the morgue."

Guto looked mystified.

"Most members of most rock bands," Berry said patiently, "have stuff in their past that doesn't lie down too easy with a career in politics. Like getting busted for dope, smashing up hotel rooms. Yeah?"

"Ah . . . right," said Guto. "But no. Not me. Once got busted for Woodbines in the school lavatories, I did. But drugs, no."

"Hotel rooms?"

"The hotels in these parts, nobody would notice."

"Mr. Clean, huh?"

"Mr. Bloody Spotless," said Guto. "Well, you know . . ."

"Yeah."

Guto grabbed his pint with both hands. At which point, a thought seemed to strike him and he put the glass tankard down on the bartop and said seriously, "I never asked – are you a reporter?"

Berry started to laugh. He laughed so hard he thought he was going to lose control of his bladder. He laughed so hard people began to stare at him.

"What did I say?" said Guto.

Berry shook his head, tears in his eyes. He was thinking of

261

the po-faced front-bench bastards in the House of Commons. He was thinking of the Energy Secretary making a careful state-ment at the bottom of his manicured lawn in the Cotswolds. He was thinking of his dad and a particular senator.

In the normal way of things, none of this would have seemed funny enough to make him lose control in a public bar.

He wondered, after a few seconds, if what he was really doing wasn't crying.

"I'm sorry," Berry said, getting his act back together. "Yeah, I'm a reporter, but I don't think I came here to report. I think I came to go to a funeral."

Guto said nothing.

"My pal died," Berry said. "Tomorrow he gets cremated."

"Oh Christ," said Guto. "Giles Freeman, is it?"

Berry looked hard at the nationalist guy. What did he know about Giles Freeman? "I'm looking for someplace to stay," he said. "One night, maybe two."

"Every hotel in this town is booked solid," said Guto.

"That's what I heard."

"Giles Freeman, eh?"

"Yep. You knew him? I guess he knew you."

"We met," said Guto. "Just the one time. But memorably. Looking for a posh place, are you?"

"Huh?"

"To stay."

"I'm looking for a bed."

"My mam is feeling aggrieved," Guto said. "She does bed and breakfast all through the summer. Now, when everybody wants to stay in Pontmeurig, I have to tell her: forget it, Mam. What is it going to look like, you taking in party workers or reporters? *English* reporters, for God's sake! Me out there on the hustings and you cashing in. So, very aggrieved she is feeling."

"What's the charge?" Berry noticed Guto was suddenly

looking at him the way business people the world over looked at Americans.

Guto's eyes gleamed. "Thirty-five quid a night?"

"Th . . . ?"

"Big breakfast, mind," said Guto.

Guto's mother was a small, scurrying, squeaky creature with an agonisingly tight perm. In a living room so crammed with little jugs and vases and thousands of polished plates that Berry didn't like to move his arms, she told him seriously that Guto would be the death of her.

"She is delighted, really," Guto said. "She's never had an American to stay. What's your name anyway?"

"Morelli."

"That's an American name?"

"Don't be so rude, Guto," Mrs. Evans snapped. She smiled at Berry and her teeth moved. "We had some Morellis, we did, at the back of us in Merthyr. Do you know Merthyr . . . ?"

"Of course he bloody doesn't, Mam. Listen, Morelli, we can't do hash browns or steak and eggs for breakfast. Well, eggs are OK, but . . ."

Berry told them he was vegetarian.

"Oh dear, oh dear, we haven't any of that," wailed Mrs. Evans, squeezing the corners of her apron in anguish. "What will you think of us?"

"Toast?" said Berry. "Marmalade?"

"An American vegetarian?" said Guto, aghast.

"He'll be the death of me, this boy," said Mrs. Evans.

CHAPTER XL

Berry spent the night under a mountain of blankets in a bed like a swamp. He slept surprisingly well, and, at eight-fifteen on a grey Pontmeurig morning, came down to a table set for one, with a spare napkin. There was thick toast, thin toast and toasted rolls. There were three kinds of marmalade.

"These jars are new," Berry said.

"I sent Guto for to wake them up at the shop," Mrs. Evans explained. "I still don't feel right about it. I can't have you paying for a proper breakfast."

It occurred to Berry that Mrs. Evans did not know she was charging thirty-five pounds a night.

"Guto had to leave early to prepare for his Press conference," she said. "He'll make a terrible mess of it, I know he will. He'll say all the wrong things."

He already did, Berry thought. "He'll be fine," he said.

"Do you think so?"

"Guy's a natural politician."

"He won't win, I'm afraid," Mrs. Evans said. "And then he'll come on with all this bravado. And then he'll drink himself silly."

"They say he has a good chance."

Mrs. Evans shook her head. "Any chances he has he'll ruin. That kind of boy. They offered him a job once, down in Exeter. Head of the History Department. He wouldn't have it. That kind of boy, see."

"This is great," Berry said, munching a slice of toast with ginger marmalade.

"It's not a proper breakfast."

"It's my kind of breakfast," Berry said. "Can you tell me where I find the police department in this town?"

There were two public buildings in Pontmeurig built in the past five years. This morning Berry would visit both. One was the crematorium, the other was the police station.

The police station was so modern it had automatic glass doors.

"Who's in charge here?" Berry said.

"I am," said an elderly police constable behind the latest kind of bulletproof security screen. "So they tell me." His voice came out of a circular metal grille.

"You don't have detectives?"

"Detectives, is it?" The constable looked resentful. "What is it about?"

"It's about what I guess you'd call a suspicious death," said Berry.

The policeman's expression remained static. He picked up a telephone and pointed to some grey leather and chrome chairs. "Take a seat, my friend," he said. "I'll see if Gwyn Arthur's arrived."

Above the security screen, the digital station clock was printing out 8:57 a.m.

The huge oak hatstand was a determined personal touch in Detective Chief Inspector Gwyn Arthur Jones's new office, where everywhere else was plastic or metal or glass and coloured grey or white. Berry decided the Chief Inspector might be the only guy in the CID who still wore a hat.

"I can appreciate your concern," Gwyn Arthur said. "I can even understand your suspicions." He spread his long fingers on the plastic of his desktop. "But none of us can argue with a post mortem report."

He took an envelope from a drawer of the desk. "You realise I don't have to show you this."

"Good of you," Berry said.

"Trying to be cooperative I am. As I say, I can understand your suspicions."

Before consenting to discuss Giles Freeman, the Chief Inspector had spent a good ten minutes lighting his pipe and asking Berry a lot of questions about himself. Casual and leisurely, but penetrating. He'd examined Berry's ID and expressed considerable curiosity about American Newsnet before appearing to accept that Berry's interest in this case was personal, as distinct from journalistic.

"This is the autopsy report, yeah?"

"You can skip the first three-quarters if you aren't interested in things like what your friend had for breakfast on the day he died. Go to the conclusion."

"I already did," said Berry. "Some of these medical terms elude me, but what it seems to be saying is that Giles died of a brain tumour. Which is what we were told."

"Indeed," said Gwyn Arthur. For a Welshman, he was surprisingly tall and narrow. He had a half-moon kind of face and flat grey hair.

"I don't get it."

"What don't you get?"

"This stuff. These . . ." Berry held up the report. "This mean bruising, or what?"

"More or less. Abrasions. Consistent with a fall on a hard surface. Consistent also, I may say, with a blow. Which occurred to the doctor who examined him in the hospital and who passed on his suspicions to us."

"He died in hospital?"

"No, he died at his home. Let me explain from the beginning."

"Yeah," said Berry. "You do that."

Gwyn Arthur Jones talked for twenty minutes, puffing his pipe and staring down at his fingers on the plastic desk. He talked of the doctor's suspicions that Giles had been in a fight and Giles's insistence that he'd fallen in the Castle car park.

"Which, considering the state of his clothes, was plausible enough. And was not something we could contest as, if there was another protagonist, we have not found him. Or her – who can tell these days? And I would add that the doctor did suspect at the time, from the way Mr. Freeman was behaving, that there might have been brain damage. He wanted to make an appointment at Bronglais Hospital in Aberystwyth, but your friend flatly refused and discharged himself."

Berry smiled. "Sounds like Giles."

"They parted with some acrimony. Personally I think the doctor ought to have exercised his prerogative to prevent your friend from driving. Still, he appears to have made it home, without mishap, to Y Groes. Where, it seems, his luck ran out."

Claire Freeman, who told the police she knew nothing of Giles's fall, had been out when he arrived home. She was not expecting him back from London until that evening.

Gwyn Arthur said, "Why did he come home early, do you know?"

Berry shrugged. "Any chance he had to get out of London, he took it. He was kind of obsessed with Y Groes – with having this bolthole, you know?"

Gwyn Arthur sighed. "It is a common aberration. Among the English."

"So what happened?"

"There is a schoolteacher in Y Groes. It seems she had become quite friendly with Mr. and Mrs. Freeman and was giving them lessons in the Welsh language. She was among a group of people who saw him lying in the car park on the Thursday night and went to help him. The following day, Mrs. McQueen – that's the teacher – learned that your friend had discharged himself from the hospital and gone home. So, in her lunch break, she went up to his house to see if he was all right. She knocked and got no reply, so she looked through the downstairs windows and saw a man's body, in a collapsed state, on the floor of one of the rooms. She went to the pub for help and two of the customers went back with her and broke down the rear door."

Berry was picturing the judge's house, the back porch near the window he'd prised open with a screwdriver on a late summer's afternoon.

"Mr. Freeman had probably been dead for over an hour by the time they got to him."

Gwyn Arthur took another envelope from a drawer. "Do you want to look at these?"

"What are they?"

From the brown envelope Gwyn Arthur pulled a dark-grey folder, about six inches by eight, on which was printed, in black, the words DYFED-POWYS POLICE.

"As I say, it did look somewhat suspicious at first. Mrs. McQueen telephoned the police. I drove across, with the scenes-of-crime officer. These photographs were taken before the body was moved."

Berry felt a little sick, tasted ginger marmalade. He opened the dark-grey folder.

"They would have been produced at the inquest, had there been one," said Gwyn Arthur.

The pictures were in colour. They'd been taken with a flash.

Berry flinched.

Giles's lips were drawn back into a twisted parody of a grin. Both eyes were open, the left one purple and black. The bruising spread down one side of Giles's face and mingled with the freckles.

Another picture was taken from further back and higher up, like the photographer had been standing on a chair.

"Shit," Berry breathed.

It showed Giles sprawled crookedly, arms extended. All around him were scattered black books. One had its binding partially torn away, and curling pages lay around.

Tissue-thin. Berry could hear the pages whispering.

Next to Giles's head was a red dragon's head, spitting faded, threadbare fire into the dead man's right ear.

"The study," Berry said, going cold. "He died in the study."

"You have been in this house?"

"Once," Berry said. "Just once. What happened to the books?"

"He appears to have had some kind of, er, final fit, should I say? Obviously grabbed at the shelves to try and prevent himself falling. Dragged out the books. Quite a frenzy."

"So you ordered an autopsy."

"Naturally. The state of the room suggested a possible struggle. Oh, yes, we had the portable incident room on standby, I can tell you. But by teatime it was clear we had all overreacted. These things happen."

"Brain tumour."

"It had been forming for – well, who knows how long. Weeks, months, years? His wife tells us he had been suffering from very severe headaches. Mrs. McQueen confirms this. Perhaps, you yourself . . ."

"No. He never mentioned headaches."

"You see, with a condition like this, his apparent black-out in the car park . . . Hit his head on a car bumper, he said. All consistent. It is a great tragedy, but that's all it is. Natural causes. No inquest. Unless there's something you feel you can add?"

"No," Berry said. "Nothing I have to add. Thanks, Inspector."

Gwyn Arthur Jones put the slim photo-album back in its envelope. "I'm very sorry."

"One thing," Berry said. "His wife, Claire."

"Quiet little girl," said Gwyn Arthur.

"Where was she when they found Giles?"

"My, you are a suspicious chap," said Gwyn Arthur with a half-smile. "Mrs. Freeman was quite a short distance away, at a friend's house, as it turns out. Mrs. Dafis, is it? I don't know without looking up the statement. Obviously she feels very bad about not being there when her husband arrived home and him dying like that, on his own. I hear the funeral is today."

"You going?"

"Well, see, I don't mean any disrespect, but not appropriate, is it, now?"

"Guess not."

"See, even if he'd gone to Bronglais, as the doctor wanted, the chances are it would have been too late, the size of that bloody thing. Any time he could have gone."

"Malignant? I was kind of shaky on the big words."

Gwyn Arthur's pipe had gone out. He laid it on the grey plastic desktop and looked at it.

"As the devil," he said. "As the bloody devil."

CHAPTER XLI

They came in from the Lampeter end, George twice stopping to consult the map, slowing at every signpost.

Terribly galling, because he was normally such a fast driver, often recklessly so in his wife's opinion.

"Pretty obscure place," George grunted. "Don't want to get it wrong."

"You don't want to get there at all," Elinor said icily.

"Elinor, I still say . . ."

"And *why* do you think we weren't told?" Elinor demanded. "Because I didn't tell her about *his* death. As simple as that."

"I can't believe," George said, slowing the Volvo for another signpost, "that she would be quite so petty."

"You mean, not so petty as me?"

"That is *not* what I said. Elinor, for Christ's sake, will you stop this."

"We can't be far off," Elinor said and affected a shudder. "I can feel it somehow."

George sighed and kept quiet. He was a rumpled man with hair of nicotine and white. He'd never really taken to his son-in-law, she thought. George avoided people in high-profile jobs. He wasn't a high-profile person. He'd never minded his daughter being a photographer, though, because the photographer was the one person guaranteed always to be *behind* the camera.

She was like him in a way. Claire. George's daughter. Wife of Elinor's dead son-in-law.

271

The shock, for Elinor, had been quite stunning. And to chance upon it, without warning, in Giles's own newspaper, spread on the ceramic worktop after breakfast, four brief paragraphs of obituary, a quote from the editor, immense flair . . . terrible tragedy . . . so young . . . will be hard to replace.

Elinor had *liked* Giles. He'd been strong in his opinions, forthright. Whereas George had always been so *grey*. She'd been sure that Giles would, after a few weeks, realise the impossibility of living in Wales and lead Claire back. Lead. That was it. He'd always been a leader. That was what she'd liked about Giles, that staunchly English quality of leadership.

"I don't know where we're going to stay," George was saying. "You do realise there's a by-election on."

"We'll find somewhere," Elinor said, more briskly than she felt. "Just get us there."

"It's four miles," George said. "That's what the signpost said. But you know what they say about Welsh miles."

The aftershock had been the discovery that Giles's funeral was not to be in London. Elinor had learned this by telephoning his paper. She'd phoned the number in Y Groes about twenty times, of course, and got an answering machine, Claire's voice . . . in Welsh! She'd refused to leave a message after the tone. "Claire, I'm sorry, I refuse to leave a message," she'd said once, voice faltering, and hung up, regretful and feeling rather stupid.

At the paper, the political editor said he too was surprised that the funeral was being held in Wales, although with both Giles's parents being dead he supposed there was no special reason for it to be done in London. And with the by-election on, there'd at least be enough reporters out there to make a respectable showing.

Elinor had been glad, at least, to learn that Giles was not to be buried in the churchyard at Y Groes. Even the ceremony would not be held there.

And yet she did wonder why.

And still she had not spoken to Claire. Her daughter's reaction on their appearance at the funeral was something she could not even attempt to predict. She accepted that they had not parted on the best of terms, but for the girl to avoid her own mother at a time when a mother was needed the most . . .

George had taken a hopelessly circuitous route and they had turned into the road linking Aberystwyth and Pontmeurig, entering the grim valley of the disused lead mine.

Feeling at once sorrowful, offended and inadequate, Elinor experienced the pinprick of a small tear. Her daughter was a widow. A widow and childless.

"I suppose she'll marry again," George said suddenly, as if he'd picked up her thoughts. Which was something he never did, being far too insensitive.

"What do you mean?"

"She's young. I suppose if she stays out here, there'll be lots of chaps . . . that is, I mean . . ."

"Stays?" Elinor's body went as rigid as the stark towers of the lead mine. "Stays *here*? Are you *quite* mad?"

Guto was in deep shit.

Berry had seen it coming, a whole dump-truck load. Guto underneath, apparently oblivious of the danger.

The man steering the dump truck, one sure finger on the wheel, was F. C. W. "Bill" Sykes, Political Editor of the *Daily Telegraph*, one of fourteen reporters and two TV crews, ranged in a three-quarter circle around the candidate. Television lights were belching hot glare into the makeshift gladiatorial arena in the shabby lounge of the Drovers' Arms.

They were mob-handed now, no longer the inoffensive affable guys in the public bar last night. Notebooks and pocket cassette machines next to the cups at their elbows. No alcohol, just hard caffeine. They meant business.

Berry Morelli had covered one British by-election before and knew they were basically all the same: every morning, for about a fortnight, each of the political parties would hold a Press conference with the candidate and some heavy back-up from Westminster – a Minister or a Shadow Minister or, on perhaps one occasion, the party leader. In Plaid Cymru's case, Berry guessed, the leader would show up pretty often, on account of the party had only three MPs to pull out.

They must be saving the big guns for later. Guto was doing his first conference solo, accompanied by only one minder – Plaid's General Secretary, a diffident guy in tinted glasses. This afternoon they'd be out on the streets, canvassing, pressing the flesh, as they put it. And then, each night there'd be public meetings to address.

Hard grind.

And this morning, the baptism of fire.

It started with a question about an act of vandalism perpetrated by the Welsh Language Society against a leading high-street building society which had been unwise enough to refuse a mortgage application in Welsh.

"Ah, well," Guto explained, "they are youngsters with a mission and sometimes they get carried away."

"Usually by the police," Ray Wheeler said from the table nearest Guto's. There was laughter.

"All right then, old boy," rumbled Bill Sykes, "While we're on the subject of brushes with the law . . ."

He was unfolding a cutting from Wales's national newspaper, the *Western Mail*.

"Let's get this one out of the way, eh?" Sykes said kindly. "Clear the air. This business of you being questioned by the constabulary about minor injuries inflicted on some poor chap from

London who'd had the temerity to buy himself a farmhouse near here. Small incident in a pub, I believe."

"*This* pub, Bill," Charlie Firth said. "May even have been this very room. This is where they hold the auctions, isn't it?"

"Was it *really*?" said Sykes, as if he didn't know. "Anyway, let's polish it off now, shall we? Then we can all have a nice peaceful campaign. What exactly happened, Mr. Evans?"

The room fell into a hush.

What the hell was this? Mr. Clean? Mr. Bloody Spotless? Berry caught Guto's eye and raised an eyebrow.

Guto appeared unconcerned.

"Well, you know," he said to the silent, expectant Press, "I feel a bit offended. I cannot understand why you boys are concentrating on this one little incident. Here I am, the party hard-man, scarcely a night goes by without I don't beat up an Englishman . . ."

The head of the General Secretary of Plaid Cymru swivelled through ninety degrees. Berry couldn't see his eyes behind the tinted glasses but he was pretty sure that here was one worried man.

". . . and you pick on the one occasion when I am standing by that very bar across the hall, minding my pint of Carlsberg, and suddenly I am at the centre of a most regrettable kerfuffle for the sole reason that I happen to be in the path of a gentleman who falls off his stool."

There was a hoot of derision from the floor.

He's on a tightrope here, Berry thought. These guys catch him out in a lie, he's finished. He was surprised to find himself caring, just slightly, that Guto's campaign should not come to an ignominiously premature conclusion. Even if the guy *was* staging the bed-and-breakfast scam of the century.

"Then why did the police find it necessary to question you?" demanded Gary Willis.

Berry could see one of the TV cameramen going in tight on Guto's face. He could see Shirley Gillies urgently adjusting the level on her tape-recorder.

"I think perhaps," said Guto, glancing across the room, maybe not so sure of himself now, "that you should direct that question at my good friend, Chief Inspector Gwyn Arthur Jones. Not for me to answer on his behalf, is it?"

Playing for time, Berry thought. But these guys have all the time in the world.

"Come now," said a rat-faced reporter Berry didn't recognise. "Let's not evade the issue. The inference is that you feel so strongly about English people buying up all the best property in these parts that you're liable to lose your temper when faced with a blatant example of . . ."

"I think . . ." Guto's voice was raised.

"I think perhaps you should give the question rather more serious consideration before you answer, Mr. Evans," said Bill Sykes with magisterial menace.

"Come on, Guto," Charles Firth said. "Let's have the truth."

He's had it, Berry thought sadly. They're gonna rip him apart.

Guto raised a hand to quell the murmurs. "I think we can resolve this very minor issue . . ."

"Not minor for you," somebody said.

". . . if I introduce you to a friend of mine."

At the back of the room, a metal-framed chair fell with a clang as a man got to his feet. "Terribly sorry," they heard, a kind of Chelsea purr. "I do seem to have a knack of knocking furniture over in this place."

Everybody turned, including the TV cameramen. Everybody except for Berry, who was standing at the back of the room next to the guy who'd deliberately knocked his chair over.

And was therefore the only one to see Guto expelling a mouthful of air in manifest relief before his beard split in delight.

You bastard, Berry said under his breath. You smart son of a bitch.

"I was bloody worried for a minute or two, though," Guto confessed to him outside. "Couldn't see a thing for those flaming lights. I thought, Christ, what if he's not there? What if he was pissing up my leg all the time?"

The reporters had shuffled off to the Plas Meurig for the next two party Press conferences. They were almost in carnival mood. Berry had watched amazed as Bill Sykes had shaken Guto by the hand and Ray Wheeler had patted him on the shoulder. Suddenly they love the guy, Berry thought. He turned it all around.

The merchant banker from London – the guy who'd bought the farm and a bruised nose – had raised a hand to Guto, politely rebuffed the exhortations from the Press to elaborate further on the story and slid into the Mercedes waiting on a double yellow line outside the Drovers'.

"I confess," said Guto, "that I am developing a certain respect for the English. He came up to me, you know, after the *Western Mail* ran that piece. No hard feelings, old chap, all this, buys me a drink. Well, both a bit pissed, we were, see, when it happened, and he knew the damage it could do. So he says, look, boy, I'll come along and make a public statement if you like."

"What can I say, Evans? You blew them away."

Guto grinned evilly. "I did, though, didn't I?" He glanced around to make sure the reporters were out of sight, then he leapt up and punched the air. "Oh boy, thank you, English! Thank you, God!"

"You asshole," Berry said. "You . . ."

He fell silent. Around the corner came a hearse driven by a man with a bald head who nodded at Guto as he passed. Apart from the bald man, the hearse was empty.

"Gone to fetch your mate," Guto said.

Berry nodded. "How far's the crematorium from here?"

Guto took off his Plaid Cymru rosette and put it in a pocket of his jacket. He was wearing the black tie he'd borrowed from Dai Death. "Not far," he said. "We can walk."

CHAPTER XLII

The funeral service for Giles Robert Freeman was pathetically brief. A throwaway affair, Berry Morelli thought, compared with old Winstone's London send-off.

The entire business took place in the new Pontmeurig crematorium, the first the town had ever had, Guto explained. Built because, when attempting to extend the local cemetery, the council had hit a massive shelf of hard rock which meant that any future graves would have had to be dug with dynamite.

At the end of a wooded lane behind the hospital, the new crematorium looked, from the outside, like a small factory with two discreet steel chimneys hardly hidden by recently planted trees, especially in December.

The chapel inside was maybe a third full, mainly due to the Press contingent. Reporters had filed in, fresh from the Conservative Simon Gallier's conference, as the organ drone began. Only a handful of people had been in place when Guto and Berry had arrived. Berry didn't recognise any of them at first, although a young woman in a black suit and gold earrings looked vaguely familiar.

The minister had begun the service before Berry realised that another woman, sitting in the front row two or three yards from the coffin must be Claire Freeman.

He'd met Claire maybe a couple of times, never spoken much with her. She was the quiet type.

Now he was staggered by how different she looked. And it

wasn't only her hair, which he remembered as blonde and was now almost black.

He wondered if poor old Giles would recognise her. And then wondered why that thought had come to him.

The coffin of pale pine sat on a plinth covered in black velvet. Would it slide away when the moment came, or just slowly sink? Berry looked at the coffin and tried to banish the image of Giles with his empurpled eye and his hands clawing at the black books.

Not meant to be there, the English.

Giles would be here for ever now, filtered into the Welsh air through the steel chimneys.

But why not a mellow grey stone in a corner of the church-yard at Y Groes, where wild flowers grew and the air was soft with summer even when it wasn't summer?

The minister was a young guy with what Berry now recognised as a local accent. Each word was enunciated in that rounded, robust Welsh way which still didn't cover up the obvious fact that the minister didn't know a damn thing about Giles. When you listened to the words, rather than the music of the words, you realised it was just a bunch of platitudinous crap which could have applied, Berry thought, to some John Doe they'd pulled out of the river.

There was just one hymn. An English hymn that Berry had never heard before. As the congregation sang, with little gusto, he read the words on the flimsy service sheet they'd been handed.

Love is kind and suffers long
Love is meek and knows no wrong.

What did this have to say about Giles Freeman? Anything at all?

Berry began to feel angry. Was this how it ended? They just

signed the guy out, quick as they could, and drew a neat line underneath. Would they give him a plaque somewhere: Giles Freeman, immigrant, didn't last long?

He looked over at Claire. She wore a plain, black dress and no jewellery apart from a heavy Celtic cross around her neck. Over the back of her chair was slung a faded, green waxed jacket, the kind Giles used to wear. It didn't seem like a tribute.

Claire's blonde hair, the couple times he'd met her, had always been neatly trimmed, cut close to the skull. Her new dark hair was longer and wilder. And Berry thought she seemed taller somehow, maybe the way she carried herself.

Although she wore no make-up that he could detect, she had with her a glamour he didn't recall.

Each time he looked at Claire he noticed that the other woman, in the black suit and the earrings, seemed to be looking at her too. He remembered where he'd seen this woman now. In the street last night. The one he'd wondered if she was a whore. He felt bad about that now; she didn't strike him that way at all today.

"Who's that?" he whispered to Guto. "Woman in the earrings."

Guto looked at him suspiciously. "It's Bethan," he whispered back. "Bethan McQueen."

"Ah," said Berry. The schoolteacher referred to earlier by Chief Inspector Gwyn Arthur Jones.

As the congregation sank down after the hymn, he heard the sound of stiletto heels on the chequered tiles at the entrance, and then a slim woman of sixty or so came in, followed by a harassed-looking man tucking the end of his tie inside his jacket. There was a black smudge on his forehead. They sat across the aisle from Berry. The woman did not look at the man. But, after a short while, she too began to look hard at Claire Freeman, as if there was something there she couldn't quite believe.

Berry tried to work out if anyone was with Claire and came to the conclusion that the people nearest her just happened to be occupying those seats.

She was alone, and she didn't look as though she cared.

He searched her face for tearstains, any signs of grief. The face was without expression but calm and womanly and strong.

And sexy? That dark glamour?

Jesus Christ, Morelli. He felt uncomfortable, ashamed. He wanted to be out of here, and then he felt ashamed about that too. Ashamed at the relief he felt at the end, five minutes later, as the coffin drifted away below his eyeline, the machinery working smooth, silent magic under the velvet-covered plinth.

Giles had gone.

Without a sound. Without a word in his memory.

He looked at Guto and saw that Guto was looking at the woman in the gold earrings, Bethan McQueen, who was looking at where the coffin had been and was pale.

Outside, amid the leafless trees, she joined them.

"That's it then," Guto said. "That's the lot. Don't mess about, do they, the English?"

"They mess about as much as anybody," Berry said. "That's what's so . . ."

"I feel very empty," Bethan McQueen was saying. "It wasn't a funeral, it was . . ."

"Waste disposal," Berry said. He kicked morosely at the ornamental light-green, crystalline gravel around the crematorium building.

"Bethan, this is Morelli. He was a friend of Giles Freeman." Guto turned to Berry. "Bethan was teaching him Welsh."

"Without great success, though, I am afraid," Bethan said, solemnly shaking hands with Berry.

Reporters came out in a bunch, Charlie Firth taking out one of his thin cigars, Ray Wheeler saying, ". . . down the pub and give the poor sod a decent wake, eh?"

The sixtyish couple hung around the doorway, apparently waiting for someone. The woman pointed at the man's forehead and he took out a handkerchief and wiped away the black mark.

"What did you mean," Bethan said to Berry Morelli, "by waste disposal?"

"I wouldn't mind so much, but the bloody thing was serviced a fortnight ago," George Hardy said. "I don't suppose you happened to notice a Volvo garage in the town."

"You fool." Elinor's features were pinched with contempt. "Is it likely?"

"Suppose not. I wish she'd come out. Get this over."

"All you've ever wanted, George, is to get things over."

Claire did come out then. She was with the minister. They shook hands and then spoke briefly in Welsh. The minister went back into the crematorium. Claire approached her parents.

"I wondered if you would come," she said.

The sky had darkened, with a warning of rain on the gathering wind.

"Hello, Claire," said George. "We had a dreadful journey and then the car broke down two miles from here and we had to be towed in. You look marvellous, doesn't she, Elinor?"

George always came out with the wrong things, or the right things in the wrong order. But what were the right things in this situation? How were you supposed to approach a daughter who had deliberately kept you in the dark about the sudden death of her husband?

And who was not the daughter you remembered.

"Yes," Elinor said. "She looks . . . well."

Claire kissed her father and looked calmly at her mother.

Elinor could stand it no longer. "Oh, Claire ..." Face crumbling, though the muscles were fighting it. "Why?" She was furious with herself for this.

Claire stepped back. The wind caught her dark hair, which seemed three times as long and dense as Elinor remembered it.

"I wrote to you," she said. "The letter's probably waiting for you at home."

"Why didn't you *phone*?" Elinor's eyes were glassy with frozen tears. "I learned about it in the *newspaper*, for God's sake!"

Claire said, "I'm sorry. I find this difficult to explain, but I could not invite you here. If you were going to come it had to be your decision."

She's so remote from us, Elinor thought. Look at her, with her shaggy mane and her faraway eyes.

"How do you feel, darling?" George was saying. "Are you all right?"

Claire smiled with dignity and composure.

"I am adjusting," she said.

"We should offer our condolences to Claire, I guess."

"I think you'll find," Bethan said, "that she doesn't need your condolences." She turned her back on the chapel entrance. "I have to go. I'm sorry."

Berry watched her walk away down the gravel path. "I think I need to talk to her."

"I don't think so," Guto said.

"She was the one who found Giles, right?"

"Listen, Morelli, leave her alone, she's had problems."

"*Giles* had problems."

"I know, but she cannot help you. Her husband died, see, a few months ago, of leukaemia. She has not come to terms with that. Her nerves are not good, they've taken her off work."

Plaid's bearded hard-man seemed oddly ill-at-ease, Berry thought.

"I've known her a long time. Fond of her, see."

Clearly, Berry thought.

Plaid's General Secretary appeared at Guto's elbow. Away from the TV lights, he'd taken off his tinted glasses. "You have twenty minutes to get some lunch, Guto, then we're off to Eglwys Fawr."

"Eglwys Fawr?" Gusto was dismayed. "That's practically North Wales. We really have to start by canvassing the barbarians?"

"Work North to South of the constituency, I thought. Then back again."

"You are the boss," Guto conceded. "See you tonight, Morelli?"

"Sure, but I may have to barter over the bill. Or maybe tell the tabloid boys how much you're charging."

"You wouldn't . . ."

"Try me."

Guto scowled at him and followed the General Secretary down the crematorium drive. Claire Freeman and the older couple walked past Berry; none of the three even looked at him.

At the bottom of the drive Guto turned and called back, "Remember what I said about Bethan, Morelli. I don't know what you want here, but she can't help you, OK?"

Berry was suddenly alone on the ludicrous green gravel in front of the modern disposal plant that ate Giles Freeman.

A line of Bob Dylan's went through his head, something about pitying the poor immigrant, who wishes he'd stayed at home.

He tried to analyse how he felt. Whether he was out of his mind or there was something happening here. He couldn't get a handle on any of it. All too . . . Words like amorphous, nebulous and numinous came into his head. Crazy stuff.

Rain began to tumble on him, and he ran down the drive and back into the town.

CHAPTER XLIII

This, Elinor thought, frozen into silence, could *not* be happening.

The ghastly little pointed spire loomed up in the centre of the windscreen and she almost screamed in revulsion.

"Rather pretty, really," George said, and Elinor shrivelled him into the back seat with a blowlamp glare.

Claire drove the Land-Rover like a man, spinning the huge utility steering wheel, dark hair bouncing as she tossed the big vehicle through the gears. As though she were a farm girl who'd been driving Land-Rovers and tractors most of her life, Elinor thought in dismay.

It was, of course, all George's fault.

When the garage in Pontmeurig had said it would take a day, perhaps two, to get the parts, he ought to have told them to forget it and had the vehicle towed to the nearest Volvo dealer, no matter how far away that was.

But not George.

Not compliant, feeble George.

Elinor and Claire had been drinking dreadful instant coffee in some dismal teashop, saying stiff, formal things to each other when George had returned from the garage with the bad news.

"Problem is, there's nowhere to stay in this town," he'd said. "By-election, you see."

And then, without even looking at Elinor, he'd turned automatically to his daughter and said . . .

Actually asked her, without even thinking . . .

"Don't suppose there's any chance of you putting us up for the night, is there, Claire?"

Elinor had wanted to pour her coffee over his head.

But she could not help noticing that, for the first time, Claire had appeared discomfited. "I'm not sure that would be wise."

Elinor was damn sure it wouldn't be wise, having long ago sworn never to set foot in that abominable house again.

"Well, unless you can lend us a tent," George said with a silly laugh, avoiding his wife's blazing gaze, "I don't know quite what we're going to do. The garage chappie said Aberystwyth was about the nearest place we could hope to get in, and apparently several of the hotels there are closed for the winter. Bloody inconvenient."

"It's absurd," Elinor said.

And then Claire had said, "Look, if it's only for one night, perhaps –"

"No!" She couldn't stop herself.

"I was thinking of the *Tafarn*," Claire said. "The village inn."

And now the Land-Rover was rattling down from the hills, out of the forestry, Elinor next to Claire in the front, George in the back. Claire had told them she'd acquired the second-hand farm vehicle from someone called Dilwyn, in exchange for Giles's car. Which Elinor thought was a disgusting thing to do within a few days of his death, as well as a disturbing indication that Claire was now committed to living in a place where a Land-Rover was considered a sensible mode of transport.

A grey squirrel shot out of the hedge, apparently intent on hurling itself under their wheels. Claire ignored it.

"Look out!" Elinor yelled, but Claire neither braked nor swerved.

"You've run over it!"

"Perhaps." Claire didn't even look in the mirror.

Elinor was profoundly shocked. "What's happened to you, Claire? What's *happened* to you?"

"Don't be ridiculous, Mother." Claire tossed her ragged black mane. "They're vermin."

Elinor was hunched in the corner, well away from her daughter, wrapping her arms around herself, shivering inside.

Claire spun the wheel as they rolled out of the trees and past the sign that said simply Y Groes. The lumbering vehicle went across the river bridge with only inches to spare either side. The inn lay before them, and above it reared the church, its squat tower massive from this angle, its weather vane pricking a pale halo in the cloudy sky.

"Stopping raining, anyway," George observed from the back seat.

CHAPTER XLIV

It took Berry all of twenty minutes to find out where Bethan McQueen lived.

First off, he went into the Welsh Pizza House and ordered a plain cheese and tomato from an English guy who wore a white plastic apron. On the apron a drooling red dragon brandished a knife and fork. The pizza was crap, but the guy thought Bethan McQueen might be the girl who lived over the bookstore.

Hampton's Bookshop had a window display featuring the new Ordnance Survey maps, local travel guides and a handful of books – in both English and Welsh – about the history of Wales. Most prominently displayed was a paperback with a man's face superimposed over a map of Wales. The face looked thoughtful and ended in a beard with a forked tip. The book was called *Glyndwr, The Last Prince*. It was by a Dr. D. G. Evans.

"Naw," Berry said aloud. "Couldn't be."

He went in out of the rain.

"Dreadful weather," said an elderly man, looking up from a copy of the *Spectator* spread before him on the counter.

"Could be worse, I guess," Berry said.

"It *was* worse a few nights ago. The river almost burst its banks."

Berry picked up the Glyndwr paperback and turned it over and saw another bearded face in a black and white photograph on the back.

"Holy shit," he said.

"Sold seven copies in the past couple of days," the elderly man told him proudly. "Mostly to journalists more interested in the author than the subject."

Berry put the paperback on the counter with a ten-pound note. "Guess that makes it eight."

"Actually, they're remainders," the bookseller confessed. "Touch of inspiration, though I say it myself. As soon as I heard Plaid'd picked him as the candidate, I rang the publishers and offered to do a deal for however many copies they had left. They were only too pleased, only having managed to get rid of a couple of thousand."

"When'd it come out?"

"Five years ago? Six? Not much interest, you see, outside Wales, in Owain Glyndwr." He wheezed out a laugh. "Actually, not much interest *inside* Wales until now. But that's business. You have to seize the moment. If he wins I'll doubtless flog the lot, if he doesn't I'll still have made a reasonable profit."

Berry said, "Listen, can I ask you . . . Does Bethan McQueen live here?"

"Ah." The bookseller folded the paperback into a brown paper bag and handed Berry his change. "The lovely and intriguing Mrs. McQueen." He pointed to the ceiling. "Up there."

"Intriguing?"

"Oh well." He smiled ruefully. "Beautiful widow living quietly and discreetly. Never any visitors . . . Well, this chap –" he pointed to the Glyndwr books "– on occasion, but never for very long. I'm a terrible old gossip, as you may have gathered, so pay no heed to a thing I say. There's a short alley next to the shop door. Just inside that you'll find another door in a recess. Ring the bell. I don't know if she's in."

"Thanks." Berry stepped out into the rain and then dodged into the alleyway. The door in the recess was plain, no glass, and painted some indiscernible colour. He pressed the bell-push and waited, not able to tell if it was working.

Until the door opened and Bethan McQueen stood there in white jeans and a turquoise sweater of soft wool.

"Mr. Morelli."

"Hi," Berry said, suddenly lost for words. "I, ah . . . I have this feeling we should talk."

"About Giles Freeman?"

"And maybe other things."

Bethan McQueen said, "Did you tell Guto you were coming?"

"Sure did."

"And what did he say?"

"I don't recall the exact words. But he seemed to be indicating that if I bothered you I could expect to have him clean the street with my ass."

Bethan McQueen turned on a small, impish smile. "You had better come up," she said, "while he's safely out of town."

"Tea? Or coffee?"

"Tea, please. No milk."

"I'm glad you said that, I don't think I have any milk. Do you like it strong?"

"Like crude oil," Berry said. While she made the tea he took in the apartment. It looked temporary, like a storage room for furniture that was destined for someplace else. There was a big sofa with a design involving peacocks. He sat in one of a pair of great fireside chairs with loose covers in a floral print. Too big for the room, like the enormous Welsh dresser in honeyed pine. The dresser was empty save for a few books.

As Bethan returned with a tray, two white cups with saucers on it, and biscuits, there came a hoarse crackle from outside and then a tannoyed voice announced:

"THIS IS SIMON GALLIER, YOUR CONSERVATIVE CANDIDATE. I SHALL BE AT THE MEMORIAL HALL AT SEVEN-THIRTY TONIGHT WITH MY SPECIAL GUEST, THE SECRETARY OF STATE FOR TRADE AND INDUSTRY, THE RIGHT HONOURABLE JOHN GORE. I HOPE TO

SEE YOU THERE AND WE WILL BOTH WELCOME YOUR QUESTIONS
ON LOCAL AND NATIONAL ISSUES."

Then the same message – presumably – was repeated, in
Welsh.

"He's English, this Gallier," Berry said, taking a cup and
saucer. "But he's learned Welsh, right?"

"I believe –" Bethan perched on an arm of the sofa "– that he
has been on some sort of crash course. Two weeks' work at a
residential centre. Very intensive."

"Like, they wake you up in the middle of the night, flash a
light in your face and make you answer personal questions in
Welsh?"

Bethan smiled.

"That the kind of course you had Giles on?"

Bethan's smile became a frown. "Don't think me rude." She
looked him hard in the eyes. "But who exactly are you?"

Simon Gallier's speaker-van made a return trip up the street.
"DON'T FORGET. SEVEN-THIRTY AT THE MEMORIAL HALL. AND
MAKE THOSE QUESTIONS TOUGH ONES!"

"That's a tough one," Berry said.

"You do not know who you are?"

He drank some tea.

"Who do people *think* you are?" she asked.

It was the strongest tea he'd ever been served. It had to be at
least a six-teabag pot.

"I'm sorry," he said. "I'm not helping the situation, am I? I,
ah . . . I'm a reporter. I work for an American news agency in
London. Giles was my friend. Originally, what happened was
this guy we both respected – dead now – he told me to dissuade
Giles from throwing everything up and moving to Wales. So I
came out here with Giles – early in the fall this was – to look at
his cottage. And there was . . . something there I didn't take to,
OK? Now Giles is dead. That's it. That's everything. Basically."

292

This was what reporters were supposed to be able to do, reduce the Bible to a paragraph.

And edit all the meaning out of it.

Bethan McQueen drank her tea slowly, watching him.

"Giles was my friend too," she said eventually. "I tried to teach him Welsh, and I failed. It was a disaster. I came to feel that the lessons were doing him harm. When I learned about his . . . tumour, it was as if I had personally, you know . . ."

"Finished him off?"

"Yes."

"That's crazy, Beth."

"Bethan."

"Sorry."

"No, *I'm* sorry. My husband called me Beth. I am being stupid."

"If we're getting into self-flagellation here," Berry said. "Most likely, *I* killed him. I failed to persuade him not to come here. Didn't hardly try. If he'd been in London maybe he'd have gotten some medical attention instead of pushing himself like he did, to move out here in record time, commuting to and fro, all that."

"I don't think that is what you're saying, is it?" Bethan said.

"I'm sorry . . . ?"

"You said you think you might have killed him because you failed to persuade him not to come here. You are implying he died because he came to Y Groes."

"Well, no, I . . ."

"That is not what you were implying?"

"I . . . Shit, I don't know." Berry rubbed his eyes, drank more tea. She was forcing him to say things he hadn't even put into thoughts.

"Look, give me your cup," Bethan said. "I should not have tried to poison you."

"What?"

"Nobody can drink tea as strong as that. Except for me when I am feeling beaten, which is most of the time at present."

Berry held out his cup. "It was wonderful tea. I mean that. Seriously."

"You are joking. I'll make some fresh."

"Listen, forget the tea. Siddown please."

Bethan put her cup and saucer on the floor and sat down on the sofa. She reached forward and flipped the switch on the side of an archaic three-bar electric fire.

"This is kinda hard," Berry said. "It's like we're walking around each other, keeping a distance. Like suspicious dogs. Trying to provoke each other into snapping or something. Listen, how about we go for dinner tonight? Always presuming there's some place other than the Welsh Pizza House where we can actually *get* some dinner."

"I'm sorry. I mean, I really *am* sorry. I have to go to Simon Gallier's meeting. In my role as Guto's secret agent. I have to report back."

Berry thought about this. "Well, would you mind if I tagged along? I have to file some kind of piece to the agency tomorrow. I do need to see this guy Gallier in action."

"All right."

"Good. Maybe we can figure out how to approach this thing. Always assuming there's something that needs to be approached."

"Mr. Morelli, I've lived with this for so long that I don't know who to trust any more."

"Berry, for Christ's sake."

"Bury?"

"As in strawberry. My name."

"Oh."

They stood up. Bethan straightened her sweater.

"I would love to say you can trust me," Berry said. "Only I'm not sure I can trust myself. I'm notoriously neurotic."

She faced him from the other side of the monster sofa with the brilliant peacock fans on it.

She said, "Do you believe Giles died because he came to Y Groes?"

"I . . ."

"It's important. Do you believe it?"

Berry shook his head. "Also, I'm indecisive."

"Well, I believe that Robin . . ."

"Robin?"

"My husband. I believe Y Groes killed Robin. I hate that village, Mr. Morelli. I'd like to see the church fall down and every stone of every building smashed and pounded into the ground."

PART SEVEN

THE NIGHTBIRD

CHAPTER XLV

ENGLAND

Miranda had been absolutely determined not to do this. A clean break was the only way. They simply didn't need the hassle of each other any more.

The problem was she'd got rather pissed on the plane – private plane owned by the company, no expense spared when you were working with these people, lots of Champagne, none of this Sangria nonsense – and the thought of ferrying all her luggage out to Daddy's place had been too tedious.

Besides, the Spanish resort where they'd been shooting – two days for about six seconds – had been a sort of hot Bognor, the kind of location which dictated at least an hour in the shower absolutely as soon as one reached civilisation.

So Miranda let herself into Morelli's flat and made straight for the immersion heater. It was supposed to be one of those rapid ones, but she decided to give it twenty-five minutes, because an hour in the shower was a long time for Morelli's primitive cistern to cope with.

She picked up the mail and put it on his desk. No point in trying to pretend she hadn't been here – Miranda would have been the first to agree that her personal ambience was not the easiest to dispel.

OK then.

She switched on every heater she could find, flung her case into the middle of the floor and stripped off most of her clothes. Sometimes feeling rather cold could be quite a luxury.

Miranda hated Spain. On the other hand, she did rather enjoy doing commercials. So many well-known serious actors were doing them these days that people tended to think that if you were in one you must be a rather respected figure too.

She wandered into the bedroom. Duvet still thrown back. He obviously hadn't returned from Wales. What an utter plonker he was. Always worrying about the effect he might be having on the great cosmic scheme of things, or the effect he ought to be having. "Taking responsibility, kid," was how he'd put it, explaining that you shouldn't eat meat if you weren't prepared to kill your own.

Morelli was a mass of conflicting neuroses. How could anyone be the young Al Pacino on the outside and mid-period Woody Allen underneath?

Miranda marched into the bathroom and ran the shower. She gave it a couple of minutes to heat up and was about to step in when the phone bleeped.

She decided to go ahead regardless, but remembered then how annoying a telephone could be when one was showering – the shower never quite managing to drown out the bleeps. So she decided to unplug the thing. But, of course, curiosity won in the end and she picked it up and affected a Deep South sort of voice.

"Thiyus iyus the Morelli res'dence."

A man's voice, educated, not young, said: "Oh, is that *Mrs.* Morelli?"

"It most certainly isn't!" snapped Miranda, reverting to type.

"Oh dear. Well, would it be possible to speak to Mr. Morelli? I'm afraid this is about the seventeenth time I've tried over the past two days."

"I regret to have to tell you," Miranda said, "that he's in Wales. Please don't ask me why."

"Wales, eh?"

"Wales."

"Well, would you happen to know precisely where in Wales he's gone?"

"Somewhere full of grim mountains and dead sheep, I expect," said Miranda, beginning to feel rather chilly standing there in the altogether. "Would you like to leave a message?"

"Look, if I'm barking up the wrong tree, cut me off or something . . ."

Don't tempt me.

". . . but it wouldn't be a village called Y Groes, would it?"

"Called what? They all sound the same to me."

"Y Groes. Spelt I-Grows."

"Oh, well, look, I believe he has spoken of some such place, yes. But I really couldn't be certain."

"Ah. Do you know if he's staying at the inn there?"

"I can't honestly say where he's staying. Look, can I take a message?" Over her shoulder, Miranda could hear the beckoning patter of the hot water.

"You see, it was about Y Groes that I wanted to speak to him. Are you a friend of his?"

"Friend, ex-lover, confidante – and highly qualified to pass on messages." Come on, you old fool, spit it out.

"Perhaps I should explain . . ."

Must you?

"My name's Peters."

"I'm writing it down."

"Canon Alex Peters."

This has to be a first, Miranda thought morosely. I'm standing here tit-and-bum naked, talking to a vicar.

"I conducted the funeral service for Winstone Thorpe. Perhaps your, er, friend mentioned him."

Miranda barely managed to suppress a groan.

"You see, I was chatting to your friend after the funeral, and he told me how poor Winstone had begged him to discourage young Giles Freeman from making his home in Wales. Of course, I was born and brought up in South Wales and I'm afraid I was rather dismissive about the whole thing. Nonsense, I said. Lovely place, lovely people."

Get on with it! Miranda was grinding her teeth.

"Then, you see, I read about Giles's death, and it said he'd been living at Y Groes, and immediately I thought about Martin Coulson and this awful man Ellis Jenkins."

"I really think I should leave a message for Berry to ring you when he gets back," Miranda said, goose pimples on her arms now.

"You see, I didn't know until I read about Giles's death that we were talking about Y Groes. Which, of course, is where Martin died so tragically a couple of years ago. Do you know the case I'm referring to?"

"I don't think so, but –"

"Died in the church. Twenty-five years old. Dreadful. And then Jenkins refusing to have him in his churchyard. Caused quite a stir in church circles. So I thought I ought to pass this on to Berry Morelli, as he'd seemed rather anxious, a little unsure of what he ought to do."

"Oh, he *always* seems anxious . . ."

"It's probably of absolutely no relevance. Though I confess to being rather curious about where Giles Freeman was eventually buried."

"Well, I'm afraid I really can't help you there," Miranda said. "Look, I'll get Berry to ring you, shall I? What's the number?"

Canon Alex Peters gave her a number. "I'm at Woodstock,

near Oxford. In retirement. Not much else to think about, you see. As I say, probably nothing, but, if he should happen to ring you from Wales, pass on my number, would you?"

"Oh, I will," Miranda said. And then, just a tiny bit curious herself by now. "Look Mr., er – Canon –"

"Peters. Alex Peters."

"Of course, I wrote it down. Listen, I shall probably regret asking this, but why wouldn't they let this chap be buried in the churchyard?"

"Ah, well . . ."

"Yes?"

"Well, because he was English, my dear."

When she got back to the shower it was lukewarm.

Miranda shrieked in rage and frustration.

"God, Morelli," she rasped through her teeth, groping for his bathrobe and discovering he'd taken it with him. "Wherever you are, I hope you're really *suffering* for this."

CHAPTER XLVI

WALES

Elinor said, "I hate this room."

She didn't hate any particular part of the room. She didn't hate the Victorian bed. She didn't hate the deeply recessed window, or the low-beamed ceiling. Or even its size – rather cramped, with that enormous wardrobe.

"I suppose," said George Hardy, with heavy resignation, "that I'm supposed to ask you why you hate the room."

Still wearing her funeral dress, Elinor sat on a corner of the bed, glazed gaze fixed on the window through which she could see, in the late-afternoon light, the rooftops of the cottages opposite the inn, the winter-browned oak woods on the edge of the village and the misting hills beyond.

She was wondering if all this – the car breaking down, having to come here – was fate's fumbling attempt to heal the cuts she and Claire had inflicted on each other.

Wasn't working, though, was it? Anyone could see the wounds had only widened.

"I don't *know* why I hate it," Elinor said.

George said, "I think I shall ask that fellow if I can use his phone, give the garage a ring in Pontmeurig." George pronounced it Pontmoorig. "Make sure the parts will be here tomorrow."

Elinor, distant, still staring out of the window, said, "Should have had it towed away. Back to England, if necessary. We could have taken a taxi."

304

George didn't bother to reply.

Elinor stood up and turned back the covers of the bed to see if the sheets were clean. Unfortunately, they had the look of being freshly laundered. She sat down again, on the edge of the bed.

As she sat down this time, the bed shifted and a floorboard creaked.

"Better ring the office too," George said. "Get them to stall any clients."

"We won't be here for ever, George."

"Can't count on anything these days." Tidy George unpacked two clean shirts and hung them in the wardrobe. "Good job you're so efficient," he said brightly. "Enough clothes here to last the week out."

Elinor was determined not to rise to this bait.

"Handling it awfully well, though, isn't she?" George said.

"What?"

"Claire. I was quite surprised."

And relieved no doubt, Elinor thought. He could never deal with women's tears. Blubbing, he called it once. Only once – she'd almost had his eyes out.

"No, she's a tough girl," George said admiringly. "What d'you think of her new hairstyle? Quite fetching, I thought. I'd almost forgotten what her natural colour looked like."

"George." Elinor dug her nails into the bedspread. "Go and make your phone calls."

The floorboard creaked again as she stood up.

That night must have been an encouraging one for Simon Gallier, Conservative Parliamentary Candidate for Glanmeurig.

There weren't enough chairs in the Memorial Hall in Pont; groups of people were blocking the firedoors and clustered in the passageway to the lavatories.

Novelty value, Berry Morelli thought. It was obviously a real night out for many members of the audience. Most of the men wore suits and ties.

He was standing under the platform, searching the crowd for Bethan McQueen and failing to spot her. Feeling a hand on his shoulder, he turned expectantly.

"We're down here, mate," Ray Wheeler said. "One space left on the Press table."

"Oh. Sure. Thanks." Berry allowed himself to be steered to a chair between Shirley Gillies and Bill Sykes.

"Mind boggles, eh?" Sykes grated. "Bet old Johnny Gore's never pulled a bigger crowd since his wedding. Oh, sorry, John, didn't see you there."

"Evening, Bill," said the Secretary of State for Trade and Industry, leaning across the Press table and then whispering, "Afraid I'm going to be a trifle boring tonight. Don't want to outshine the boy."

"Poor old Johnny," said Sykes, as the Minister hefted his considerable bulk up the three wooden steps to the platform. "Couldn't outshine a ten-watt bulb."

"I was wondering," Berry said, "what ole Winstone would've made of all this. Think he'd've come?"

"Not a hope," said Bill Sykes. "You wouldn't have got Winstone back to Wales for a lorryload of Glenfiddich."

It struck Berry that you could get a hell of a lot of Glenfiddich on a lorry. More than enough to make a cynical old hack overcome his prejudices. He made a mental note to raise this with Sykes when the speeches were over.

There were a few cheers as Simon Gallier stepped onto the platform. He was built like a front-row rugby player, had prematurely greying hair and a shambling, untrimmed moustache like, Berry thought, a badly made yardbrush.

Gallier made a tough, rousing speech, full of commitment to

Wales and the language, a few Welsh phrases scattered strategi-
cally around. When he threw these in, there were odd noises of
appreciation. English immigrants, Berry thought. Token Welsh
wouldn't cut much ice with the locals.

His perception surprised him. He must be getting the measure
of this strange, mixed society.

The Secretary of State for Trade and Industry was indeed,
even by comparison with Gallier, extremely predictable. Almost
as boring as the questions people asked afterwards. Berry suspected most of the questioners were plants. These guys were
preaching to the converted. No opposition here – except, he
thought, amused, for Bethan sitting somewhere back there
discreetly absorbing it all for Guto's benefit. Mata Hari.

"One of Johnny's better efforts, I thought," grunted Sykes as
the Minister sat down for the last time.

"Oh, Berry," a voice breathed in his ear.

As Gallier's applause died, Berry turned to find Shirley Gillies
contemplating him, a bijou smile dimpling her plump, downy
features. She said, "You must be getting really fed up, stuck
in the Drovers' all night." She dipped her eyelashes. "I was
wondering . . . why don't you wander back to the Plas Meurig
for a couple of drinks before turning in?"

The implication was clear.

He couldn't believe it; she was genuinely turned on by all this
shit. Wow. Was there a name for a person who was erotically
stimulated by the cut and thrust – with the emphasis on thrust
– of party politics?

"Thing is, ah, I arranged to see someone later," he said, trying
to sound regretful. "Thanks, though, Shirley."

"Oh, right, OK," said Shirley. "Just a thought."

It was going to be somebody's lucky night. Maybe even Bill
Sykes's, depending how legless the alternatives were around
midnight.

As they stood up, the hall clearing, people talking in bunches, Berry said to Sykes, "When you said Winstone wouldn't come back to Wales, you meant because of the bad time he had covering that story in the sixties, the murder of the two farmers?"

"Ha!" Bill Sykes snapped a rubber band around his notebook. "Winstone never covered that story. He wasn't even born then. Indeed, that's the whole point."

"Huh?"

"Now *there's* a mystery for you, old boy. Remind me to tell you about it sometime, eh?" Bill began to rub his knees. "Not good for the joints, these damn chairs."

"Hey, come on, Bill, t–"

Tell me now, he'd been about to say, but there was a hand on his shoulder again and this time, to his relief – relief and a frisson of something more interesting – the hand belonged to Bethan.

She was wearing her white raincoat, Guto's beautiful spy.

"Can we be seen talking?" Berry said out of the corner of his mouth. "Or should I leave a message in the dead-letter drop?"

"Actually, this is probably the one place we are safe," Bethan said. "If Guto sees us together one of us will need to seek asylum in England."

"Right. Ah . . ." Good a time as any. "I was gonna ask. Guto – Guto and you . . . ?"

"He thinks I need to be protected," Bethan said.

"By him."

"Of course. He thinks living alone is not good for me. He thinks I am in danger of having a nervous breakdown."

"What do you think?"

"I think a nervous breakdown would be quite a relief," Bethan said softly. "Come on, let's go."

*

It was George who made the discovery, just as they were getting ready for bed.

"That's it!" he announced, sitting on a corner of the bed, flinging down a sock. "I'm going to find out what's causing it."

He's drunk too much, Elinor thought. "It's only a loose floorboard," she said.

"Getting on my nerves."

Elinor had more to worry about than a creak. It had been a most unsatisfactory evening.

She'd been almost hopeful at the start – Claire turning up at the inn at around seven, joining them for dinner. Roast lamb, of course. All the Welsh seemed to be able to cook was lamb. George enjoyed it.

There'd been nobody else dining at the inn, theirs the only table with a cloth. The little white-haired licensee had served them himself, reasonably courteously. An opportune time, Elinor had judged, to raise the issue of what was to happen now.

"Why don't you come and stay with us for a while, give yourself time to think things out?"

Claire had told her nothing needed to be thought out and then said, "We'll never agree about this, Mother, you must surely have realised that."

George had said, "Let the girl get over it in her own way." And Elinor had found herself wondering if, for Claire, there was really anything to get over. It was clear their marriage had not been as well founded as she'd imagined.

"I shall come and visit you, of course," Claire said. "Sometimes."

"I should hope so," her father said in his jocular way, his second cigarette burning away in an ashtray by his elbow.

"Knowing how much you would dislike coming to my grandfather's house."

Elinor had felt something coiling and uncoiling in her

stomach. *Tell me I've got it wrong. Tell me you aren't going to stay here . . .*

"Let's just enjoy our meal, shall we?" Claire had said.

Later, in the bar, everyone had greeted Claire in Welsh, switching to English when they saw she was not alone. She'd introduced them to her "friends", a thin man with horrible teeth and a couple, he bearded and hefty, she red-faced with little beady eyes and an awful gappy Welsh smile. All were appallingly friendly to Elinor and George, who was persuaded to play darts and allowed to win.

Not Elinor's sort of evening.

"Hey, look at this –" George had the floorboard up.

"Put the bloody thing back, for God's sake, George –"

"No, look –" He appeared ludicrously unattractive, sprawled on the floor, hair awry, white belly slopping out of his underpants, arm down a hole in the floor.

"Some kind of book, I think. Hang on . . . Here it comes."

George brought it into the light. "Probably a valuable first edition or something. Oh . . ."

The light from the centre of the ceiling fell on an ordinary stiff-backed notebook from W.H. Smith.

"Can't win 'em all," said George. He stamped on the floorboard. "Least I've stopped the damn squeak."

"What is it?" Elinor said, in bed now, wearing a long-sleeved pale-blue nightdress.

George opened the book. "Sir Robert Meredydd," he read. "Thirteen forty-nine to fourteen twenty-one. Can't be *his* notebook, anyway, it's written in Biro. Couple of diagrams, rough sort of plan, pages of unintelligible scrawl. Doesn't look very interesting. Why do you suppose it was under the floorboard?"

"I don't know. And I don't care."

"Probably a bloody treasure map." George laughed and tossed

the book on to his bedside table. "Remind me to give it to that chap Griffiths in the morning."

"I wish it was morning now," Elinor said.

"I don't, I'm bloody tired."

"You're drunk."

"What, on three pints and a Scotch?"

"There's an awful tension in here. In the air. Can't you feel it?"

"Only the tension in my bladder," George said coarsely, pulling on his overcoat. "Excuse me."

As he stumped off to the bathroom across the landing – nothing en-suite in this place – Elinor pulled the quilt around her shoulders and picked up the notebook to take her mind off how much she hated this room. The book was not particularly dusty, obviously hadn't been down there long.

It fell open at the reference to Sir Robert Meredydd and Elinor saw that the date 1421 had been underlined twice and an exclamation mark added.

She looked at the diagrams. One appeared to be a rough map of the village with a circle marking the church, shading denoting woodland and a dotted line going off the page and marked "trackway".

Half the book was empty. The last note said something like "Check Mornington".

Elinor put the book back on the table, on George's side.

She'd hated those people in the bar tonight. Most of all she'd hated the way they and Claire had exchanged greetings in Welsh, Claire seeming quite at home with the language.

Elinor hated the sound of Welsh. Nasty, whining, guttural. If they could all speak English, why *didn't* they?

Her father had never once spoken Welsh to them at home. Yet had turned his back on them, returned to the so-called land of his fathers – and then, apparently, had spoken little else.

There was something rancid in the air.

When George returned they would have to put out the light, and the room would be lit from the window, which had no curtains and was divided into eight square panes. And the room would be one with the silent village and the night.

CHAPTER XLVII

Shadows clung to the alleyway along the side of the Memorial Hall. It was lit only by a tin-shaded yellow bulb on the corner of the building. Berry walked close to Bethan. He liked walking close to Bethan, though he wasn't too sure who was protecting whom.

Neurotic chemistry.

They came out on the parking lot below the castle. Any place else, Berry thought, they'd have had floodlights around a ruined castle this big. Made a feature of it. In Pontmeurig they seemed to treat their medieval monument like some shabby industrial relic, hiding it with modern buildings, parking cars and trucks as close as they could get to its ramparts.

Plenty cars here tonight, as many as in the daytime.

"Business has never been so good," Bethan said, as they crossed the road to Hampton's Bookshop. "The licensees are hoping that whoever wins the by-election will die very soon so they can have another one."

"Where's Guto's meeting tonight?"

"Y Groes," Bethan said quickly and pulled her keys from her bag.

"What time's he get back?"

"Alun's driving, so he'll have a few drinks afterwards. Half-eleven, twelve."

"Gives us a couple of hours to talk before he comes looking for your report."

"He won't tonight. Close the door behind you."

Bethan led the way upstairs, flicking lights on. In the flat she switched on a single reading lamp with an orange shade, went to plug in the kettle.

"How long you lived here?" Berry said.

"Only a few months. After Robin died, I went to work in a school in Swansea, but then they offered me the head teacher's job in Y Groes."

"Hold on," Berry said. "I thought you were at Y Groes before."

"Yes, but not working there." Bethan came through from the kitchen in jeans and sweater, coat over her arm. She threw it in an armchair, sat on an arm of the sofa. "I'll start at the beginning, shall I?"

"OK."

She told him she'd been born in Aberystwyth, where her parents still lived. Went to college in Swansea, came back to teach at the primary school in Pontmeurig then at a bigger school in Aber. Met Robin McQueen, a geologist from Durham, working at the British Geological Survey Centre just south of the town. When they married they'd been delighted to be able to rent a terraced cottage in Y Groes, even though it would be a fifty-mile round trip to work each day for both of them.

"It all seemed so perfect," Bethan said. "Robin was like Giles – overwhelmed by the setting and the countryside and the beauty of the village itself. The extra driving seemed a small price to pay."

"How long were you there, before –?"

Her eyelids dropped. "Under a year."

"Listen, you don't have to –"

"There is very little to say. He complained increasingly of feeling tired. Put it down to the travelling and the stress. The stress, he – The survey team were being told to investigate Mid-Wales to find areas where the rocks were suitable for burying nuclear waste. Robin, of course, was fiercely *anti*-nuclear. He considered resigning. But then we would have been forced to leave the area – nothing else round here for a geologist. Then, worst of all, he found two prime nuclear-dumping sites in the Nearly Mountains, five miles from Y Groes, can you imagine that?"

"Awkward."

"So he was tired and under terrible stress and he flew into a rage if I suggested he should see a doctor. And then –"

The kettle puffed and shrilled. Bethan got up. Berry followed her into the tiny kitchen.

"And then he *did* see a doctor," she said dully. "And of course it was too late." She poured boiling water into a brown teapot. "Far too late."

Bethan pushed the fingers of both hands through her black hair. "We had not quite two weeks," she said.

"Jesus," Berry said softly.

"My neighbour at the time, Mrs. Bronwen Dafis, told me one day – being helpful, very nice, very understanding – that Robin would be dead before the weekend."

"She was medically qualified, huh?"

"It emerged that she had followed a corpse candle from the church to our door."

"Followed a *what*?"

"In rural Wales," Bethan said, "there are many signs and portents signifying death. The corpse candle is said to be a tiny light which floats a few feet above the ground. Identifying the house of a person who will soon die. Or perhaps someone will see his own corpse candle, trailing behind him along the lane."

"People believe that?"

"That is the very least of what some people believe. There is something, also unique to Wales, I imagine, called the *teuli* or *toili*. The phantom funeral. A funeral procession may be seen carrying a coffin or pushing the coffin on a bier or a cart. Perhaps you are in some lonely place at night or twilight, and the cortège passes right through you."

"Legends. Folklore. Country bullshit, right?"

"Of course." Bethan poured two teas. "Strong enough?"

"Fine. These stories . . . must scare the crap out of kids."

"Except," Bethan said, "in Y Groes."

"Why'd I have a feeling you were gonna say that?"

They carried the mugs back into the living room. Bethan put on the electric fire. They sat, one on each arm of the peacock sofa.

"All this furniture from the cottage?"

Bethan nodded and told him how, heartbroken, she'd at first put the furniture in store and taken a job, any job, in Swansea – in spite of the entreaties of her neighbours, several of whom had seriously urged her not to leave.

"Obviously, they wanted me to stay because I was a Welsh-speaker and they needed younger blood. The young people leave this area in their hundreds, to find work. And because, well, that is what young people do, they leave their roots behind. So you have many villages which are full of old people. And immigrants."

"Ah."

"But not Y Groes. It is perhaps the only village in Wales where everyone is Welsh. And Welsh-speaking."

"Everyone? What about the Welsh people who bring their wives and husbands who happen not to be Welsh –?"

It hit him.

"Aw, hey, come on . . ."

Bethan shrugged.

Half asleep, Elinor thought at first, as anyone would, that it must be the wind.

And then she heard the unmistakable beat of wings.

The bed shifted as she sat up.

"What was that? What *was* it?"

George grunted.

"Did you hear it? George, did you *hear* it?"

A clear, cold night outside. A quarter moon in the top-left square of the deepset window.

Elinor shivered in her cotton nightdress.

"I was asleep," George complained. "For God's sake, I was *asleep*."

"It's stopped," Elinor said. "It was a bird, I think."

"Owl, probably."

"Owls don't peck at windows."

"I wouldn't know. I'm not an ornithologist." George wrenched at the blankets, turned over.

"Stopped now." Elinor spoke faintly and sank back on the pillow.

"Go to sleep," George mumbled. "We'll be away from here tomorrow, God willing."

Eyes wide open, she wondered how much influence God might exert in a place like this. She was no more a theologian than George was an ornithologist. But she was a woman and he was a depressingly unresponsive man. There were things that he would never begin to understand.

She lay on her back looking up at the beamed ceiling, only white bars visible, found by the sparse moonlight.

"George," she said after a while, unmoving in the bed.

"What?"

And came out with it at last. "I think she's pregnant."

George turned over towards her. "What on earth makes you say that?"

"Oh, you probably wouldn't understand, but I can feel it about her somehow – the way she moves, her colouring, her skin tone. Not much more than a month perhaps, but it's there."

"Oh dear. That *would* be difficult, especially in a place like this.

317

How would she support a child? She's a freelance. No maternity leave for a freelance."

"I'm probably wrong," Elinor said, sorry now that she'd blurted out what was on her mind. She'd always had cause to regret confiding her deeper feelings to bluff, shallow, well-meaning George.

"Hope you are," George said. "Although I'd quite like to be a granddad one day. Completes the picture."

Within minutes he was snoring. Always make the best of things, that was George. Elinor turned on to her side and after a while began to drift unhappily towards the blurred frontier of sleep.

Was pulled back by that hideous noise again.

The measured, sharp taps on the windowpane, the convulsion of wings.

Rolling over in her lonely terror, she saw the shadow of the nightbird against the moon-tinted glass.

In a flat, cold silence, as if the sound of the world had been switched off, it brandished its dark wings at her, a spasm of black foreboding.

And vanished.

She turned to face the wall. And did not sleep again, nor look at the window, until morning came in a sickly pink mist.

CHAPTER XLVIII

Berry came down to breakfast and heard voices from the sitting room next door.

"Bethan has been here since seven," explained Mrs. Evans, setting down his three kinds of toast. "Been following the Tory campaign, she has. Well, I never realised this electioneering was so complicated."

Ten minutes later, as she carried his plates away, he heard her open the sitting-room door. "I'm taking your tea and coffee into the dining room. It's not friendly to leave Mr. Morelli on his own."

Guto's reply was unintelligible but audibly grumpy. He shambled in a couple of minutes later wearing a torn sweat-shirt with something in Welsh printed on the front and a lot of exclamation marks. "Morning, Morelli," he said without enthusiasm.

"Bad night?"

"Don't even fucking ask," said Guto, reversing a dining chair and sitting down with his legs astride the seat and his chin on his hands over the backrest.

Bethan followed him in, contrastingly elegant in black, with the big gold earrings. "Guto has decided his meeting in Y Groes was not a success," she said carefully.

Mrs. Evans returned with matching tea and coffee pots in some ornate kind of china, put the coffee pot on the table in front of Guto. "I've told you about sitting like that, you'll ruin that chair."

"Oh, Mam, not this morning, for Chr– Not this morning, please."

Mrs. Evans put down the teapot. "*Two* black-tea drinkers?" She said. "There's coincidence. Strong or weak?"

"I like mine strong*ish*," Bethan said. "I am afraid *he* likes it so it corrodes the spoon."

Guto threw her a penetrating look which said, And how the hell do you know that?

"Berry was at the Conservative meeting last night," Bethan said quickly, pouring tea. "They served tea afterwards," she lied. "He was complaining about the Tory tea, how weak it was. This is lovely, Mrs. Evans."

Guto's look said, Oh, *Berry*, now, is it?

"Anything else you want," Mrs. Evans said, scurrying off, "I'll be in the kitchen."

"Yes, yes, thank you, Mam," Guto said irritably.

"So what went wrong?" Berry lit a cigarette.

"I truly cannot fathom it, Morelli," Guto said. "You know Y Groes, you've been there?"

Berry nodded.

"Not a soul in that village does not speak Welsh, am I right, Bethan?"

"You're right," she said. "And you are remembering that when Gwynfor won his by-election to become the first Plaid MP, back then, it was said he had one hundred per cent support in the Welsh-speaking communities of Carmarthenshire – in Llanybydder and Rhydcymerau."

"Right," Guto said bitterly. "Of all the places, this was the one I was the least worried about. Didn't even think about what I was going to say in advance. I'd march into the school hall to universal cheers. Hard-man of the nationalists, hero of the hour."

He rocked backwards and forwards on the dining chair.

"You know how many were there? Nineteen. Nineteen fucking people!"

Berry reckoned Simon Gallier must have pulled nearly four hundred. OK, Guto's meeting was in a village, but, shit . . .

"Another notable chapter in the annals of apathy, it was," Guto said. "And worse still – get this – most of the nineteen were from farms and hamlets a few miles away. I should say there were fewer than five actual residents of Y Groes. And they were the people who knew me, come out of politeness – Aled from the pub, Dilwyn Dafis, Dewi Fon. What is it we learn from this, eh? What do we fucking *learn* here?"

"Maybe the meeting wasn't publicised enough," Berry said.

"Bollocks. Nothing happens in these villages that everybody doesn't know about. Apathy, it is. Typical of this area. Makes you sick."

He looked despondently at the floor. Bethan looked at Berry. The look indicated she could maybe explain this, and apathy was not the word she would use.

"Look, I have to go," Bethan said.

"And I have to change, for my Press conference," Guto said. "Jesus, what if the hacks have heard about it?"

"Any of them there?" Berry asked.

"No. And with only twenty-one people in the bloody room, I can be sure of that, at least. But they'll have heard, see. Word travels fast. I tell you, if it goes on like this, I'm finished, man."

"It won't, Guto," Bethan said. "Believe me. It is not like other places, that village. I know this. And you have over a week, yet." She squeezed his arm.

Berry thought, he's worried about this getting out and he just told the entire story to a reporter.

He didn't know whether to be flattered or insulted that neither Guto nor Bethan seemed to consider him a real journalist.

*

When Guto, reluctantly be-suited, had left for the Drovers', Berry wedged himself into the telephone alcove of Mrs. Evans's china-choked sitting room and called American Newsnet, collect.

"I was beginning to think," Addison Walls said, "that the telephone system had not yet been extended to Wales." He sounded like he had a cold.

"It got here at the weekend," Berry said. "Just nobody could figure out how to connect the wires. So, how much you want me to file?"

"I don't want you to file a thing," Addison Walls said. "I read every damn word printed about that by-election and, as I predicted, it's all shit and of purely domestic interest. So what I'm lookin' for is you back here by tonight, yeah?"

"Ah, I don't think I can do that," Berry said.

There was a long pause during which Berry could hear Addison trying to breathe.

"I hear you correctly? I said I needed you back here by tonight, and you said –"

"I said I didn't think I could make it. Like, you know, my car broke down."

"You drive a pile of crap, Morelli, whadda you expect? So take a train. If there's no trains, take a bus. Fuck it, grab a cab, but get your ass back here by tonight, OK?"

"Addison, listen," Berry said. "How about I take a couple days' vacation –"

"Nearly December, Morelli. You took all your vacation."

"OK, I'll take some of next year's."

"Morelli, Goddamn it –" He heard Addison Walls blow his nose. "Listen, we're up to the eyes here. Paul went sick, I can't see the top a my desk for fuckin' influenza remedies that don't fuckin' work. You know what, Morelli, you've become a real weird guy. So, listen, you don't show up tomorrow, I am not gonna be all that worried. Give me an opportunity to test out my new shredder on your contract."

"Addison, hey, come on . . . Just two days is all I'm asking."

"You getting the general direction of my thinking, Morelli?"

"Yeah." Berry felt some perverse kind of euphoria filling up his head. "Yeah, I think I'm finally piecing things together."

"Good," Addison Walls said, and he hung up.

The sun was out, pale but definitely out, and the street sparkled after an overnight frost. Berry could see the broken denture of the castle walls, a sign pointing to the Welsh Pizza House – lousy name, lousy pizzas. Feeling suddenly very strange, very different, he began to walk up the street. Saw Guto's mom coming back from the shop with a teeming basket over her arm and a headscarf over her perm. Felt a crazy kind of affection for Guto's mom.

Guto too. He'd make the right kind of MP. Always be in trouble, always say the wrong things to the wrong people. Berry liked that.

But how much of a chance did Guto really have? Why didn't Y Groes want him? Heart of the Welsh-speaking heartland.

He could get back to London in four, five hours. He could spend most of today here and still get back to London by tonight. Maybe come back next weekend, see how things were going.

Sure. No problem.

At the top of the street, past Hampton's Bookshop but before you got to the bridge, there was a teashop which also sold Welsh crafts. Mainly lovespoons, which were made of wood and were intricately carved and came in a variety of sizes. Berry wondered what they had to do with love. Maybe he'd ask Bethan, who ought, by now, to be waiting in there. An arrangement they'd made last night.

They'd talked until eleven-thirty, then Berry had said he

ought to go because Guto would be home and Mrs. Evans would want to get to bed. He hadn't *wanted* to go. Christ, no.

As he approached the teashop, he could see her sitting in the window, black hair tumbling into a black cowl-neck woollen sweater.

She'd told him last night how she'd done this dumb thing, gone to the education department and suggested they close down the village school. How she felt the school had been corrupting generations of kids. She'd found it hard to explain why she thought this. Said he'd need to meet the other teacher to understand.

Berry had told her about breaking into the judge's house that day with Giles. He'd told her about the study, the deep, dark atmosphere of hate.

"Yes," she'd said. "Yes."

He hadn't told her about the room whispering, *sice . . . sice . . .* because he wasn't even sure that had happened.

The education department had told Bethan to take two or three weeks off. They figured she had to be nuts, trying to get her own school shut down, maybe heading for a breakdown.

I think a nervous breakdown would be quite a relief.

He walked across the road to the teashop. She had her back to him, talking to someone maybe. He caught a flash of gold earring as she tossed her hair back. No way could this woman be insane, but then, who was he to judge?

CHAPTER XLIX

Inside the teashop it was very dim, all the furniture stained as dark as the lovespoons on the walls. Which was why, from outside, you could only see the person sitting in the window. Why he hadn't seen the other two people at Bethan's table.

It was the older couple who'd been at Giles's funeral. The guy with white hair, yellow at the front, and deep lines down both cheeks. The woman thin-faced, harsh hair rinsed an uneasy auburn, looking like copper wire.

"Berry, this is Claire's mother and father."

"Oh." Somehow, he'd thought they must have been relations of Giles, rather than Claire. "Hi," he said, pulling out a chair.

Bethan introduced him as a friend and colleague of Giles's, down here for the election. "Mr. and Mrs. Hardy had to spend the night at the *Tafarn* at Y Groes. They are having problems with their car."

"But we're getting it back this morning," George Hardy said. "That's why we're here. Claire dropped us off."

Berry turned to the woman. He'd heard her muttering "Thank God", when her husband talked about getting the car back.

"You don't like it here?"

"Not really our sort of place, I'm afraid," Elinor Hardy said, tight-voiced.

"Not being *snobbish* or anything," George assured Bethan. "Good *God*, no. Wonderful place for a quiet summer holiday. Just that at this time of year it seems a little cold and remote and it's not quite what we're used to. Certainly never had to wait two days before to get what seemed quite a simple problem with the cam belt seen to."

"We didn't get much sleep, I'm afraid," Elinor said. The skin under her eyes was blue, Berry saw, and it wasn't cosmetic. She was fingering her coffee cup nervously. He wondered why Claire had put them in a teashop and just left them.

"Bloody bed kept creaking," George said. "Had to get down on my hands and knees and mess about with a loose floorboard underneath to stop it. Good God, I'd forgotten – Elinor, why didn't you remind me?"

From an inside pocket of his overcoat he pulled a slim, red, hard-backed notebook. "Found it under the damned floorboard. Meant to give it to the manager chap this morning."

"Unlikely to have been his anyway," Elinor said.

"Suppose not. Must belong to somebody, though, and he'd be better placed than us to find out who, obviously."

Bethan said, "You found it under the floorboard in the bedroom? Can I see?"

George passed her the book. "Keep it, if it's of any interest. Odd little hand-drawn maps of the village, that sort of thing. Probably mean more to you than me."

"Thank you." Bethan made no attempt to look at the notebook, slipping it into her bag.

"If you find any treasure, send us a few bob, won't you." Ignoring his wife's withering glance, George laughed and coughed and pulled out his cigarettes. "Don't mind, do you? Only things that seem to *stop* me coughing these days."

A waitress appeared, glum girl of about seventeen. Bethan said, "Can I order you more coffee?"

Elinor grimaced.

"Just one pot of tea, then." Bethan told the girl, *"Un te, plis."* Pointed at Berry. *"Dim laeth."*

PHIL RICKMAN

Berry saw the woman flinch when Bethan spoke Welsh. She was in some state.

The hell with tact. He said, "I hear that Claire . . . she has this amazing aptitude for the Welsh language."

Elinor said tonelessly, "Has she?"

George Hardy looked at his watch, stood up, cigarette in hand. "Think I'd better pop round the corner to the garage, see how they're getting on with it. Have to stand over these chaps sometimes. Nice to meet you, Miss . . . er. Yes."

When he'd gone, squeezing his overcoated bulk past the racks of lovespoons, his wife just came apart.

She leaned across the table, seized Bethan's wrist. "Look, I don't know anything about you, but please will you help me?"

"Of course." Bethan was startled. "If I can."

"I'm sorry, I don't usually behave like this. But I don't *know* anybody here, do you see?" Berry saw her eyes fill up. She let go of Bethan's wrist, pulled a paper napkin from a wooden bowl. "Pen."

Berry handed her his.

"I want to give you my telephone number." She began to write erratically on the napkin, talking as fast and jerkily as her wrist was moving. "Want you to promise to ring me. If anything happens. You see Claire, don't you? Of course you do. Teaching her . . . that language."

Bethan said, "I –"

Berry's eyes said, Don't contradict her, let her talk.

"Something's happened to her. She's not the same."

"No," Bethan said.

"You can tell that, can't you? You've only known her a short time, but you can see it."

"Yes."

"I won't say –" Elinor put down the pen, folded the napkin;

327

Bethan took it. "I won't say we were ever terribly close. Dreadful admission, but I have to be frank. Have to."

She looked defiantly from Bethan to Berry and back to Bethan.

"Often felt closer to Giles. He would tell me things she concealed. And now he's dead. And we weren't told. Weren't invited to the funeral, you know."

"That's awful," Bethan said.

"She said," Elinor pulled another napkin from the bowl, dabbed her eyes. "She says she wrote to us, but she couldn't invite us here. We had to decide. For ourselves." She blew her nose, crumpled the napkin in her hand. "Never saw a letter. Read about it in the paper. Suppose she didn't tell us because . . . when my father died . . . we were about to leave for a holiday and I didn't tell *her*. None of us went to his funeral. I didn't want *her* going, didn't want her anywhere near him again."

"Oh," said Bethan. "Of course. You're the judge's daughter."

"He was a bastard. I think that's the first time I've ever used that word."

"Why?" Berry asked gently. "Why was he a bastard?"

"You don't want to know all that. No time, anyway. George'll be back soon. With the car."

"You said you didn't want him near her again. I remember Giles telling me specifically that Claire never met her grandfather."

"She didn't *remember* meeting him. We were once foolish enough to bring her here. As a small child. He . . . went off with her. I thought . . . that he wasn't going to bring her back."

Bethan said, "Went off?"

"I don't know where they went."

"To the woods? To the church?"

"Does it matter? Please, all I want . . . Just ring me sometimes. Tell me how she is and if . . . You see, I think she might be expecting a baby. Perhaps that's why she's changed. I pray that's all it is."

"Not the best time to have a kid," Berry said. He felt very sorry for the woman. Obviously wasn't able to confide in her husband. Something not right when she had to pour it all out to strangers in a café.

Elinor Hardy straightened up, threw the crumpled napkin in the ashtray with two of George's cigarette butts. "You must think me a very stupid, hysterical woman."

"No," Berry said. "All the people you could've told this to, we're the ones least likely to think that."

"I'll be better when I'm out of here. I know it's your country, but I don't like it here. Feel vulnerable."

. . . not meant to be here, the English . . .

"Car goes wrong and you're suddenly stranded. Strange language, different attitudes. Birds pecking at your window in the night."

Bethan's expression did not change at all, but Berry felt she was suddenly freezing up inside.

"Birds?" Casually. Hiding it.

"Pecking . . . tapping on the window. Kept waking me up in the night. Wasn't an owl, I saw it. Or I may have dreamt it, I don't know. I'm in a terrible state. I've got to get out of here, it's gloomy. I'll go and find George. Look, you will ring me, won't you?"

"I'll ring you before the weekend," Bethan promised.

"Thank you. I don't even know your name."

"Bethan. Bethan McQueen. Mrs. Hardy, you *are* leaving today, aren't you?"

"Oh, yes," Elinor said. "Count on it."

When she'd gone, Bethan rose silently, paid the girl, collected her bag and her white raincoat from the table. She walked out of the café and along the street, Berry following. She didn't speak. They came to the bridge and Bethan crossed the road and walked back towards the town, on the castle side. The frost had melted now, but the sun had gone in.

When they reached the castle car park, Bethan said, "Your car or mine?"

Berry unlocked the Sprite. They got in. Berry started the engine. Not easy. Blue smoke enclouded the Sprite, which now had a cough worse than George Hardy's. Berry backed it round, pointed it at the road.

"Where we going?"

"Turn left," Bethan said. "Across the bridge. Keep going. You'll see a sign pointing over the Nearly Mountains to Y Groes."

"I know it."

"Pass it," Bethan said. "Keep straight on."

"But where are we going?"

"Christ knows," Bethan said. "Somewhere where nobody has ever thought they've seen the bird of death."

CHAPTER L

Every second farm they passed seemed to have a political poster pasted to a gate or a placard sticking out of a leafless hedgerow. Berry counted seven for Gallier (Con), three for Evans (Plaid) and two each for Labour and the Liberal Democrats.

"Could be worse," he observed. "All over the world, farmers are notoriously conservative."

She didn't reply. She was sitting as upright as was possible in a bucket seat full of holes and patches.

At least the Sprite was responding, losing its bronchitis now they were into open country. He'd been getting a touch paranoid about that, having told Addison Walls his car had broken down and therefore been half-expecting it to do just that.

Superstition. Everywhere, superstition.

Five miles now into the hills north-west of Pontmeurig, and disillusion was setting in. At first he'd been stimulated by all that "your car or mine" stuff on the castle parking lot. Now the space between them was a good deal wider than the gap between the bucket seats, and he didn't know why.

She said suddenly, "Death fascinates the Welsh."

The first time she'd spoken since they passed the sign to Y Groes.

"Corpses and coffins and funerals."

"Signs and portents," Berry said.

"You see these farms. Each one an island. Farmers never visit their neighbours. But, when one of them dies, people will come from miles around to his funeral. All the roads to the chapel

331

lined with cars and Land-Rovers for half a mile in each direction. On the day of a big funeral, the traffic police send for reinforcements."

"Bethan, what is the bird of death?"

She didn't reply.

"Where are we headed?"

"Keep driving," she said.

After a few miles they came to a T-junction, Aberystwyth to the right, Machynlleth to the left.

"Make a right here?"

She pointed to the left. "Quickest way out of the constituency."

Sure enough, after a couple more miles there were no more political posters. The landscape became rougher and a lighter, more faded shade of green. Kind of like the Nearly Mountains, snow on the high ground giving the crags a 3-D outline.

Presently, they drove down into a pleasant town, with a wide main street and a Gothic clock tower.

"This is the town that ought to have been the capital of Wales," she said. "Perhaps the earliest centre of Welsh civilisation."

We had the sociology, Berry thought, now we get the history lesson. What is this, a school outing?

"But that's not why we're here," she said.

"So why are we here?"

"Because at the top of this street is the best restaurant in this part of Wales," Bethan said. "Vegetarian meals a speciality. Park anywhere along here."

Berry grinned. A long, slow Italian grin.

"No. No! No! No!"

"I'm sorry. My wife is rather distraught."

"Nooooooo!"

"We lost our son-in-law, you see."

332

Elinor strode out then, straight through a patch of oil, ruining her sensible pigskin walking shoes.

"Is there no chance for later today?" George pleaded.

"What can I do," the mechanic said, "if they send me the wrong parts? Look, I will show you a copy of the order we dictated to them over the phone –"

"Never mind, I believe you," George said. "It's just bloody inconvenient."

"Quite an old Volvo, see."

"Volvos last for ever," said George, affronted.

Some minutes later he caught up with Elinor.

"It's really not my fault, you know."

"It's never your fault."

"Look, what we'll do –"

"I won't go back there. I'll sleep on a park bench first."

"Dammit, there isn't a park. Nor any benches. But what I was about to say . . . We've got a few hours. We'll have lunch at that Plas Moorig place and see if they can't find us a room. Any room. How about that? Please . . ."

Over lunch, Bethan said, "I want not to think about it. Just for a while."

"OK. Fine."

"Tell me about you."

"Oh, shit."

Bethan started on her fresh salmon salad. "What is that stuff?"

"It's a vegetarian canelloni."

"I know *that*, but what is it?"

"Well, it's got spinach and stuff inside." He sampled a segment. "It's OK."

"For Wales."

"No, it's real good. Jesus, you Celts are so touchy."

He'd taken off his jacket, revealing a green sweatshirt probably older than Guto's, if less torn. In black Gothic lettering across the chest it said, AMERICAN WEREWOLF IN LONDON.

"You haven't told me about you," Bethan said. "You just said, 'Oh shit,' and then we were sidetracked by the food."

"OK. I'm from New York originally, but I was brought up and educated in seven different states on account of my dad kept moving to further his career until it wouldn't go any further and he decided it was time he became a power and influence in the land."

"What did he do? What was his job?"

"I just love it when people say that. I hate it when they say, hey, you related to Mario Morelli?"

"Who is Mario Morelli?"

"He's my dad, the bastard."

"I had gathered that."

"OK, Mario Morelli is maybe America's number-one TV anchor man, known coast to coast. A household name, like that – what's that stuff you put down the john?"

"Harpic? Toilet Duck?"

"Yeah, he's a real toilet duck. Only the great American public doesn't want to know that on account of he has this mature elegance and charms the matrons with his dazzling Italian smile."

He told her about Mario Morelli's role in the Irangate cover-up. He told her how his conscience wouldn't let him sit on this information when it seemed they were going to get away with it.

"Like, I don't want to come over as this big idealist. But when your dad's a national hero and you know what kind of asshole he really is . . . OK, in the end, it made no difference. Most of it came out. And Mario Morelli came out of it as this caring patriot. He did it for his country, all this shit. Cue for selfish, radical un-American activist son to leave town. Or leave country in this case. So I came to England and I find England's suddenly become a place where it's cool to make a million over-night and they're looking up to America as this big, successful younger brother who *got it right*, for Chrissake. That's about it. My vegetarian cannelloni's getting cold."

He ate some cannelloni, then he said, "One thing I kinda like about Wales is that it's just about the most obscure country in Western Europe, now even Belgium has the EC, but it doesn't seem to look up to anybody."

"Wrong," Bethan said. "Wrong, wrong, wrong."

"Wrong, huh?"

"You've only been exposed to people like Guto, who are the most vocal but not typical. For most of this century Welsh people have been looking up to anybody prepared to notice they're even there. Especially the English."

"You're talking as a nationalist. It's an outdated concept."

"How else can we defend what is ours? The English wanted more water for Liverpool and Birmingham, so they came into Wales and flooded our valleys. Whole Welsh villages at the bottom of English reservoirs. And the humble Welsh people went to work for the English water boards and said how good they were and how well they looked after their employees."

"Sure, yeah, but –"

"I know, that was years ago. But they are doing it again. Only this time they're flooding us with people and they're drowning our language and our culture."

Berry put his fork down. "You know," he said. "You're beautiful when you're defending your culture."

"Sir, with my hand on my heart, I can tell you that, even if you were prepared to sleep standing up in the third-floor broom-cupboard, I would not be able to accommodate you."

The proprietor of the Plas Meurig Hotel (two-star) was a

short, plump Englishman in a double-breasted fawn-coloured suit which matched the walls of the hotel lobby.

"I'm prepared to pay over the odds, if necessary," George said.

"Sir, I've turned away Conservative Members of Parliament who are prepared to pay *well* over the odds. I've turned away a senior editor from Independent Television News with a cheque-book as thick as the New Testament. I swear if I could get an extension block put up in five days, I'd call in the builders now and apply for planning permission later. I could be making a fortune. But I am utterly full and there's nothing I can do about it."

"Well, where else would you recommend?"

"In this town, to be quite honest, there's nowhere I'd actually *recommend*. But I seriously don't believe there's anywhere you'd get in anyway."

"Let's not be stupid about this," George said to Elinor outside. "It's going to be a damn cold night. I think we should ring Claire."

At the top of the wide street, on the same side as the restaurant, was a very old building with flags protruding from its deep-grey stonework.

Bethan said, "This is where Owain Glyndwr convened the first Welsh parliament in 1403. By that time he was in control of most of Wales – the nearest we ever came to ruling ourselves."

Inside, there was a tourist reception area with books about Wales and about Owain Glyndwr, including Guto's paperback.

"I bought one, you know," Berry said. "Still in the car."

"It's really very good," Bethan said. "You should make time to read it."

They saw a replica of Glyndwr's parliament table, pictures of the man himself, one of him sitting solemnly in state. The only real distinctive thing about him, Berry reckoned, was the fork in his beard, like somebody had tried to cleave his head apart from underneath.

"Hold on," he said, as they emerged onto the street. "I just realised who this guy is. He's Owen Glendower, from Shakespeare. *Henry the Fourth Part One* or *Part Two*, I can't remember. The point being –"

"*Part One*, I think," Bethan said.

"The point being that Owen Glendower was a horse's ass. Pompous, full of shit –"

"The point being," Bethan snapped, "that Shakespeare was biased. The real Owain was a fairly modest, cultured man who studied law in London, had many English friends and would never have gone to war with England if he hadn't been faced with a completely untenable –"

"OK, OK." Berry held up his hands. Few other people were in sight on the wide, cold street. Bethan was facing him on the pavement, small lips tight, fists clenched by her sides. This was not about the rights and wrongs of Welsh nationalism or whether Owain Glyndwr was full of shit.

Her fists unclenched. She looked small and alone and without hope.

"I think," she said slowly, "I think I am ready now to have my nervous breakdown."

CHAPTER LI

The Rhos Tafol Hotel was a white-painted former farmhouse about six miles west of Machynlleth. It overlooked the placid Dyfi estuary, beyond which mountains lay back, pink and gold in the last light of the last day in November.

The Rhos Tafol dated back to the seventeenth century and had a suite with a four-poster bed. OK, a *reproduction* four-poster. But four posts were four posts.

Tenderly, he kissed a small, pale left breast. "How would you feel," he said, "about *another* nervous breakdown?"

The sky over the inn was like bronze tinfoil, the cottages around it coloured ochre and sepia and clustered together like chocolates.

Yes, it was beautiful. She had to agree. It cast its spell.

And inside the beauty it was only a village, only houses with front doors and gardens and electric cookers and televisions. It could not harm her.

This was because, before leaving Pontmeurig in the Land-Rover, Elinor had taken two valium.

Claire steered them casually, one-handed, over the bridge. "You never know, having to come back here – it might be destiny."

Destiny, Elinor thought. Dessss-tinny. Fated to see it like this, in what passed for sunset. To understand why they were all so attracted to it.

"Or it might simply be incompetence and inefficiency," George growled, trying to hold a match to his cigarette as they jolted to

338

a halt in front of the inn. "Can't for the life of me understand how they managed to send the wrong damn parts."

Destiny and fate and beauty, Elinor thought, drifting. I shall leave tomorrow and still look back with a degree of hatred.

"Perhaps we should have taken it to Dilwyn's," Claire was saying. "Dilwyn is very good at improvising."

"Don't want a Mickey Mouse job," George said, opening his door, peering out. "Don't know why you can't have a proper car, Claire. Hell of a way to the ground from these things."

"You said that yesterday," Elinor said, opening her own door, putting a foot into the air, giggling.

"Mother, wait . . ."

But she fell into the gravel. She was crying when Claire went to help her to her feet. "Don't mind me, darling," she said miserably, clutching her handbag to her chest.

Night came and they did not leave the reproduction four-poster bed, did not go down to dinner.

She clung to him for hours.

He woke intermittently, hearing voices from the bar below. Mainly voices speaking Welsh. Local people, farmers. He and Bethan must be the only guests.

It occurred to him that in only a few hours' time he was going to be out of a job. He could, of course, steal quietly out of bed and drive like hell through the night, reaching London by dawn, just time to shower and shave and change and present himself at Addison's desk by nine-fifteen. Then again . . . He hugged Bethan tightly. She moaned softly. Her body was slick with her own sweat, nothing to do with the sex. He hoped she was sweating out all the pain.

He slept.

Woke again. No noise from the bar now. Bethan stirring in his arms, mumbling, "Which of us is sweating?"

"Don't wish to be ungallant," he said, "but I think it's you. I also think –" licking moisture from her shoulder "– I also think I love you. Is this premature?"

"You don't know what you are saying."

"Do too."

"We've talked so much, you think you've known me for a long time, but it was only yesterday. What I think –"

"Don't care what you think. No, yes I do. I care."

"I think having so much to talk over, things we'd never told anyone . . . that is a great stimulant."

"Like Welsh lovespoons," Berry said.

She kissed him. "What are you talking about?"

"Those lovespoons. The long wooden ones. Aren't they some kind of Celtic dildo?"

For maybe a couple of seconds, because they'd pulled the curtains around the bed and it was too dark to see her face, he had the impression she thought he was serious.

Then a small hand closed around his balls.

"No, hey . . . I didn't mean it . . . Bethan, geddoff . . . I'll never . . . Bethan!"

After a third, rather more languorous nervous breakdown, she said, "I have *got* to have a shower."

"OK."

"Alone! You stay and read Guto's book. It is the least you can do for him now."

"Because I went off with his woman?"

"I am *not* his woman."

"Well, he obviously –"

"Shut up and read the book."

He looked at his watch on the floor by the bed. It was three-fifteen in the morning. They'd been in bed since about four-thirty yesterday afternoon.

Hell, he'd left all his stuff at Mrs. Evans's. What was she

going to think? More of a problem, what was Guto going to think?

As they'd had no cases – and not wishing to make anything *too* obvious – they'd carried everything they could find out of the Sprite's trunk. Bags full of useless stuff lay under the window, on top of them the two books – Guto's *Glyndwr* and the red notebook George Hardy had given Bethan.

Berry switched on a bedside lamp with pictures of Tudor houses on the shade. He heard the rush of the shower. He began to read, the way journalists read official documents when they have only twenty minutes to extract the essence.

She was right about Glyndwr. He was an articulate, educated guy who'd probably had no ambitions to rule an independent Wales. This had been a lost cause since the last official Prince of Wales, Llywelyn, had bought it in the thirteenth century. All the same, people in Wales – where there seemed less of a social gap between the peasants and the landowning classes – felt they were getting a raw deal from the English king, Henry IV. And Owain Glyndwr had been pushed into confrontation when some of his own land was snatched by one of Henry's powerful supporters, one Reginald de Grey, who seemed to have had it in for Glyndwr in a big way.

Guto's style was straightforward, fluid and readable – and maybe as biased as Shakespeare in its way. But Berry was prepared to give him the benefit of the doubt as he read the enthusiastic account of Glyndwr's rebellion which, at one stage, had put almost the whole of Wales under his control. Guto implied that a Wales under Glyndwr and his parliament would have come closer than anywhere else in Europe to some kind of medieval democracy. It was an appealing theory.

The book was fairly dismissive about Glyndwr's reputation as a wielder of supernatural forces – a side of him which had certainly caught Shakespeare's imagination. The only lines Berry could remember from *Henry IV* were Glendower claiming,

I can call spirits from the vasty deep.

Oh, sure, somebody had replied, or words to that effect. But are they really gonna show up when you do call for them?

Dr. D. G. Evans quoted Shakespeare some more, Glendower boasting,

> *... at my birth*
> *The front of heaven was full of fiery shapes.*
> *The goats ran from the mountains, and the herds*
> *Were strangely clamourous to the frightened field.*
> *These signs have mark'd me extraordinary;*
> *And all the courses of my life do show*
> *I am not in the roll of common men.*

There had been claims, Guto wrote, that Glyndwr had been trained in Druidic magic and could alter the weather – a couple of his victories were put down to this ability. All crap, Guto said: the English view of the Welsh as wildmen from the mountains who, having no military sophistication, needed to put their faith in magic.

Nonetheless, Guto conceded, all this stuff added to Glyndwr's charisma, put him alongside King Arthur as the great Celtic hero who never really died and one day would return to free his people from oppression.

Prophecies. Signs and portents and prophecies.

Bethan came out of the bathroom, a big towel around her. She looked wonderful, black hair all tangled, skin aglow in the warm light of the Tudor lamp.

"Feel better?" He tossed the book on the bed, rose and filled the electric kettle sitting there with tea and coffee and biscuits

342

and soft drinks. One worthwhile extra that inns had picked up from the motel trade.

Bethan sat down on the edge of the bed, towelling her hair.

"What happened to him? Glyndwr."

"He retired, defeated," Bethan said through the towel.

"Checked in at a retirement home for aged rebels, huh?"

"By the early 1400s, he was losing ground," Bethan said patiently. "It all fell apart and Owain just disappeared. He had a daughter near Hereford and one story suggests he went to live with her."

"In England?"

"I am afraid so. But at least he could still see the Welsh hills."

"Sad."

"All Welsh history is sad."

"Jesus, how would the Welsh survive without self-pity?"

"Unfair," Bethan said. "But tonight, I am prepared to excuse you."

"Bethan . . ." He hesitated. "Is this the first time since . . . ?"

"Robin. Yes."

"How do you feel about that?"

She put the towel down. Faced him across the bed. Her eyes were brown and luminous in the lamplight. "Glad," she said. "I have tried to feel bad but I don't. I wish we could stay here for a very long time."

Pouring boiling water on four teabags – it wasn't a very big pot – he thought, I don't have a job to go to, neither does she.

"We can stay here a while," he said. "Buy a change of clothes." He ran a hand across his chin. "Razor. Toothpaste."

"No," she said. "We can't. You know we can't."

"Maybe we're both chasing shadows."

Bethan said, "You wanted to know about the bird of death."

"Right now I can do without the bird of death."

She said in a rush, "The bird of death is supposed to come at

343

night and tap on your window. It's an omen, like the *cannwyll gorff* and the *toili*, the phantom funeral. Sometimes it flutters its wings. At night, this – unnatural. Sometimes . . ." Bethan clutched the towel around her breasts. "Sometimes it has no wings at all."

"Why couldn't Claire's mom have simply been disturbed by an owl?"

"Oh, Berry," Bethan said in exasperation. "I am not saying she actually *saw* anything. It's what she *believes* she saw or heard or whatever. Yes, you're right, it's all nonsense. These things don't even exist – except, somehow, in the minds of people living in Y Groes."

"I didn't say that. I never said it was nonsense."

"Meaning?"

"Meaning I'm prepared to believe there's something essentially weird about the place." He poured tea, passed her a cup. Gave the pot a stir and then poured a murkier brew for himself. "We're talking about this now?"

"Yes."

"OK, let's lay it all on the table and push it around. Robin died suddenly. Giles too. Suddenly, but natural causes. Who else?"

"Dilwyn Dafis, who runs the local garage. He had an English wife, a young secretary. He met her on holiday. Within a year or so of coming to Y Groes, she was dead. Breast cancer, I think, and it spread very rapidly."

"That's three."

"A couple of years ago, the Church in Wales sent a young Englishman as curate to ap Siencyn. I don't know much about this, but he had some sort of fall in the church. Broke his neck."

"Four. Three natural causes, one accident."

"And a suicide." She told him about a child leading her to a body hanging from a tree by the river bank.

"*You* found him?"

She nodded, lowered her heavy eyelids. With one small breast exposed, she looked like a creation of one of those Italian painters Berry didn't know enough about. Botticelli, maybe. No, too slim for Botticelli, hair too dark. Aura too sad.

"You had a bad time," he said. Understatement.

"And then there was another one, about the same time as the suicide."

She reached down for the red notebook. "This is his, I'm sure. He was a historian of some sort. He came to the school once. He was writing a book about relations between Wales and England in the late medieval period, had some theory involving Y Groes. He wouldn't tell *me* about it, a little Welsh schoolteacher. He was a very pompous man. Nobody really liked him and yet they humoured him, let him stay at the *Tafarn*."

"Could they stop him?"

"The *Tafarn* does not provide overnight accommodation. They have a dining room for local functions, but no bed and breakfast."

"What about Claire's mom and dad? They stayed there."

"Only, presumably, because Claire requested it. And yet Aled gave this man – that's Aled the landlord there – he gave this man Ingley a room. An unpleasant, prying English academic. That is curious, don't you think?"

"And he died, this guy?"

"A heart attack, they said. Found dead in bed."

"Police called in?"

"No need." Bethan riffled the pages of the red notebook. "The local GP, Dr. Wyn, examined him, said he knew of his heart condition and signed a death certificate."

"Why'd this guy conceal his notebook under the floorboards?"

Bethan shook her head.

"How do you know it was his?"

She opened the notebook. "Little maps of the village, rough

plans of the church. Very detailed notes on a late-medieval tomb. Pages of references to different textbooks. Addresses. And look at it." She passed him the book. "It's quite new. The pages are a little dusty but not in the least yellow. It obviously had not been under the floor very long."

Berry sighed. "Problem about all this – you got half a dozen deaths. OK, all premature. But all of them *explained*. No mystery here. Nothing you could tell the cops."

He dropped the red notebook on top of the Glyndwr paperback. "Paranoia, Bethan. That's what they'd say. And what about Claire? She's English; nothing happened to her."

"You heard what her mother said. She was taken to see her grandfather as a small child. He disappeared with her. We don't know what happened then. All I know is that, while Giles was desperately struggling with basic Welsh, Claire was mastering the grammar and pronunciation at a speed I could not believe. And there are other things. *You've* seen the changes, her mother's seen it. It's uncanny. Eerie."

"True," he conceded. Reached across the bed, pulled her into his arms. "But what the hell can we do about it?"

"I'm only relieved," she said, wet hair against his chest, "that her parents managed to get away before . . ."

CHAPTER LII

Did George *know* she was on Valium?

She thought he must. How could anyone be expected to cope with reality as dismal as this without a little something to place a distance between one and it?

George did not, of course, need anything himself. Some sedative side of his mind seemed to be turned on automatically whenever life threatened to cross the pain threshold.

He certainly enjoyed his dinner again.

The little licensee had gone to great pains to make sure they were comfortable, lighting a log fire in the dining room where they ate alone. Serving lamb which George said was more tender and succulent than any he'd had before, even in the most expensive restaurants.

She had no opinion on this, did not remember tasting it.

The wine, though, she drank some of that, quite a lot in fact.

"Steady on, Elinor," George had said, predictably, at one point.

At which she'd poured more.

"Another bottle, Mr. Hardy?" The little landlord, dapper at George's elbow.

"Oh, I don't think –"

"Yes please," she'd said to the landlord.

Thinking of the combined sedative punch of valium and alcohol and deciding she needed to be entirely out of her head if she was to sleep the night through.

"When's Claire coming?" Pushing her plate away.

"She isn't." George lighting a cigarette, blue smoke every-where. "She's picking me up first thing, then we can get the car back. Won't take them more than half an hour once they've got the parts. So I told Claire not to bother coming over, we'd be having an early night."

"An early night?" Elinor croaking a mirthless laugh as a log collapsed in the fireplace. "Bit late for that now."

"Have some coffee."

"Don't want coffee, thank you. The Welsh can't make proper coffee. Nescafe and Maxwell House are all one ever gets in Wales."

"Actually, what I didn't want –" George leaning across the table, voice lowered "– was another night in that awful bar, all this bonhomie."

"Oh, I hate it too, George. I shall drink here."

"Please, Elinor . . . We'll be away tomorrow."

"You bet your miserable life we will. If we have to flag down a long-distance lorry driver and show him my drooping tits."

"Elinor!" Through his teeth. ". . . God's sake."

"Perhaps I'd've been better off with a lorry driver, what do think, George? Common people have fun."

"Are you coming?" Getting to his feet, taking his cigarette with him.

"Did you ever imagine, George, that the day would come when you'd want to get me to bed only to save embarrassment?"

"Yes," George said brutally.

She awoke thinking the night was over.

A reasonable mistake to make. There was a brightness beyond the curtains, before which all the furniture in the bedroom was blackly silhouetted.

But her watch showed 3:55 a.m.

Elinor, in a white nightdress, slid her feet into her wooden

Scholls, made her way unsteadily to the door, turning the handle slowly because, for once, her husband was sleeping quietly, no snoring.

At least the radiators in this place worked efficiently. It must be a freezing night outside, but the atmosphere in the bedroom was close, almost stuffy. Same on the landing outside.

She locked herself in the bathroom, two doors away, used the lavatory. She was disappointed but not surprised that the combination of drink and Valium had failed to take her all the way to the daylight. Washing her hands afterwards, she could not bear to look into the mirror over the basin, knowing how raddled she must look, still in last night's make-up for the first time in thirty-odd years.

She had no headache, but was certainly on the way down from wherever she'd been, despising herself utterly.

Why had they come? What had she been trying to prove?

Come to pay their last respects to their good and upright son-in-law. And to be at their daughter's side in her hour of need.

A joke. Claire had not needed them for years and would never need them now.

She bent her head over the sink, turned on the taps again. Feebly splashed water on her face, left great lipstick smears on the towel wiping it off.

This time she did look up into the mirror. And in her sick clown's face she saw her father's eyes.

"Your fault," she hissed. "All this. I hope your soul is rotting."

Her father's eyes did not flicker.

She turned away, pulled back the bolt and switched off the bathroom light, thankful for one thing: at least they had not set foot in his house. Not that Claire had invited them. Not once.

When she returned to their room, George was lying on his side, face to the wall. "Mmmmmmph," he said.

At home they had twin beds. Next year, she decided, she would move into a separate room.

How far off morning?

The watch said 4:21.

But the light through the curtains was brighter. It could not be long.

She stood by the window; her hand moved to lift up the curtain ... and pulled back. Suppose that bird was there again?

Beyond the drawn curtains it grew brighter still, blue-white like constant lightning.

"Errrrmph." George rolled over.

Elinor forced herself to pull back the curtain a little, and she looked down into the village street.

The street was blue with cold.

Radiantly blue. A mat of frost the colour of a midsummer sky was rolling out over the river-bridge towards the inn.

Along this chilly carpet a figure moved.

He had a long overcoat of grey, falling to the frosted road, and a wide-brimmed hat which shadowed his downcast face. He moved like a column of smoke, hands deep in the folds of his coat.

She could not see his feet or hear his footsteps, only a sharp, brittle sound, perhaps the frost itself. He left long, shallow tracks behind him but, as she watched, the marks in the frost healed over and the bright-blue ground shone savagely cold and mockingly untrodden.

The figure advanced towards the door of the inn, and with each of his steps the temperature dropped around Elinor, as if the radiators were shutting down in great shudders. Her body began to quake, her teeth to chatter, and the fingers holding back the curtain were numbed.

Reaching the door of the inn, the visitor paused, the cold

rising from him like steam, brought a hand out of his pocket as if to knock.

It was not a hand but the yellow, twisted, horny talon of a bird of prey.

"Shut up! Stop that screaming, you stupid, bloody drunken bitch!"

Her body arched at the waist, her neck extended as if she were trying to vomit.

"Are you totally insane, woman? Shut up! Do you hear me, you bitch?"

On his feet now, between her and the window, George grabbed her by the shoulders and threw her down on the bed. "Stop it!"

She looked up into her husband's bulging, sleep-swollen eyes.

Hands clenched around her bony shoulders, he lifted her from the bed then slammed her down again.

And again.

This time her skull crashed sickeningly into the headboard of Victorian mahogany.

George's eyes were opaque.

He smashed her down again, lifted her up, smashed her down, a rhythmic motion, grunting, "Stop it."

Stop it.

Stop it.

Stop it.

PART EIGHT

THE RED BOOK OF INGLEY

CHAPTER LIII

They watched each other over the breakfast table, different people now. She wore yesterday's black cowl-neck sweater and the big gold earrings; his sweatshirt still identified him as an American werewolf in London. But they were different people.

The Rhos Tafol's dining room overlooked the estuary, shining cobalt in the chill morning. There were perhaps twenty tables in the room, all stripped bare except for the one where they sat, by the window.

December.

"We could just walk away from it." Berry spread marmalade on dry toast.

Bethan looked down into her boiled egg. He loved the fall of her eyelids; it was what put him in mind of the women in Renaissance paintings.

"Or not," Berry said.

They'd lain and talked about it until the dawn streaked the Dyfi. She'd told him about Claire in the river Meurig, washing away the English. And about Claire's photos; the tree that vanished, whatever that meant.

He'd told her about old Winstone – whatever *that* meant.

Also about Miranda. Who was funny and diverting but belonged to the person he used to be before last night.

"So." Crunching toast.

Bethan said, "When I came back from Swansea to be head teacher – less than six months ago, I can't believe it – I thought

I was going to change everything. Let some light into the place. It was pretty hard to do, coming back."

"I don't know how you could."

"The way I rationalised it, it was going to be a kind of memorial to Robin. Modernising the school, changing the outlook of the children. It was a mission. But –"

"You didn't realise what you were taking on."

"I was *very* determined. Nothing left to lose. Ready to fight centuries of tradition. And Buddug."

"Buddug's this other teacher."

"The name Buddug," Bethan said, stirring the tea in the pot to make it blacker, "is Welsh for Boudicca, or Boadicea."

"The hard-nosed broad who took on the Romans," he remembered. "Drove this chariot with long knives sticking out the wheels, relieving whole legions of their genitalia."

"I had never thought of it quite like that, but the way you depict it, it does seem horrifyingly plausible, yes."

"She's like that, this Buddug?"

"She's worse," Bethan said.

"And what you're saying is you think you might accomplish now what you couldn't when you came back from Swansea?"

"I am not alone this time," Bethan said, and his heart took off.

"C'mon, honey." She turned over, coughed. "One more time for Berry." She turned over again, caught.

"She is very old," Bethan said.

"We don't discuss her age. It upsets her. When I'm in London, this guy checks her over every few weeks. You can still get the parts, if you know where to look."

He followed the estuary back towards Machynlleth. "I like it here. I like feeling close to the sea. You wouldn't care to stay another night, think about things some more?"

"I told you last night, I should *like* to stay here a very long time." She sighed. "Keep driving, Morelli."

"One point," Berry said, pushing the Sprite into the town, towards the Gothic clock tower. "You're a nationalist, right? Guto's a nationalist. This Buddug and all the people in Y Groes, they're nationalists too."

"Why, then, did Guto go down like the proverbial lead balloon?"

"Precisely."

"You have to live in Wales a long time to work it out," Bethan said. "And just when you think you've understood the way it is . . ."

She ran the fingers of both hands through her hair, as if to untangle her thoughts.

"You see . . . There are different kinds of Welsh nationalism. There is Plaid Cymru, which envisages a self-governing Wales with its own economic structure – an independent, bilingual state within the European Community. And there is another sort which you might compare with the National Front, the Ku Klux Klan, yes?"

"Extreme right wing."

"Except they would not think of themselves like that. They are protecting their heritage, they feel the same things we all feel from time to time, but –" She sighed again. "I'm afraid there are some people for whom being Welsh is more important than being human."

"And – let me guess here – this type of person sees Plaid as a half-baked outfit which no longer represents the views of the real old Welsh nation, right?"

"Yes. Exactly. *Da iawn.*"

"Huh?"

"Very good. In moments of exultation, I revert to my first language."

"So that's what it was," Berry said, remembering moments of last night.

Driving south in worsening weather, Berry wondered why neither of them had put a name to what they were up against. Six deaths. Accident, suicide and natural causes. All English people, no other connecting factor. They couldn't be talking murder. Not as the law saw it.

"Bethan," he said. "Can we discuss what happened to Giles?" Sparse sleet stung the screen.

"*Listen* to me now," she said, as if this had been building up inside for some while. "There is one thing I haven't told you."

Above the whine of the wind in the Sprite's soft top, she revealed to him the truth about Giles's "fall" in the castle car park in Pont. Why they'd kept quiet about it.

"Giles himself was particularly anxious people should believe it was a fall. I think he was embarrassed. Does that make sense to you?"

"I guess it does. Say the two guys are arrested, there's a court case. And then everybody working with Giles in London knows he got beat up on. In his beloved Wales. Yeah, I can buy that. No way would he want that out, the poor sucker."

Bethan squeezed his hand on the wheel. "I am so relieved. I was worried you would think we covered it up to protect ourselves."

"Guto, yes. You, no. So who were they, these guys?"

"Just yobs. Troublemakers. Guto threw one in the castle ditch. I would know them again. We all would."

"If it came out," Berry wondered, "is there any way we could use it to turn the heat on this thing? This guy, Inspector Jones –"

"Gwyn Arthur."

"Yeah. Seemed approachable."

"He is a nice man. But Giles did not die as a result of the attack. What could Gwyn Arthur really do now?"

"If only there'd been an inquest . . ."

"But what would it reveal? The medical evidence says he had an enormous tumour. What I would ask is, why did he *develop* the tumour? Why did Robin develop leukaemia? Why did the hiker hang himself by the river? Why did the professor . . . ? It's not something an inquest can go into, is it?"

"Paranoid delusions, Beth. Bethan. Listen, this may seem a distinctly American way of looking at things, and I apologise in advance, but is there anybody we could *beat* the truth out of?"

"Not my style," Bethan said.

"Naw, me neither."

"I am glad to hear it. But, look, there *are* still people we can talk to. I know . . . Why don't you stop at the next phone box."

"We aren't gonna see any dead people, are we?" Berry was uncomfortable. He hated these places.

"Don't be a wimp. They cannot harm you."

He shuddered. "Bad enough seeing those pictures of Giles."

"I know," Bethan said quietly. "I was there when they were taken."

"Jesus, I'm sorry." He kissed the top of her head. "Forgive me?"

"I shall think about it," she said.

"Bethan! Is that you?"

"Hello, Dai. Where are you?"

"In the embalming room, come on through."

Berry felt his legs giving way.

"Only kidding," the bald man said, pushing through the purple curtains. "Oh, I'm sorry, Bethan, I thought you had Guto with you. Bugger won't go within a mile of the embalming room, see." He chuckled.

Bethan said, "This is Berry Morelli. He and Guto have a similar attitude to death."

Dai shook hands with Berry. The undertaker's hand was mercifully dry, no traces of embalming fluid. "Morelli. Italian, is it? You want to go to that pizza place next door, show the buggers how to do it properly."

Berry shook his head. "No way you can teach an Englishman to make a pizza."

"This could be true," Dai said. "The trouble with an Englishman, however, is he doesn't believe there is anything he cannot do. Come through to the office."

The office looked out over a cleanly swept, white-walled yard. Over the top of the end wall they could see a segment of Pontmeurig castle.

There were four hard chairs with purple velvet seats and a desk. It had a phone on it and a diary, four brass coffin handles and a thickset man with crinkly grey hair.

Bethan said, "Berry, this is Idwal Roberts. He is the Mayor of Pontmeurig."

"Hi, Mayor," Berry said, shaking Idwal's hand. "Berry Morelli. Don't get up."

"I can never quite bring myself to sit on a chair in here," Idwal Roberts said, short legs dangling over the side of the desk. "Don't want to feel I'm here on business, see."

"One day," said Dai, "we'll bring you in feet first, you bugger. Now, Bethan . . ."

"This is difficult," Bethan said. "And in confidence, please."

"Of course," Dai said. "Sit down. I have told Big Gladys to make some tea."

"Idwal, you remember that night at the Drovers' . . . Well, of course you do."

"Oh, *that* night," Idwal said. "I told you, we should have gone to –" He looked at Berry in alarm. "Not police, this chap, is he?"

"He's a friend of Giles's," Bethan said. "And of mine. No, he's not police."

"Only, I thought, with this, you know –"

"Idwal, relax," Dai said. "I am not so short of work that I *want* you to have a stroke."

"And we were talking," Bethan said, "that night, before the trouble, about Y Groes, if you remember. Dai was annoyed that Giles Freeman had managed to secure a house there when he could not. And you said –"

"I suppose I said I would not want to live there myself."

"Correct," Bethan said. "You said, I think, that it was ungodly. Why did you say that?"

"What are you getting at here, Bethan?"

"Just tell me why you said that."

"Well, I suppose . . . I'm a chapel man, see. Always been a chapel man."

"Yes, and the only chapel in Y Groes is Dilwyn Dafis's garage before it was converted."

"Well, see, it isn't just that . . ." Idwal began to fill his pipe. "This is only my own thoughts, Bethan."

"Yes, fine. Go on."

"Well, this is a non-conformist area. Every village has at least one chapel."

"At least," Bethan said.

"But I remember, when I was a youngster, my dad telling me how they almost had to have a missionary expedition to take the chapel to Y Groes. Known as Y Groesfan then, the crossing place. And the only village without a chapel. Only the other side of the Nearly Mountains, but it might have been some pagan place in Africa, the way they campaigned and raised the money."

"Who campaigned?" Berry asked.

"Ah, well, see, this is the point. There was a farmer – I forget his name – who moved up towards Eglwys Fawr for a bigger farm and became a convert to the chapel. And he still kept a field in Y Groesfan, on the edge of the village there. And he said, I will give this field for a chapel to be built there, and everybody began to raise money, in Eglwys, in Pont, in chapels down as far as Lampeter and Cardigan. It became a . . . how do you say it in English . . . ?"

"*Cause célèbre*?" said Berry.

"Exactly. A *cause célèbre*. Everybody gave money for the new chapel in Y Groesfan. And I am asking myself why. What was there in the history of this village that everybody should instinctively put their hands in their pockets to raise the money for a chapel, when there was no demand from the inhabitants. No demand whatsoever, even though many doors were knocked upon and Bibles proffered."

"But surely, it's a *church* village?"

"Pah!" said Idwal, puffing contemptuously on his pipe.

"So they raised the money and they built the chapel," Bethan said. "What happened then?"

"Oh, it went very well for a time. Like, as I say, a missionary conquest of some pagan place in Africa. People travelled from miles around to attend services at the new chapel. Like a pilgrimage, see. The first motorcoach outings from Pont were to Y Groes – they'd got the name changed now, as well, to reflect its new status. The cross. Oh, it was wonderful, for a while."

"And what happened?" said Berry.

Idwal shrugged. "Some say it was the war. Or that it was like everything that burns so bright. Soon extinguished. But myself, I think there is something in that place that needs to be cleaned out before the Lord can enter in. It seems to me . . ."

There was a loud tap on the office door, and it was shouldered open by a large girl whose hair was streaked in gold and purple like the curtains in the chapel of rest. She was carrying a tea tray.

"Thank you, Gladys," Dai said.

"Will you be going over to Y Groes, Mr. Williams, because you've another appointment at twelve. Do you want me to put them off?"

"I'm not going anywhere, girl. Why would you think that?"

"Well, no, I just thought, with the murder. Put it down here, shall I? If Mr. Roberts will move his legs."

"Murder?" Berry said.

"Oh hell, Gladys," Dai said. "Murder is a different thing altogether. Police do their own fetching and carrying with a murder."

"Only they've found something else now, Jane was telling me from the café. More police cars gone chasing up the Nearly Mountains."

"Bloody tragic," Dai said, and it was not clear whether he was talking about the death or the fact that, because it was murder, he had not been called in to remove the body.

"Poor girl," Idwal said. "First she loses her husband, and now . . ." He shook his head.

"No," Bethan whispered. "Oh, please, no –"

"Oh, Christ," Dai said. "I thought you knew – I thought that was why you were asking all this?"

CHAPTER LIV

The police car pulled in behind Gwyn Arthur's fraying Fiesta. Detective Sergeant Neil Probert got out and looked down to where his chief was standing, at the bottom of a steep bank, about twenty yards from the road.

Probert, the Divisional natty dresser, was clearly hoping Gwyn Arthur would climb up and join him at the roadside. But when the Chief stood his ground, Probert wove a delicate path down the bank, hitching up his smart trousers at the waist.

"Thinking of joining the Masons, are we, Neil?" enquired Gwyn Arthur. "Come on, man, the mud's all frozen!"

"Except for that bit," he added with malicious relish as Probert squelched to a halt in a patch of boggy ground, where all the ice had been melted by the heat from the Volvo's engine.

The big blue car had gone down the bank and into a tangle of thorn bushes. Three police officers were cutting and tearing the bushes away for the benefit of a female Home Office pathologist who was rather attractive – certainly the best thing they could hope to encounter on a December morning in the Nearly Mountains.

"I spoke to the garage, sir," Probert said, squeezing brackish water from the bottoms of his trousers. "He picked up his car at just after nine-thirty. Appeared quiet and preoccupied but not otherwise agitated. Enquired at the garage about a hardware shop and they directed him to Theo Davies, where he bought twenty feet of rubber pipe."

"Not dissimilar, I take it," said Gwyn Arthur, "to the hose we see here affixed to the exhaust pipe."

"Indeed, sir," Probert said.

"In that case, Neil, it looks like a wrap."

"Yes, sir."

"Would you like to have a look at him, in case anything occurs to you?"

"No thank you, sir."

"He doesn't look bad. Pink and healthy. Kind it is, to a corpse, carbon monoxide."

"So I understand, sir."

Gwyn Arthur nodded. "All that remains, it seems to me, is for Mollie to furnish Forensic with a few traces of blood of the appropriate group."

"Hang on, Gwyn, I'm not even in the bloody car yet," the pathologist called across, and Gwyn Arthur smiled at her.

"Just a point, Neil. Did anyone see him arrive at the garage?"

"Yes, sir. He was in a blue Land-Rover driven by a young female. Assumed to be his daughter."

Gwyn Arthur nodded. Shortly after the discovery of her mother's body, the back of its head a mess, he'd spent ten minutes talking to Mrs. Claire Freeman. Obviously in shock, but remarkably coherent, Mrs. Freeman had told of picking up her father, as prearranged, at eight-fifteen and driving him to Pontmeurig. It had been agreed that Mr. Hardy would return with the car to collect his wife. His manner, as described by his daughter, was in no way suspicious. Indeed, he had several times expressed the hope that the car would be ready to collect so that he could take Mrs. Hardy home.

"If you find a pen, Mollie –"

"I know, I know . . ."

In a plastic sack at Gwyn Arthur's feet was an AA book, found on the passenger seat, partly under the dead man's head. Across the yellow cover of the book had been scrawled,

I'm so sorry. I do not know why it happened. I loved her really.

That poor girl.

In thirty years of police work, Gwyn Arthur had several times encountered people around whom tragedies grew like black flowers. This was definitely the worst case – compounded by her being stranded in a remote village in a strange country.

He thought fleetingly of the death of Giles Freeman, of the American who had come to the station with his undisclosed suspicions. Undoubtedly, there was more to this than any of them realised, but the details were likely to be deeply private, and what good would come of digging it over now? It was a wrap. He had a result. Murder and suicide, a common-or-garden domestic. Leave it be.

Chief Inspector Gwyn Arthur Jones: firm believer in compassionate policing.

"Oh, and BBC Wales have been on, sir. I think they might be sending a crew across from Carmarthen."

"Get back to Mike from the car, tell him to phone and tell them they'll get more excitement out of the by-election."

Gwyn Arthur jammed his hat over his ears, picked up the plastic bag containing the AA book and followed Probert up the bank.

"Tell him to give them a quote from me," he said. "Say we aren't looking for anyone else in connection with the incident at this time."

Within the hour, reporters and crews from both BBC Wales and its independent counterpart arrived in Y Groes. Neither attempted to interview Claire. They had no luck with any of the villagers either, in that all those approached refused to give an interview through the medium of English. The licensee of *Tafarn Y Groesfan*, Aled Gruffydd, sounding very tired and nervous, said a few words to the reporter from Radio Cymru, the BBC's Welsh-language radio station. Translated, it came down to: "This is a terrible tragedy, and we do not want to make things any worse. Just let it go, will you?"

Max Canavan, of the *Sun*, was the only reporter who attempted to talk to the woman who had lost her husband and her parents in separate tragedies within a week. The door of the judge's house was opened to him by a huge, bearded man who informed the reporter in a conversational tone that if he did not leave the village immediately he would not leave it with his arms unbroken.

Deprived thus of a story which might have opened with "Tragic widow Claire Freeman spoke last night of her grief and horror . . ." the national newspapers ignored what was, after all, only a domestic incident.

CHAPTER LV

So overgrown were the walls of the house with some sort of evergreen creeper that its gabled attic windows looked like the eyes of a hairy sheepdog under pointed ears.

Frightfully Gothic. Even when they retired, she thought, some clergymen just had to find a typical vicarage to hole up in.

She parked the Porsche proudly in the driveway. It was only a secondhand one, with two substantial dents on its left haunch which she'd refused to let them repair. But it looked even better for that. Miranda liked her cars – and her men, come to that – to convey an impression of having been around.

This Canon Peters clearly had been around. He wore a crumpled cream suit, and his clerical collar, if indeed he was wearing one, was hidden behind a beard like those supplied with the more superior Father Christmas outfits.

"My dear," he said, flinging back the door. He had to be over eighty and yet he was looking at her, Miranda noticed, with the eyes of a man who thought that if he played his cards right he might be in with a chance here.

"*Ex*-lover, eh?" Canon Peters said. "What can the boy be thinking of? And a Porsche too! Two visions to break an old man's heart. Come through, my dear."

Phew –! He hadn't been like this on the phone.

Miranda followed the old clergyman along a dim hall and then into a big warmly toned room, its walls painted the creamy colour of his suit.

"Drove Triumph Spitfires for years," he was saying. "Now the sods have taken away my licence. Bloody eyesight test."

"Didn't seem to me that your eyes were terribly deficient," Miranda said.

"Fiddled the test, if you ask me. Thought I was too old for a sports car. Bloody bureaucrats. Like a drink?"

"Perhaps not," said Miranda, who had once had her own licence taken away, as a result of a mere couple of double gins. Well, perhaps three.

"Suppose I'd think twice too, if I had a Porsche. Coppers love a Porsche."

"They do indeed. Now, Canon Peters –"

"Alex, please. Sit down, my dear." He brought himself a whisky and sat next to her on the chintzy sofa, an arm flung across its back behind her. "I didn't really expect you to come."

Miranda was surprised too. When the Canon had phoned, she'd been lying on Morelli's bed watching morning television – some awful ex-MP who thought he was God's gift – and feeling somewhat at a loose end. She'd traded in her Golf for the Porsche the previous day, the result of a particularly gratifying bank statement, and was trying to think of somewhere moderately exciting to exercise it.

But Wales?

Alex was saying, "I can see you're hooked on this thing already." On a coffee table he had a six-speaker ghetto-blaster of the most overt kind.

"Let me play you what I recorded from the radio. I listen to Radio Wales every morning, sentimental old sod."

He pressed the "play" key. "Missed the first bit, I'm afraid. By the time I realised it was significant, damn thing was half over."

... *was found brutally beaten to death in a bedroom at the village inn. Mr. and Mrs. Hardy had been forced to spend the night at the inn after their car broke down. The couple, who were from Gloucestershire, were in the area to attend the funeral of their son-in-law, who died suddenly last week. Mr. Hardy, who was sixty-four, was found dead later this morning in his car in a remote area about three miles from the village. Police said they were not looking for a third person in connection with the incident.*

"There," said Alex, switching off the ghetto-blaster. "I think we can take it, don't you, that these two people were Giles Freeman's in-laws?"

"It certainly looks that way. Gosh."

"Did you try to contact your friend Morelli?"

"Oh yes," Miranda said. "In fact, that's partly why I'm here."

After the Canon's call she'd rung American Newsnet to enquire if they had a number for Berry Morelli in Wales and been told that Berry Morelli, as of this morning, was no longer working for the agency.

"What?"

"He fired himself," Addison Walls had said.

"Is he still in Wales?"

"Your guess is as good as . . . No, hell, he's there all right, the weirdo bastard."

"But what's he *doing* there?"

"Listen, lady, if I knew that . . ."

So, in the end, what had really done it for Miranda was the thought that she might be *missing* something.

That what Morelli had been rambling on about was not, in fact, the purest load of old whatsit, but something rather extraordinary – *and she wasn't part of it.*

This, and having no actual work in prospect for at least a month.

And owning a Porsche for the first time in her life and having nothing exciting to do with it.

Miranda's plan was to milk the Canon and drive across to Wales with whatever goodies he had to offer – and a lot of tyre-squealing on the bends.

"Martin," she said. "You mentioned somebody called Martin. Who died."

"Poor Martin, yes. Super chap in his way."

"So what happened to him?"

"Sure you won't have a drink?"

"After you tell me what happened to this Martin."

"You're a hard woman," Alex said, and he recalled how he'd met Martin Coulson some time after his retirement, while doing a spot of part-time lecturing at a Welsh theological college.

Coulson had been a student there, an Englishman, though you wouldn't have thought it, Alex said, to hear the boy speak Welsh.

"I'm no expert, mind. I was brought up in the Rhondda and left there at seventeen. My own Welsh is rudimentary to say the least. But my colleagues were enormously impressed by this young man's dedication. Actually, what it was was an obsession which lasted throughout his time at college. And his achievement was publicly recognised when he was declared Welsh Learner of the Year at the National Eisteddfod."

"What an accolade," Miranda said dryly.

"And after he was ordained he was keen to work in a Welsh-speaking parish. So the bishop decided it was time Y Groes had a curate. I think, actually, he was getting rather worried about Ellis Jenkins, the vicar there. Jenkins had been very well known as a poet, writing in English and then increasingly in Welsh and getting his work published under the name Elias ap Siencyn – ap Siencyn being the Welsh version of Jenkins. Anyway, the reason they were worried about him was that his work was becoming . . . shall I say, a little esoteric. And yet somehow strident. Rather extreme in an anti-English way."

371

"Loony Welsh nationalist vicar?"

"Lots of them about, my dear. Never read R. S. Thomas?"

"I've never even read *Dylan* Thomas," said Miranda shamelessly.

Alex Peters made no comment on this. Miranda had taken note that the author's name which seemed to occur more often than any other on his own bookshelves was Ed McBain.

"Of course, Ellis Jenkins didn't want a curate, but he had no choice in the matter. So Martin, all enthusiasm, fluent in Welsh, goes off to Y Groes, and within three months . . . he's dead."

Miranda waited while Canon Alex Peters filtered whisky through his beard.

"The inquest returned a verdict of misadventure, although I was not convinced."

"You thought he'd been murdered?"

"Oh, good Lord, no, I thought he'd committed suicide."

"Oh," said Miranda, disappointed.

"He came to see me. Must have been about three weeks after going to Y Groes to take up his curacy. In a terrible state. Thin, hollow-eyed. Obviously hadn't been eating properly, or sleeping much, I would have said. We had a long discussion. I wanted him to stay the night but he refused. You might think, my dear, that we're all bumbling, stoical chaps, but I can tell you, a clergyman in the throes of emotional crisis is a dreadful sight to behold."

"Was he a poof?" asked Miranda, this being the only emotional problem she could imagine the average clergyman having to come to terms with.

"Oh, nothing like that. Nothing *sexual*. No, quite simply, the much-lauded Welsh Learner of the Year had got up in the pulpit for the first time, about to deliver his maiden sermon to the assembled villagers of Y Groes – and, believe me, that parish is one of the few left in Britain that still pulls 'em in on a Sunday.

So there he is in the pulpit, fully prepared, rehearsed – and he can't do it. Won't come out."

"How d'you mean?"

Alex Peters threw up his arms. "He finds he simply can't preach in Welsh!"

"I don't understand," said Miranda.

"Neither did he. This man was good. I mean *very* good – one chap at the college told me he sometimes thought Martin Coulson's Welsh was more correct than his own, and he'd lived all his life in Lampeter. And yet, whenever he got up in the pulpit at Y Groes, he was completely tongue-tied. And not only that, he found he was increasingly unable to speak Welsh to the villagers he met socially or in the street. I'll always remember what he said to me that afternoon. He said, 'You know, Alex, when I'm in Y Groes – as soon as I get out of the car – I feel like a damned Englishman again.'"

Miranda thought to herself that Martin Coulson must merely have come to his senses after wasting all that time learning a language that was about as much use in the civilised world as Egyptian hieroglyphics. The best thing he could have done was get on the first available train to London.

"I didn't know how to advise him," Alex Peters said. "I wondered whether Ellis Jenkins was intimidating him in some way. I suggested he take a few days' holiday and think things over, but he insisted on going back. It's always been a source of great regret to me that I didn't go with him for a day or two – how much help I'd have been, with no Welsh to speak of, is debatable. But, as one gets older, these things prey on one's mind."

"I gather he went back then."

"Afraid so. I phoned him once or twice to find out how he was getting on. 'Fine,' he said. 'What about the Welsh?' I said. 'Done any preaching?' 'Not yet,' he said, 'but I'm working up to it.'

"So what happens next is Jenkins abruptly decides to take

a holiday. Never been known before. So, off he goes to North Wales on the Saturday, and the following day Martin ascends the steps of the pulpit, looks out over the congregation, opens his mouth to deliver the opening words he's presumably spent all night preparing – and has the most appalling nosebleed. I leave you to imagine the scene. Blood all over the pulpit, Martin backing off down the steps and rushing out. Service abandoned in disarray. All this came out at the inquest."

"How horrid," Miranda said.

"Next day they find the boy unconscious on the floor of the church. Cracked open his head on the pointed corner of some tomb. Rushed to hospital. Five days in a coma, then gone."

"Why did they decide it was an accident?"

"Well, he'd had quite a lot to drink, apparently, and he wasn't used to it. There *was* evidence that he was very depressed. That from me, of course – Jenkins was away at the time of Martin's death, and he was being rather vague and bland about the whole business. And there was no suicide note, and so the feeling was that he must simply have had too much to drink, wandered into the church in the dark, tripped and bashed his head on the tomb. The idea of somebody deliberately smashing his head into the stone didn't appeal."

"But you thought –" Miranda was finding this rather distressing now. No fun any more.

"I suppose I had the idea of him kneeling there and being suddenly overcome with despair and throwing back his head and – crunch. Sorry, my dear, but you did ask. *Now* can I get you a drink?"

"Yes please," she said. "Just a tiny one. Lots of soda."

Forty minutes later she was roaring westwards – though very much in two minds now about the whole thing.

Thinking seriously about all this, what you had was not an

intriguing mystery but something really rather squalid: the story of a grim, unpleasant place where people couldn't settle down and had become unhinged and killed themselves or each other out of sheer depression.

When she'd pressed him, Canon Peters had shrugged and said he just felt there were certain places you ought to avoid if you possibly could.

"Yes, but *why* . . . ?"

"Oh, I don't know, my dear. Why do some places, some people seem to attract tragedy? Is it isolation? In-breeding? Perhaps it's something endemic to the whole area. Why was Winstone Thorpe so bothered about Giles Freeman moving up there? I don't think we'll ever reach any kind of conclusion. But I had it on my conscience that I might have fobbed off young Morelli. And well, you know, after failing to save Martin . . ."

Miranda had been vaguely intrigued by this vicar person, Ellis Jenkins.

"Ah." The Canon had looked sort of wry. "I did meet him once, at a conference in Lampeter. Spindly chap, staring eyes. And the stories, of course."

"What stories?"

"His obsession with the old Celtic church – back at the dawn of Christianity in Britain. And what came before it."

"And what did come before it?"

"Oh, Druids and things. All tied in with his preoccupation with being Welsh and the Eisteddfod and the Bardic tradition."

"Tedious," Miranda said.

"Very, my dear."

Miranda had graciously declined another drink and whatever else Canon Alex Peters might have had in mind. She hadn't even stopped for lunch at any of the rather inviting Oxfordshire pubs. The tang of adventure in the air seemed to have dissipated, leaving her quite moody and almost oblivious to the fact that she was driving an actual Porsche.

Morelli was arguably the most uptight, paranoid, insecure person she'd ever been close to. Was he really the right person to be paddling about in this grotty little pool of death and misery?

Miranda prodded the Porsche, and it took the hint and whizzed her off towards the Welsh border.

CHAPTER LVI

Berry found it disturbing the way his whole life had been dramatically condensed in just two days, his horizon reduced to a shadow.

Was this how it happened? Was this what it did to you? Drew you in, and before you knew it there was no place else to go, and the sky was slowly falling?

He was walking from the little square behind the castle, through the back streets to Guto's place to pick up his stuff, pay his bill, thank Mrs. Evans.

And then what?

Not yet noon, but it was like the day had given up on Pontmeurig; the atmosphere had the fuzzy texture of dusk.

He thought about Giles, who, once he'd seen Y Groes, was sunk. Nothing else mattered but to escape to the place – a place where the future, for him, was an illusion.

He thought about the Hardy couple, how desperate she'd been to hightail it out of here and how everything had pushed them back in until, different people by now – they had to be different people – they'd destroyed each other.

Different people.

He'd come here two days ago just to clear his own mind, settle his obligations. Now – he could hardly believe how quickly and simply this had happened – *he had no reason to go back*. The link with London and, through London, with the States had been neatly severed.

And there was Bethan.

Looking at it objectively, he had to face this – Bethan was part of the trap.

Maybe they were part of each other's trap.

Through the front window he could see Mrs. Evans inside, dusting plates – a job which, in this house, must be like painting the Brooklyn Bridge. And she saw him and put down her duster and rushed to the door.

"Oh, Mr. Morelli –" she wailed.

"Hey, listen, I'm real sorry about last night, only I got detained and –"

"You haven't seen Guto, have you?"

No he hadn't, thank God.

"Only he've gone off in a terrible mood again. Came home last night moaning about being betrayed and giving it all up, his – you know – the candidate's job. He doesn't mean it, mind, but he's terrible offended about somebody."

A somebody with black hair and big gold earrings and eyelids you could die over.

"How, ah, how's his campaign going?"

"Oh dear, you haven't seen the paper?"

On the hallstand, among about a dozen plates, was a copy of that morning's *Western Mail*, folded around a story in which Conservative candidate Simon Gallier was suggesting that support for Plaid Cymru was rapidly falling away. He had based his conclusion on a Plaid public meeting in the totally Welsh-speaking community of Y Groes which, he claimed, had been attended by fewer than a dozen people.

"– And when he saw that, on top of everything, well –"

"I can imagine."

He could also imagine how Bethan was going to feel about this. What a fucking mess.

"Can I pay you, Mrs. Evans?"

"You aren't leaving, are you?" She looked disconsolate.

"I, ah, think it's for the best. That's three nights, yeah? One hundred and –"

"You only stayed two nights!"

"I shoulda been here last night too."

"Go away with you, boy. Two nights, that's eighteen pounds exactly."

He didn't want to screw things up further for Guto by telling Mrs. Evans that even two nights, at the rates quoted by her son, would come out at seventy pounds. He made her take fifty, assuring her that all Americans had big expense accounts. Then he went to his room, shaved, changed out of the American werewolf sweatshirt and into a thick fisherman's sweater because it wasn't getting any warmer out there.

Then he carried his bag downstairs, thanked Mrs. Evans again, assuring her (oh, boy . . .) that things would surely work out for Guto, and took his stuff to the Sprite on the castle parking lot.

Loaded the bag into the boot, keeping an eye open for the hard-man of the nationalists. Guto was a guy with a lot to take out on somebody, and he sure as hell wasn't going to hit Simon Gallier if Berry Morelli was available.

He got into the car and sat there watching the alley next to Hampton's Bookshop over the road, waiting for Bethan to emerge.

They'd parted outside the funeral parlour, he to pay Mrs. Evans, she to go home and change. They had said not one word to each other about Elinor and George Hardy.

After half an hour it was very cold in the car and he started the engine and the heater. She knew where he was. She'd come. What if she didn't?

He looked across at the flat above the bookshop but could detect no movement. And yet she couldn't have gone anywhere because her Peugeot was right there, not fifteen yards away.

But what if she *had* gone away? What would he do if he never saw her again? If that part of the trap were suddenly to spring open?

He couldn't face it. He needed to be here now not for Winstone or Giles, who were beyond any help, but for Bethan. Accepting now that this was why he'd let his job slide away. This was how his life had condensed – around her. There was no way he could leave here without her. But there was no way she was going to leave until –

A blink of white in the alleyway, and she came out and walked quickly across the street to the car.

Berry closed his eyes and breathed out hard.

Bethan got into the car and slammed the door and they looked at each other.

And he said, "I know. Drive, Morelli."

The village had been called Y Groesfan, and this had interested Dr. Thomas Ingley.

Y Groesfan meant "the crossing place", suggesting a crossroads. And yet no roads crossed in the village; it was a dead end.

What other kind of crossing could there be?

The origins of the village were unknown, but the church was the oldest in this part of Wales, and its site, the mound on which it was built, was prehistoric.

Most of the graves in the churchyard dated back no further than the 1700s, but the tomb of Sir Robert Meredydd in a small chapel to the left of the altar was late medieval.

Around the time of Owain Glyndwr. It was recorded that Glyndwr, as a young man, had been to Y Groesfan in the late summer of 1400 to "pay homage". This was only weeks before he was declared Prince of Wales following a meeting of his family and close friends at his house Glyndyfrdwy in northeast Wales.

All this Bethan had learned from the red notebook found under a floorboard by the late George Hardy.

"But why does it have to be relevant?" Berry asked.

They were heading east from the town now, towards Rhayader, close to the very centre of Wales, where the executive council of Plaid Cymru had met to decide on a candidate for the Glanmeurig by-election.

"The last two people to hold this notebook are dead," Bethan said, the red book on her lap.

"That scare you?"

"Left here," Bethan said. She pointed out of her window. "That church is Ysbyty Cynfyn. See the big stones in the wall? They are prehistoric. The church is built inside a neolithic stone circle. It used to be a pagan place of worship; now it's Christian."

"Like Y Groes?"

"Probably."

"You want to stop?"

"No. Can we go to England, Berry?"

"We sure can," he said, surprised. "Any particular part? Hull? Truro?"

"Not far over the border. Herefordshire."

"Any special reason for this?"

Bethan opened the red book. "There's an address here. Near Monnington-on-Wye. Do you know the significance of Monnington? Did you get that far in Guto's book?"

"Uh-huh." Berry shook his head.

"You can look out from there and see the hills of Wales."

"I think I understand," Berry said.

CHAPTER LVII

He liked less and less having to go into the oak woods, particularly in winter. Without their foliage, the trees could look at you.

And into your soul.

He did not look at them, could not face them. As he walked, he stared at the ground. But he could see their roots like splayed hands, sometimes had to step over individual knobbled fingers.

Remembering being introduced to the woods as a boy, as they all had been. Taught honour and respect for the trees, fathers of the village itself.

And once, aged eighteen or thereabouts, bringing a girl into the woods one night in May and feeling afraid at the inferno of their passion.

Gwenllian. His wife now.

He told himself he was doing this for her. Ill she was now, most of the time. Did not want to cook, would go into no bedroom but their own, wept quietly in the afternoons.

Looking only at the ground, he almost bumped into the oaken gate.

Rheithordy.

Looked up then, and into the face of the rector.

Cried out, stifled it, embarrassed.

Ap Siencyn, in his cassock, standing at the gate, motionless, like one of the winter trees.

"Rector," Aled said weakly.

Only the rector's hair moved. Even whiter than Aled's and longer, much longer, it streamed out on either side, unravelled by a little whingeing wind which the oaks had let through as a favour.

The rector spoke, his voice riding the wind like a bird.

"You are a coward, are you then, Aled?"

"Yes," Aled confessed in shame. "I am a coward."

There was a long silence then, the wind cowed too.

"We shall have to leave, I know," Aled said.

"Indeed?"

"We . . . I . . . There used to be this exhilaration. A delight in every day. Contentment, see. That was how it was."

"And you do not think we have to justify it? Nothing to pay, Aled?"

"But why upon me? Me and Gwenllian, all the time?"

"Perhaps it is a test. A test which you appear to be on the point of failing."

"But when there's no contentment left, only a dread –"

"It's winter, Aled. In winter, the bones are revealed. In winter, we know where we are and what we are."

Aled said, "Death himself walked from these woods last night, and across the bridge and to the door of the inn." The pitch of his voice rose. "*We heard him knocking, with his claw, a thin knocking . . .*"

The rector said mildly, "You've known such things before."

"It's changed," Aled said. "There is . . . something sick here now."

The rector did not move yet seemed to rise a full two feet, and his white hair streamed out, although there was no wind now.

"How *dare* you!"

Aled shook his head and backed off, looking at the ground.

"You puny little man." He was pointing at Aled now, with a thin black twig, like a wand.

"I'm sorry."

"If you go from here, you must go soon," the rector said.

"Yes. There are relatives we can stay with. Over at Aber."

"You must get out of our country."

"Leave Wales?"

"And never return."

"But what will we do?"

"No harm will come to you, I don't suppose," the rector said. "Unless you try to come back here."

Meaningfully, he snapped the twig in half and tossed the pieces over the gate so that they landed at Aled's feet.

"It's building again, you see," ap Siencyn said deceptively gently. "You must be aware of that. You must surely feel it growing beneath us and all around us."

Oh yes, he could feel it. Almost see it sometimes, like forked lightning from the tip of the church tower.

"It's like the rising sun on a cloudless day," the rector said. "Always brighter in the winter. Rising clear. And those who do not rise with it, those not protected, will be blinded by the radiance."

Aled thought, this man talks all the time in a kind of poetry. Perhaps it is a symptom of his madness.

But the parish owned the inn and many of the cottages and so he, in effect, was ap Siencyn's tenant. And in other ways, Aled knew, ap Siencyn had the power to do good and to do harm. He looked down at the two pieces of the twig at his feet and saw where his choice lay.

"Don't leave it too long, will you, Aled? Make your decision."

"Yes," Aled said. He walked back through the woods towards the road, and the oak trees watched him go.

CHAPTER LVIII

"I felt it was right, see," Guto said. "Meant to happen. All my life, the disappointments, the frustrations – all foundations for it. I mean, Christ, I *needed* this."

Dai Death said, "Oh, come on, man. Not over yet, is it?"

"It is for me. I'll tell you when it ended . . . that meeting in Y Groes. I just can't convey to you, Dai, what it was like. Thinking, you know, have I come to the wrong bloody hall, or what? Another pint, is it?"

"Not for me. And not for you either. Finish that one and get a sandwich down you."

"Bloody mother hen," Guto grumbled.

Well, all right, he was drinking too much, he knew it. And in public. The party's General Secretary, Alun, had warned him about this – "half the voters are women, never forget that" – as they drove across to Aber for a lunchtime conference with two other Plaid MPs. The other MPs had been encouraging. You could not really get an idea until the final week, they said. But Guto had followed campaigns where a candidate who'd been strongly tipped initially had dropped clean off the chart in the first few days.

By the weekend the results of the first opinion polls would be out. If they were half as bad as he expected, he'd be placed at least third . . .

"Bethan it is, though, really," Dai said. "Admit it."

Guto glared resentfully at the undertaker through his pint glass. Then he put the glass down, fished out a cigarette, the anger blown over now, leaving him subdued.

"Aye, well, that too."

And that also would have been so right, both of them gasping for fresh air – her with the trouble at school, him badly needing a legitimate outlet for frustrations which were threatening to turn destructive. Westminster, the bright lights – and what was so wrong with bright lights? He'd convinced himself – well, Christ, politics weren't everything – that when he won the election she would go with him.

When he won . . .

He could have bloody wept.

"Who *is* this Morelli?" Dai asked. "Who is he *really*?"

"More to the point," Guto said, "*where* is he?"

This was also what the girl in the Porsche wanted to know.

"Seen you on the telly, isn't it?" Mrs. Evans said at once, having watched the car pulling up outside the house and this exotic creature unwinding.

"Well, it's possible," Miranda admitted modestly.

"It's the red hair. Wasn't you in . . . Oh, what's it called now, that detective thing on a Sunday night . . . ?"

"Oh well, you know, I pop up here and there." Miranda was hardly going to remind this little woman that her best-known television persona was the girl accosted in a back street by a leather-clad thug impressed by her shampoo. "Anyway, I'm awfully sorry to bother you, but a journalist told me Berry Morelli was staying here."

"Oh, Mr. Morelli. Him you're looking for."

"I am indeed."

"Well, he left, not two hours ago."

"Do you know where he's gone?"

"Well, I never asked him, not wanting to pry, Miss –"

"Moore-Lacey. Miranda Moore-Lacey."

"Oh, lovely. He'll be terrible sorry to have missed you. Let

386

me see now . . . I wonder if my son . . . Perhaps he can tell you where Mr. Morelli is. Do you know my son?"

"I'm afraid I don't know a soul here."

"Well, you can't miss Guto. Very distinctive, he is. Black beard and a big green rosette. Can't be far away, he've a meeting to do in town tonight. He'll be at the Memorial Hall by seven. Do you know where that is?"

"I'll find it," Miranda said. "Thank you very much."

As she slid into the car, the first snowflakes landed on its bonnet and instantly evaporated.

Within ten minutes there were rather more of them and they were not evaporating quite so rapidly.

When they found Bryan Mortlake, he was splitting logs outside his house, a former lodge next to the main road. He did not stop splitting logs when they spoke to him, and he did not invite them in.

"Ingley," he said, raising the axe. "Nutcase," he said, bringing it down.

The axe hit the log dead-centre and the two halves fell from the block. One rolled over Bethan's shoe.

"Safer to stand further back," Mortlake said, looking and talking more like a retired colonel than a retired academic. Except retired colonels, in Berry's experience, were more polite.

He set up another log. "Not still hanging around, is he?"

"He's dead," Berry said.

"Oh? Well, he was still a nutcase."

"You have many dealings with him?"

"Not when I could help it. Would you mind moving out of my light. Snow's forecast for tomorrow, did you know that?"

"Dr. Mortlake," Bethan said. "Would you tell us what Dr. Ingley came to see you about?"

Mortlake brought down the axe. There was a knot in the log,

and it jammed. He looked at Bethan as if it was her fault then hit the axe handle with the flat of his hand to free it. Both log and axe tumbled off the block and Mortlake looked furious.

"Look, what's all this about?"

"We found your name and address in this." Bethan pulled the red book from her raincoat. "I am a schoolteacher in a village in West Wales, where Dr. Ingley was doing some research. When he died, his notes were passed on to me. I'm writing a history of the village and I thought –"

Mortlake snatched the book and thumbed through it for about half a minute before handing it back with what Berry assumed to be a superior, academic sneer.

"Bilge," Mortlake said.

"*What's* bilge?" Berry said. "What's he saying here? That's all we want to know."

"You a Welsh schoolteacher too?"

"I'm a friend of Mrs. McQueen. You have a problem with that?"

"Look." Mortlake hefted the axe and the log onto the chopping block and stood back panting. "Did you ever meet the man?"

Berry put a foot on the log, hit the axe handle, freed it and gave it to Mortlake.

"No," he said.

"He had a crackpot theory about Glyndwr. Who, you may remember, was supposed to have ended his days a few miles from here, at Monnington."

"We are going there next," Bethan said.

"Can't see what good that will do you. None of it's proven. There's an unmarked stone in the churchyard there, which they say is Glyndwr's grave. I doubt that."

Berry said, "What was the crackpot theory?"

Mortlake threw down the axe. "You know, half the foolish myths in British history begin like this. In my view, when someone cobbles together a lot of patent rubbish and then dies without publishing it, we should all be damned thankful and let it lie."

"Dr. Mortlake," Bethan said. "This is only a little village project. What harm can that do?"

"What d'you say the village is called?"

"Y Groes."

"Never heard of it."

"It's near Pontmeurig."

"Oh, the by-election place." Mortlake gave in. "All right, there's a legend – I mean, when you're talking about Glyndwr, half of it's legend – and the story goes that some years after his death – No, actually, there are two different stories, one says it was after his death, the other says it was when he was dying. Both come to the same conclusion – that four patriotic Welshmen couldn't stand the thought of the old hero dying in exile, came across the border and took him home. Or carted his remains home, whichever version you prefer."

Berry sensed Bethan's excitement.

"Ingley was convinced this was true," Mortlake said. "He maintained there was a place in Wales where all the heroes went to die or whatever, according to some ancient tradition. You see, it's complete nonsense – man was bonkers."

"Did he say where the place was?" Bethan asked.

"Wouldn't tell me. Big secret. As if I really wanted to know."

"What evidence did he have?"

"Oh, he claimed to have discovered the names of the four Welshmen who came for Glyndwr. He suspected there may have been some collaboration here with John Skydmore, of Monnington Court, who was Glyndwr's son-in-law. Which was why he came to me."

"You helped him?"

"He left me the names. I said I'd look into it. Didn't bother, to

389

be quite honest. I can tell a crank from fifty paces. And don't ask me for the list because I've probably thrown it away."

"Well, thanks," Berry said. "We'll leave you to your logs."

"Very good memory, though, as it happens."

"I'm sorry?"

"My memory. Very good. If it's any use for your . . . village project . . . the four men were a farmer, a lawyer, a coachman and . . . a carpenter, yes. He was said to have made an ornate coffin, fit for a prince, as they say. And their names, d'you want their names? Very well . . ."

He leaned on his axe, pursed his lips. "Vaughan – John Vaughan. Robert Morgan. William, or Gwilym Davies and –"

Mortlake paused triumphantly. He'd plucked all four straight out of his head.

"– Thomas Rhys."

He beamed.

"Don't tell me," Berry said. "He was the lawyer."

Mortlake, in a better temper now, picked up a big log with both hands and set it on the block. "You know more than I do, sir," he said.

Dusk now. A pair of black swans glided across the pond behind the church. It was cold and utterly still.

"He was right," Berry said. "Gonna snow."

The sky was taut and shiny, like a well-beaten drum.

"Snow is for the Christmas cards," Bethan said. "You won't find a country person who likes it."

"This is a wonderful place," Berry said, putting an arm around her.

Like Y Groes, Monnington was a dead end. Like the immediate environs of Y Groes, the surrounding land was soft and peaceful. But, although the church was in a secret place, approachable only by foot along a shaded green lane, the landscape around was opened out, mostly flat, the hills serene in the distance.

They found one small, unmarked stone close to the entrance of the church. There was nobody around to ask if this was the supposed grave of Owain Glyndwr.

"This is totally England," Berry said. "You know, this is more like the real old England than any place I ever went to. No cars, no ice-cream stalls, no parking lots, no information bureaux."

"I wish I could interpret what we've learned," Bethan said, pulling away and going back to the stone which might or might not be Glyndwr's.

"Did I gather by your reaction that the families of these four patriotic Welsh guys still live in Y Groes?"

"I can't be sure. Yes, there's a Dewi Vaughan. F – O – N, he spells it, the Welsh way – how they spell it now, rather than then, I should imagine. And yes, he's a carpenter. Like his father before him. Davies – Dafis. Several of those. Thomas Rhys, well –"

"Very weird," Berry said. "Judge Rhys feels he has to return to preserve the family tradition. He leaves his house to his grand-daughter, his chosen heiress. She changes her name to Rhys. Her husband, who is irrelevant to all this –" his voice dropped "– dies."

"And she's possibly pregnant, don't forget."

"So Giles has served his purpose," Berry said. "Jesus, I hate the thought of all this. Sorry, what'd you say then?"

"I said, if it is Giles's baby."

"Hey, what –?"

"I don't *know*," Bethan said desperately. Snatching up the hood of her raincoat so that he couldn't see her expression, she moved quickly away through the graveyard, a ghostly white lady in the dusk.

CHAPTER LIX

He almost didn't wear a tie.

In fact, if the Plaid Cymru president had not been lined up to speak, he thought he would have had difficulty persuading himself to go at all.

At seven o'clock he entered the Memorial Hall through the back door and peeped into the main hall from behind the stage, convinced he'd be looking at half-a-dozen people and about three hundred empty chairs.

To his surprise, there must have been over two hundred in the audience already.

A big turn-out for the humiliated hard-man.

He was still feeling depressed and cynical when he climbed on to the platform at the Memorial Hall and took his seat next to the party president, who was going through a patch of unprecedented popularity.

Celebrity night.

By the time they were ready to begin, there must have been nearly five hundred crammed in, and a full complement of Press. He got an encouraging smile from the plump lady from BBC Radio, who seemed to fancy him. But all the rest, he was sure, had come to watch the official public funeral of Guto Evans's election hopes.

Since the report in the *Western Mail*, he was convinced, people had actually been avoiding him in the street, out of embarrassment.

Fuck 'em, he thought. You've got nothing left to lose, boy, so fuck 'em all.

And he did.

He came to his feet feeling like one of those athletes on steroids. Full up with something anyway, and it wasn't the drink, thanks to Dai Death.

Somebody asked him the old question about where he stood on Welsh terrorism, petrol bombs and the burning down of property to deter immigration. To his surprise, he didn't give the careful, strategic answer he'd spent hours working out. Instead, he lost his temper and heard himself saying how much the great Glyndwr would have despised the kind of pathetic little wankers who could only come out at night with paraffin cans.

Politics, he roared, was a game for adults, not spotty adolescents.

Aware that this must sound pretty heavy coming from a man who looked like a sawn-off version of Conan the Barbarian, he felt a surge of pure adrenalin, like red mercury racing up a thermometer. Or one of those fairground things you slammed with a mallet and, if you were strong enough, it rang the bell. For the first time since the London banker had performed the knocking over of the chair right on cue, Guto Evans, fuelled by rage and bitterness, was ringing bells.

For over forty-five minutes, he fended off hostile questioners with the ease of a nightclub bouncer ejecting tired drunks. He didn't care any more what he said to any of the bastards.

"Ladies and gentlemen," the Plaid president, looking shell-shocked, said when Guto finally sat down, "I think you have seen tonight an example of precisely why we selected Guto Evans to fight this by-election. And why Guto Evans, without any doubt, is going to be the next MP for Glanmeurig!"

And up in Eglwys Fawr, Guto thought cynically, as the

audience responded with vigour, the Tories will be saying exactly the same thing about Simon Gallier.

On his way out, men he didn't know patted him on the shoulder, and three women kissed him.

Groupies, by God.

Unfortunately, not that young, the three women – in fact, not much younger than his mam, really.

But, bloody hell, *this* one was . . .

She had definitely come to the wrong place, dressed like that.

"Mr. Evans, I wonder if I might have a word."

"The night is yet young, darling," Guto said, his system still flooded with that desperate, high-octane, who-gives-a-flying-fart-anyway adrenalin. "Have as many as you like."

They spent the night in a glossy new hotel on the edge of Hereford. Country inns were out as far as Bethan was concerned. No oak beams, no creaking floorboards, no "character".

This room was done out in calm and neutral pastel shades. And that included the telephone, the TV with video and satellite receiver, the bedside lamps with dimmer switches and all the envelopes and containers of stuff which nobody ever opened but which showed the management really cared.

Towel-swathed, Bethan came out of the shower into this hermetically sealed haven, where Berry Morelli was sprawled across the pastel bed, trying to screw up the colour-coordination with his bright-orange undershorts.

"Sooner or later," he told the ceiling, "you're gonna have to tell me whatever it is you haven't told me."

She didn't look at him, went over to the dressing table and began to untangle her hair.

Facing his image in the mirror, she said, "Did you read the same thing as me into those notes about the church and the tomb?"

Goddamn red book again.

"Could be," he said. "Sir Robert Meredydd. Died 1421. That would be within maybe a year or two of Owain Glyndwr. You're saying this Meredydd actually *is* Glyndwr? That these guys brought him back to Y Groes and secretly entombed him under a false name?"

"Well, there we are. Possible, isn't it? I have also thought of something else. Dewi Fon, the carpenter. Davies, the coachman? Dilwyn Dafis runs the garage at Y Groes. Repairs vehicles, does a bit of haulage. It's a very old business. I didn't realise quite how old."

"That's wild," said Berry. "I mean, that is *wild*. You're suggesting this guy Dilwyn's ancestor built some kind of special funeral cart or horse-drawn bier or whatever they had in those days to fetch Glyndwr home. And five centuries later the family's still in the transport business. Who's the fourth man, the farmer?"

"Morgan. There is only one Morgan family in Y Groes, and Buddug is married to the head of the tribe."

"The ball-slasher?"

Bethan nodded into the mirror, unsmiling. "The Morgans have farmed there since . . . who can say?"

Berry said, "Are we imagining all this?"

She said sharply, "You mean am *I* imagining all this?"

He went over and put his hands on her shoulders, didn't try to dislodge the towel. She carried on combing out her hair as if his hands weren't there.

"Bethan, I'm taking a deep breath, OK? What makes you think that if Claire is pregnant we may not be talking about Giles's baby?"

She did not reply, went on combing her hair, although the tangles were long gone.

Through the mirror, he saw what looked like old tears burning to come out. She blinked them away.

He felt suddenly angry but said nothing – where was the use in pressurising her?

But then, abruptly, she put down the comb, wiped her hands on a pastel tissue and told his reflection, without preamble, why she'd gone to Swansea after Robin's death.

When she'd finished talking, he went over to the window and looked down to where sporadic night traffic was circumventing the construction site for some new road.

He really wanted to believe her.

But how much of this could you take? Things getting weirder by the minute.

"Stupid of me," she said. "I did not want to tell you, but you pushed."

He turned back and started towards her.

"No," she said.

He sat down on the bed, put his hands over his face and rubbed his eyes in slow circular movements.

He said, "And it really couldn't have been his, Robin's?"

"No."

"Bethan, I don't only want to believe you. I *need* to believe you."

"That is not good enough," she said.

sice ... sice ... sice ... the air said. Tissue-thin pages whispering.

Bethan tossed her head back, stared at the ceiling. The chasm between them was about a hundred miles wide.

You and me, The Gypsy said, *we in same shit. One day you find out.*

What Bethan had told him was that, approximately three weeks after Robin's death, she had discovered she was expecting a baby. Because she knew in her own mind that this could not be Robin's child, she had moved to Swansea where no one knew her. And where the pregnancy had been terminated.

"I did not kill my baby," she emphasised quite calmly. "I killed *its* baby."

"It?"

"The village. Y Groes."

Oh, Christ.

He had no idea how to follow this up. Either she'd tell him or she wouldn't. His lips kept forming questions, but the questions never made it. Only one.

"How could you go back?" he asked. He'd asked her that before.

"How could I not go back?" she replied.

"And do you work with Morelli?" the Bearded Welsh Extremist asked. Every few seconds somebody on the way out would slap him on the back and say something jolly in Welsh.

"You have got to be joking," said Miranda.

"Well, what do you want him for?"

"I don't actually *want* him," Miranda said frankly – no point in trying to bullshit a politician; they were all far too good at it not to spot it coming from someone else. "I just want to pass on some information which might help him."

"I see," said the BWE, whose name she couldn't remember, except that it sounded vaguely insulting. "Well, I don't know where Morelli has gone but I do know who he is with." His eyes were smouldering, she thought, in rather a dark and brooding way, like some sort of Celtic Heathcliff. "Tell me," he said, "have you anywhere to stay?"

"Well, I have," Miranda told him. "But it isn't much of a place."

"Oh, well, good accommodation is hard to find with this election on."

"You're telling *me*. I wound up at some faded Victorian dive called the Plas something or other."

His eyes stopped in mid-smoulder and widened. "The Plas Meurig? You managed to get a room at the Plas Meurig?"

"I realise there's got to be a better hotel somewhere, but I *was* in rather a hurry."

He appeared to be regarding her with a certain respect, on top of the usual naked lust. But before she could capitalise on this, an efficient-looking man with tinted glasses and a clipboard slid between them. "Guto," he said. "Problems, I'm afraid. Tomorrow night's meeting with the farmers' unions. Bit of a mix-up over the hall at Cefn Mynach. Liberal Democrats have got it, so I'm afraid . . . Look, I did try for an alternative venue to Y Groes, but it's central for the farmers."

"No way, Alun," snarled Guto. "I wouldn't go back there if the alternative was a bloody sheep-shed in the Nearly Mountains."

Miranda thought, *Y Groes* . . .

Lowering his voice, this Alun said, "Come on, Guto. We should see it as a challenge. We can build on tonight's success, regain our position. You're acquiring an enviable reputation for turning the tables."

"Aye, and the Press will show up in force when they find out," said Guto. "No, forget it, postpone it."

"We can't postpone it. We'll come across as unreliable. Look, I shall make sure there's a good crowd this time. We can even take most of one with us. Come on, man, you did well tonight."

"Alun," the Extremist said. "I am getting a bad feeling about this."

Oh my God, Miranda thought. Not another one.

CHAPTER LX

Berry Morelli slept uneasily. Bethan did not sleep at all.

Outside, even in Herefordshire now, it was snowing lightly but consistently.

They had not touched one another.

The room had caught an amber glow from the road-construction site below. And in this false warmth Bethan was remembering a close summer evening, a bitter argument with Robin, who was always tired and fractious but insisted it was nothing physical. She remembered storming out, nerves like bare wires, and being soothed at once as the air settled around her, as comforting as soft arms.

It did this sometimes, the village. Was absorbed through the skin like some exotic balm. The soporific scents of wild flowers on a breeze like a kiss. Your churning emotions massaged as you walked down the deserted street, past the *Tafarn*, the church tower soaring from its grassy mound, venerably beneficent.

Robin raging alone inside their terraced cottage at the top of the street, while Bethan was wafted away on the silky, cushioned wings of the evening.

She remembered the air lifting her gently over the stile to the meadow that sloped to the river, trees making a last shadow-lattice on the deepening green.

Remembered yielding her body gratefully to the soft grass, letting the breezes play in the folds of her summer dress. There seemed to be several breezes, all of them warm, making subtle ripples and swirls and eddies.

And she had fallen asleep and dreamed a child's dream of the *Tylwyth Teg*, the beautiful fairy folk.

Awoken in the moistness of the night, the dampness of the grass, the cold wetness between her legs, the bittersweet tang of betrayal, a lingering faraway regret.

And no memory at all of what had happened.

Of what.

Or who.

"Guto," she said. "Git-toe. It really is a super name."

"Thank you," Guto said dubiously. He was trying not to be charmed by this creature who, only minutes earlier, had been chanting git-toe, git-toe through clenched teeth, in concert with the rhythm of her loins.

What also filled him with a certain perverse delight was the thought that, in order to bonk this terribly English Englishwoman, he had actually infiltrated Simon Gallier's fortress, the Plas Meurig, and was about to spend a night within the hallowed portals free of charge.

Whatever the result, it had certainly been an experience, this by-election.

"You might as well tell me," he said. "How the hell did you manage to persuade them to let you have a room? And not just any room, for heaven's sake . . ."

He was looking up suspiciously at an ornate Victorian ceiling across which misshapen plaster cherubs frolicked amid gross moulded foliage.

"Isn't it so utterly tasteless?" said Miranda and giggled, a sound which reminded Guto of the tinkling door chimes in Pontmeurig's new health-food shop which he'd entered for the first time during this afternoon's canvassing.

"It might be tasteless," he said. "But it's probably the best room they've got."

An awful thought had crept up on him. They wouldn't, would they?

"Hah!" Miranda sprang up in the bed, wobbling deliciously. "I know what you're worried about!"

"What am I worried about?"

"You think I've been planted, don't you? You think I'm an expensive bimbo hired by the opposition to discredit you. You think any second now the door's going to fly open and chaps will crowd in with popping flashbulbs. You do, don't you? Admit it!"

"Was a thought," Guto mumbled gruffly.

"Hah!" Miranda shrieked and rolled about laughing. "Oh, how utterly wonderful that would be!"

"Shut up, woman," Guto hissed. "Everybody'll know you've got somebody in here."

"Oh, I love it when you call me 'woman'."

"Well, come on, enlighten me. How *did* you get into a hotel that's been claiming to've been booked up solid for weeks?"

"I'm not going to tell. I have my methods."

"Now look, I'll . . ."

"*Will* you, Guto? Will you really? Do you think you still have the strength? Well, in that case I'll tell you just a little. It all comes down to judicious use of that famous phrase 'Do you know who I am?' which never works with the police these days but still tends to put hoteliers in the most awful tizz, especially in small-town snobby dumps like this. So don't worry any more, OK?"

"Who said I was worried?"

Miranda dug into the bedclothes. "Oh dear, he's utterly flaked out, isn't he, poor little Welsh thing. All right, I'll give him half an hour to recover. And you can use the time to tell me all about this dreadful village where people go to die."

"Y Groes?" Guto fell back into the pillows. "I suppose I died there myself, in a metaphorical way. In the theatrical sense of presenting your famous one-man show and no bugger applauds."

"Did you know a chap called Martin Coulson?"

"Met him the once. Briefly, like."

"I was talking to this old vicar who believes Coulson committed suicide because he was brilliant at speaking Welsh but he couldn't get a word of it out in the pulpit. Does that make any sense to you?"

"Aye, I remember now – he spoke Welsh to me. I switched over to English pretty smartly, mind, when I realised how good he was."

"Typical."

"Well, I was brought up in the Valleys. Welsh is only my second language, see. You don't like to be put to shame in your own country by an Englishman."

"Good heavens, no."

"And you say this vicar thought he topped himself because he couldn't turn it on in the church?"

"That was what he said."

"Sounds highly unlikely to me," Guto said. "Red hot, he was. And it's not an easy language to learn. This is what you wanted to tell Morelli?"

"More or less." She told him how Berry Morelli had gone to Y Groes with Giles Freeman and returned feeling very funny, disturbed over some sort of dubious psychic experience. "And when Freeman snuffed it suddenly, he got very upset. And now these other two people, Giles's in-laws . . . Well, gosh, it's even made me think. It's a lot of deaths, isn't it?"

"Probably more than you know," Guto said. "But it's all explained and, after all, they were –"

He'd been about to say they were all English, but stopped himself on the grounds that she could do a man a lot of damage, this one.

"Well, I'm going there tomorrow night," he said.

"I heard."

"So, if you want to tag along, it'll be one more in the audience."

"Super," Miranda said. "I look forward to it. Where do you think Morelli's gone? Will he be there tomorrow?"

"How should I know?"

"It's snowing again," Miranda said, switching out the bedside light so they could see the white blobs buffeting the long window. "Quite hard, too."

"Berry, wake up. Please."

He turned his head into the steam from a white cup of black tea.

"What's the time, Beth?"

"Nearly four-thirty. I'm sorry to wake you, but my thoughts are killing me."

He sat up, took the cup. Waking wasn't so hard.

"Please can we talk. About everything."

"We can try, kid," Berry said. He'd called her Beth and he'd called her kid, and she hadn't reacted. She must be serious about this.

"OK," he said. "So what are we into here? One sentence. One word. Say it."

Bethan said, "Magic."

"That's the word," Berry said. "That's the word we've been walking all around and poking at with the end of a stick on account of we don't like to touch it."

"Perhaps there are two words," Bethan said.

"And the other one," Berry said, taking her hand, "is black. Right?"

They sat on the edge of the bed in the overheated hotel room, holding hands and drinking tea and watching the snow fall, feeling more afraid now the word had escaped.

CHAPTER LXI

Hotel staff had cleared most of the snow from the car park, but Berry had to dig out the Sprite, which coughed like hell and turned the air blue with acrid smoke.

"Could be pneumonia," he said anxiously, driving into the centre of Hereford, where the early-morning streets had a first-fall purity that would last maybe until the shops opened.

The snow had stopped soon after dawn, but the bloated sky suggested this was only an interim gesture of goodwill.

The city library was almost opposite the cathedral and at this hour they had no problem parking right outside. Waiting for the library to open, they wandered the cathedral grounds, an ancient island cut off from the city by a soft white sea.

Bethan said, "If it snows again we may not make it back for days. We'll have problems anyway; it could be a lot worse in Wales."

Berry thought it would be no bad thing if they didn't get back for weeks, but he said nothing.

On the way here, they'd talked about the baby.

He said it was the most insidious case of rape he'd ever heard of. "Some bastard has to pay."

Bethan thought this was unlikely. "I'm sure, you see," she told him, "that when I was offered the head teacher's post - at the express request of the school governors, I've since discovered - it was expected that I would return very pregnant. And of course the baby would be looked after while I was at the school - very

404

caring people in Y Groes. And the child would grow up like all the rest."

"What would that mean?"

"I can't explain it very easily. They are children of Y Groes. Steeped in the Welsh traditions – traditions which no longer apply anywhere else, not to this extent anyway. Although the community is . . . clings, if you like, to its church, this church is different. There's an element in the religion of the village which is almost pre-Christian. It accepts all the eerie, psychic things – the *toili* and the *cannwyll gorff* and the bird of death – as part of life's fabric. All right, that's not unusual in itself, rural West Wales is riddled with superstition, but here it's a way of life."

"But the church is Anglican," Berry said now, under the massive spireless tower of Hereford Cathedral. "Like this place."

"Not so simple." Bethan was wearing her pink woolly hat and a red scarf wound twice around her neck. "The old Celtic church was the earliest form of Christianity in Britain and it probably absorbed many elements of paganism. Nobody knows for sure what its rituals were, or its dogma. I suppose we can say the two earliest known religious influences in Wales were the Celtic church and . . . what remained of Druidism, I imagine. Intermingled."

"It says in Guto's book that it used to be suggested Owain Glyndwr had been trained in Druidic magic. Like, he was some kind of sorcerer who could alter the weather and –"

"Call spirits from the Vasty Deep," said Bethan. "Yes. Obviously, Guto is deeply dismissive of all this. He wants Glyndwr to have been some sort of pragmatic early social-ist with a deep commitment to democracy and the classless society."

"What do *you* think?"

"I think Glyndwr was probably fumbling in the dark like the

rest of us," Bethan said, taking his arm. "You need a thicker coat, Berry, you must be freezing."

In the library they paused to glance through the morning papers. Over Ray Wheeler's story in the *Mirror* was the headline:

W – KERS!
GUTO BLASTS THE BOMBERS.

Bethan shook her head wryly. "The things an election campaign can do to a person. Not three weeks ago he was saying that, while he deplored the methods, he could fully understand the motives of anti-English terrorism."

They went up some stairs, and Berry said to the guy in the reference section, "We're interested in aspects of Welsh folklore. The, ah –"

"*Gorsedd Ddu*," Bethan said.

"I don't think I've heard of that," the guy said, and Bethan assured him this was not so surprising.

They spent more than an hour bent over a table, exploring maybe twenty books. At one stage Berry went down and moved the Sprite to avoid collecting a parking ticket. When he returned, Bethan announced that she was satisfied there was nothing to be learned here.

"This mean there's nothing actually documented on the, ah . . . ?"

"*Gorsedd Ddu*. Probably not."

Before they left the hotel Bethan had given him a very brief history of the Welsh bardic tradition. Of the Dark Age poets, of whom the best known was Taliesyn. And how, in the nineteenth century, Edward Williams, who called himself Iolo Morgannwg – Iolo of Glamorgan – had identified himself as the Last Druid in Wales and set about single-handedly restoring the tradition.

It was Iolo, an inventive antiquarian scholar not averse to forging ancient verse to prove his point, who established what was to become the National Eisteddfod of Wales – the annual gathering of poets and singers and cultural leaders honoured as "bards".

The inner circle of which was the *Gorsedd* – whose members appeared in white ceremonial costumes such as the Druids were believed to have worn.

"You mean it's all crap?" Berry had said, astonished. "The great Welsh bardic tradition was *dreamed up* by this guy, bridging a cultural gap between the nineteenth century and the Dark Ages? It's all bullshit?"

"Well, let us say, ninety per cent bullshit. But it did fulfil a need in the Welsh people to . . . exalt their heritage, I suppose. It gave them this annual showcase for the language and the poetry. The Welsh love to show off."

"And they conveniently forgot about the antisocial side of the Druids – like human sacrifices in the oak groves under the full moon, all that heavy ritual stuff?"

"Ah, now, some Celtic scholars say the Druids did not sacrifice people or even animals – that was just stories put about by the Romans. We only have people like Julius Caesar to rely on for concrete information about Druidism. But, yes, the organisers of the *eisteddfodau* have even forgotten that the Druids were pagan. It has always been a very God-fearing festival."

They collected all the books together and took them back to the man in charge of the department.

"Nothing?" he said. "Are you sure you've got it right about this *Gorsedd*, er –"

"*Ddu*," Bethan said. "It means black. The Black *Gorsedd*. Yes, but don't worry, there is nothing wrong with your books."

"Oh, we do know that," he said.

*

They sat a while in the car with the engine running, for heat. "Where's that leave us?" Berry said.

No more snow had fallen and last night's was already being trampled into slush.

Bethan said, "They talk about the *Gorsedd Ddu* in some places like you talk of bogeymen, to frighten the children. Eat your greens or the black bards will get you. Or the *Gwrach y rhibyn*."

"What's that?"

"The *Gwrach*? A sort of Welsh death-hag. A monstrous woman with black teeth and leathery wings who's supposed to scare people to death and then steal away their immortal souls. She's a vengeful demon who preys on those who have sinned."

"Jeez, what a country. What do the black bards do?"

"Well, the inference is that, while the white bards –"

"– as invented by this Iolo guy –"

"I wish I hadn't told you that, now. Yes, the white bards, while they are amiable pacifists, the *Gorsedd Ddu* are supposed to have very real magical powers. They are stern and cold and . . . perhaps vindictive."

"Question is," Berry said, "do they exist? This is the bottom line. And, if they do, do they have any more of a solid foundation than the old guys at the eisteddfod or are we just looking at a bunch of fruitcakes?"

"And if they have –" Bethan leaned back in the ruptured bucket seat, the side windows and the screen all misted, blurred ghosts of people walking past. "If they have foundation . . . powers . . . what can we do about it anyway?"

"Magic's not illegal any more. Not even black magic."

"Killing people is."

"How can we say that? Natural causes, accidents, suicide and, OK, a murder now. But it's solved."

"Yes, it sounds silly. Utterly."

"We're saying there's a – an atmosphere, whatever, generated here. Which causes outsiders – say, people not protected by the village or by this aura of Welshness, whatever that means – either to lose the will to live, to fail in what they most want to do –"

"Like Giles failing to learn Welsh – to be a part of something he so much admired –"

"Right. Or have their negative emotions take over. Lose their normal resistance to unacceptable or downright brutal behaviour. Like ole George Hardy. Suburban solicitor beats wife to death. In short, go nuts."

"Or," Bethan said, "if we try to explain the deaths from natural causes, to get into such a state that even their bodies stop fighting."

"OK. Like the immune system breaks down or something of that order. My knowledge of these things is no more than the average hypochondriac. So they're exposed to diseases, tumours form that never would've, heart diseases worsen and, well, yeah –"

"I've always found it bitterly ironic," Bethan said bleakly, "that Robin, who was so opposed to nuclear power, should die of a condition so often said to be induced by radiation escaping from nuclear installations." She shook her head sadly. "Radiation."

"Was he happy in Y Groes? Was it like he'd imagined?"

"He – Oh, what does it matter now . . ." Bethan was twisting her scarf. "The truth is we never really had much of a marriage in Y Groes. Almost as soon as we moved in, he began to be tired and irritable. The stress of the move and the travelling and having to search for nuclear dump-sites – that was what he put it down to. We used to go for walks together, along the river bank, up to the woods, and he would go so far and he just became . . . bone-tired, you know?" She turned away, stared hard at the people-shapes passing the misted car window. "I'm going to cry."

"Let's get outa here." Berry flung the Sprite into gear, rubbing the windscreen clear, moving into a line of traffic on the one-way system out of town.

"We really *are* insane, aren't we?" Bethan was shouting at him. "Tell me we're insane! Tell me we're imagining it all, fabricating something out of thin air to account for a lot of people's bad luck. Look, for God's sake, take me home, Morelli! Don't you have a job to go to?"

"No," he said. "And you don't want to go home. You know where we have to go."

"No . . ." Bethan was shaking. That is, she was sitting there very still, but he knew she really was shaking inside. "We can't."

"How else?" He also was shouting now, against the gear-threshing of a big delivery van alongside them. "How else we gonna find out one way or the other? How else, without we go in there and start kicking asses till we get some answers?"

"You don't know what it's like!" Bethan screamed.

A lorry's brakes hissed . . . *sssssssssssssssssssssiiiice!*

He turned into a stream of traffic crossing a wide bridge over the Wye.

"You came back, Beth. Nobody said you had to take that job. You'd killed its baby and you came back."

Bethan wept, biting hard into her lower lip until blood came.

CHAPTER LXII

The radio had described the road over the Nearly Mountains as "passable with care".

On the way to Pont, with his wife Gwenllian in the passenger seat, Aled had driven with considerable concentration, knowing of old what this road could do with a coat of snow on its back. On the return journey, alone now, his driving had been sloppy, his mind on other things, and he'd taken a corner too fast and ploughed the van into a snowdrift.

Digging himself out with the shovel he always kept in the back from November until May, Aled could see the tip of Y Groes's church tower, a light haze around it, wispy blue. While the sky above him, as he shovelled snow from around the van wheels, was thick as pastry.

He was going back. He had put Gwenllian, who did not understand these things, on the bus to Aber where her sister lived. But he was going back.

What alternative was there? He was the keeper, like his dad before him, of the most beautiful inn in the most beautiful place you would find anywhere. This was what he told himself.

He threw the spade in the back of the van. All around him the Nearly Mountains were tundra, no visible blade of grass. The slender creature about two hundred feet away was a fox, ears pricked, loping off when it saw him, black against the snow. Everything in black and white from up here, except the sky over Y Groes.

By the time he arrived back in the village – not yet ten o'clock

– the sky had deepened to a lurid mauve, the colour pouring in from a circle in the clouds like a hole sawn in a sea of ice for Eskimos to fish. It was as if the church tower had stabbed out the hole.

In the village, the light scattering of snow had already melted. For the first time Aled did not like the fact that there was so little snow here while so much lay on the lower ground of Pontmeurig. For the first time it seemed less than healthy. The ochre and grey stone shone with moisture, like a film of sweat. The whitewashed buildings had a mauvish glow that made him think of the glow in the faces of people on radium treatment.

It's gone too far, Aled thought.

"Going to snow again, though," Guto observed hopefully. "Why don't we call it off now?"

He wasn't inclined to risk any journey which might so delay his return to Pontmeurig that it would be difficult to slip unseen up the stairs at the Plas Meurig and into Suite 2, where the woman at the centre of all his finest fantasies would be waiting in exquisitely expensive French knickers.

There had been a few amazing moments last night when the result of the Glanmeurig by-election had seemed a matter of little consequence.

"No way," the General Secretary of Plaid Cymru pronounced. He glared at the sky through his tinted glasses – permanently rose-coloured, Guto thought – and then consulted his personal organiser. "Saturday tomorrow, OK? Big day. And you have meetings scheduled all next week. This is a crucial one. We can't be seen to be avoiding discussions with the farming organisations. If *they* want to call it off, fine, but we cannot."

"But, Alun, nobody will come! It'll be just like last time, and where does that leave us?"

Alun spread his hands. "We're not dependent on the villagers, this time. It just happens to be a central venue. Farmers, this is, Guto. And tell me, what does every farmer have?"

"A bloody big chip on his shoulder," said Guto.

"A four-wheel-drive vehicle," Alun said patiently. "Enabling him to get to places otherwise inaccessible. Which is why they won't call it off. Deliberately – to see what you're made of. Fortunately, we also have two Land-Rovers at *our* disposal, one for you and me and one for Dai and Idwal and the boys from rent-a-supporter, so you will not be lonely this time. Anyway, it isn't going to snow that hard, according to the forecast. And you will come across as tough and dynamic and totally reliable."

"Piss off," said Guto.

"Will you be staying another night, Miss Moore-Lacey?"

Miranda was an inch or two taller than the proprietor of the Plas Meurig, but the way she looked at him made it seem like a couple of feet.

"Possibly," she said.

His thin smile was barely perceptible on his plump face. "Would it be possible for you to let us know by lunchtime, do you think?" Slightly less deference than yesterday, she thought. Might have to deal with that.

"I'll see," she said airily and walked briskly through the hotel foyer to the front door, slinging her bag over her shoulder as a gesture of dismissal.

Outside the door she giggled, feeling almost light-hearted. Wondering how many points one was entitled to for a Neanderthal Welsh nationalist. Having woken her up at some ungodly hour for the purpose of giving her one for the road, Guto had slipped away before eight, confident of passing relatively unnoticed among all the Tories and Liberals milling around waiting for an early breakfast.

As she walked out to the Porsche, a man with one of those

motorised things on his camera took about half-a-dozen photographs of her. Miranda waved gaily to him. Famous actress spotted in Wales. Hah!

All the main roads had been cleared of snow; the by-roads were not to be trusted, the radio said.

"We shall be all right then," Bethan said, "at least as far as Pontmeurig."

Ahead of them, the mountains were pure white and flat as a child's collage.

"You ever break into a tomb?" Berry asked. "Any idea how it's done? Jemmy? Jackhammer?"

Bethan began to worry about him. She wished she had not told him about the baby. He was unshaven, the blue-jawed tough-guy now, hair as black as her own falling over his forehead as he spun the wheel to ease his car between a snowdrift and the hedge of a steep incline. But there was a gleam of something unstable in his eyes. Something to prove – to himself, to his father. And to her now. Which she did not want.

"I'm not crazy," Berry said.

Bethan said nothing.

"Just I hate secrets. Hate cover-ups."

"So I've gathered," Bethan said.

"Way I see it, if the big secret of that place is that Owain Glyndwr's body is there, and people somehow are dying so that secret can *stay* a secret, then it's time the whole thing was blown open. What we have to do is finish Ingley's work for him."

"Ingley died," Bethan said. They had come the roundabout way because of the snow and were entering the valley of the lead mine.

"We gotta blow it wide open. Let the historians and archaeologists in there. Be a find of national importance, right? Bring in the tourists. Let in some air."

414

This morning the abandoned lead mine was bleakly beautiful, its jagged walls like some medieval fortress – the dereliction, all the scrappy bits, under humps of snow. In a place like this it would survive for ever, Bethan thought. Until its stones and the rocks were fused into one in the way the snow had united them today.

Wales has no future, the poet R. S. Thomas had written. No present. Only a past.

A past guarded with vengeful fury.

Somewhere around her stomach, Bethan felt a sense of insidious foreboding. Berry Morelli, like Ingley, like Giles in his way, had become ensnared.

"Berry," she said. "Please. Turn round. Let's go to an expert. Go to the University. Find some help."

"No way," Berry said. "Academics don't take one look at a little red notebook and say, wow, let's get over there. They take years. Go to committees. Seek funding to establish official research projects. Only time they move fast is when it's clear that, if they don't, all the evidence is gonna disappear. I guess that is the kind of action we have to precipitate."

"It won't let you, Berry."

"It? *It* won't let me? Jesus." The road widened out and he ground his foot and the accelerator into the floor.

"Listen," Bethan said. "How are we going to do this alone? Just two ordinary people. Two ordinary *scared* people."

"All my life," Berry said, "it seems like I've been a scared person. Neurotic, wimpish." Un-American, he thought. "This is where it ends."

Or you end, Bethan thought.

PART NINE

CELTIC NIGHT

CHAPTER LXIII

When they made love that afternoon it was almost like a ceremony. This, in spite of the fact that it took place in the flat above
Hampton's Bookshop, in Bethan's single bed, and to the banal
cacophony of duelling speaker-vans, Tory and Labour, from the
street.

A tender ritual, Berry thought. A parting ritual. But why
should either of them be thinking like that?

They held each other and then he kissed her moist and
beautiful eyelids as if for the last time.

"How about I go to Y Groes alone?" he said. "Nobody there
knows me. It makes sense."

She surprised him. "All right," she said.

"OK." He got up, pulled his jeans and fisherman's sweater
from a chair.

"We'll go separately," she said. "You go in your car, I'll go
in mine – if it will start after two days in the car park in this
weather."

"That's not what I meant."

"It's the best you'll get."

They dressed, went out to the kitchen. It was three-thirty.
Soon the light would fade.

"Tea?" Bethan said.

"Let's go to that teashop by the bridge. I'll buy you a lovespoon."

She smiled. "I don't think I can look at another lovespoon
after what you said about them. Hold on a minute, I'll be back."

She went back into the bedroom and he heard her opening

419

the wardrobe. She returned in seconds and said, "It's snowing again. Try this for size."

It was a fleece-lined flying jacket of brown leather, as worn by fighter pilots in the Second World War.

"Robin's?"

"It's the only thing of his I kept. He'd always wanted one. I bought it for him the Christmas before he died. It cost me almost a week's wages."

Berry said, "I can't."

"Please . . ."

It was not a perfect fit, but it was close. Bethan adjusted the shoulders and arranged the huge, fleecy collar. "It's to say all the things I haven't felt safe in saying. Well, not in English anyway."

"You said them in Welsh?"

Bethan shrugged. "Maybe. Come on, let's go."

There was nobody else in the shop. They ordered a pot of tea, no milk. Sat down, but not in the window. Berry was still wearing Robin's flying jacket, which was kind of bulky and too warm in here, but he didn't feel he should take it off.

They looked at each other in silence for maybe half a minute, and then Berry said, getting down to business, "You see any point in confronting Claire? I met her a couple times, but I can't say I know her well enough to raise something like this."

"It might be worth talking to her," Bethan said. "There are things she ought to know by now. She's been brain-washed, of course."

Literally, Berry thought remembering what she'd told him about Claire's head in the writhing Meurig.

"I would have to go alone," Bethan told him.

"Why?"

"Because I doubt she'd speak English to you."

"That far gone?"

"That far gone," Bethan said. "However, I should like to try someone else first. I have a feeling."

"Someone in the village?"

Bethan was nodding as the teashop door was flung open and a young woman stood there and gazed at them. She was frowning at first, but then a slow, delighted smirk spread over her finely sculpted features.

She wore a bright-yellow coat and a very short skirt. Her hair was vividly red.

"Oh my God," she said, looking Berry up and down. "Bloody Biggles flies again."

Bethan thought she'd never seen anyone look so astonished – gobsmacked, Guto would have said – as Berry Morelli when the elegant red-haired girl walked over to their table and sat down.

"Ugh." Inspecting the contents of their cups and wrinkling her nose. "Not one black tea, but *two* black teas. If it wasn't so revolting, it would be almost touching."

Berry said, "This, ah, this is Miranda. She's full of surprises. I guess this must be one of them."

"Isn't he wonderful when he's embarrassed?" Miranda said, holding out a hand tipped with alarming sea-green nails. "You must be Bethan. I've heard lots about you from Guto. Do stop squirming, Morelli."

"And I a little about you," Bethan said guardedly, shaking the hand.

"Now don't you worry your little Welsh head, darling," Miranda said. "I haven't come to take him away." She was the kind of woman, Bethan thought, who, if she did plan to take him away, would be entirely confident that this would pose no long-term problem.

"Pardon me for asking, Miranda," Berry said. "But what the fuck are you doing here?"

"Gosh," Miranda said. "I think he's regaining his composure. All the same, not the most gracious welcome for someone who's come to assure him he may not be bonkers after all."

"Coffee, Miranda?"

"No thank you, I can see the tin over the counter." Miranda wrinkled her nose again. "I'll come straight to the matter on which I've travelled hundreds of miles in appalling conditions. Have you by any chance heard of one Martin Coulson, former curate of this parish?"

"I didn't know that," Bethan said. "About the difficulty he had speaking Welsh."

"Like you were saying about Giles." Berry filled their cups from the pot; Miranda winced at the colour of the tea. "Inside that village the language becomes a total mystery to the English, no matter how well they were picking it up before. Like a barrier goes up."

"It was very good of you to come and tell us," Bethan said. "Thank you."

"How many coincidences can you take?" Berry shook his head. "Clinches it, far as I'm concerned."

"And what are you going to do about it?" Miranda demanded.

"The bottom line," Berry said. He lit a cigarette, watched her through the smoke, wondering where she'd go from here.

"I think it's all rather exciting," Miranda said, and they both looked at her, Berry with a rising dismay. He might have known she wouldn't have come all this way just to tell him about the death of an obscure country parson. She'd realised there was something intriguing going down and she wanted in.

"Listen, I realise it isn't my place to – But keep the hell out of this thing. Please." Realising even as he spoke that this was just about the last way to persuade Miranda to back off.

"He's right," Bethan told her seriously. "It's not exciting. Just very sad and unpleasant."

"Well, thanks for the warning." Miranda smiled sweetly at them both, abruptly picked up her bag and sailed towards the door. "I'll see you around, OK?"

She walked away down the street without looking back. Welsh snowflakes landing tentatively, with a hint of deference, in her angry red hair.

They cleared most of the snow from the Peugeot, chipped ice from the windscreen. "It's terribly cold for December," Bethan said, patting gloved hands together to remove the sticky snow. "We rarely see much of this before New Year."

It was coming down in wild spasms, the white-crusted castle looking almost picturesque against a sky like dense, billowing smoke.

"You're right, of course," Berry said. "One of us gets stuck, we at least have a second chance."

The engine started at the fourth attempt. Bethan let it run, switched on the lights, pulled her pink woolly hat over her ears.

"OK," she said. "You follow me. When we get there, we park behind the school, out of sight."

The equipment was in the Sprite, behind the seats. Early that afternoon they'd been to see Dai Death who, in turn, had consulted his friend, the local monumental mason, supplier of gravestones over an area stretching from Pont down to Lampeter. Dai had been suspicious, but he'd done it – for Bethan.

"But first," Berry said, "we go see this friend of yours."

"I doubt I have any actual *friends* there," Bethan said. "This is just the one person I can think of who won't bar his door when he sees me coming."

CHAPTER LXIV

Up in the Nearly Mountains, headlights on, the snow was all there was. It came at the windscreen at first in harmless feathery clouds, like being in a pillow fight. Could send you to sleep, Berry thought.

The higher they climbed, the denser it became. Cold cobs, now, the size of table-tennis balls. The two small, red tail-lights of Bethan's Peugeot bobbed in the blizzard.

"Get me through this, baby, I'll buy you an overhaul," he told the Sprite, pulling it down to second gear on a nasty incline, wheels whirring. Ice under this stuff up here.

At least the snow was a *natural* hazard.

we in same shit, you find out . . .

Like all his life had been propelling him into this. Leaving the US with his ass in a sling, so to speak. The disillusion of London and an England full of yuppies and video stores and American burger joints. Old Winstone dying on him. Giles.

All this he saw through the snow.

No family. No job. Now everything he had was out here in this cold, isolated graveyard of a region where people saw their own mortality gleaming in the darkness.

Everything he had amounted to a geriatric little car and – maybe – a woman who needed the kind of help he wasn't sure he had the balls to provide.

But, if all his life was converging on this woman, it had to be worth walking into the graveyard, just hoping the Goddamn corpse candle wasn't shining for him.

For the first time since putting on Robin's flying jacket he went into a hopeless shivering fit, scared shitless.

Only five-thirty and Y Groes was midnight-still and midnight-dark.

Berry parked next to the Peugeot behind the school and got out, closing his driver's door just as quietly as he could, and looked around, disturbed.

"This is weird," he said and wondered how many times he'd expressed that opinion in the past week.

But, yeah, it *was* weird. No snow falling any more, only a light covering on the ground, a passing nod to winter, an acknowledgement that the season was out there but wasn't permitted to enter without an invite.

"The blue hole," Bethan said, taking off her woolly hat, shaking her hair; it was warm enough to do that. "It might be quite natural. One of those places where the arrangement of the hills –"

"You believe that?"

"No," she said. "Not entirely."

The sky was clear; you could even see stars, except for where the black tube of the church tower rose in the east. But only a few meagre lights in the houses. Power cut maybe.

He breathed out hard. "Beth, listen, from now on, we have to start believing all this other stuff is real. The corpse candles, the bird of death, the whole cartload of shit. Because in this place it *is* real. We left the civilised world behind, we don't play by those rules any more."

"I think I always did believe they were real," she said.

"Beth, before we go in there, I just wanna say –"

Bethan put the pink hat back on. "Save it. Please."

"But if –"

"I know," she said.

*

425

Aled looked far worse than she remembered. Perhaps it was the light from the oil-lamp in the porch which yellowed his skin, made his eyes seem to bulge. His white hair was stiff, no spring to it, and his Lloyd George moustache misshapen and discoloured.

"Bethan." Disappointment there, but no real surprise; even his voice sagged. "Why do you have to do this to me?"

He didn't even seem to have noticed Berry Morelli standing behind her.

"You don't know why I've come yet," Bethan said.

"Oh, I know, girl. I know all right. And I'll tell you, you didn't realise when you were lucky. Take your friend with you and get back to Pont. If you can still make it."

"Still make it?"

"With the snow. That is all I mean."

"No, it isn't all you mean," Bethan said firmly. "Let us in, Aled."

"We open at seven."

"Good. That leaves us plenty of time to talk."

"Bethan, you don't want to do this. Too many people –"

"I'm allowed to do it. I'm Welsh."

"But *he* isn't." Aled didn't look at Berry.

"I'm not English either," Berry said. "And I'm not polite, so –"

"No." Bethan put a hand on his arm.

But Aled sighed and stepped back then and held open the door from the inside. Bethan walked in and Berry followed, and Aled closed the door and bolted it, top and bottom. "No lights," he said. "Snow brought down the power lines. Go through to the dining room where we can't be seen from the street."

Through the dining-room window, they could see a small yard and the church hill rising sheer beyond it, palely visible because of its light dusting of snow. Aled made them sit around

426

a square dining table, one of only five in the room. Then he lit a candle in a glass holder on the table – the only source of light or heat; just dead ash and the husk of a log in the grate.

"For a schoolteacher," Aled said, "you don't learn anything, do you, girl?"

The convoy assembled at six in the castle car park. A Range Rover, a Daihatsu and a little Fiat Panda which was all Dai Death had been able to borrow from the garage at short notice.

Guto was furious when he saw who was piling into the six-seater Daihatsu.

"You said supporters," he snarled at Alun, the General Secretary.

"It'll be fine," Alun whispered back. "A little adventure for them."

"I hope there's a bloody pub there," Charlie Firth was saying, getting into the back between ski-jacketed Shirley Gillies with her Uher tape-recorder on her knee, and Bill Sykes in an ancient overcoat with a vicuna collar. Ray Wheeler was in the front with young Gary, Giles Freeman's replacement, and a farmer called Emlyn, who was driving.

It was still snowing, and there must have been four or five inches of it on the ground.

"Flaming cold," Firth said.

"We'll just have to bunch together," said Shirley. She was on her own tonight, TV news having been affected by a judiciously timed cameramen's dispute about overtime payments.

Idwal Roberts, tweed trousers stuffed into his Wellingtons, looked at the Fiat Panda and then looked at Dai. "You're sure this thing is four-wheel-drive?"

Dai pointed to the appropriate lettering on the little car's rear door. Idwal looked unconvinced.

"I'm sorry, I've forgotten – which paper are you with?" Alun asked Miranda, who was looking startling in a huge lemon-coloured designer parka with lots of fake fur.

"*Gardening News*," Guto told him.

Alun, seeming somehow less efficient in a leather flat-cap and without his tinted glasses, gazed up at the dark and tumbling sky. "It was supposed to stop tonight."

"You dickhead," said Guto.

"Yes, yes," Aled said, anguished. "But there is no way anyone can ever prove it. And what good would it do anyway?"

Bethan began to feel sorry for him. He was worn and tired, his wife had left him . . .

"She will come back," Aled said. "When she is well again. When the winter is over."

"A lot of it left to come," Berry said.

"Yes." Aled stared into the dead fireplace. "I don't know, something has changed, gone wrong, isn't it?"

"Maybe it was always wrong," Berry said.

"No. It was *not* wrong." Aled's face was ragged in the candlelight. "How could it be wrong? We were preserving that which was ours. A shrine, it was. Is."

"Not 'is'," Bethan said. "You don't believe that now."

"I don't know. Why are you asking me these things? There is nothing you can do, except to save yourselves. Perhaps."

Berry said, "How can it not be wrong if people are dying?"

Aled put his face into his hands, peered slowly over his fingertips. "Ones and twos," he said. "That was all it ever was. It was so strong, see. They could not withstand the exposure to it. Some of them simply went away. Fine. But over the years, some . . . Ones and twos, that was all."

Bethan's pity evaporated. "Ones and twos? What does that mean, Aled? Minor casualties?" Hands curled into fists, pressing

428

hard into the tabletop. "Expendable English people, like Martin Coulson and – and –"

"Yes, yes – I was so sorry. He was a good man, Robin. A fine man. And I did try to talk you out of it, the cottage, once. Do you remember that day? But they see this place and there is no stopping them. Seduced, they are. You know that." Eyes wide, full of futile pleading.

Bethan said quietly, "The *Gorsedd Ddu*."

"No. I will not talk about that."

"Ap Siencyn then."

"If you know, why do you ask me?"

Bethan hadn't known. Not for certain. "And the others?"

"Judge Rhys?" Berry leaned into the candlelight.

"Yes, Judge Rhys, and now –"

"Morgan?" Bethan demanded. "Buddug? Dilwyn? Glyn Harri?"

"Yes, yes, yes! And the rest are scattered all over Wales, I don't know how many, I only run a pub. Oh God, what have I done?"

"Ap Siencyn," Bethan said. "Tell us about him."

"What is there to tell that you do not know? The minister, he is, and the *dyn hysbys*."

"What's that?" Berry said.

"The wise man," Bethan said. "The conjuror. The wizard. Most villages used to have one. Someone who knew about curing illnesses and helping sick animals and –"

"Like a shaman?"

"I suppose."

"He cure people?"

"Some people," Aled said.

"And what about the others?"

"We do not ask," Aled said. "It has been a good place to live."

"Where does the *Gorsedd* meet?" Berry demanded.

Aled screamed out, "What are you trying to do to me?"

And the candle went out, as if someone had blown on it.

CHAPTER LXV

The first vehicle in the Plaid Cymru convoy drew up to find the village school in darkness.

"What the hell –?" Alun jumped down from the Land-Rover and strode to the school door.

"What did I tell you?" Guto roared after him.

Miranda stepped down into half an inch of snow. "So this is Y Groes." She paced about, kicking at the thin white dust with the tip of her boot. "It's almost warm here, isn't that odd?"

"I can't understand it," Alun was saying, walking round the building, looking into windows. "I was talking to the FUW not two hours ago. They said it was definitely on. I said, 'Look, if there is any change, get back to me.' I gave them the mobile phone number, everything."

"Oh, gave them the mobile phone number, did you?" Guto leaned against the bonnet of the Land-Rover and started to laugh.

"What's wrong?" Alun was affronted.

Headlights hit them, the Daihatsu crunched to a stop, and presently Bill Sykes wandered over, his long overcoat flapping. "Are we here, old boy?"

"We seem to have a problem, Bill," Alun said.

"The problem is Alun," Guto told him. "He is a city boy. Alun, do you have your mobile phone on you?"

"It's in the Land-Rover."

"Well, if you go and get it, I think you will find the words NO SERVICE emblazoned across its little screen."

"No way. That phone functions everywhere around here. It's the best there is."

"Dickhead," said Guto. "They haven't even got television in Y Groes."

"You're kidding."

Guto stepped back and held open the door of the Land-Rover for his colleague. When Alun emerged, the five reporters were clustered around the Plaid candidate in the beam of the Land-Rover's headlights. They turned to face the General Secretary, all looking quite amused.

"Right," Alun said briskly. "I don't know why it's been called off, but it obviously has. Well ... As you can see, it's stopped snowing, so I don't think we'll have any problems getting back. I think the least I can do is buy you boys a couple of drinks. The pub is just over the bridge."

There was a small cheer.

"You're a gentleman," said Ray Wheeler of the *Mirror*. "A nationalist and a gentleman."

Dai and Idwal arrived in the Fiat Panda, and Guto explained the problem. "I'm not having a drink," Dai said. "Bad enough getting here as it is."

"Well, have an orange juice," said Guto, as Miranda appeared at his shoulder, frowning.

"I've just had a peep round the back," she said. "Morelli's car is there, parked very discreetly under some trees. And another car, a Peugeot, I think."

"Bethan's car?" said Dai sharply. "They came to see me earlier, wanted to know about –" He looked across the village to the church hill. "Oh, bloody hell."

They knew Aled was shaking because the table was shaking.

"Go," he said. "All right? Go from here."

Berry found his lighter, relit the candle.

"Draught," he said.

"Remember what you said when we got here?" Bethan asked him.

"OK. Not draught."

The candle flared and Aled's white face flared behind it. "Can you not feel it, man?"

Berry didn't know what he was supposed to be feeling. He looked around the room and out the window. It was still not snowing. There were still no lights.

"The snow will melt before morning," Aled said.

"No chance. You shoulda seen it on the mountains."

"The village is generating its own heat," Bethan said. "Is that what you're saying?"

"Bethan, I once told you, see, this village makes demands."

"I remember."

"Demands, you know – sacrifices."

"You did not say anything about sacrifice."

"The old Druids, see," Aled said. "They did not sacrifice each other, their – you know, virgins, kids. None of that nonsense."

History lessons, Berry thought. Wales is all about history lessons.

"But I've heard it said they used to sacrifice their enemies," Aled said. "Their prisoners. A life's a life, see, isn't it? Blood is blood."

He stood up. "That is the finish. You have had enough from me."

Bethan was too shocked to speak.

Aled picked up the candle and they followed him out of the dining room and through to the bar, where he unbolted the oak front door.

"Opening time soon," he said. "And you won't want to see the Morgans, will you?"

"One more thing," Berry said in the doorway.

"No. No more things."

"You have a flashlight I could borrow?"

Aled did not reply but went behind the bar and fumbled about and then presented a long black torch to Berry.

"Rubber," he said morosely. "Bounces, see."

The crescent moon was curling from the tower like a candle flame. A huge, symbolic corpse candle, Bethan thought.

The smell in the December air was a little like the summer-night smell of wild flowers, but heavier, sweet with decay, as though the flowers had sprouted unnaturally from the dead earth, like bodies in rotting shrouds thrusting their hands through the grave dirt. The ground, with its thin veneer of snow, had a blueish, sometimes purplish tint, like the cheeks of the newly dead.

Bethan felt sick. She felt Y Groes closing around her, bloated with blood, greasy with human fat.

"I want to leave," she said. "Now."

"Not till we take a look at the church."

"I will not go in there."

"I'll go in then."

"Did you realise what he was saying just now? About sacrifices?"

"I'll think about it later. Right now, I need to see that tomb."

Bethan cried out, "What good will it do now?"

She stood at the top of the deserted street, her back to the bridge, white raincoat drawing in the unnatural incandescence of the night so that it turned mauve.

Irradiated, Berry thought. He felt love and fear, and he almost gave in, hurried her back over the bridge to the cars. Foot down, out of here.

Then they heard voices from the other side of the bridge and he took her arm and pulled her into the alley between the *Tafarn* and the electricity sub-station which tonight had no electricity to dispense.

Laughter.

". . . hey, Shirl, you can't be cold now."

"No, but it's awfully dark – Whoops!"

"Shit," Berry whispered. "What the hell are *they* doing here?"

"Guto," Bethan whispered back. "I can hear Guto's voice, and isn't that –?"

"Christ," Berry said. "It's Miranda."

The bunch of people crossed the bridge and they heard a banging on the pub door and Dai's voice. "Come on then, Aled. It's gone seven."

"And don't tell us the beer-pumps don't work," shouted an English voice. "Won't affect the optics."

The snow in the street seemed to sweat, and there was a kind of liquid hum in the air, as if the dead sub-station was a church organ and there was a hidden choir somewhere poised to sing out into the night.

Voice thick with growing nausea, Berry said, "What's the Welsh for *fee fi fo fum* . . . ?"

CHAPTER LXVI

Aled did not like this.

Every Friday night was more or less the same, summer or winter. By seven-fifteen, Glyn Harri would have come in, or maybe Dilwyn. Morgan, with or without Buddug, around eight.

These were the constants.

Others were regulars, not bound to a time: Dewi Morus, Mair and Idris Huws, Meirion, Dr. Wyn. And then the occasionals, who included the rector.

Tonight, gone eight now, and none of them had arrived.

There was no precedent for this.

Nearly a dozen people in the bar, but none of them locals and half of them English. Reporters. Loud people, practised drinkers.

"What's that stuff?"

Man in an expensive suit, well cut to hide his beer-gut. Late forties, going unconcernedly to seed. Leaning over the bar by the spluttering Tilley lamp, pointing to the bottle of Welsh Chwisgi.

"Whisky," Aled said. "Like any other. Blended over in Brecon."

"Welsh whisky? You're bloody joking."

"Try some," Aled said neutrally.

"Is it cheap? It should be."

"Cheaper than some. Dearer than others. There is also the Prince of Wales twelve-year-old malt. What you might call Wales's answer to Chivas Regal."

"Stone me. Better just give us a single then, Alec. No soda. Got to savour this one. Bloody Welsh whisky, Ray! One for you? Make it two then, Alec."

"We'll have the bottle," Alun, of Plaid, said generously. "Put it on my tab."

Aled brought the bottle of Prince of Wales twelve-year-old malt over to the cluster of tables. A brass oil-lamp hung from a great brown beam above them. A log fire blazed.

"Isn't this cosy?" a woman said. The chubby one, not the glamorous red-haired one.

Shirley Gillies had had two gin and limes very rapidly.

"Yeh, if you like the rustic bit," Gary Willis said, looking uncomfortable. "Not very into the primitive, personally."

"Trouble with you, Gary, is you have no soul," Shirley said. "A nice body, but no soul. I think it's rather wonderful; all the power lines down, the mobile phones useless."

"And in a pub!" said Ray Wheeler.

"I told you," Alun whispered to Guto. "I told you it would be an adventure for them."

"You know," Ray said. "This reminds me in a way of poor old Winstone Thorpe."

"Winstone's Welsh experience," said Charlie Firth. "Miserable landlady, every bugger speaking Welsh, all the pubs closed 'cause it's Sunday, and only Jack Beddall to talk to."

Bill Sykes leaned into the lamplight. "You know I really think it's time I scotched this one for good."

"Better than Welshing it," said Charlie Firth. "Although actually, this stuff's not bad. I reckon what it is, somebody bought a case of Glenfiddich and switched the labels."

"Sod off, Englishman," Guto said. "One of my mates, it is, makes this. But I shall pass on the compliment."

"Go on, Bill." Ray Wheeler topped up Sykes's glass with twelve-year-old Welsh malt. "Winstone Thorpe."

"Well ... I suppose he told you he'd been sent out on a story about two Welsh farmers who'd been shot by their housekeeper."

"Back in the sixties," said Ray.

"Definitely not in the sixties, old boy. Long, long before that. And he only had Jack Beddall on the story because Beddall's been dead twenty years."

"Oh, wonderful!" Shirley Gillies finished her drink. "A mystery story. Can I have one of those?"

"On top of gin, Shirley?" Gary passed over the Prince of Wales bottle, two-thirds empty already.

"It *did* happen. The shooting. One of those peculiar rural *ménage-à-trois* situations. The housekeeper was an English girl who innocently answered an advert and found herself sharing a bed with two hairy yokels smelling of sheepshit. Most distasteful."

"Oh, I don't know ..." Shirley giggled and looked across at Guto, who had an arm discreetly around Miranda's waist. Shirley spotted the arm and looked disappointed.

"Anyway, the girl inevitably got pregnant and the farmers, being unable to decide which of them was the father, resolved the argument by throwing her out."

"Typical," Charlie Firth said.

"Only, when she left, she took their shotgun with her and returned that night and re-plastered the bedroom wall with the pair of them."

"Heavy," said Gary Willis.

"Quite a controversial court case in its day," said Bill Sykes. "She got off very lightly, perhaps because of the baby. I can't remember whether Winstone was actually born in the prison hospital or whether she was out by then, but he certainly –"

"You're joking!" Ray Wheeler put down his glass in astonishment.

"Hated the Welsh all his life," said Sykes. "Had it instilled into him at his mother's knee that no self-respecting English person should ever venture over Offa's Dyke. Been recycling the story as a sort of parable ever since."

"Just a minute," Miranda said. "Where exactly did all this happen?"

"Oh, somewhere up North. Snowdonia way, I imagine. I think I was the only one he ever told, but he didn't go into details, even with me."

"You mean this Winstone never actually came around here?"

"He never went to Wales in his life," said Sykes. "And he warned everyone else to stay out as well. Very fond of his mother, Winstone was. So now you know. I was sworn to silence, but it can't do any harm now, can it?"

"I can hardly believe it," Miranda said in a low voice to Guto. "Just wait till I tell Morelli. The only reason he got dragged into all this was old Winstone and his Cassandra routine."

"I'm confused," Guto said. "And I think I would prefer to stay confused."

Dai Death, who had no interest in any of this, was at the bar, quizzing Aled about Bethan.

"I don't know where they went," Aled said. "But, if you find them, get her out of here. This is no joke."

"I don't know whether I should be asking you this, Aled, but why would they want to go up to the church with two crowbars and a hydraulic jack?"

Aled was silent, but Dai could tell this had cut him like splinters from a suddenly shattered bottle.

Eventually, Aled said slowly, "I shall have to tell them. If they don't already know."

"Tell who? What?"

"But I will not."

Unseasonal sweat shining on his head, rivulets rolling into his silver sideburns, Dai said, "I am finding it hard to work out who is mad here."

"Assume that everyone you meet is mad," Aled said.

Shirley had taken off her ski-jacket and unbuttoned her blouse to a dangerous extent. Charlie and Ray were taking an interest, but it was clear Shirley wanted Gary Willis.

It was very hot in the bar, the log fire superfluous in its inglenook. "Alec," Charlie Firth called out. "We'll have another bottle of that Welsh Scotch."

Aled brought the whisky and went over to the window, high in the wall behind the journalists.

Where were they?

There were few lights visible in the cottages across the street, but there was a glow about the cottages themselves and a milky layer in the air. Premature snowdrops poked out of a tub under the window. He was sure they had not been there this morning.

"Can we move the table back from the fire," the plump woman was saying. Half stripped, she was. "Too hot even for me."

He wanted to tell them to drink up and go.

In fact – the realisation flared around him, underfired with a simmering fear – he wanted to go with them.

But, if they did not go, he knew he could not stay and watch it happen, as he knew it must.

CHAPTER LXVII

Medieval, perpendicular. Two-tiered, pyramidal, timber-framed bellchamber . . .

The church was a giant monolith in its circular graveyard; its spire always seemed to be outlined against the brightest part of the sky, from wherever you were standing.

From the churchyard, you looked up and the whole edifice seemed to be swinging towards you, like a massive pendulum suspended from the moon itself.

"I can't," Bethan said. "I don't think I've ever liked old churches, even in the daylight, and I'm frightened of what this one has become. I'm sorry."

Berry had it worked out. She was saying this because she didn't want *him* to go in there. If he thought she was the one who was most scared he'd maybe back off, seek help.

No way.

He took out his car keys. "Listen, how about you go fetch the Sprite. The gear's in back. Give me time to check things out – might not even be open." It was only a couple hundred yards to the cars, and there was plenty of light.

She accepted the keys reluctantly.

"Listen, any problems, just blast on the horn, OK? Bring Guto and the guys outa the pub."

He tried out Aled's flashlight. The beam was strong and white and threw a mist into the air. He hurriedly directed it downwards, and it lit up a grave, and Bethan drew in a sharp breath.

On the gravestone was carved,

Dyma fedd Thomas Rhys . . .

Berry tried a shrug. "We had to be standing by *somebody's* grave."

He tried to ignore the smell, which was as if the grave had been opened.

A lot of whisky had been drunk. Alun, of Plaid, was looking at his watch. Miranda had fallen asleep on Guto's shoulder. Guto was endeavouring to give Bill Sykes a true insight into the philosophy of Welsh nationalism, while Charlie and Ray were sharing a cold meat pie.

Gary Willis had gone to the gents, and Shirley Gillies had followed him out of the bar.

At the bar itself, the Tilley lamp had spluttered out and been replaced with a couple of candles in ashtrays.

"Quiet in here, though, tonight," Dai said to Aled. "Where are all the locals then?"

Aled shook his head, said nothing.

"Funny buggers here," Idwal Roberts said. "Won't share a *Tafarn* with outsiders, see."

"Rubbish, man." Dai scowled. "They have never been known for that. I've been in here of a lunchtime, an English chap walks in and everybody in the place stops speaking Welsh immediately, out of courtesy. Very hospitable people. Unusually hospitable."

"Where are they then?" Idwal said. "Most places, if there's a power cut, no telly –"

"They have no tellies here anyway. No reception, see."

"Well, radio then. Not even a proper light to read a book by. What would they do but go to the pub? No, you are naïve about this, Dai."

"What I want to know," Dai said, "is what Bethan and that American fellow are up to."

"Get them out," Aled said suddenly. "Get them all out, Dai, for Christ's sake."

Behind him the telephone rang, and everyone looked up.

Dai said, "Don't imagine the phone to be working in a power cut. You forget it makes no difference."

Aled said, "*Y Groes pedwar, pedwar, chwech.*"

"Aled, is that you?"

"Yes it is."

"Aled, it's Gwyn Arthur from the police station. I'm ringing you myself because the roads are blocked all over the place and we've had to pull the cars off. Otherwise someone would have come out to see you."

"Snow's bad over there, then?"

"Worst for ten years. Aled, Aber police have been on the line, and I am afraid I have bad news. Very bad news. You should sit down if you can."

"Let's go for a walk," Shirley said, and she grabbed Gary Willis's hand.

Gary thought, ah, what the hell – and allowed her to pull him to the pub door.

The problem was, he was getting married in a couple of months and was trying to develop a new and disciplined attitude when faced with the sexual opportunities which, ironically, had seemed to come his way quite often since his engagement.

On the other hand, Shirley, by all accounts, knew the score. Had a husband somewhere and a very discreet, adult approach to this sort of thing. She was also considerably older than Gary, and so, he reasoned, it would be a sort of social service on his part.

Yeh, what the hell. They stepped out into the blue and purple night.

442

"Isn't it just amazingly . . . you know, not cold." Shirley had left her ski-jacket in the bar.

"Bit odd, really," Gary said. "Considering the conditions when we were coming over the mountains."

"I quite fancy coming over the mountains," Shirley said, grabbing hold of his tie and leading him into the street like a showman with a dancing bear.

She let him go when they reached the bridge, the river burbling below. Soft snow sat lightly and inoffensively on the top of the parapet. Shirley made a snowball and threw it at Gary. It hit him on the cheek and felt like candyfloss. Gary gathered up a handful of snow and advanced on Shirley who screamed delightedly.

Gary plunged the handful of snow down the front of Shirley's blouse. "You swine." She cackled and pulled his hand back down. "Now you'll have to get it all out."

"So I will," Gary said.

By the time they'd made their inebriated way to the far side of the bridge the blouse was off, Shirley waving it at Gary like a football supporter's scarf. Gary managed to grab a sleeve and the blouse tore neatly in half, leaving them looking down at their respective fragments and laughing helplessly.

Gary, sweating, pulled off his jacket and hung it over the bridge parapet.

They might have been on a beach in August.

Shirley unfastened her bra, took it off and twirled it around her head as she bounced off towards the woods. Gary thought she couldn't half move for her size.

"Slow down, Shirl, you'll have no energy left."

"Ho ho," Shirley gurgled. "We'll see about that, baby."

Running past the school lane, she let her skirt fall to her ankles and stepped out of it and kicked it away with the tip of a patent-leather boot.

She reached the edge of the woods and stood panting, wearing only her boots, a pair of pink briefs and a silver necklace, her back to an enormous oak tree, a ludicrous grin on her face.

Just for a moment, as he stood at the edge of the wood, fumbling with his belt, the total madness of the situation was fully apparent to Gary Willis.

He saw the oak tree, heavy with snow. He looked up at the iceberg hills, stark in the starry night. He looked across the bridge to the village, feeble glows from behind the drawn curtains of Christmas-card cottages with snow on their roofs.

He looked at Shirley and saw the sweat freezing rapidly on her grinning face, the skin of her exposed body blue and mottled. And he thought, *it isn't warm at all, it just seems warm to us.*

And then the moment passed, and nothing was clear any more.

CHAPTER LXVIII

Berry walked into the nave, footsteps on stone.

Tock, tock, tock.

Outside, it had been unseasonally, ridiculously warm. Inside the church it was winter again. When he switched off the torch, the light was ice-blue from through the Gothic windows on either side and livid through the long window at the top of the nave, beyond the altar.

He was glad Bethan was not with him, but that didn't make him feel any better about being here.

He walked up the aisle towards the altar.

Tock, tock, tock,

tock, tock,

tock.

The churches of his several childhoods, in different States, had mostly been newish buildings masquerading as places as old as this. His dad had been a lapsed Catholic, his mom a Presbyterian. And so religion, to him, had been something pointless that people argued about.

Here, tonight – shining the torch on his watch he discovered it was not yet nine o'clock – he was aware for maybe the first time of the awful power of something venerated. Like the Welsh language in Judge Rhys's study, only there was ritual worship involved here, and many centuries of it.

Whatever it was reverberated off the stones in the walls, was filtered through the mortuary light from the windows, lay rich and musky on the air.

445

And it didn't want him here.

Fuck you, he wanted to say, to make a stand, be defiant. But his full range of flip obscenities would seem pathetically peevish and infantile, and about as effectual as throwing stones at a tank.

"Help me," he said, to his surprise, and the walls immediately laughed off the words.

mee, hee, heee . . .

He switched on the torch with a thunderous clack-ack-ack, and the monstrous shadows leapt out, rearing up then settling back just on the periphery of the beam so he would know they were there, and waiting.

He drew breath and the rich air seemed to enter his lungs in staccato bursts, like something that was planning to come out as a sob. It was thick, sour-milk air, like in the judge's study, only here it had a great auditorium to waft around in and ferment.

Berry found the tomb. There was only one. It was in a small chapel to the left of the altar. A chapel of its own.

It was three feet high and five or six feet long, as long as the stone figure of the knight laid out on top, hands together, praying.

The knight wore armour and its face was worn, the expression on it blurred by the years. But the essence of this remained, and it had nothing reassuring to say. Berry thought the face might at one time have had a beard, but he could not tell if the beard was cleft.

He didn't like to look too hard at it, felt it was looking back.

There was kind of a plaque thing on the side of the tomb, with lettering. But this was in Latin and maybe Welsh too, and he couldn't make it out.

Meredydd, the guy's name, it had said in Ingley's book.

Owain Glyndwr, I presume, was what he'd figured he'd say on approaching the tomb. Let the stiff inside know it was dealing with a wisecracking, smart-assed American who was in no mood for any spooky tricks, OK?

Only the words wouldn't come out.

He thought that if, anything spooky happened in this place, there would be little question of how he'd react. He would piss himself, throw up, something of that order.

The years had not blurred a very ancient, sneering cruelty in the face of this knight that belied the supplication of his hands.

Berry didn't like him one bit and he had a sensation, like a cold vibration in the air over the knight's eyes, that the feeling was mutual.

He put out a finger, touched the effigy's eyes, one then the other. The way the centuries had worn the stone you couldn't be sure whether the eyes were closed or wide open. Berry felt exposed, observed, and was unable to rid himself of the notion that somebody was standing behind him in the cold chapel, perhaps the knight himself, a great sword raised in both hands over his head.

He tried to clear his mind of all such thoughts and made himself go through the motions of checking out the structure of the tomb, as Ingley must have done.

Before he died.

For Chrissake . . .

The body of the tomb was constructed out of stone blocks, each about ten inches by six, three rows of them supporting the top slab and the effigy.

He laid the torch down on the knight's stone-armoured breast, up against the praying hands with their chipped knuckles.

Then he turned his back on the tomb, fitted his fingers under the edge of the slab, closed his eyes, counted down from three . . . and heaved.

To his secret horror, the slab moved just enough to show him that with the equipment and perhaps a little help he could get inside.

The thought chilled his stomach.

OK. Calm down.

He knew he had to go fetch the stuff from the car, and whatever was in there he had to let out. And let some air into this place.

An act of desecration.

Sure. No problem.

Berry emerged from the chapel of the tomb holding the rubber flashlight confidently in front of him. The flashlight immediately went out.

He froze.

And the sour-milk air clotted around him and clogged his head. He felt dizzy and sat down on some pew on the edge of the nave, and then found he could not move. His thoughts congealed; his senses seemed to be setting like concrete.

Then, after a while – could have been hours, minutes or only seconds – there were ribbons of light.

And the light came now not from the windows on either side or the long window behind the altar, but from above. It descended in a cold white ray, making dust-motes scintillate in the air, and he had the idea it must be the moon and the pillars and buttresses of stone were like trees on either side and the air was pungent now with brackish scents and the residue of woodsmoke.

As the walls of the nave closed in, he looked up into the night sky and on the boundary of his vision a black figure eased out of the mist.

CHAPTER LXIX

Bethan parked the Sprite in the shadow of the lych gate and sat there for a minute or two, making her mind up.

Then she got out, slammed the door – you had to slam it or it would not stay shut – and walked back down the lane to the *Tafarn*.

What she was remembering was Martin Coulson, the curate, who had fallen and smashed his head on the tomb of Sir Robert Meredydd. And this had happened in broad daylight.

The image came to her of Berry Morelli face-down on the stone-flagged floor, unmoving, a river of dark blood flowing down the aisle. She began to run.

By the time she reached the door of the pub, the perspiration was out around her eyes; she felt clammy, wanting to shed her hat and her raincoat.

But she remembered how Owain Glyndwr, it was said, could bring about rapid changes in the weather to confound his enemies. Even Shakespeare's satire seemed to reflect this. Bethan, having studied *Henry IV* at college, knew all Glendower's overblown speeches, heard them echoing as she ran,

Three times hath Henry Bolingbroke made head
Against my power; thrice from the banks of Wye
And sandy-bottomed Severn have I sent him
Bootless home and weather-beaten back.

So Bethan took off nothing.

From the *Tafarn*'s ill-lit interior came sounds of merriment. Guto's voice, and the rest were English accents.

449

Inside the doorway she almost bumped into a stooping figure emerging from the gents' lavatory.

"Bethan! Where the hell have you been? You look all of a tizz."

"Oh, Dai." It came out as a long sigh.

"You look as if you need a drink, girl. Come and –"

"No, no, no." Bethan wiped sweat from her eyes, smearing what remained of her make-up. "You must help me, Dai. First, you have to get all those people out of there."

"Oh hell." Dai Death looked exasperated. "This is what Aled was saying before he stopped talking altogether. Everybody's gone mad tonight. Anyway, they won't go. The road is blocked at the Pont end and God knows what it's like over the Nearly Mountains. The council's out with the snow-ploughs and they're waiting for some clearance from –"

"Dai, get them out, I do not care how. Tell Guto –"

"They're all bloody pissed, girl! They don't care whether they get home or not."

"God." Bethan was almost frantic. "Then can you and Idwal get up to the church and help Berry?"

"Why, what's he doing?"

Bethan wiped her eyes again and clasped her hands in front of her, squeezing the fingers. And told him very slowly and very precisely that Berry Morelli was trying to break into a tomb which was believed to contain the mortal remains of Owain Glyndwr.

Dai looked sorrowful. She did not think he believed what she had said, only that she was insane.

"My job, Bethan," he said, "is to put them in, not get them out."

"I wish this was all a joke, Dai. I really wish it was a joke."

Dai put a calming hand on her shoulder. "All right. All right. I will go. I'll bring Idwal. A good chapel boy. We'll both go. All right?"

Bethan nodded, sagging in the doorway. The heat was awful.

Aled washed glasses and watched the English drink.

The General Secretary of Plaid Cymru appeared at the bar. "Did they say when the ploughs would be through?"

Aled shook his head.

"Where's Emlyn gone, the driver? He said he was going to see some friends, but he hasn't come back. We need a good driver now, more than ever, for these chaps."

Aled shook his head, rinsed a glass, held it up in the candlelight, stood it on a shelf behind him.

"Any use, do you think, if I talk to the police?"

Aled made no reply. His hands moved mechanically, rinsing the glasses, holding them to the weak light, putting each one carefully on the shelf.

"I can't understand it. Why is the weather so bad in Pontmeurig when here it's so incredibly mild? I've never known anything like this . . . Oh, sorry, am I in your way?"

Charlie Firth had appeared unsteadily at his shoulder, holding the plate which had held the cold meat pie he'd shared with Ray Wheeler. The plate slithered from his fingers onto the slop-mat on the bartop.

"I feel sick," Charlie said.

He said it loudly enough to turn heads. Ray Wheeler's head anyway. And Guto's. Miranda's head was still on Guto's shoulder, shifting occasionally in sleep.

"The way I see it," Charlie said, "it was either that Welsh whisky or the meat pie. I'm betting on the pie."

Aled washed another glass, rinsed it, held it to the candle.

"You listening to me, Alec?"

Aled turned his back on Charlie Firth and put the glass on the shelf behind him.

"You tried to poison me once. I said it'd never happen again."

"What are you talking about?" Alun said.

"*You* tried to poison me," Charlie Firth said, stabbing Alun in the chest with a rigid forefinger. "You're Welsh, aren't you?"

"And you, I'm afraid, are legless, my friend," Alun said jovially. "Go and sit down. We'll get you back soon, don't worry."

"Come on, mate," Ray Wheeler said. "I had half that pie, and I don't feel sick."

Aled washed another glass, impassive.

Charlie reached across the bar, snatched it from his hand and hurled it at the nearest wall. Nobody saw it connect; the light was too weak.

Aled said nothing but walked out through the door to the kitchen.

"That's it then." Guto hauled Miranda to her feet in the manner of a man well used to removing comatose companions from bars. "This looks like another of those scenes I need to avoid."

"Don't know what's come over him," Bill Sykes said. He'd removed his overcoat and his jacket, was sitting in shirt sleeves and a paisley waistcoat. Nobody had commented on the disappearance of Shirley Gillies and young Gary.

"The Welsh." Charlie Firth's face was swollen with contempt, as if he were accumulating a mouthful of spit. Behind him, Guto eased Miranda into the doorway, half-dragging her; she was dead weight. He motioned with his head to Alun, who mouthed, "We can't leave them here."

"We bloody can," Guto shouted.

"Where have you gone, Alec, you little Welsh twat?" Charlie Firth was roaring.

Alun dodged behind him to the door, shouting to Ray and Bill, "We'll find Emlyn for you. The driver. Send him back."

Outside, he found Guto on the bench to the left of the porch, with Miranda in his arms. "Come on, come on," Guto was whispering urgently.

"Yes, yes, I'm here," Alun said, searching his pockets for the Land-Rover keys. And then he realised Guto was talking to Miranda, her head cradled in the crook of his arm, blue snowlight washing over her classically English autocratic face.

Guto stared up at him, panic in his eyes. "Alun, I – I can't bloody wake her, can I?"

CHAPTER LXX

The white moon, sickle-sharp, overhung the glade. The fat trees crouched, entangling their aged, twisted branches like the antlers of stags.

Groundmist was waist-high and looked as thick as candle-grease. The trees were in a silent semi-circle within the mist. He tried to count them and could not.

Not because there were too many of them, but because his brain was working too slowly for counting, like a clockwork mechanism winding down. Also the trees were somehow indistinct, embedded in the groundmist. They were one. An old entity. A fusion of consciousness, of now and of then.

More than trees. They had strong, vibrant thoughts and the thoughts had sounds which came from far way, as if windborne. One was as high as a flute or a lamb's bleat. Another sombre and quivering like the lower octaves of a harmonium. They could have been male or female. And they were orchestrated together, one voice, which could have been speaking in no other language but Welsh.

The mist cleared a little, although it did not evaporate as much as soak into the ground, leaving solid patches like mould, like fungus.

Around an altar.

Which was not an altar of stone, as artists imagine, but of wood, the trunk of an immensely thick oak tree, split in half as if by lightning, hewn out down its centre to form a shallow cradle, almost a coffin.

sice, he heard.

Wind in the trees, air-brakes of an articulated lorry, bellows, a freezer door opening and closing.

siiiiiiiiiiiice.

There formed in the hollow of the altar, in the cradle, in the coffin, a satin-white woman with flowing red hair through which tendrils of mist drifted and curled.

The trees encircled her, their knobbled branches bowed. Stood there in the moonlight – so much light from such a slender moon – and watched her dying like an October butterfly.

Hunched on a stool in the dark beside the kitchen stove, his head in his hands, Aled wept savage tears, while the crazy-drunk reporter banged his fist on the bartop and screamed abuse at the Welsh nation.

Aled was not weeping for the Welsh nation.

He was weeping because it was the end of everything.

"... *on to the line at Aber station. Some sort of dizzy spell, perhaps ... no, nothing anyone could do ... So sorry, we are, Aled, sorry I have to tell you like this, too, but the weather ...*"

"Come out, you little twat! No sodding guts, any of you. Come out, I want a bleeding drink!"

A shattering. Glasses, newly rinsed.

The most beautiful pub in the most beautiful village in ...

Aled howled aloud at the night, at the village, at the heat, at the snow, at the *Gorsedd*.

"*What time?*"

"*Not long after seven. Apparently, she just disappeared, went out alone ... must have been confused, see, they said ...*"

Seven o'clock.

"*Bethan, why do you have to do this to me ... ?*"

He came slowly to his feet.

"I'm helping myself, Alec, all right?"

"Don't be a pillock, Charlie." Another English voice.

"Yeah, well, this way I *know* I'm not being bleeding poisoned. All right, Alec? That make sense to you?"

More glasses smashing.

But Aled's fingers were no longer shaking as he lit a candle, set it on a saucer and, holding the candle before him, went out of the kitchen the back way, through the scullery and into a stone-walled storeroom with no windows.

The storeroom had a long, narrow, metal cupboard, which was padlocked.

Aled put the candle on an old worktable, his hands flat on the cool metal cupboard door. Hesitated there a moment. And then felt about on the ledge above the storeroom door, where the key lay in grease and dust.

He undid the padlock, left it hanging from the lock as he felt inside the cupboard and found what he'd come for.

Guto and Alun lifted Miranda, all legs, into the back seat of the Range Rover.

"This is folly, Guto. Isn't there supposed to be a doctor here in the village?"

"Are you going to drive, or shall I?"

"Let me at least knock on a few doors first, get word to Emlyn to come and pick up the other reporters. Will take me no more than two minutes. We brought them here, after all."

"Stuff the party image," Guto shouted, loud enough to have awoken Miranda from any normal slumber. "For God's sake, look at the place! You'll knock and knock and no bugger will answer!"

Few of the cottages even showed the glow of candlelight or an oil-lamp now, and yet there was somehow a sense of silent, listening people behind every door.

"I mean, is this flaming normal? Atmosphere is as if there's been a nuclear alert."

"Yes. It's strange."

"So get moving, man. We have to get her to the hospital in Pont. And anyway –" Guto got in the back, lifting Miranda's head onto his knees "– I wouldn't trust the bastard doctor here, and don't ask me why."

Alun climbed into the driver's seat, Guto saying, "In fact, I wouldn't trust any bastard in Y Groes. Don't worry, Emlyn'll go back for them when he's ready."

The elderly Range Rover clattered into life, was rapidly reversed by Alun into the alleyway by the useless electricity sub-station, wheels spinning in the thin skim of snow. Guto looking over at the hills, made majestic by the snow, thinking, oh God, don't let us get stuck up there.

"Jesus," he said, a hand on Miranda's cheek. "She's not even warm. Heat. Put the heat on."

"You're joking, it's –"

"Put the bugger on full blast, man!" He smoothed Miranda's icy brow. "She can't – I mean, people can't just die, just like that, can they?"

"So who is she really?" Alun steered the Range Rover across the bridge. "Not a journalist, then."

Guto's hand moved over Miranda's throat, searching for a pulse, not knowing where it was supposed to be.

"Does it matter?" He felt his voice beginning to crack. Oh Jesus, how abruptly, and with what brutality, life was coming at him these days. Despair to euphoria to an even deeper despair.

Alun braked hard.

"Strewth, man, you'll have her on the floor."

"What is it?" Alun said.

"Whatever it is, sod it."

"No, something odd here, Guto. A jacket over the wall. And – trousers. No, a skirt. It's a skirt."

"Bloody hell, Alun, were you never young? Step on it!"

"In the middle of the road, Guto? A skirt discarded in the middle of the road?"

Following a scuffle of footprints, he swung the Range Rover off the road and into the entrance to the track that led into the woods, drove up it until it became too narrow for a vehicle.

Where he braked hard again and the engine stalled. And the headlights illuminated a wondrously ghastly tableau.

"God," Alun whispered in horror, and in awe.

He seemed uncertain, at first, about what to do. Then, efficient as ever, he calmly opened the driver's door, leaned out and was copiously sick in the snow.

Grabbing up a handful of unsoiled snow, he washed around his mouth, rubbed some into his eyes and sat back and closed them, reaching out with his right hand to pull the door shut.

At the very instant it slammed into place, Guto thought he was aware of a distant blast, someone shooting at a rabbit in the winter hills.

Hesitantly, he lifted up Miranda's head, leaned across the back of Alun's seat, looked out through the windscreen and sat down very quickly.

"Jesus," he said.

Alun sat up, put the Range Rover into reverse and looked constantly over his shoulder until they were back on the road and the headlights no longer lit a recumbent, erotic sculpture in marble, two figures coitally entwined, utterly still, frozen together for ever.

"It's a nightmare, Guto," Alun said. "It has got to be a nightmare."

Yes. Of course. Sure. A nightmare. A dream from which you had to free yourself. The difference was that, in a dream, when that thought came to you, the realisation that you were in fact dreaming would wake you up at once.

458

This was the difference.

He tried to speak, to scream at the circle of black, malevolent trees under the white moon. He tried to scream out, you are not here, you are someplace else, this is a church for Chrissake . . .

These lines only came to him as vague things, nothing so solid as words.

Sice, the mist said, blown from the bellows. The mist had risen to cover the altar, but it may have been a mist inside his own head because this was how it was in dreams.

siiiiiiiiiiiiiiiiiiiiice!

"*Sais*," Giles Freeman hissed, a red spectre staggering out of the mist in a torn and soaking suit, with a bulging black eye. "Means English. Often used in a derogatory way, like the Scots say Sassenach. Satisfied now?"

A string somewhere was pulled. A big door opened and closed. Thunk. Breath came back to Berry Morelli, air blasting down a wind-tunnel.

"DIM SAIS!" he cried out, stumbling out into the nave, arms waving. "DYDWY DDIM YN SAIS, YOU BASTARDS!"

"We never said you was, man," Dai Death said calmly. "Come on out now."

Bethan, waiting by the lych gate, saw Dai Williams and Idwal Roberts leaving the church with Berry Morelli, he gesturing at them, as if arguing. He was all right. He was not lying by the tomb, leaking dark blood over the stone flags.

Bethan's relief was stifled by the realisation that nothing had changed. The air still was fetid, the moonstreaked sky bulging over Y Groes like the skin of a rotting plum.

She did not go to him but slipped back through the lych gate and hurried a little way along the road until she saw a track winding between the silhouettes of two giant sycamores.

CHAPTER LXXI

Around the timber-framed porch for several yards in all directions, the snow was as pink as birthday-cake icing and this had nothing to do with the strawberry sky.

When they dragged his body out, Charlie Firth seemed to have a hole in him the size of a grapefruit. As if he'd been punched by a fist in a boxing glove and the glove had gone through him.

Bill and Ray dragged him out on the off-chance that he was still alive.

He wasn't.

The mistake he'd made had been to laugh when Aled had emerged from the back room holding out the double-barrelled twelve-bore shotgun and hoarsely ordering them all to leave his inn. Charlie had made some reference to old Winstone's mother and a shotgun and that she, being English, at least had the nerve to use it.

Ray Wheeler remembered Aled's hollowed-out face in the wan ambience of the candle, by then not much more than a wick floating in an ashtray full of liquid wax. He thought he remembered a glaze of tears in the licensee's eyes as he poked the gun barrel under Charlie Firth's ribcage.

Ray certainly remembered Aled reloading the twelve-bore from a box of cartridges on the bartop, Sykes shakily saying something on the lines of: Now look, old boy, no need for this, surely? The banalities people came out with when something utterly appalling had occurred.

Blood and obscene bits of tissue had been slurping out of Charlie all the way to the door and Bill was relieved to leave him in the snow. He and Ray, liberally spattered with pieces of their colleague, backed away from the body, looking for some cover in case the mad landlord should come charging out after them.

They hid in the car park at the side of the inn, behind the Daihatsu. "So where's everybody gone?" Ray said. "It's like bloody High Noon. What the fuck's wrong with this place?"

Bill Sykes ran in a crouch – how he thought that would make him less of a target for a man with a twelve-bore Ray couldn't fathom – across the road to the only cottage with some sort of light burning inside. He heard Bill hammering at the cottage door hard enough to take all the skin off his knuckles and then enunciating in his polite and formal Old Telegraph way, "Hello, excuse me, but would it be possible to use your phone?"

There was no response at all from within, where a single small, yellow light never wavered. Not even an invitation to go away.

"I need to telephone the police," Bill said loudly into the woodwork.

To nil response.

"Well, could *you* perhaps telephone the police? Tell them to come at once. Please. Just dial nine nine nine. Think you could do that?"

The cottage was silent. The air was still. The burgeoning sky seemed to have sucked warm blood out of the snow.

"Oh, bollocks to this," Ray yelled. "Let's get the fuck out of here."

In thirty years of journalism, in Africa, South America, he'd never known a place, an atmosphere, quite so unearthly. He climbed into the Daihatsu, fumbled around and almost wept with relief when he discovered the key in the ignition. Obviously nobody worried about teenage joyriders on the loose in a place as remote as this.

Bill climbed in the other side. "Ever driven one of these things, old boy?"

"No," Ray said, through his teeth. "But I reckon this is one of those occasions when I could master the controls of a bloody Jumbo Jet if need be." He leaned forward to turn the key in the ignition, feeling distaste as a patch of Charlie's blood on his shirt was pulled against his chest.

Bill said, "What about Shirley and young whatsisname?"

"I reckon they've gone," said Ray, with more confidence than he felt. "The Range Rover's gone, hasn't it? The Plaid bunch."

"True. Well, off you go then, Ray. Probably the only way we'll get to alert the constabulary."

"I don't know what the hell kind of story we're going to do on all this, do you?"

"Least of my worries, old boy. Least of my worries."

After a hiccupy start, they got over the bridge and on to the road that took them out of Y Groes. There was only one and, at first, the going was easy enough. It was not snowing and the stuff on the road was impacted, no problem for four-wheel drive.

They came soon to a signpost. Pontmeurig one way, Aberystwyth the other. "Doesn't say how far Aberystwyth is, Ray. I think we should stick to what we know."

"Yeah, OK." Ray steered the Daihatsu, headlights full on, into the hills. Where it soon became quite clear that Y Groes had got off incredibly lightly as far as the weather was concerned.

As the road rose up, they could see the church tower behind them under a sky so rosy it seemed like some sort of ominous false dawn. But before midnight?

Above and around them, however, the night was darker than Welsh slate, and then the snow began to come at them like a fusillade of golf-balls, through which they first saw the figure at the side of the road.

"Reckon this poor bugger's broken down?" Ray slowed the Daihatsu. "Or got his motor jammed in a drift?"

Bill Sykes was wary. "Nobody we, er, know, is it? Better be a bit careful here, Ray."

"Bill, it looks like an old woman."

The figure lifted a stick to stop them. They made out a long skirt and a ragged shawl tossed in the snowstorm.

Ray opened his window, got a faceful of blizzard. "Yeah, OK, luv. Can you make it over here, I don't want to get stuck in the ditch."

Advancing on the vehicle, the bundle of old clothes grew larger absorbing the snow on either side, issuing bits of shawl and ragged, stormblown hair.

"Bloody walking jumble sale," Ray said out of the side of his mouth.

"Don't you think it's a bit odd," Bill said. "This old girl out on a night like this? And don't you think –?"

"Yeh, I –"

The snow blasting in on Ray had suddenly become black and polluted with the smell of smoke and motor oil and also the four-day-old corpses in a makeshift charnel house he'd once been compelled to investigate in the Middle East.

He started to close his window, but the black snow was already filling the Daihatsu, and Ray went rigid with shock as he experienced a sensation of teeth on his chest and a slimy, probing tongue and a nuzzling and a guzzling at his bloodied shirtfront.

It was over in seconds and he was left with a heap of foul-smelling snow in his lap. When the appalling face came up in the windscreen, neither he nor Bill was able to speak; Ray's foot sprang off the clutch, and the Daihatsu spurted suicidally away into the white night.

Hearing a rustling sound and a crackling, Ray shot one final gut-shrivelling glance to the side and saw the creature hovering over the snow, kept aloft by her flapping shawl, or perhaps, he thought, delirious with fear, as the Daihatsu smashed through a barbed-wire fence, perhaps she had little wings.

As she rose and hovered, the illusion of wings was hardened by the crackling noise she made.

gwrach . . . gwrach . . . gwrach. . . .

"You said yourself this was a God-forsaken place. You said something had to get cleaned out before Christ could get in."

"It's still the House of God, Morelli," Idwal said. "And I'm no grave-robber."

"Think of it as an exhumation," Berry said.

"I will think of it not at all."

"Dai?"

"Come away, Morelli. Leave it. It'll do no good."

Directly under the tower, the moon arching like a spotlit ballerina from its weather vane, Berry could see their faces very clearly. Idwal's was sombre, unmoving. Dai's disturbed and anxious.

He tried another angle. "How much you know about this place? Why's it on a mound? Would I be right in thinking that in the old days, way back before there was a village, the oak wood covered all of this ground?"

"I don't know," Idwal said heavily.

"And I don't care," Dai said.

"So that maybe even before there was a mound – when's that, medieval, or earlier? – this was a place of worship. Sacred grove, whatever."

"What happened to you in there?" Idwal asked him, with obvious reluctance.

Worst of it, he couldn't remember. Only that, when they'd come up to him in the church, he'd been momentarily surprised to find it *was* a church and that when he looked up he couldn't see the moon.

"What does any of this matter?" said Dai.

"Of course it matters, you dumb bastards. People are dying."

"I cannot believe any of this." Dai walked off a couple of paces.

Sweltering in Robin's flying jacket, his whole body quivering with the need to do something, the stifling urgency of the situation, Berry looked up at the sky and it seemed like a great balloon, full of blood. He felt that soon the point of the church tower would spear the balloon and there'd be a never-ending gory deluge over Y Groes.

Alun had suggested to Guto that, when they reached Pontmeurig Cottage Hospital, he should be the one to carry Miranda in.

"May still be able to keep you out of this whole business."

"Oh, aye? And which of us will tell the cops about the bodies in the wood?"

"You are right, of course." Alun sighed. "This whole campaign has been jinxed. For us, that is. Why could none of this have happened to Gallier?"

The snow had started where the oak woods ended and the conifers began their stiff, sporadic ascent of the Nearly Mountains. It had been fluffy and mild at first, innocent as dandelion clocks, before the hedges had solidified into frozen walls, like the Cresta run, the snowflakes gaining weight and bumping the screen; if it had not been for the four-wheel-drive they would have got no further.

They were perhaps two miles out of Y Groes when Guto thought he heard Miranda moan. His heart lurched.

"Come on then, love." He raised her head up in the crook of his arm.

"Want me to stop, is it, Guto?"

"No, no . . . Keep going, man."

Despite all the snow, it was far darker up here than in Y Groes. Guto wound down his window to give her some air and was shocked, after the clammy heat of the village, at the chill which rushed in with a stinging blast of snow.

"Come on, darlin', please . . ." He couldn't see her eyes, but his fingertips told him they were still shut. Shielding her from the blast with his right shoulder, he wound the window back up with his left hand, thinking, oh Jesus, what does a death-rattle sound like?

The Range Rover suddenly crunched to a stop; a creak of brakes and a hopeless sigh from Alun. Guto looked up and saw in the headlights a sheer wall of white, over half as high as their vehicle.

"I'm no expert," Alun said, "but I estimate it would take ten men until breakfast to dig us through that."

Guto lowered his bearded face to kiss Miranda's stiffening, stone-cold brow.

CHAPTER LXXII

Past the iron gate now, to where the judge's house sat grey and gaunt and self-righteous in the sick, florid night.

All its windows darkened, except for one. And Bethan knew which one that was.

The light in the study was too small and weak to be the big brass oil-lamp. She approached it warily. She had to know precisely who was in the house.

She slid from tree to tree across the snowy lawn, eyes always on the window. And then, after reaching the side-hedge, she edged along it towards the house, camouflaged, she hoped, by her long, white mac.

The study window was set so high in the wall that she was able to slip into a crouch beneath it, before moving up slowly to peer through a corner.

All the bookshelves were in deep shadow except for a small circle of heavy volumes above the great oaken desk at the far end of the room opposite the window. On the desk were two wooden candlesticks with inch-thick red candles in them, alight.

A book was splayed open upon the desk. Claire was not looking at it.

Her eyes were closed but, had they been open, their gaze would have been directed on Bethan.

Who gasped and sank down to the lawn.

In her memory, the old Claire's face had seemed small and round, the brisk, blonde hair fluffed around it. Now, under the tangled dark hair, the face had narrowed, the lips tightened, the lines deepened either side of the mouth. Severity.

Bethan wanted to run back to the hedge and away.

But she carried on under the window to the front door. It had been her intention to beat hard on the knocker to indicate she was in no mood for evasion. However, the door was ajar.

It opened without a creak and Bethan found her way into the living room, all in darkness, a gleam where the moon picked out the handle of a copper kettle in the inglenook.

There was no fire in the grate, nothing of the mellow warmth she'd found in here on the night of the first Welsh lesson.

Poor Giles.

Bethan shivered, not only at the memory of a dead, snarling Giles spreadeagled on the study floor but also because the temperature in here was many degrees below the death-bearing mildness of the night outside.

This, she realised, was the reality. The heat outside, which did not melt snow, was something else.

Tightening the belt of her raincoat, she went through the open door to the inner hall, ducking her head, although she was small enough to go under the beams. To her right were the stairs. To her left, a flickering under the door, was the –

Come in, Bethan.

She was sure not a word had been spoken aloud.

Yet she went in.

"We need to move fast," Berry said. "They're gonna know we're here."

"Moving as fast as I can, man. You have the chisel?"

Berry patted a pocket of Robin's flying jacket. "Fix the light first."

Dai was wedging the torch roughly into the bottom of a

centuries-old rood screen so that the beam was directed onto the tomb.

Distantly, they could hear Idwal Roberts pacing around outside. He would not come in.

Dai looked curiously at Berry. "How do you know that?"

"Know what?"

"That they will know we are here."

Berry shrugged. "Shit, I dunno."

The Gypsy, he was thinking. She would know. Where are you tonight, lady? He grinned. He wasn't scared any more.

He thought, *Jesus Christ, I'm not scared any more.*

Dim Sais. Dydwy ddim yn Sais.

Where had that come from? He didn't know a word of Welsh, apart from *sice* itself and *da iawn.*

Weird, weird, weird.

Berry placed the chisel under the lip of the tomb, avoiding the eyes of the knight because this was just some old stone box, OK? Dai handed him the mallet and he struck the head of the chisel.

Thud-ud-ud.

Felt something crumble, give way.

He stopped. "Where's Bethan?"

"Outside, with Idwal, I should think. She didn't want to come in, either. Morelli . . . ?"

"Yeah?"

"This thing with Bethan and you. Nothing serious there?"

"What's that mean?"

"You know what it means, man, you know the way it has been for her."

"Yeah." Berry hit the chisel again. They heard fragments of loose stone fall a few inches inside the tomb. A flat kind of chink as a piece struck something and did not bounce off; rather the substance it had fallen on simply crumbled.

Dust to dust.

The torchlight flickered.

"She's not for you, boy."

"You don't think so, huh?" Berry left the chisel jammed under the lid of the tomb. Dai fitted the end of one of the crowbars into what was now a half-inch gap alongside it.

The torchlight flickered.

Berry's eyes met the smooth, years-worn orbs of the knight's eyes.

They were open now. He knew those eyes were open.

"I think maybe we aren't gonna need the jack after all," Berry said.

Bethan said, "I've come to talk about trees."

Miss Rhys, the judge's granddaughter, was bolt upright in the judge's high-backed Gothic chair, her face made harsh by candlelight which ought to have softened it. Bethan stood on the old rug, where the dead Giles had lain, both feet on the dragon's head.

Claire said, "My tree or yours?"

"You found your tree," Bethan said. "I want to find mine."

"Why?"

"I want to chop it down," Bethan said simply.

Claire Rhys looked at her with contempt.

"Well?" Bethan did not move.

"Have you asked Buddug?"

"If I had been five days in the desert, I wouldn't ask Buddug for a cup of water."

"Go away," Claire said. "Go and ask Buddug."

Bethan moved towards the desk, intending to knock a candlestick over in her face.

"Come any closer," Claire said calmly, "and I shall have to harm you."

Bethan stopped. The room had grown very cold, she thought, under the influence of its mistress's displeasure.

She said, "What have you become?"

Claire smiled. "You never really met my grandfather, did you?"

Bethan said nothing.

"I've discovered, to my shame, that he was rather a weak man. He knew he had to return here, that he could not break the chain. So he left my grandmother and my mother in England and he came back. He came back alone."

Bethan was momentarily puzzled. Then she felt nearly ill.

"He ought, of course, to have brought them with him."

The village, Aled had said, demanded sacrifices.

"But he was weak, as I say. He left them and he returned alone."

. . . the old Druids, see, they did not sacrifice each other, their . . . you know, virgins, kids. None of that nonsense. But I've heard it said they used to sacrifice their enemies.

"You brought Giles as your little sacrifice," Bethan said, her voice like dust.

"And also atoned for Thomas Rhys," Claire said. "Don't forget that. I had to complete what he could not."

She meant her parents. She'd given her parents in sacrifice to Y Groes and to whatever lay in the tomb and whatever it represented.

He was only English, Sali Dafis had said.

"You were very stupid," Claire said. "You and your child could have belonged here. You could have lived in the warmth, at the heart of our heritage and watched it spread and grow and flourish like a lovely garden."

"Once the weeds had been killed," Bethan said.

"Your words."

"And Glyndwr will rise again, like the legends say, springing from his tomb with his army behind him to free Wales from the oppressor."

Miss Rhys spread her hands. "We are not naïve. Glyndwr is dead and buried."

And then her voice rose, horribly close to Buddug-pitch.

"But the Bird is aloft. And Death walks the roads in his long coat. And the shit-breathed hag – *Gwrach y rhybin* – the hag is on the wing again."

Bethan turned away, almost choking.

They had both crowbars wedged under the lip of the tomb, the effigy on top slightly askew now.

The torch flickered.

Dai stood back. "I think we are there."

"How you figure we should play it? Slide it?"

"If we both get this end," Dai said, "we can lift it and then swing it to one side. Are you prepared then, Morelli?"

"For?"

"For whatever is . . . there. Spent most of my life with stiffs, see," Dai said. "You were a bit jumpy back at the depot, if I remember rightly."

"These are old bones. Old bones aren't the same."

Dai smiled, the torchlight glancing off his bald skull. "And you reckon it's old Owain Glyndwr in here? Well, tell me, Morelli, how will you know?"

"Be more obvious if it isn't."

"You mean if it's empty."

"Is what I mean." Berry stood at the head of the tomb, hands grasping the stone lip an inch or so from the eroded cheeks of the knight. "OK, Dai? We gonna count down from five and then lift and swing? Four, three, two, one –"

The torch went out.

Berry heard the grating thump of falling masonry. An icy, numbing pain bolted up his arm.

When the torch came on again, Dai was holding it. Berry

looked down and couldn't see the end of his own left hand beyond the lip of the tomb, beyond the smirk of ages on the face of the knight. He was in agony, knew his wrist was broken, maybe his arm too. And, worse than that, he was trapped.

Dai was walking off into the nave. "I'm sorry, Morelli," he said over his shoulder. "But a man has to make sacrifices if he wants to retire to paradise."

It was all shatteringly clear to Bethan now.

"And Dilwyn's wife? A harmless little typist from the South-East?"

Miss Rhys stood up. "We've spoken enough, Bethan. Time you left, I think."

"It doesn't bear thinking about. How can you live with it?"

"In comparison to what the English have done to the Welsh over the centuries, it's really rather a small thing, wouldn't you say? I should have thought that you, as a teacher –"

"But I don't have to live with it," Bethan said. "I can tell whoever I choose. Beginning with the police."

"Bethan, I used to be in journalism," Claire said wearily. "I learned a lot about the police and the law. What it amounts to in this case is that the police don't believe in magic and, even if they did, no offences have been committed under the *English* legal system. Now go away and dwell upon your future."

When she calmly blew out both red candles, Bethan's nerve went; she scrabbled for the door handle and got out, feeling her way along the walls, through the hall, into the living room where the moon glanced off shiny things, and out into the blood-washed night.

She had to find Berry, get him away from that church, if Dai and Idwal had not persuaded him already to forget the fantasy of dislodging a tradition cemented through centuries.

She came out of the gateway, between the sycamores, looked

up and down the country lane over the sweating snow. The Sprite was still parked where she'd left it. She looked in the back and saw that the hydraulic jack and crowbars were missing. Berry had gone to desecrate the tomb.

Trembling with anxiety, Bethan ran through the lych gate into the circular graveyard where the atmosphere was close and clinging and the sky was low, red and juicy. She could see across the village – still no power down there, houses lit by glow-worms – to the Nearly Mountains, hard and bright with ice.

Bethan stopped and stiffened as a hand clawed her shoulder, spun her around.

Buddug seemed to tower over her, bulky in a dark duffel-coat, her big face as red as the sky.

"A question you have for me, is it, little bitch?"

474

CHAPTER LXXIII

They would come for him in time, he knew that.

It was not dark. The light from the sky leaked in from the long window, crimson.

He was too weary now to endure the pain of struggle, wanting to lay his head down on the tomb in exhaustion. But the only part of the tomb his head could reach was the head of the effigy, his eyes looking into its eyes, its lips . . . He turned away in revulsion and the movement dragged on his trapped arm and the pain made his whole body blaze.

He'd looked and felt around for something to wedge under the slab, next to his arm. Something he could lean on, hard enough perhaps to make some space to pull the arm out.

But Dai had taken away the jack and both crowbars and even Robin's flying jacket which Berry had hung over the rood screen while they worked on the tomb.

"Scumbag!" he screamed, and the walls threw it back at him with scorn. ". . . bag, ag, ag."

The stone knight shifted, settled on Berry's arm; he thought he could hear his bones splintering, getting ground into powder. From the other side of the church wall, he heard the movement in the snow which he'd earlier assumed was Idwal Roberts.

"Idwal! Help me, willya!"

The cry was out before he could stop it.

No way could it be Idwal out there. No way could it have been Idwal first time around, when he and Dai were busy with the crowbars. Idwal had been dismissed or was dead or was a party to the betrayal.

Which was not a betrayal of him so much as of Bethan.

Was there anybody left in these parts who had not at some time betrayed Bethan?

He wept for Bethan and because of the pain, because he was trapped. Because, sooner or later, they were going to come for him.

Bethan looked up into the split veins and the venom. Black eyes and yellow, twisted teeth.

"*Gwrach*," Bethan spat.

Buddug did not move at first, but something leapt behind her black pebble eyes. And then her enormous turkey-killer's hands came up with incredible speed and lifted Bethan off her feet and hurled her into the church wall.

Bethan's head cracked against the stone and bounced off, and Buddug whirled and brutally slapped her, with bewildering force, across the face so that her head spun away so hard and so fast she thought her neck was breaking.

"The first thing we learn at school," Buddug said, not even panting with the exertion, "is to be polite to our elders."

Bethan fell in a heap to the soft snow and sat there, half-stunned, her back to the wall, feeling the blood running freely from her nose or her mouth. Her glasses had gone.

"And the next thing we learn –" Buddug bent down and dragged her to her feet, tearing her white mac at the shoulders "– is to stand up when we are spoken to."

Bethan lolled, feeling her eyes glazing.

"Don't you go to sleep!" Buddug hit her again with a hand that felt as sharp and heavy as a wood-axe.

Buddug hissed, "You killed our baby."

Bethan tried to speak. Saw Buddug's hand raised again and shrank back against the wall.

"We like them to be pure-bred if possible," Buddug said. "Dilwyn's was a mistake. The child has to work harder, see, because of its mother."

"You're sick," Bethan whispered through swollen lips. "Go on, hit me again. What more can you do?"

"Idwal!" They heard from inside the church, a weak and despairing cry. "Help me, willya!"

Bethan's heart sagged in her limp body. Buddug's lumpen features cracked with glee.

"They say he loves you, the American," Buddug said. "Do you love him?"

Bethan desperately shook her head.

"You will not miss him, then, when he is gone. They will leave him tonight to see how much he can do to himself and then, in the morning –"

Bethan rocked her head from side to side to shut this out.

Buddug pinched Bethan's cheeks together to make her look at her. "*And then, in the morning –*"

"What are they doing to him?"

"No matter," Buddug said, ignoring the question. "He will be long gone by then. He will know that soon."

The knight smiled a victor's smile with reddened lips.

From outside Berry heard the sound of scuffling, heard talking in Welsh, a voice cry out in pain.

He recognised the voice at once.

"Bastard!" Berry screamed at the Goddamn knight, his control gone. "Motherfucker!" All the words that had seemed so pathetic still seemed pathetic.

He pushed the fingers of his left hand as far as they would go into the gap between the slab and the walls of the tomb, rammed the arm in so that both arms were parallel under the knight's dead weight.

He waited two minutes like that, conserving his strength. Then he wrenched hard on the trapped arm and simultaneously heaved upwards with the good left arm.

The knight shifted and he felt an appalling weight on the left arm. The good arm.

He cried to the rafters in his agony and passed out with the pain.

When the long, bitter cry came through the church wall, Bethan pushed Buddug aside and made a rush for the corner of the building and the doorway.

Or intended to.

She'd moved less than a couple of feet when one of Buddug's great hands caught her by the throat and squeezed on her windpipe. She is going to kill me, Bethan thought. Like the ducks, like the chickens in the farmyard.

"We do not walk away when we are being spoken to," Buddug said and squeezed harder.

All was quiet within the church.

"Will not be long, now," Buddug said.

"Why are you doing this?"

"Do not make yourself ridiculous," Buddug said.

Bethan thought of the *Gorsedd Ddu*, who judged the traitors and the cowards.

She thought, we must hear each other's agony and hopelessness before we die.

"*Dewch*," Buddug said, taking Bethan's arm. Come.

"No."

With little effort, Buddug twisted the arm until Bethan, gritting her teeth, felt the bones begin to crack.

Sobbing, she nodded and Buddug propelled her across the churchyard to the top of the steps.

*

A meagre light appeared.

He opened his eyes and saw both arms under the stone, and there was no pain now, but he could not move at all.

And beyond the chapel, visible through the lattice of the rood screen, the little light, like a taper.

The light did not move. It seemed to cast no ambience. Like the light through a keyhole, something on the other side of the dark.

Berry felt no pain, only sorrow and profound misery.

CHAPTER LXXIV

When the blizzard eased a little, Guto and Alun left the Range Rover with its nose in the snowdrift and walked away in different directions.

Alun's mission was to climb to the top of the nearest hill with his mobile phone to see if he could get a signal and, if he could, to send for the police. And the ambulance.

Which was too late now, anyway. Snow matting his beard and freezing there, coming over the tops of his Wellingtons with every step, Guto looked down on the Range Rover. Left with its sidelights on and its engine running to keep the heater going, quite pointlessly, for Miranda Moore-Lacey.

Guto didn't have a mission other than to walk. He should have stayed in the heat, laid Miranda's body out in the snow. At the thought of this, he rammed his hands bitterly down into the pockets of his presentable Parliamentary candidate's overcoat and ploughed on.

Years since he'd walked the Nearly Mountains, and that had been in decent weather; he hadn't the faintest idea where the hell he was.

However, reaching the crest of a ridge, he found he was looking back towards Y Groes where the sky still was streaked with this unhealthy red, shining out like the bars of an electric fire in a darkened room. An electric fire in the dark always conveyed a sense of illness to Guto; his mam used to leave one in his bedroom when he was sick. Years ago this was, but the impression remained.

He wanted a drink. He wanted several drinks. He wanted to get blind pissed and forget the wasted years between being a sick kid in an overheated bedroom and a big, arrogant, macho politician with a hard line in rhetoric and a posh English chick in French knickers.

Stupid to think that he could make all those years worthwhile at a stroke. The rock band that almost got to make a record, the book that almost sold five hundred copies. The posh English chick in French knickers who almost survived two whole days of being Guto Evans's woman.

He glared down at the village of Y Groes with savage loath-ing, vowed to avenge Miranda in some way and knew he wouldn't because he'd always be too pissed to function in any more meaningful way than punching the odd wealthy immi-grant. And in just over a week's time he'd be a member of the biggest political group in Wales: the FPCC – the Failed Plaid Candidates' Club.

Overtired, overstressed, overweight, Guto staggered on through the snow and the self-pity, hard to decide which was denser. The endless snow seemed to symbolise both his past and his future. As soon as he crunched a narrow path, the sides fell in.

Looking down at his plodding wellies, he did not notice the shadowy figure walking up the hill towards him until it was upon him.

"*Noswaith dda*, Guto."

Guto did not recognise the man. That the man recognised him was no surprise; people usually did these days.

"You live near here?" Guto asked him. "You have a phone?"

"I've come from there." The man gestured towards Y Groes. Guto couldn't see him too clearly; he seemed to be wearing leather gear, like a biker.

"Poor bugger," Guto said, in no mood for diplomacy. "They let you out, is it?"

Guto felt the leather-clad man was smiling. "They let me out," he agreed.

"Good," Guto said.

The snow stopped, the air was still for a time. Guto looked at his watch, feeling this was significant. It was 12:05 a.m.

Something companionable about the stranger. Something odd, too. Something odd about the leathers he was wearing, and what would a biker be doing in the Nearly Mountains at midnight in a blizzard? Guto glanced at the man but could not see him clearly; there was a haze about him.

They stood together on a snowy hummock, as though they were having the same hallucination, looking down towards Y Groes. Guto noticed that the sky over the village had lost its red bars, as if someone had unplugged the electric fire. The sky over Y Groes was just like the sky everywhere else: charcoal grey and heavy with suppressed snow.

"No time to waste, Guto," his companion said and clapped him briskly on the back.

"You're right," Guto said. "Thanks. *Diolch yn fawr.*"

He turned away, tramped off down the hill back towards the Range Rover. When he turned around, the man had gone, but there was a kind of heat below his left shoulder where the hand briefly had touched him.

He almost bumped into Alun, who had come over the rise, his mobile phone in his gloved hand. "Who were you talking to?"

"Some bloke," Guto said.

"I got through," said Alun. "Gwyn Arthur Jones is sending to Carmarthen for the police helicopter. They say we should go back to Y Groes and wait."

"OK." Guto got in the front of the Land-Rover with Alun, not wanting to look at what lay on the rear seat.

Alun reversed the Range Rover for almost half a mile until they came to a sign indicating a lay-by and he was able to make a three-point turn and they went back towards Y Groes, as Guto always knew they would.

"God, I feel sick," Miranda said in his ear, inducing icy palpitations down his spine. "What time is it?"

Snow swirled around the Fiat Panda, tucked into the side of the inn. "What have I become?" Dai Death said. "Tell me that."

"What have you always been, man? A covetous bugger." Idwal Roberts sat in the driver's seat, where he'd been for the past hour, trying to get the car radio to work. "Pontmeurig was not good enough. No, you had to find your paradise. Look at it. You call this paradise?"

"I didn't believe it. And then I did." Anguished, Dai pummelled his knees.

"I told you," Idwal said. "I warned you not to go in there."

"And then – was as if I was seeing everything through differ-ent eyes. I just dropped the bloody stone on his arm. I did that! Me! How is it I could do that? How?"

"You tell me."

"Seems like a dream to me now. Maybe it was a dream. Come back with me, Idwal."

"I will not."

"See, I go back there afterwards –"

"You told me."

"– when the snow has started and the fever has gone from my head. And I go back into the church, see –"

"Yes, yes. But *where* have they taken him?"

"– Bloody tomb open, bloody statue thing in pieces, shattered."

"But what was in it, Dai? Did you look?"

"Oh, Jesus," Dai wailed. "Don't go asking me that."

*

"A question you have for me, is it, little bitch?"

"I don't want to know," Bethan said, and knew immediately this was the wrong thing to say.

Buddug smiled horribly.

As a wind blew out of nowhere, she forced Bethan down the river bank to the edge of the water. Bethan looked up. Even without her glasses she could see the church tower had lost its grip on the moon, which seemed to be swimming away on a churning sea of cloud.

"Look, Buddug! Look at the sky!"

"It will pass," Buddug said. The wind had seized her ragged hair, making it writhe like serpents. She was the *Gwrach y rhibyn*. The death hag. She pulled Bethan into the shelter of the bridge. "I will tell you how it was," she hissed into Bethan's face, with a gush of vile breath.

"No!"

"We all came to see. A beautiful summer night, it was, the sun going down. And you in your white summer dress. Like a bride."

"And my husband already dying." Bethan tried to turn her head away and Buddug seized her cheeks between thumb and forefinger.

"Indeed, perhaps that was the very night he *began* to die," Buddug said, the muscular fingers of her other hand caressing the bruised skin on Bethan's neck with dreadful tenderness.

"No . . ." Bethan closed her eyes, felt and smelled Buddug's warm, putrid breath, began to cough.

"You closed them that night, too . . ."

Bethan jerked both eyes open, looking into Buddug's yellow teeth, the black gaps between them, the breath pumped through those gaps like poison gas.

"You did not care," Buddug said dreamily. "You were in thrall to the night and the sweet smells and the old magic. And as you lay with your legs spread . . ." A heavy gust of wind came through the bridge, with a surge of snow.

"*Gwrach!*" Bethan screamed through the wind. "*Gwrach! Gwrach! Gwrach!*"

Buddug had both her butcher's hands around Bethan's throat now, holding her at arm's length and looking from side to side, down at the river then up at the church and the heaving sky, with the sudden realisation that something fundamental had altered. "What have you done, bitch? What have you done to the night?"

"*Gwrach!*"

"You are . . . *cachu.*" Buddug's eyes burning red like coals.

Bethan felt a thumb going up into her larynx, its nail probing like a knife. She felt the skin parting, her throat constricting, tongue out, eyes popping.

"And when I can see in your eyes that your time is upon you," Buddug told her, "I shall tell to you the name of the father of your child."

Bethan felt herself rising above the horror of the night and the hag's slaughterhouse hands and graveyard breath. Rising into the Wales of her childhood, low tide at Ynyslas, a fire of driftwood on her birthday, the view from Constitution Hill at sunset over the last ice lolly of the day. She heard lines of poetry: Gwenallt, Dic Jones the bard and finally, sonorously, in English, the haunted cleric, R. S. Thomas:

to live in Wales is to be conscious
At dusk of the spilled blood
That went to the making of the wild sky

Between the snowflakes, she felt the hot splashes of blood on her face, opening her eyes at the deafening blast, Buddug's hands still around her throat but no grip in them any more.

And Buddug, no head to speak of, most of it in fragments down the front of Bethan's torn once-white raincoat.

PART TEN

NOS DA

CHAPTER LXXV

The other side of midnight people began to emerge from their homes in coats and scarves, carrying lamps and torches, all very muted, hardly saying a word to each other. Like survivors of some bombing raid. Mair Huws, from the post office, and Eirlys Hywels silently helped Bethan take off what remained of the raincoat and wrapped her in an old tapestry cape, leaving the bloody mac draped over the bridge, dripping into the river.

Aled was crouching alone just inside the alley between the inn and the sub-station where the wind could not reach him. By the light of his torch, propped up against a brick, he was slipping another cartridge into his shotgun.

"What are you looking at?" He stood up and pointed the twelve-bore vaguely around him. In fact, nobody was looking at him except Berry Morelli, smoking a cigarette, one sleeve of his flying jacket flapping empty.

"Well, Aled. What can I say? You blew her head off. Dump the gun now?"

Aled shook his head. "To the rectory I have to go."

"Hey now, Aled," Berry said. "Think about this. Just take –"

"What is there to think about?" Standing with the gun hanging loose in his limp hands, white hair bedraggled, Aled put on a stark smile. "Mass-murderer I am now, isn't it?"

"When we explain to the cops –" Berry said, but Aled shook his head.

"Explain. Explain this?" He chuckled sourly. "Where do you

489

begin? No, what I am doing is giving you an easy explanation, isn't it?"

Berry said, "Grief-stricken madman goes on the rampage with shotgun."

Aled smiled ruefully. "You are a little ahead of me, boy."

Berry looked at the little white-haired mass-killer and saw some kind of flawed hero.

"Go on, you bugger," Aled said. "Leave me be. Go to your woman."

"Why'd you do all this, Aled? There's nothing gonna bring her back."

Aled said, "Listen, man, an accident. I have no reason to think otherwise. I blame no one for that. I –" he patted his jacket pocket, spare cartridges rattled "I don't want the third degree, Morelli. Don't know why I turned away. Been coming on a long time probably."

"One more question, OK?"

Aled sighed. "I ought to shoot you as well, you nosy bugger."

"The tomb. Unless Glyndwr had curly horns –"

"Morelli, it never mattered what was in that tomb. The *Gorsedd Ddu* has *always* looked after this place, long before Glyndwr. *Y Groesfan*, the crossing place, where the warriors and heroes and the men of magic came to die. People have lived here half-aware of this for centuries. What they brought back, the four, was – I don't know – the *spirit* of Glyndwr, isn't it? Or something. How do you say it in English – the essence?"

Which they corrupted, Berry thought. They took the magic, and they wove that into the tapestry of this place. He thought of what he and Bethan had learned in the library over at Hereford yesterday. The impression they'd formed of the latter Druids as purveyors of a degraded version of the Celtic religion.

This was the tradition continued by the *Gorsedd Ddu*.

"Can of worms," Berry said, thinking of graveyard worms, grown fat on the dead. "How could folks live with all that?"

"Ah, Morelli, you will never understand. It's powerful, see. It works. What else in Wales is truly powerful these days, other than our traditions?" Aled's top teeth vanished into his snowy moustache. "Excuse me, I am going to take the air."

"No way I can talk you out of this?"

"Not unless you have a bigger gun," Aled said.

Berry watched him walk away across the bridge into the snow.

He discovered Bethan was at his elbow, wrapped in some kind of Welsh rug.

"He's gone to kill ap Siencyn," Berry said. "I don't see him coming back."

She gripped his only visible arm.

"No," Berry said. "He knows where he's at. I think."

"Just goes on, doesn't it?" Her voice was hoarse and fractured; she kept massaging her throat. "On and on."

"Something ended here tonight. You must feel that."

"Nothing truly ends with guns," Bethan said.

Berry shrugged, which hurt his broken arm. "How do you feel now?"

"How do I look?"

Bruises besmirched most of her face. The skin was purple and swollen around both eyes. Her lip was twisted and her cheeks blotched with blood, some of it her own.

"You look wonderful," he said.

"Your poor arm. Is it very painful?"

"Not like in the church. Christ, I don't think I ever felt more – you know – than when I was lying with both arms jammed in the Goddamn tomb and there's this candle drifting towards me across –"

Bethan looked up sharply.

"Don't panic," Berry said. "It was Aled. The dissident. His, ah, wife died."

"Gwenllian?"

"Accident in Aber. What pushed him over the edge, I guess. Sign that, when something goes real bad, it ceases to discriminate between the English and the Welsh."

"Or traitors and the cowards," Bethan said.

"I liked him. Whatever happened here tonight, whatever lifted, it was in some way all down to him. Not me or you. *He* did it."

He licked his forefinger and rubbed a blood-fleck off her nose. "What happens in the church, Aled puts down the candle and he levers up the slab so I can get my arms out, and then we kick the slab clean off the tomb and smash the shit outa the fucking effigy. He does most of that, I'm hurting too much."

Bethan said slowly, "So you know now what was in the tomb."

"Yeah."

"Do I have to ask?"

"Bones," Berry said. "Bones. Like you'd expect. Only *not* what you'd expect. Soon as the air got inside they more or less crumbled away. But, yeah, we saw what it was."

"And?"

"Aled figured it for a ram."

"A ram? As in . . . sheep?"

"Yeah. Make what you want outa that. Me, I don't want to think too hard about it. I lost enough sleep already."

The rotors of the police helicopter were heard, a distant drone and then a clatter. And with the clatter a searchlight beam swept the village.

"Best place to land, I think," Chief Inspector Gwyn Arthur Jones said, "is the school playground. What do you think, Neil?"

Sergeant Neil Probert only grunted. Flying at night through

intermittent snow, he'd been terrified most of the way. Even the pilot did not look exactly happy. He'd made them wait an hour until the snow had eased, before deciding it was safe to make the trip at all.

Neil had not spoken since the searchlight had picked up the Daihatsu on its side at the bottom of a gulley, and Gwyn Arthur had ordered the pilot to go in low enough to ascertain that they were both dead, the two men who'd been flung out into the snow. They could not have been anything *but* dead.

"Tell you one thing, guv," said the pilot now, a Cockney called Bob Gorner. "You won't catch me doing this number again."

"Ah, worst of it is over, man," Gwyn Arthur said scornfully. "Right now, come on, let's go round the village once again before we land."

There was still apparently no power in Y Groes. Plenty of little glimmerings, though, candles, lamps. Far more than you'd expect after midnight even in a town the size of Pont. Something was up, Gwyn Arthur thought. No question.

The police helicopter circled over the pub – lots of wispy little lights around there – and then over the church and back again towards the river.

"OK, take her in then, Bob. No wait – what's that?" Gwyn Arthur leaned forward in his seat.

Neil Probert, feeling queasy, didn't move, just closed his eyes and muttered, "Where?"

"By there . . . See it? Figure scurrying along the bank. Could've been a child. Gone now. Under the bridge, maybe?"

"Want me to go round again, guv?"

"Yes, one last time, then we'll land."

Neil Probert groaned.

When the searchlight beam had passed over, Sali Dafis came out from under the bridge, small and lithe, elfin in a black tracksuit. The air was temporarily still, a break between snow salvos.

The body of the big woman still lay on the bank, headless. Partially covered in snow, in various shades of pink and a kind of crimson which was close to black.

Sali looked down at the body, then up at the church tower, then down at the body again, and finally up at the bridge, to her left, where her *nain*, Mrs. Bronwen Dafis, had appeared.

Old Mrs. Dafis leaned over the bridge parapet and watched Sali silently.

Sali crouched beside the body in the snow. She began to brush away some of the soft, white snow, and then the hard pink snow. Finally the ice-blood around Buddug's neck.

She glanced up again at the bridge, and Mrs. Bronwen Dafis nodded.

So did the woman now standing next to her, the younger one. Whose face, the girl could tell, even from this distance, was equal in its severity.

Sali plunged her small, white hand into the gore.

Rheithordy.

The gate was open.

But no light shone from the house, not a candle-glimmer.

He knew where the rectory was, though, could sense its bulk, although there was no feeling of a building about it.

Sometimes it was a building, and sometimes it was just a part of the woods, the oak trees crowding the lawn, almost shoulder-ing the rectory itself, as if feeding sap to their brothers in its frame.

Aled walked to the front door of the rectory and the snow went with him, flurrying around his body. He felt a sudden power – *he* was bringing the snow. He was the bad-weather man.

The door was unlocked. He turned the knob and it opened

and the smell came out at him, mouldy, brackish, the smell of the oak woods in decay, only ten times as strong as it would have been in the wood itself.

"Rector!" Aled's voice was harder and colder than the snow that came with him.

What did he know of ap Siencyn? Who *was* the man? The latest in an ancient line which sometimes has been interrupted but never for long because the wrong men would not last in this parish – if they were Welsh they would move away, if English . . .

"Rector!"

Poking the gun before him, Aled entered the hall, scattering snow.

He kicked open the doors, one by one, saw still rooms tinged with snowlight through steep, multi-paned windows.

No firelight, no candles.

He knew, then.

Abruptly he turned and stalked out of the rectory into the night, where they were assembled around the entrance.

Snarling, breathing in spurts, Aled crouched and blasted both barrels into the night and into the company of ancient oaks gathered before him on the rectory lawn.

There were four shots; he had obviously reloaded.

Groups of people stood in the snow outside the *Tafarn*. Nobody spoke.

Bethan watched the faces of the people and saw a complexity of human emotions, from shock and bewilderment, through tired acceptance, to a kind of relief.

Among the people conspicuous by their absence were the mechanic Dilwyn Dafis; his mother Mrs. Bronwyn Dafis, the seer; skeletal Glyn Harri, the village historian. And bluff, bearded Morgan Morgan, farmer, and husband of the late Buddug.

Bethan wondered for whom the *cannwyll gorff* shone now.

"Over?" Berry wondered.

The police helicopter was almost overhead. The villagers began to drift away, many into the *Tafarn*.

Bethan said, "You won't tell Guto, will you?"

"Huh?"

She said, "That there was a ram in the tomb."

"I don't understand. And where the hell *is* Guto?"

"Probably in the bar with Miranda celebrating his victory in the by-election."

"Jesus, how long was I *in* that church?"

Bethan would have smiled but her facial muscles weren't up to it. "He believes he had a vision in the Nearly Mountains. There is a folk-tale about the Abbot of Valle Crucis in North Wales. How one morning on the Berwyn Mountain the Abbot is approached by a figure out of the mist which turns out to be Owain Glyndwr. And Owain says, Good Morrow, Abbot, you are out early, something like this. And the Abbot says, No, you are out a hundred years *too* early. And Owain vanishes, never to be seen again."

"Until he runs into Guto on the Nearly Mountains?"

"Guto is not laughing about this. He claims there was a miracle, which he won't talk about. . . . Glyndwr, you see, was probably closer to Guto's kind of democratic nationalism than to the . . . the *evil* conjured in Y Groes. Whichever part of Glyndwr they thought they had here, it was brought against its will. I'm sure of it. I have to be sure. Or else . . . or else we're *all* of us evil, aren't we? But . . . well, Guto is convinced he will now win the by-election."

"Who knows?" Berry said. "Maybe we did let something else outa the tomb. The whole point – the whole secret of this – is not what actually happened but what you *believe* happened. Hey, am I getting mystical, or becoming Welsh, or what?"

Bethan pulled him into the shelter of the *Tafarn* porch. Through the door they could see a lot of people quietly drinking, helping themselves; no landlord any more. The atmosphere was like an overcrowded hospital in wartime, full of assorted casualties, people looking around wondering what happened and who was left alive.

Windblown snow hit the porch in a cloud. Berry stared at it, expressionless. Bethan said, "What are you thinking?"

"Trying to figure out what happens now," Berry said. "Apart from getting my arm fixed. Sitting around waiting till I can drive again. Watching the bruises heal on your face."

"And then you'll go back. To London?" Keeping her expression as neutral as she could, given the condition of her face.

He shook his head.

"To America?"

"No way. I got no roots left anyplace. Maybe I should stick around awhile until something suggests itself." He tried to hold her eyes. "Maybe I should learn Welsh."

Bethan flung an arm around his neck and kissed him, which hurt them both quite a lot. "Start with this . . . *Fi'n caru ti.*"

"Tea? Hold on, I got it. You're saying 'I'd like a black tea, no sugar . . .'"

They smiled stupidly at each other. "Yuk, how utterly nauseating," Miranda said, coming out of the bar, sipping a vodka and lime. "How is it that other people in love are so unbearable?"

She stood with them on the porch, red hair a little awry, but otherwise as elegant and unruffled as ever. "That bastard Guto," she said.

"What'd he do now?"

"He's dismissed me," Miranda said petulantly. "Until after the election. He thinks I won't be good for his image. How ungrateful can you get? Besides, he's awfully funny in bed. I mean, what am *I* going to do until after the election?"

Miranda took a big, sulky sip from her vodka and lime. It seemed to Berry that Guto had a point here.

"Well," he said thoughtfully, watching Bethan out of the corner of an eye, his spirits suddenly up higher than the helicopter. "I can get you a ten-inch lovespoon, but you got to buy your own batteries."

"This the last time, guv?"

"One final look. No, hang on, listen, you hear that? Can you cut the engine a second?"

"It's a bleeding helicopter, guv, not an Austin Metro."

"Sorry, Bob, stupid of me. It's just I thought I heard . . . well, a shot. Never mind. Look, there's the child, do you see her?"

"Where?" said Neil Probert, eyes closed.

"Wake up, you dozy bugger. What do you make of that?"

"Sorry, sir." Neil leaned over Gwyn Arthur's shoulder. The searchlight had picked up the small girl on the main street.

"Skipping along, see. Not a care in the world, as if she's going home from school. And *what* bloody time is it?"

"One twenty-five, sir."

The child looked up at the helicopter, directly into the searchlight's glare, and even from this distance they could tell she was grinning.

"Kids," said Gwyn Arthur, forgetting for a moment that he was investigating at least one suspicious death. "What are the bloody parents doing? And what's that all over her face? Toffee?"

The child skipped gaily up the street. "Oh Christ . . ." said Neil Probert. "Who's this?"

"Jesus . . ." Gwyn Arthur breathed. "Get us down, Bob."

The man with the shotgun was stalking the child along the street.

"Get the fucking thing down!"

"Yeh, yeh, got to be the field, though."

"Can't you get any closer?"

The man was perhaps three yards behind the girl. He raised the gun to his shoulder.

"Sod the fucking field!" Gwyn Arthur screamed. "Go in."

The pilot glanced wildly from side to side, judging distances, road levels. "Gonna damage it, guv."

"So it's damaged . . . Go in!"

They were so low now, churning up the night, that the man's white hair was blown on end. He went into a crouch, the gun aimed at the back of the child's head.

"Hit him in the fucking whatsits – land on him or something."

The girl stopped.

She turned round.

The man's hair and his clothes were quivering in the swirling air.

He lowered the gun.

The girl's hair was unmoving in the rotor-driven maelstrom. She stood quite still in the spotlight, staring at the man.

The man stood there for long, long seconds before sinking slowly to his knees in the snow and fumbling with the shotgun and something else.

"What's –?" Neil said.

"A twig," Gwyn Arthur said, suddenly calm. "Pen. Pencil. I don't know. But he's fitting it under the trigger guard."

Aled rose from his knees, the shotgun upright on the ground, its barrel tucked under his chin. The child watched him lift a foot, bring it down the side of the gun to where the twig, pencil, whatever protruded from the trigger guard.

Neil Probert turned away.

"OK," Gwyn Arthur said quietly. "Pull back. Land in the schoolyard. Don't scare her any more."

The starburst of blood and brains covered a very wide area of the snowy street.

Bob Gorner said, "She ain't scared, guv. Tell you that for nuffink."

The child had turned her back on the mess and was skipping back up the road, past the *Tafarn*, towards the cottages, to where two women were waiting. They each took one of the child's hands.

"She's in shock," Gwyn Arthur said uncertainly.

But Neil Probert knew what the pilot meant. He sank back, closed his eyes, the sweat cooling on his brow.

Bob killed the searchlight and took the chopper into an arc towards the school.

None of them spoke.

For a moment it seemed the child had thrown a shadow ten times her size across the snow. A monstrous shadow, with the illusion of small, hard wings flapping at its shoulders.